To Janeth
All the Best
[signature]

Bittersweet Tones of Love

Sarah Salem

Continued from …
Twisted Forms of Love

AuthorHouse™
1663 Liberty Drive
Bloomington, IN 47403
www.authorhouse.com
Phone: 1-800-839-8640

© 2014 Sarah Salem. All rights reserved.

No part of this book may be reproduced, stored in a retrieval system, or transmitted by any means without the written permission of the author.

Published by AuthorHouse 10/28/2014

ISBN: 978-1-4969-4923-3 (sc)
ISBN: 978-1-4969-4924-0 (hc)
ISBN: 978-1-4969-4922-6 (e)

Library of Congress Control Number: 2014919051

Any people depicted in stock imagery provided by Thinkstock are models, and such images are being used for illustrative purposes only.
Certain stock imagery © Thinkstock.

This book is printed on acid-free paper.

Because of the dynamic nature of the Internet, any web addresses or links contained in this book may have changed since publication and may no longer be valid. The views expressed in this work are solely those of the author and do not necessarily reflect the views of the publisher, and the publisher hereby disclaims any responsibility for them.

To my dear daughters:
You are my gift.

Acknowledgments

I WOULD LIKE TO THANK my wonderful family: my daughter, you mean the world to me; my mother, sister, brothers, and brother-in-law, for all your wonderful backing and encouragement; and my wonderful friends, for believing in me.

I also would like to thank my editors, for all their direction and assistance.

I couldn't have done it without you.

Chapter One

It was a Friday afternoon on a cool, cloudy fall day. I stood outside a closed old gray wooden door. I contemplated knocking on the door for a few minutes; I then glanced around briefly. I took a deep breath, quickly glancing at my four-year-old daughter, Nora, whose little hand was tightly held by mine. I gave her a wide, reassuring smile. Her big brown eyes were anxious. I had to hide my anxiety behind a calm exterior. With a shaky hand, I reached to knock on the door. This was the place I had wanted to break away from, but my twisted destiny had led me straight back to it. This time around, I wasn't alone though; I was with Nora. As I waited for someone to open the door, I recalled the events that happened since my car accident.

A couple of weeks after my husband Yusuf's death, my mother, Mona, went back home, and I took an airplane to Nova Scotia. I needed to be next to Nora, who was staying with my friend Cameron and her husband, Troy. Because of my awful circumstances and my injuries from the accident, I had been laid off of my job, and I would be collecting unemployment for months to come. The sight of Nora brought me to tears. I felt a mixture of relief and pain down in my chest. I realized that I was still suffering from the effects of the horrific events that had happened to me.

Cameron and Troy were both relieved and happy that I was safe and also delighted to share the happy news they had received soon after landing in Nova Scotia. Cameron was finally pregnant after trying to conceive for so many years.

The mild, cool fall weather in Nova Scotia was somewhat soothing for the first couple of days. I spent some time sitting on their balcony overlooking the beach. The small two-bedroom apartment they were renting temporarily until they bought a house was well laid out. The open concept in the kitchen and living room and the bright, colorful, casual furniture set against a crisp backdrop of white floors, walls, and ceilings at first gave me the illusion of being on vacation. I should've felt happy and free. Nora whined most of the time for my attention, which was exacerbated by my withdrawn feelings, causing me to ignore her. I found myself remaining silent most of the time. But my silence was interrupted by sudden changes of my mood. I snapped at the wrong time for the smallest, most insignificant misbehavior by Nora. Alone in my despair, I wondered what type of mother I was becoming. I felt helpless and scared.

I valued Cameron and Troy's attempt to get me out of the shell I had quickly formed around myself. I felt as if my life had changed from a thrilling scene to a frozen, feeble-looking picture. I tried to act as normal as I could. It was as if Yusuf's accident and death had killed something in me. I felt really empty at times, and at other times, I felt full of rage. After two weeks, I knew that I had to figure out my living situation. I couldn't exploit my friends' kindness, especially when they were happily planning to welcome the new baby in their lives.

I kept in touch with Mother on the phone. She told me that she had to bring Father back home because he was ill. At first, when I heard of Father's illness, I was somewhat skeptical. Was he reaching for attention, using his health as an excuse? I really didn't feel remorseful toward the news and was disappointed by Mother's weakness. She was once again making horrible decisions by welcoming Father back into her life. Hadn't he ruined all our lives enough already?

At that moment, my former life gushed back into my head. I recalled my torn-up country, Lebanon, my father's selfishness and continued abuse, my mother's weakness, my horrific childhood, and my husband, Yusuf, a lunatic con-artist, a man who burst out of nowhere to become my husband and terrorize my already traumatized life. A month after the accident, my body still went rigid at the horrendous memory.

A couple of weeks later, I received a call from Mother. She was calmer than usual, possibly because Father was around the house; he was controlling her ability to speak freely.

A few minutes into the conversation, she said, "I have to tell you something. It's about your father." She sighed.

I replied, "Okay."

"Your father has cancer. We just found out a few days ago." I frowned, but somehow, I felt really calm on the inside. She continued, "He went for a surgery to open up the blockage in his pancreas. The doctor found that his organs were enlarged and inflamed." We were both silent for a few long seconds. She continued in a tight tone. "The doctor is giving him weeks."

I hoped to feel a squeeze in my chest, but I remained calm and quiet. I closed my eyes. I couldn't really interpret my feelings about this news. What type of emotionless robot had I become?

I said, "How come the doctor operated on him? Didn't he see the signs of cancer?" I really didn't understand. Was the doctor that ignorant?

"The doctor had been trying to get him to take a blood test for the last year, during which your father had to be on a strict vegetarian diet for a couple of weeks. Your father refused to change his high-protein diet. You know how your father always enjoyed his food." She sighed again.

I let out a sigh too, shaking my head and scowling. I did remember Father's love for food. He always made sure he had plenty of chicken, beef, and fish. His portions alone were as big as my mother's and the kids' combined. I recalled how hungry we were growing up. How angry I was looking at Father's oversized plate! His egoism turned against him; it was sullen and cold with sharp edges. It stabbed him straight in the gut. Should I feel something with this new discovery? At this point, I shouldn't feel bitter and cynical. I wanted to feel remorseful.

My mother continued in a brittle, low tone, "Will you come and bring Nora soon? I've missed you both a lot. Even Chady has been asking about the both of you lately."

I pressed my lips tight together; my chest got tighter too. I didn't want to hear that. When did Father ever care about me or my daughter? We never even existed in his agenda. I ended the call with Mother soon after. I promised her that I would try to come as soon as I could. I felt lost. But I knew I had to make a decision. Did I really want to see my father during the last few weeks of his life?

A couple of days later, I was on my way back to Ontario. I had to be with Mother and my siblings; my family needed me to be around. I also had to see my father; I had decided that that was the right thing to do. During the cab ride, I started to feel something finally. I felt apprehensive. I hadn't seen my siblings for a while. How would I feel when I saw Father's ill face? How would I react to his weakness when I was much stronger?

***

The door swung open. A beautiful, bleached-blonde young woman stood in front of me. She wore tight jeans and a simple white shirt. I smiled. I recognized her right away, of course. She was as pretty as the picture I had seen. She still resembled Mother but in a wilder, more exotic way. I could tell that she was stressed despite her wide, welcoming smile. Her big brown eyes shone. I hugged Jasmine as tight as I could with my injured hand between us. She was slightly taller than me. Her slim shoulders felt warm and inviting. I could hear her quietly crying, while my eyes were still dry.

She spoke in a wobbly voice. "I've missed you, Sis. I've miss you so much!"

Now my eyes were starting to water.

I said calmly, "I've missed you too. You look gorgeous. Even better than the picture Mother showed me when she came to see me."

She pulled back a bit. Sniffing back her tears, she said, "You didn't change one bit. You are still as beautiful as always."

I wanted to laugh. I knew that couldn't be true, since I'd been looking way too dejected for years. But at least my face wasn't as pale as it had been weeks earlier.

I heard Nora say, "Mommy, who is this?"

I couldn't believe I'd forgotten about Nora. I looked around myself. I didn't even notice my brothers and mother, who were waiting to greet me. I was, after all, overwhelmed by Jasmine's touching welcome.

I looked over at Nora and said with a smile, "This is my sister. She is your aunt, sweetie."

Jasmine picked up Nora's small body and hugged her tightly. Nora still looked a little perplexed. I moved on to greet the twins. I gasped. They were at least a couple of inches taller than I was. They were almost thirteen years old—both had straight, brown hair; their bangs covered their foreheads. Their brown eyes were welling with tears. I didn't know what happened, but the sight of them brought my emotions to life. I felt hot tears on my face. The twins were more than brothers to me; I had practically raised them with Mother. I took turns hugging them. Each of the twins in turn insisted on carrying me around for a few seconds. I guessed they wanted to show me that they were all grown. Then they each grabbed Nora and tossed her into the air lightly. She was giggling loudly. She only knew her uncles and aunt from the pictures that I had shown her. She was meeting my family for the first time. I was glad she was happier and not as fretful as she had been earlier that day.

Hady was a tall young man. He looked very handsome with his dark-brown hair brushed to the back, his round face clean-shaven. His big brown eyes were moist. His full lips kissed my temple and both of my cheeks. He then gave me a tight squeeze. I felt sad all of a sudden, as if I had missed a decade already, not just a little over four years. I hadn't seen any of my siblings or my parents since Nora was born. Yusuf even picked up the couple of letters Mother had left me at her work. He made it too clear that he never wanted me to see my family.

Mother was behind Hady. She still looked the same as when I had met her weeks before in Montreal. She was my height, about five feet two inches. Her eyes seemed tired, with dark circles surrounding them. Her face appeared a bit pale, and her slightly graying hair was shoulder-length. All the abuse she had received in her life was starting to show in her features. Despite the fact that she looked worn down by her destiny, Mother's beautiful bone structure helped her somehow defy her age and the years of agony she had already lived through.

After we all settled in the living room, which seemed smaller than I remembered, maybe because Mother filled the small, open living and dining room area with better-looking furniture from what I recalled. It was still simple but no longer mismatched. It had a couple of warm beige leather sofas, a coffee table, and a square dining room table, and even the TV sat on a proper stand. I glanced around myself. I wondered where Father was. My heart sank slightly at the thought of him.

Gazing at my family, one at a time, with my eyes narrowed, I asked, "Where is Dad?" Their facial expressions changed considerably.

Mother's voice came as a low tone. "In the hospital. He was in a lot of pain. His doctor said yesterday that he should stay in the hospital until …" She didn't continue with her sentence. There was no need to. The whole thing about my father's health situation still felt somehow unreal. She added, "Hady was going to drive Jasmine and me soon. You can come if you want."

I gulped hard. All of a sudden, my throat felt dry. "I will come."

A couple of hours later, I was walking toward the hospital. I felt a little shaky when my family turned to enter his room, but I followed. The room was dimly lit, and the windows were dark since it was past 7:00 p.m. I looked over where my family stood. I took a deep breath, preparing myself to see Father. And when I did, I turned my gaze away right away. I needed to adjust my eyes to him. Slowly, I turned back to face him. I could hardly breathe. Was that my father? His face was pale and scrawny. His eyes were looking into empty space, dull and lifeless. I recalled my grandpa Mouhdy's dead blind eyes from ages ago. Father looked as if he was only a shell of his former self. I took a deep breath, swallowed my anxiety, and then moved closer. I wanted to say something, anything. My words were stuck deep inside my throat. I couldn't even pull them out.

I hesitated, and then I heard Mother saying to him, "Chady, Hannah is here. She came back."

He turned his face toward me. Could he see me? I didn't know what to expect at this point. I came closer. I held his skinny hand. It was cold. With a trembling voice, I said, "Dad, um, I … I …" I really didn't know what to say to him. I couldn't tell him that I came to watch him die. I wanted to shed tears. I wanted to do the normal things people did during these circumstances. Why couldn't I cry?

He wet his dried-up lips with his white tongue and said faintly, "Hannah, is that you?"

I nodded my head lightly, as if he could see me. I knew I had to speak up. "Yes. It's me, Dad." I added hesitantly, "How are you … um … feeling?"

His lips curled into a lifeless smile. "As good as a dying man," he said breathlessly.

I felt a squeeze in my chest. I couldn't say anything else. Should I give him false hope, when he already knew he was dying?

With great effort, I said, "We all care about you, Dad. We want you to be better."

He shook his head, as if he was dismissing that thought. I glanced at Mother. She had tears in her eyes. I wondered what she was feeling right then, watching the man who completely ruined her life, the man who caused her endless agony, the only man she ever knew, and the father of her five children helplessly dying. I closed my eyes. I didn't want to be there. The memory of Yusuf's accident came crawling down my head. This time, I couldn't dismiss his image. I just couldn't, not when Father was dying in front of me. I looked at the walls surrounding me. I had to get out *that moment!* I felt myself walking out of the room. My head was empty, but my heart was suffering from deep agony, as if my body was facing multiple feelings at once, not knowing how to react. I walked around the hospital.

I heard footsteps behind me a few minutes later. I stopped. I turned to meet Mother's gloomy gaze. She came close to me. She tucked a strand of my hair behind my ear and lightly touched my face. At that moment, I thought of something; I knew it was somewhat tactless to ask, but since my life was full of inappropriate events, I decided that it would be okay to pose that particular question.

I mumbled, "Did Dad know about his brother Nader?"

She sighed. I scrutinized her facial expression. She didn't say no right away, so I knew Father knew. I wondered if he even cared to know the pain his brother caused me. I wondered if he even believed Mother.

Mother shook her head lightly and then sighed right before she said, "Hannah, this is not the right time. Don't you think?" She didn't want to discuss it. Maybe I shouldn't have even opened my mouth.

When I went back to the room, Father's eyes were closed. Jasmine said that they gave him more medication to sedate him. I sat close to him, studying his face.

In a brittle voice, knowing that he couldn't hear me, I said, "Father, I wish you were a real father to me. I was dying to be loved by you. Your lack of love got me in so much trouble and will always leave a void deep inside my heart. Always." My tears started to fall on my face. I felt a sudden despair and hopelessness. I felt like a little child. I added, after trying to wipe some of it out, "No one will ever fill that void, Father."

Back at Mother's house, my brothers had already placed my suitcases in the basement. The room was small and gloomy. I arranged my things with difficulty since I could only use one arm. Luckily, Jasmine came to help me set up my new living quarters. I looked around. This was mine and Nora's new place to live.

***

Days passed stiffly and agonizingly slowly. I visited my father with my family almost every day. When I brought Nora, Father just looked at her. He was probably under heavy sedation and perhaps didn't even recognize her when I told him who she was. One day, I came without Nora. Mother's neighbor was babysitting her. Father was in and out of a coma. His body and organs were swelled with fluid. His breathing sounded like he was underwater. The doctor said he could pass at any time.

We were all by his side and watched the light completely fade out of his eyes. His feet were slowly turning cold. It was as if his soul was slowly escaping his body. All of a sudden, he stopped breathing. Liquid came out of his open blue lips. I looked at him, feeling frightened. I would never see Father's frown again. I would never hear his loud, terrorizing voice in my ears. His dead hand would never reach out to hurt me. Why was I not happy? Why was I now weeping for his loss? Why did it hurt so much to lose someone who could never show me love?

Chapter Two

IN LINE WITH OUR FAMILY'S Muslim practice, Father's funeral took place as quickly as possible after his death. We went to the mosque the next morning, where a funeral prayer was offered, during which Father's body was being washed by my brothers and a few male volunteers from the mosque. Mother, my sister, and I looked really modest with our white-and-black loose-fitting dresses. We covered our hair with hijabs, a Muslim hair cover. I only recognized a few people—my mother's neighbors.

I glanced around the large, clean, humble room, where statues and pictures were not permitted as decoration. Only the words of God and prayers were printed all over. My face was dry from tears, and I felt too exhausted even to breathe. I sat on the carpeted floor next to Mother and Jasmine and a few other ladies from our community. The Muslim burial prayer had just concluded, and we were listening to the imam's last words. Nora was wrapped in my arms. She was cranky and wanted to be glued to me at all times. I couldn't blame her, with the strange life we had had so far. I couldn't even think about the next day or even the rest of the day. I was still tormented by thoughts of my father's dead body, which I had seen this morning before he was taken to his burial. It brought agonizing memories. Yusuf was constantly on my mind; I couldn't get him off, no matter how hard I tried.

I recalled the day Father passed away, only the day before. Images flashed right before my eyes. The man was responsible for my horrifying childhood and teenage years, and yet I still had a little hope left until I met Yusuf, who demolished that hope. I was there when he died too. The two men accountable for my horrific destiny were now dead only weeks apart. *What a twisted fate,* I thought.

Father's body was to be buried after the prayer. Muslim women seldom accompanied the body to the gravesite, Mother decided to stay behind while my brothers and uncle Waleed attended, followed by many men from the community. The procession was led by the mosque's imam.

After the burial, we women went home to prepare for the evening *azza,* which was a three-day mourning period, where visitors could drop in during certain evening hours to read the Holy Koran and to offer condolences, supplication, and comfort.

***

A few weeks passed. One Saturday morning, we were sitting in Mother's small dining room, and Mother, Jasmine, and I were individually wrapped up in our own little worlds. We were all looking into space while drinking our morning coffee. We were not even speaking to one other. I felt like a city that had just been demolished by a tornado—calm, foggy, and completely destroyed. Nora came running toward me and sat on her favorite spot, my lap, almost knocking my coffee over, as usual.

I moved Nora to sit on an empty chair next to me. *The twins must still be in bed,* I thought. Hady had moved out a couple of years ago and worked at a car factory. I looked around. Apart from Nora, this room was full of women who were all shattered by our men. Even Jasmine, who was only twenty years old, managed to be married at age eighteen to a man who was another abuser. I wanted to cry and laugh at the same time. Was there some sort of curse in the family? What was wrong with our fate with men?

Right after Jasmine married and Hady left the house, Mother had decided to kick Father out, hoping to save the twins. As soon as she heard of Jasmine being harmed by her husband, she insisted that she come back home. Since then, Jasmine had filed for and been granted a divorce. Mother learned at last that by keeping Father, she was going to lose all her children to abusive partners. I realized that when someone ran away from his or her horrific destiny, he or she mostly got sucked into another horrifying one. *Lesson learned,* I thought while I sighed cynically. I sipped more coffee, and as I swallowed the bittersweet taste, I also swallowed a pain I felt in my chest. I sucked it deep inside. I was still afraid to think ahead, afraid to feel a hint of hope, afraid to be let down once again. I glanced over at Jasmine. She had Nora on her lap and was tickling her. I smirked sulkily.

Jasmine didn't seem as shattered as I felt, maybe because her horrible marriage was brief and her husband didn't threaten to kill her. He wasn't a dark, dominating criminal. I watched as Nora giggled. I knew I'd been ignoring her lately. I was really trying my best to be normal. *Maybe she should be my new light of hope,* I pondered. I knew that I needed to plan a better life for her and possibly a better future. But when I recalled my circumstances, I felt down. Once again, I was a jobless, twenty-three-year-old single mother. I had no education, no career ... I didn't know what happened to me all of a sudden. I got up and went outside into the small, cold backyard. I didn't want anyone to see me as I cried. Unfortunately, I heard Mother's voice. Why did she have to follow me? I turned to her; my face was filled with tears.

She said worriedly, "What happened to you all of a sudden?"

I must have looked as embittered as I felt on the inside.

I snapped, "Nothing happened; that's the problem. It's as if I'm back to ground zero. I have nothing ... no money, no education. I live in a matchbox, this time with my daughter." I turned away, leaning against the old chopped-wood backyard railing.

Mother's tone was calm. "Hannah, sweetheart, remember that with all that you went through, you are still alive." I shook my head.

My voice was ringing when I said, "Alive! I am alive!" I shouted, "Yippee! I am alive!" I pointed at my head. "But I'm dead here." I pointed at my chest. "And here. Only my body is moving. And I wish it wasn't. I wish I was dead right now." She came closer to hug me. I snapped my body away. I didn't want anyone to hug me. My body went stiff all of a sudden.

Mother said evenly, "Hannah, you are not alone right now. You have your daughter. She needs you." She added, "We are all here for you," and then sighed profoundly. "The poor girl has no father. You want to deny her right of having a mother too?"

I started weeping and then cried out, "What good was my father to us? I wish I never had a father! What good was he? Tell me! And Nora's father is better off dead than alive." Then I ran to the washroom. It was the only place I wouldn't be interrupted momentarily. I needed to be alone, with no one around me, at least for a few minutes.

***

As the days passed, I tried to figure out the best way to plan for my dim-looking future. Maybe a wise decision this time could faintly brighten it up somehow. I was collecting money from my unemployment, which would run out in another eight months. I had to figure out something before then. Feeling pitiful wasn't going to solve anything.

I quickly decided that I could take a few courses. I needed to land a job before my unemployment ran out. I didn't want Nora to suffer from lack of money. I really wanted to be able to provide for her the best that I could.

A week later, I started taking secretarial, English, and French courses. I recalled when I was sixteen years old, right after my family and I first emigrated from Lebanon to Canada, I could only speak in Arabic and French, merely a few words of English. Well, I came a long way since then, because I became fluent in English. I knew that being English-French bilingual would help me land a good job. Being busy was helping me slowly put my past behind me. I wished I could burn the memories and not just block them deep inside my brain. I knew that those memories would come back and wreck me one day.

Months had passed during which I completed these few courses. I felt proud to be able to reach at least one good goal I had set for myself. During the last few months, between my courses and looking after

Nora, I had no time to think. Not thinking was the best thing I could do for myself. Maybe there would be a light at the end of the tunnel; perhaps there was still a chance that I would be normal one day. I knew that I needed a car, which could help my chances of landing a job, not having to worry about long distances and transportation. I really had to overcome the horrifying feeling of being behind the wheel once again, which was going to bring up some ugly memories of the accident. I knew that I had to do what I had to do.

I also kept in touch with Cameron and Troy. I would never forget the great support and comfort they gave me while I was in Montreal and Nova Scotia, and I was glad to find out that they had a baby girl. I knew how much they yearned to have a girl from the way they adored Nora.

Mother worked as a cook in a busy Middle-Eastern restaurant and Jasmine as a hairdresser at a big, upscale salon nearby. They were both productive, and I wasn't. That knowledge made me feel despondent and useless. I hated to be slothful like Father was. The same day, I saw an ad for a used Nissan. It was small and affordable. I spoke to the owner right away, and by the end of the next day, I was driving again. A half hour after getting behind the wheel, I was more at ease. I picked up Nora and took her to Burger Land, a fast-food restaurant with a kid's play area. While she played in the kids' room, I looked at the hiring section of the newspaper. My Nissan used up all the savings I had managed to accumulate for the past few months.

After an intensive search, I landed a nearby receptionist job at a telecommunication company. I even found Nora a babysitter for when no one was available to look after her. The wage wasn't enticing, but it was my first step toward moving forward.

Chapter Three

It was during the month of July, on a Saturday evening. I brought some plates and cutlery to place outside on a small plastic table. We would have dinner while enjoying Mother's small backyard, which was blooming with different colored flowers all around. *At least she is always busy doing something,* I thought. She was always creative when it came to gardening and cooking. Jasmine and I, unfortunately, didn't inherit her creativity. We just enjoyed the sight of her beautiful garden and the wonderful taste of her exquisite food.

Mother had been working all day that day. I was off, and Jasmine had finished earlier; we both were left in charge of cleaning and cooking.

Ten minutes later, we were sitting around the table. Once again, the boys were out and about. I was sitting between Nora and Jasmine. I noticed that Mother was looking gloomy. She even frowned while looking at the table and plates of food, which consisted of macaroni and cheese, fries, chicken wings, and Caesar salad.

She said disappointedly, "I can't believe you girls were once married. You should have seen all the food I used to make when I was even younger than you. When Mother or my mother in-law came to visit, I would make sure to make the best food for them."

I didn't want to add to her agony and say, "What food?"

Jasmine asked, "What's wrong with macaroni and cheese and chicken wings?"

The chicken wings were the easiest; Jasmine picked them up on her way back home.

Mother glared at her. "It's children's food, not grown people's food."

Nora said happily, "I love macaroni and cheese; it's my favorite."

I said faintly, "Mine too."

Mother rolled her eyes and then added snappily, "I don't know how you girls are going to find husbands again."

"Do you want to bet?" Jasmine said, hiding a mischievous smile and her giggles inside her throat.

Mother frowned. She said thickly, "You, Jasmine, do worry me. At least your sister here is from work to home."

Jasmine rolled her eyes right before grabbing a chicken wing.

***

The next day, during the early afternoon, Jasmine and I lay in Mother's backyard after cleaning her whole house. Thankfully, Mother had already informed us that she was bringing some readymade food home.

I wore a black two-piece swimsuit Yusuf had gotten me years earlier, and Jasmine wore a two-piece red suit. We were tanning, taking advantage of Mother's absence. She had a big catering order and would be gone all day. She wasn't around to give us a disapproving lecture about the way we exposed our bodies even within the privacy of her backyard. Nora was playing with the new toys I had bought her a few days ago while she watched her kids' show on TV. The sun was burning my bare back. I turned to face the sun, putting my sunglasses back on. Jasmine turned too. She briefly glanced at me right before she sipped her ice water.

She mumbled, "You should come with me tonight, Hannah." I looked at her. Her wavy hair was tucked into a bun.

I asked, "Where?" even though I already knew the answer to that. That would give me time to think about my answer. Jasmine had been trying to convince me for a couple of months to join her and her friends at a nearby nightclub. I refused her invitation, because it was absurd. The idea of me facing a normal, happy crowd was scary. The thick shell I had formed around myself kept me safe and sound. I hardly even socialized at work with my coworkers.

She said, annoyed, "To the club, Sis. Where else? Come on! You really need to get out. You are like Mother said, work-home, work-home." She sighed before adding, "Your birthday is in only a few days."

I wanted to laugh at the way Jasmine spoke, as if she had been born a free-spirited woman. When I first moved back, Jasmine startled me with her character transformation. I couldn't identify the woman she had become. I wondered what had happened to the quiet, reserved girl I once knew. I closed my eyes tight. I was content the way I was. I didn't need to get out. That could cause me so much discomfort.

She added, "I will do your hair and makeup. You will look like a hot mama!" I raised my brows lightly.

Hot mama! What was wrong with Jasmine? I sniggered lightly.

"Hannah. It would mean so much to me if you came. Come on, Sis."

I mumbled, "Jasmine, am I supposed to please you on my birthday?" I giggled lightly. "Would you like a present to go along with that too?"

Jasmine giggled along with me and then added, "You are beautiful, Sis, and soon to be a twenty-four-year-old woman. Having a little fun won't hurt." She then grabbed her ice water and again sipped from it.

I sighed and, surprising even myself, said, "Fine. I will go."

Jasmine squealed happily, and then she made a tune out of her next sentence.

"Finally, the widow is out and about to have some fun!"

I frowned and snapped lightly, "I hate the word *widow*."

"Are you kidding me, Sis? You are like the youngest, sexiest widow I have ever met."

I replied gallingly, "That's because the only other widows you have seen so far are Grandma Amina and Mother. So I am not taking that as a compliment." Then I felt a cool splash on my arm.

"Jasmine, are you kidding me?" I yelled out while splashing her with my icy water. Soon, both of our icy waters had landed on our sunbaked skin. We were both laughing loudly when I heard a loud voice.

"What on earth is going on in here?" We both turned to meet Mother's angry glare.

I said in a shaky voice, "Mom, I thought you were working all day?"

She snapped, "Well, the catering order got canceled, so I came back to see my daughters half naked in my backyard." She then turned away while cursing under her breath and slammed the backyard's glass door angrily behind her.

Later on that day, Mother agreed to my uncle Waleed's wife Soha's invitation to spend the rest of the weekend at her place. Uncle Waleed had sponsored us to Canada years ago, a couple of years after he had sponsored my grandma Amina and his brother Wael. Right after dinner, I took Nora to the babysitter; I then came back home to get ready for my nightclub event. I tried not to think about it. The only club I had managed to go to was a strip club. Jasmine assured me that the two clubs didn't compare. I wondered if I knew how to dance or have fun. I really didn't wish to feel awkward and foolish. Jasmine promised never to leave my sight.

Jasmine expertly started with my hair. She cut it evenly and layered it a bit. Her hands were moving with confidence. An hour later, my hair was still long. The mousse she had applied made it look frizz-free and wavy. I loved my new bangs, which helped define my small facial features. It even gave me a super-young, innocent look. My makeup was simple and yet perfectly applied. I was surprised to see how talented Jasmine was. She managed to transform me from geek to chic in no time. And she even gave me one of her sexy dresses to wear. It was blue, sleek, and a few inches above the knee. Her black sandals fit my feet almost perfectly, adding five inches to my short stature. I was really hoping I didn't trip and break a leg, since I couldn't recall the last time I was in heels.

Jasmine went to get ready quickly while I stood in front of the mirror scrutinizing the new me, which looked nothing like me. I didn't even remember when the last time I looked half decent was. Jasmine emerged in the living room. She looked stunning, with her long brown, blonde-highlighted, wavy hair. Her makeup was immaculate, and her short, tight, black dress defined her curvy but slim figure. Her cell phone rang. She answered by saying, "Are you here? Okay, we are on our way out." She turned to me and said, "Let's go. Travis is waiting for us."

I got in the car and said hello shyly. Travis, the man behind the wheel, was somewhere in his thirties. He was average with slightly curly hair and pale skin. He had a little black moustache that gave him a manly look. Jasmine mentioned that she knew him through a close friend. I noticed that she stuttered as she mentioned the "close friend." Jasmine also declared that she was going to meet a few more friends at the club. That thought made me more apprehensive. I was hoping Travis wouldn't speak to me at all.

As soon as I settled into the back of the car, Travis glanced at me through the car's rearview mirror. "Hannah, I've heard so much about you. I am glad to finally meet Jasmine's lovely sister. You girls somewhat look alike."

I glanced over at Jasmine. I wondered what she had said.

I cleared my throat lightly and said, "Thank you. Nice to meet you too." I wasn't sure what else to say. I felt way too tense to even open my mouth.

Travis smiled into his rearview mirror. I was thankful he then directed his conversation to Jasmine. Before we got to the club, we had to make one more stop. A tall, pretty blonde girl got into the car. She wore a short white dress with white sandals.

"Hey, guys," she said loudly. Then she turned to me and added, "You must be Hannah, Jasmine's sister. Oh! You look gorgeous!" I smiled at her shiny, beautiful blue eyes. "My name is Claire."

I shook her hand lightly saying, "Nice to meet you, Claire."

Travis turned on some hip-hop music. I had started to relax a bit by the time he parked the car.

The parking lot was full. There were people standing around their cars, many of them smoking cigarettes. Most girls wore short dresses, loads of makeup, and high-heeled sandals. I felt better. I thought Jasmine, Claire, and I were way overdressed.

We all walked toward the club's entrance. There were a few people ahead of us in line. A sharp-eyed, tall African American doorman man asked me abruptly, "ID please."

I swallowed my anxiety, as I briefly remembered Yusuf when he was trying to get me into the Las Vegas clubs. My hand shook slightly when I showed my ID. I was more than old enough.

Once we were inside, I turned to my sister and whispered, "Jasmine, how come they let you in? You are not twenty-one yet."

Jasmine was turning twenty-one next month. She seemed puzzled when she looked at me.

"I am old enough. Nineteen is the legal age requirement in here." She sighed. "My gosh, Sis, sometimes I think you came from a faraway jungle."

I shrugged before I replied, "I didn't come from a faraway jungle; I came from hell."

Her eyes narrowed, and she seemed remorseful all of a sudden.

"Oh! Sorry, Sis." She then hugged me lightly. "You will be okay; I promise you that."

I didn't notice that Travis and Claire were staring at us until I looked around. They both had a repentant expression on their faces. I blushed, starting to feel awkward and discomfited; I wondered if they knew anything about my previous life. Travis insisted on paying for all of our cover charges.

I followed everyone to another entrance. A big, crowded place was set under a dim light. Moving spotlights were jumping around. Waitresses wearing short, skin-tight black dresses were shifting around as swiftly as they could around the swarming crowd. They had to hold their trays way up over their heads. As soon as I stepped in, I started bumping into people, realizing that I hated the jam-packed crowd, who were moving in so many directions. I felt a sudden anxiety and repulsion.

As I glanced around, my face felt frozen. I felt someone holding me by the hand and pulling me. I gazed in front of me. I saw Jasmine's long hair under the dim light. I would hate to lose her right then. I could definitely suffocate and die. The music was so loud. I couldn't even hear myself think, which was something I didn't mind. I really didn't wish to use my messed-up brain cells. I noticed that they were playing top-forty hits mixed with some Latin music. Most of the people were dancing. Some were just moving their heads to the tune. I wondered if there was a designated dance area, because people danced everywhere. All of a sudden, Jasmine stopped. Then I heard her shout into my ear, "What do you want to drink?"

I didn't know what I should drink, maybe a soda. "Pepsi!" I shouted at her as she gave me an odd look. I wondered why.

"Pepsi at a bar? I will get you something better, a cooler. Just drink it slowly." I noticed that there were several people in front of us. Were they all waiting to be served? I couldn't even see the bartender. The lights over the bar were bright. A few minutes later, I noticed two male bartenders. People had to shout their drink orders into their ears. That was what Jasmine did. She gave him the money and grabbed two bottles of wine coolers. She gave me my cooler and then tipped hers to mine. "Cheers."

I smiled curtly and drank my first sip of an alcoholic drink. I liked it right away. It tasted like carbonated lemonade. I sipped some more, realizing how thirsty I was. Then I noticed Travis with Claire. He was buying a couple of drinks.

My drink was almost done. I just reached to place it on the bar. Jasmine looked at me, stunned.

"Take it easy, Sis. You will get drunk soon."

I lifted my shoulders lightly. I had never been drunk before. Then I recalled when I got sick on my wedding day ages ago and the flu syrup. I felt a squeeze in my chest at the memory. Yusuf was angry because I drank most of the large bottle in one day. He accused me of wanting to get drunk on it. I enjoyed the feeling of numbness then. I wouldn't mind feeling it once again. My brain needed to go on holiday.

Travis came closer. He handed me another bottle of cooler. I glanced at Jasmine. She gave me a murky smile. I couldn't comprehend it, but I smiled lightly, accepting the drink. I wanted to reach over to my purse to pay him.

Jasmine stopped me by placing her hand on mine. "You don't have to pay him. It's his treat."

I turned to face him and thanked him.

Jasmine once again shouted in my ear, "Let's dance!"

I shook my head lightly. I didn't wish to move an inch. I was afraid to bump into people.

She insisted, "Let's dance, Sis. Come on." She pulled me by my hand again.

I finished my second drink quickly. I needed my hand to push through the crowd. My head was starting to get numb. I liked the feeling of numbness. Maybe soon, all the ugly thoughts in my head would evaporate. I smelled something weird, a mixture of strong cologne and faint sweat.

Jasmine spotted Claire. She was dancing with a medium-height man. He had dark-brown spiky hair and a clean-shaven face, which was an olive complexion. His eyes seemed dark under the dim light. He was good-looking, I would say, with a mischievous, cute smile. Jasmine moved closer to them. The man's face lit up at the sight of her as they exchanged a hug. She then said something to him. He looked toward me, smiling, and then came closer. He gave me a light hug. He was shouting, "Hannah! Nice to finally meet you. I'm Henry."

I smiled lightly before shouting back, "Nice to meet you!" Then I heard myself giggle. I felt good.

Jasmine was shouting something to both of them when all of a sudden some of the crowd came in between us. I looked around myself, feeling lost. Somehow, the people who came between us were all giants. I couldn't even see Jasmine anymore. Then I felt a hand pulling me toward a broad male chest. His white shirt was half buttoned. I stared, horrified and frozen, at his black chest hair.

How did that happen? How did I end up in here?

The tall man had his hands around me and was moving me to the Latin music. It was a song I liked, "Livin' la Vida Loca." I tried to pull away. My heart was racing rapidly, but the crowd kept on pushing my head toward his hairy, sweaty chest. *Crap! Where is my sister?*

I pulled away once again, and then I heard him shout in my ear, "What's your name?"

I shook my head lightly at him. I really needed to find my sister. Then I heard myself say, "I don't have a name." My head was spinning.

"No, really."

What is wrong with him? Why would a man want to force a woman to dance?

"Loca. My name is Loca." Then I pushed him away once again. I felt someone pulling me by my arm. I was alarmed. *What now?* I looked around and saw Henry. I felt relieved right away. At least he knew my sister.

Henry looked at the man and shouted, "She is with me, man." He then placed his arm around my shoulders and guided me to where Jasmine was.

This place is ridiculously insane! I will never come back again!

Soon I was dancing with Jasmine and Claire again. Henry disappeared for a bit, and then I spotted him again with more drinks. He handed a drink to each of us. He then said something to Jasmine in her ear. She turned to me, her face beaming.

She said, "I will be right back." Then she disappeared into the crowd.

I sipped my drink while trying to coordinate dancing and drinking all at once. It was really hard, especially when my brain cells were somehow getting disconnected. I emptied my bottle. I had to concentrate on my dancing. I really didn't wish to look too silly to the rest of the crowd. I noticed that Claire wasn't around. Henry was dancing closer to me. He had both of his hands around my waist. I was glad in a way; his hands balanced me somehow. He drew me closer. He smelled of strong cologne. The beat was getting faster. A few more songs played while we danced. I felt myself spinning, or maybe the room was spinning, I wasn't sure anymore, but as soon as he drew me closer again, I held on to him because I was about to fall down. I had both my arms around his neck. I even felt his face and warm breath around my neck. I didn't care to know what he was doing. I smiled, feeling happy, way too happy. I wanted to shout out loud.

He took me by my arm, heading toward the bar. Bumping into random sweaty people didn't bother me anymore. I didn't mind if they all even hugged me at this point.

"I have to go to the washroom!" I shouted to Henry. "Where is the washroom?"

My speech sounded slurry. He led me toward a bright entrance. I didn't want to be under the light. I would rather be in the dark, but I went in. There were a few ladies going into the ladies' room too. I just followed them. Once I was done, I washed my hands and scurried back. Henry was waiting for me with another drink. I giggled happily and then drank the bottle in a few gulps. I didn't know what I was doing next. I found myself dancing again. Henry's body was once again too close to mine. I felt a little sweaty and really disengaged from reality. I held on to him tighter.

"I think you are drunk. You need some fresh air," I heard him say.

I was glad he was holding my hand because at that point, I couldn't coordinate properly. I felt a light breath on my face.

I heard him say, "You are lovely," while drawing me closer.

I didn't know what I said back; my voice was some sort of an echo. I couldn't have made sense anyway since I felt as if I didn't exist. I felt something cool under me when I sat down. Where was I? I saw trees, and then I felt a little cooler.

Henry held my hand and said, "Are you okay?"

I nodded, but soon after, I felt that I was about to be ill. I couldn't confess this feeling to Henry; it was way too embarrassing. I fought the urge for a few minutes. Then I ran toward the tree. I found myself on my knees, while I emptied my whole stomach's contents. I couldn't think of Henry's disgusted reaction. I didn't know why I felt that sick. I felt Henry's hands moving my hair away. *That is way too distracting,* I thought. I wanted to just disappear from there and be at home, cuddled next to Nora under the covers. I felt his hands helping me back onto my feet. He handed me a little serviette. I wiped my lips and face lightly. I couldn't even look over at Henry when he sat down next to me. All of a sudden, I felt really tired. I felt my head tilting toward his shoulder. He drew me closer; then I felt nothing.

His hazel eyes were glaring at me, the way they always did. He was moving closer. I knew he wanted to hurt me. It was from the way he strolled with his long legs, and his jaw was too tense. I gasped when he held me by my shirt. I was terrified. Did he know that he was dead because of me? Was he seeking revenge? His hands came to smack me across the face; I moved my hand swiftly to stop him. Then I panted as I opened my eyes. I saw my hand close to my face, as if I were protecting it. My neck hurt from tilting my head, which felt warm. I lifted it lightly. *Where am I?* I looked around. There were trees. I was sitting on a bench. I turned to face the man sitting beside me. *Henry!* I swallowed hard. Had I been sleeping on his shoulder for a while? How did I end up here?

I heard him say, "Are you okay?" I glanced at him shyly. Feeling embarrassed, I wondered where Jasmine, Travis, and Claire were.

I stuttered, "S-s-orry. I am really sorry. I don't know what happened to me." I didn't even look at him.

He said apologetically, "It was my fault. I shouldn't have brought you more drinks. I should've seen the signs of you being drunk." He looked into my eyes. "I just wanted you to sober up before we went back. I don't want Jasmine to kill me."

My voice was husky. "How long have I been here?"

"Just half an hour. You should be able to walk straight now. No more Smirnoff Ice for you!" he said and laughed.

I got up and straightened my dress. I smiled at him. He had a boyish face.

I wondered how bad I looked right that moment. *I should go straight to the washroom,* I decided as I started to walk back.

"Your purse!" he yelled out.

I turned to grab my purse from his hands and walked more steadily toward the club entrance. I had never thought getting drunk would feel that awful. But then again, right before feeling awful, there was a feeling of disconnection from reality—a sensation I really enjoyed.

I checked the time. It was 12:30 a.m. In less than two hours, I had managed to make a huge mess out of myself. After I came out of the washroom, I found Jasmine. She looked really worried. There was a man behind her. He was tall with a fair complexion, dark hair, and big dark-brown eyes. He was really handsome.

Jasmine said, "What happened to you, Hannah? Henry texted me back saying you were okay. But what happened?"

I frowned and looked away. "Nothing." I really didn't wish to speak of the awful embarrassing moment I experienced with her friend Henry.

Then I heard the tall, handsome man say loudly, "Hannah, nice to meet you. Jasmine has told me so much about you. I am Nathan."

I smiled at him and shook his hand.

I turned to Jasmine. She said, "Sis, Nathan is um …"

"Her boyfriend," Nathan added. Then he smiled.

My eyes grew wide. Jasmine had a boyfriend? Mother hadn't killed her yet! Jasmine's expression was somewhat embarrassed but relieved. Maybe she wanted to share Nathan's type of friendship with someone. I smiled at the both of them. I wanted Jasmine to feel at ease about me knowing of Nathan.

"Nice to meet you, um, Jasmine's boyfriend … I mean Nathan," I said playfully. I still felt a little lightheaded.

"Hey, Nathan!" Henry's voice came from behind me.

I blushed at the recent encounter I had had with him.

"Hannah, Henry, have you guys met?" Nathan said.

I pressed my lips together. *A little too much,* I thought. He even met my obnoxious, foolish ill self.

I said faintly, "Yes. We did." I turned to Henry, who smiled lightly. I smiled too. I guessed what happened wasn't too bad.

We stayed another hour, during which I completely stayed away from alcoholic beverages and out of trouble. Jasmine and Nathan danced together. I slowly got over what had happened earlier and danced with Claire and Travis after Henry had to leave suddenly. That night, we left with Nathan. During the car ride, I watched as he grabbed Jasmine's hand. I wasn't sure whether to be happy or fearful for her. I really didn't want Jasmine to get hurt by yet another man.

Chapter Four

A FEW MONTHS HAD PASSED when one Saturday morning, I was cleaning the dishes after Nora's breakfast in the kitchen, before I made coffee for myself. Mother was at Soha's house. The twins had some sort of sports practice. I was hoping I could spend time with Jasmine, maybe go to the mall, since she mentioned last night that she had the day off, but I could hear her steps upstairs, as if she was already up and getting ready to go somewhere.

Nora was going to full-time school, The twins picked her up on their way back home from school and stayed with her until I came back home from work. At work, I tried to associate with my coworkers; I just needed to have more confidence. I shopped for a few new modest outfits and styled my hair differently. Right after the night at the club, I decided not to look like a miserable widow anymore. I started to look for a small, affordable apartment that was big enough for Nora and me, and at the same time, I was looking for a better job with better pay. I really wanted to move ahead in life.

I called Jasmine from the living room.

"Yes?" she answered.

"Do you want to have coffee with me?" I really needed some company. I felt really lonely and pessimistic.

"Sure, but I don't have much time. I have a wedding to go to."

I frowned. I hated the word *wedding*. I quickly made us coffee. Soon, I noticed that Nora was missing. I called her name.

"Yes, Mommy!" her tiny, high-pitched voice replied from the basement.

"What are you doing?" I really hoped she wasn't creating a disaster downstairs. That was her favorite thing to do.

"I am getting ready!"

"For what? Too early for that, Nora. Come here and watch some TV." I felt better when I could see her around me, behaving.

"Coming!" she said. I heard her steps loud and a little heavy. My eyes grew wide when I saw her. What was I supposed to do with this girl? She had on a pink-and-white dress. Her hair was straight, thick, and long. She wore some lipstick and eye makeup all over her little face, and on her little feet, she had my favorite pink sandals.

I tried to sound angry when I said, "Seriously, Nora!" I really should have sounded angrier. I should have had a frown on my face, but I couldn't; she looked way too cute.

She handed me a brush, and trying to move her hair away from her little round face, she said grumpily, "I can't brush my hair right! Tiffany said that she was going to the Kids' Zone today. I want to go too."

"Really! Says who? Don't you think you should ask first? Plus, it's only ten in the morning, way too early for Kids' Zone."

"Mommy!" She stomped her feet with my sandals. I frowned. What a temper on this girl!

"I can brush your hair," I added softly, while walking toward the living room

Without a word, she turned to sit on the carpet next to me. Every time I brushed a piece, she screamed, "Ouch!"

I sighed and said, "Why won't you let me take you to the hairdresser? They will only cut a little bit of your hair. I promise."

She shrugged and snapped, "Mom, no! Princesses don't cut their hair."

I rolled my eyes. "Sorry, Princess Nora, I forgot."

When I was finally done, Nora got up to inspect herself in front of the mirror. I sighed. I then saw Jasmine coming down. I smiled She looked really pretty in a long, sleek, off-the-shoulder green dress. Her makeup and hair were immaculate, as usual.

"Jasmine! Look at you!" She smiled happily.

After we sat at the kitchen table, I asked her a question that had been on my mind for a while.

"Jasmine, how on earth were you able to convince Mother to let you marry Mike? He is not Muslim, not even from the Middle East?"

She sipped some coffee and was silent for a bit.

"After you left to marry your lunatic man, I felt all alone here. Then I met Mike." She looked into space and then added, "I couldn't live under Dad's rule anymore. And so I married Mike as soon as I turned eighteen years old. Stupid me, I thought I was going to skip all the Middle-Eastern and Muslim men after seeing what happened to you and Mother."

I asked, "Mother didn't mind?"

She shrugged her shoulders. "She did at first. She wouldn't speak to me for a while. It was very hard for me." She had a scowl on her face. "When Hady moved out, I called, seeking her help after Mike hit me. After that, Mother asked Dad to move out and requested that I move back with her. She even encouraged me to get a divorce."

I bit my lower lip hard. I was glad Jasmine was saved.

After studying my face, she added, "How about you, Sis? Why don't you want to find a nice man who wants to look after you?"

My heart squeezed as I recalled of all the men in my life. I really wanted to laugh at the phrase "wants to look after you." All the men who had come into my life had purely one objective—to destroy me. I felt sulky all of a sudden. I wished I had never mentioned anything to her.

I said cynically, "I don't believe in that. I feel as if I am already doomed." I sipped some coffee and added, "Most men want to own you just so they can destroy you." I looked away from Jasmine's gaze. I didn't want her to see the pain in my eyes.

"Don't generalize, Hannah. I think you need to stay positive."

Positive! How could I be positive after what had happened to me? I had become afraid of my own decisions. I didn't trust my judgment anymore. I hated all men. They were all the same!

She added, "I think Henry likes you."

I frowned; I didn't want to think of the embarrassing moment I had had with him.

I said, "What makes you think so?"

"Well, for one thing, he keeps asking Nathan about you. I heard that he is single now." I didn't know he had a girlfriend when I met him at the club.

I slumped my shoulders slightly; that subject didn't interest me.

She added, "Nathan met him a few months ago through Travis. I heard his parents are pretty loaded."

I gave her a curt smile. "Good for him." I wasn't flattered knowing that Henry liked me; nor was I impressed by the fact that he was single with money. In fact, I hardly felt desire or excited about anything. Sometimes, I wondered if my feelings had died completely.

"I'm not ready yet, Jasmine. I need lots of time."

"Lots of time to become old and wrinkly? Come on, Hannah. Open up your heart. You're too young to bury yourself alive."

I frowned, and then I snapped, "What heart? My heart is dead. It's now a black stone." I wanted to conclude that ridiculous conversation. I didn't want to waste a tear over my pathetic life that day. As I was trying to calm down, I heard Nora's voice calling me from the living room.

"Mommy, can we go to Kids' Zone soon? Please, please …"

I took a deep breath. "We'll see, Nora. I don't know yet." I rolled my eyes and added, "In the afternoon, but only if you behave?"

I could hear her bouncing up and down, yelling out, "Yay!" I sighed, annoyed. Maybe I could bring an exciting book to read while she played. I wished I knew where her friend Tiffany lived just so I could bring her along with us. At least Nora could have some company.

Jasmine's phone rang. She picked it up and was soon on her way out, but she turned to me and gave me a hug, adding, "You have a heart of gold, Sis … not a heart of stone."

Yeah right! I thought scowling. *A long time ago, I had a super-foolish heart.*

The twins walked into the house fifteen minutes later. After washing up, they went into the living room. I heard Nora scream.

"Mommy, I want to watch my princess show!"

I took a deep breath; the whining and fighting over the TV had started already.

Nora came into the kitchen. She had tears in her eyes. "My uncles won't let me watch my princess show." She was whining, rolling her lower lips.

Trying to keep my voice down, I said, "Nora, you have to take turns! You can't watch shows about princesses all day. Maybe you should read a book."

She stomped her bare feet a few times on the ground. I wondered what she had done with my pink sandals.

"I don't want to read; I want to watch my princess show," she repeated angrily a few times.

Nora was way too stubborn! I gave up. I really wished I had my own place just so we could have more privacy.

Later on that day, I decided to go to the mall, right before I took Nora to the Kids' Zone. She insisted that I buy her a little princess dress from one of the big department stores.

When I was about to pay with my debit card, the short West Indian cashier associate said, "Would you like to put that on our store's Visa card? If you apply today, you can get 20 percent off your purchase."

I thought about it for a second. I was always reluctant to apply for a credit card. I didn't know why. I was perhaps afraid to overspend, or it could be because Yusuf always made me pay with his fraudulent credit cards.

I said, "Why not? How long does it take?"

"Half an hour at the most. You will get your actual credit card by mail, but we'll use the number you will receive from the company to make the purchase today and get the discount. All I need is two pieces of ID."

Half an hour later, I came back to see if the credit number was ready, just so I could finish and get it over with. Nora had been whining for a while.

The friendly associate called the credit card company again. I frowned. I waited by the cashier desk. I hoped the procedure wouldn't take much longer.

After a few minutes, she said, with a tense smile on her face, "I am so sorry, ma'am. You weren't approved for the credit card."

I frowned before replying, "Why not? I don't understand."

She gave me a piece of paper with a number.

"Call this number; they will explain it to you better."

I felt really annoyed. I didn't feel like calling anyone else when all I wanted was just to pay and go. I had waited a half an hour for no reason. *Why wasn't I approved?* I wondered, right before I paid for my purchases using my debit card.

It was already past 4:00 p.m. when I arrived at the Kids' Zone.

Twenty minutes had passed, during which I kept an eye on Nora until she settled in and was playing happily on her own. The Kids' Zone was crowded with loud children of all ages from toddlers to preteens and parents. When the pizza arrived, I went to call her. She was playing with a girl who was about her age. She had long, thick blonde hair, big blue eyes, and a red-pink dress. I gazed at the both of them, stunned. Their dresses, hair, and hairstyles and the way they talked—it was as if they had copied each other.

As soon as Nora saw me, she jumped up, saying excitedly, "Mommy! Tiffany came!"

I smiled. Nora wasn't just bluffing about meeting Tiffany. Finally, I met Ms. Tiffany, whose name was always on Nora's lips ever since she started school.

"Hi, Tiffany!"

Tiffany looked at me shyly.

I added, "Pizza is ready. Tiffany, you can join us if you want."

Nora held Tiffany's hand and guided her over to our table. They both sat down and started nibbling on their food while speaking nonstop. I noticed that both girls were really talkative. I just watched them, periodically grinning at the way they spoke mostly about princesses; they were really entertaining. Ten minutes later, a slim blonde woman, slightly taller than I was, who seemed to be somewhere in her late twenties, walked toward our table. Tiffany smiled when she saw her.

"Hi, Mommy," she said.

Her mother replied, "Hi, Tiffany. I was looking for you all over!" She had an angry blue gaze, and her fair skin looked flushed. I blushed instantly.

I cleared my throat. "Sorry! It's my fault. I should've asked you first if Tiffany could join us." I added after seeing her frown disappearing, "Would you like to sit down?"

She smiled politely. She sounded hesitant. "I have more pizza and fries too."

I said, "My name is Hannah, and this is my daughter, Nora," looking at Nora.

"Mandy." She shook my hand and then, after turning to face Nora, added, "So you are Nora! We finally meet. Tiffany always talks about you." Nora blushed lightly, shying away.

I smiled. "Same here. For the last few weeks, all I heard was Tiffany this and Tiffany that." Mandy laughed along with me.

Mandy and I went to collect her things from her table. At least I was going to have company other than my book. Time flew. Mandy was fun and free-spirited. She reminded me of Jasmine. I learned that she was divorced with only one child and she lived very close to me. At last, Nora could have some true friends. I briefly recalled the gypsy life we had once had.

Mandy and I even exchanged numbers to arrange plans for the girls to meet. Despite the fact that Mandy was easy to talk to, I hardly spoke about myself to her. I really didn't want to bring up any sad moments. When she asked me about Nora's father, I was thankful the girls weren't around. Without looking at her, I replied that her father had died in an accident and that his memory still hurt. I could tell that she was really sympathetic. I hated sympathy.

Chapter Five

It was on a Friday, during my lunch break at work. I skimmed the number the cashier had given me from the department store while I sat at my desk. I was trying to make up my mind about whether to throw the piece of paper away or to call the number on it. It had been almost a week since I was disapproved for the department store credit card. Was there something I didn't know? I briefly recalled the check scam. I wondered if Yusuf had done anything else to ruin me. I made my decision as I felt my heart pound.

A man answered on the other line; he was polite. After giving him my information and replying to some security questions, I was placed on hold for another twenty minutes.

"Ma'am, could you confirm your previous residence at …?" He then gave me an address I was trying to erase from my memory—Yusuf's condo.

I replied faintly, "Yes."

"It shows here that there are a Visa, Master Card, and couple of department store credit cards with an owing unpaid balance."

My heart sank. I shook my head. What credit card? What was going on?

"I've never owned a credit card. The only time I wanted to apply was a few days ago."

"That's not what shows here. You haven't made a payment for a while now. Your file was with collection for three and half years already."

Collection? What on earth?

"I didn't know anything about that. I swear I never applied for anything." I was running out of breath. I was scrutinizing my brain. How could that be?

"Ma'am, there is nothing I can do. All I know is that your credit score doesn't look very good right now. I could mail you the credit report if you want. It's from a few credit cards, owing a little over twelve thousand dollars. And with that, you can make payment arrangements."

I hung up with him. *That is crazy. Crazy!* I thought angrily. Each time I tried to take one step forward, I was pushed back a few steps and suddenly had to deal with another unfortunate event. I called the local bank and asked them about what it took for someone to apply for a credit card. I was ignorant when it came to credit cards, since I had really never had to physically apply for one. Yusuf took the initiative to apply for so many on my behalf. I was told a few years back that all they needed was a complete application with personal information and a signature with one piece of ID, but lately, the procedure of getting a credit card was more secure, with the additional requirement of two pieces of valid picture ID.

I sat at my desk, looking blankly in front of me. I was remembering Yusuf's words when he brought me a few forms to sign. He claimed that with those signed bank documents, I was part of his wealth just in case anything happened to him. Like a fool, I signed, just to get him off my back, not knowing that I was signing my financial freedom away instead. And as a substitute for being part of his wealth, I was part of his scam. I was just like most of the people he had swindled and cheated. I was no different. And, with all the credit cards that were in my name, I was in debt with a total amount of over twelve thousand dollars.

I also recalled the $2,900 check he wrote for himself, cleaning out my bank account. The bank had reimbursed me then, but I doubted they would reimburse me yet again, since years had passed since he applied for those credit cards. My chest felt way too congested. I couldn't breathe anymore. How come I didn't think of the document he made me sign at the beginning of our marriage? Maybe it was because I wished I didn't exist at that time, especially that particular day. I was never focused and was always drowsing away, feeling tired. I only became more focused when Nora was born—I knew she needed me. I did promise myself that I would never shed one more tear over pathetic Yusuf, but I couldn't stop the tears that came down my face. Was I ever going to wake up from my nightmare?

Later on that day, on my way back home, I got a call from Mandy. She asked me if I wanted to come over with Nora. I hesitated at first. I was once again at a low point in my life. I really didn't wish to meet anyone. When Yusuf died, I promised myself that I wasn't going to look behind me or feel self-pity. That merely distracted me from moving forward. But that day, I couldn't see in front of me. I could only look behind me. My horrific past just flooded back into my head like a long preview of my upcoming future.

Mandy welcomed both Nora and me with a wide smile. I smiled shyly at her. I was looking around me, all astonished. She really had a beautiful place. The entrance was wide with a large mirror on the side. I turned away from my reflection; I hated to look at myself when I felt glum. The entrance led to a curved stairway, which led to the second floor and was surrounded by rooms. I glanced to my left at an elegant, immaculate room. I could tell it was the guest sitting room from the way it was decorated—a couple of paintings, contemporary dark-brown couches with light-brown and yellow cushions, and a large center round glass table. I followed Mandy.

She opened an interior white French door that led to her kitchen, which was on the right side of the entrance. I wondered how many rooms this house consisted of. Mother's house was less than half the size, because the rooms were like sardine cans. The room in the unfinished basement I was staying in was definitely less than half the size of Mandy's kitchen. I was really impressed. I had almost forgotten about my trouble, looking around me. I didn't even notice Nora's disappearance. I asked Mandy about it.

"Tiffany probably took her to either her room or her play area."
I smiled and sat at the kitchen table island. Nora would love to play.
"Coffee?"
"Yes, thank you, with milk and sugar please."

She placed my coffee mug in front of me. I sipped some, realizing how delicious it was. Mandy brought some lemon cake. I liked her spacious white-painted kitchen. It was bright, especially since the blind that led to the backyard was open. Her granite kitchen table island combination could seat up to eight. The cabinets were white, making the kitchen look really spacious. I took a peek at her backyard, which looked stunning too. It was large and green, surrounded by flowers on both sides. I tilted my head a bit. There was a medium-sized covered swimming pool.

"Would you like to sit outside?"

I smiled shyly. "That's okay. It's good here." I didn't know why I had an overwhelmed feeling. That day was the wrong day to come there—after finding out that my credit score was way down. How was I going to get out of this mess? All of a sudden, I felt cynical; but I tried not to show it.

"You look pretty young!" Mandy said.

I smiled. "I'm twenty-four."

She frowned, while giving me a sincere look. "You look much younger but still too young to lose a husband. It must be hard on you as a single mom."

My gloomy day suddenly zoomed back into my head. I took a deep breath and held back my tears; it was so hard … I had to look away for a few seconds; I didn't want to burst into tears in front of her. Mandy would think that I was absurd. I simply nodded my head. Mandy seemed to live a happy, spoiled life. She wouldn't understand. I wanted to shift the conversation to Mandy.

"How long have you been divorced?"

Mandy's face was calm, as if the subject of divorce didn't bother her one bit.

"Around three years. He wasn't husband material. We agreed that I would raise Tiffany. And when he's in town, he sometimes takes her to his place."

"Does he travel a lot?"

"He does. Even when we first got married, he was always gone. To him, making tons of money was more important than raising a family." She sighed. But she didn't look hurt, as if she had accepted that fact.

I bit my own tongue. Was that the only reason they divorced? A husband being absent to support his family was some sort of a hero in my opinion. I wondered if Mandy knew how cruel some men could be.

"Do you work?" I asked. I no longer wanted to speak of her husband. What was wrong with me?

"Sometimes I do some bookkeeping for my father. This house needs full-time care, as you can see." She frowned. I tried not to roll my eyes.

"What does your father do?"

"Dad is a plastic surgeon."

I smiled.

She added, "Now he expects me to do his bookkeeping for free since he bought me this house when Larry and I got divorced."

I was glad she couldn't read my mind right then. What an arrogant woman! I mean, did she have any clue how poor people lived?

"It must be hard to keep up with the bills." I didn't know why I had asked that. That was way too personal. But Mandy didn't seem to mind.

"Larry and I had a divorce agreement. We had to divide our assets." She sipped her coffee and smiled.

Those must be some loaded assets, I thought sullenly. I sipped some coffee and faked a smile. Why did I even come here? I had never felt that embittered before. I wanted to change the subject again. I really didn't want to speak of bills either. A moment later, in a fake happy tone, I said, "Tiffany is so cute!" Mandy probably had already realized I was an awkward, out-of-her-depth woman.

She smiled. "Tiffany. Tiffany, she drives me crazy. I swear you'd think that she was some sort of royalty or something. She loves Nora." She sipped some coffee. "Does Nora refuse to let you cut her hair too?"

I nodded with a smile, giggling lightly. We had finally hit a home run. We should only speak of our daughters. That subject didn't make me feel self-conscious or cynical.

A couple of hours passed. I had been calling Nora for the last half hour for us to go. She refused to come down. I hated having to drag her down the stairs. But I had no choice. I went to Tiffany's room. I gasped when I saw it. Her room looked as if it were part of a fairy-tale story, exactly how a princess room should look. The walls were painted pink and white. Pictures of different princess characters were all over the walls. Her double bed appeared to have been just transformed by a fairy-tale godmother. It was an enchanting princess sleigh bed, crafted with a white finish, roses, ribbons, and bows. I knew why Nora didn't want to go anywhere. What was I supposed to do? I had to carry her. She was in the corner glaring at me as if I were her evil stepmother.

I said quietly, "Nora, sweetie, we have to go home."

She turned her shoulder away from me. I bent down to pick her up. She started screaming instantly, kicking me so many times with her feet.

"I don't want to go to Grandma's. I hate it there. Mom, no! *No!*"

I had to contain myself to keep from blowing up. I didn't really need this to be the way I ended my crappy day.

"My uncles won't let me watch my princess shows! Mommy, please!" Her tears covered her face.

I restrained myself from crying too. But there was nothing I could do. I really wished to give her a better life when she was born. And I felt as if everything had turned against me, *everything!* Even Nora.

"Nora, when we move, I will bring you a princess bed, I promise." I managed to carry her, her shoes, and my purse while getting kicked by both her feet. I scampered down the stairs, headed to the door. I glanced over at Mandy. I couldn't control the tears that came flowing down when I said, "Thanks for the coffee. I have to go."

I didn't wait for her reply. I loped outside, opened the car door with difficulty and despite Nora's screaming and kicking, I dropped her on the backseat. I fastened the seat belt, ran to the driver's side, and got behind the wheel. I needed to get out of there. Agreeing to come there was a big mistake.

Chapter Six

The next day, on a Saturday morning, I was going through a newspaper, sitting at Mother's dining room table. I was looking for a vacant place to live, something affordable. I didn't even mind if it was simply a bachelor apartment. I would decorate the bedroom for Nora with her princess theme. I really wanted her to be happy. I was trying to be the best mother I could be, in spite of my unfortunate circumstances.

The next few days had passed by with so much difficulty, ever since I found out about my credit history. I was not focused during work. At home, I tried to have more tolerance, but I found myself yelling at Nora constantly because she was being more than fussy; plus, I couldn't help my stretched-out patience, which was always clipped suddenly. Sometimes, I got angry as soon as she started whining. I was really doing my best not to go insane.

I knew I had to move out soon. I needed to give Nora some stability and maybe find some peace of mind for myself.

I applied at a few apartment buildings nearby; I had to fill out many applications for approval. I didn't understand the reason behind the application. I didn't have to do that when I subrented from Amanda or when I rented Cameron's basement apartment in the past. At the end of the following week, I called about the applications that I had filled out. They all had the same answer.

That same night, I lay in bed next to Nora. My chest was painfully congested. I recalled the calls that I had made about the applications. I was rejected; not even one application went through. Apparently,

I had a low credit score. If I had known that the application meant going through my credit history, I would have saved myself the agony of having any hope. I looked around the cramped area around me and took a painful breath. I was stuck there forever. There was no use in shedding more tears. I just hid my head under the blanket, enduring yet another sleepless night.

Mandy called me a couple of days later. I was surprised when I saw her number. Didn't she think I was an odd, absurd woman already? What did Princess Mandy want from me? I took a deep breath and answered it.

"Hello, Mandy. How are you and Tiffany?"

Her voice came soft and appealing. "I am good. Well, I was just thinking maybe we could take the girls to the Kids' Zone. Tiffany has been asking to see Nora since last week."

I was glad she didn't ask me to come to her place. I didn't wish to get bruised with Nora's feet once again.

She added, "I wanted to speak to you about my neighbor's friend. He wants to rent his basement apartment."

My eyes grew wide. I hoped he wouldn't require me to fill out another application.

"Really?" I said breathlessly.

"Yes, I heard that he's a quiet, reserved man. His wife passed away years ago. The rent is so cheap, and you will be so pleased with the space."

I didn't know what to say to her.

She continued, "I saw the place before I called you. I really didn't want you to be disappointed if it looked like crap,"

I was pleased by her kind gesture. Mandy hardly knew me. *I shouldn't have misjudged her,* I thought. I cleared my throat before I said, "Thank you, Mandy. That is so sweet of you. I really didn't wish to trouble you!"

"No trouble at all, Hannah. That was the least I could do."

Our conversation continued over the phone. Somehow, I got rid of some of my uneasiness. I thought Mandy was spoiled, a lucky woman. Well, she still was but with a kind heart. I had never speculated that she would ever call me back after my last visit. And here she was helping me find a comfortable place for me and Nora. Right after Kids' Zone, Mandy called the man's number to see if he would show me his place. I left Nora with Mother. I really didn't want her to be disappointed if we couldn't afford the place. Tiffany refused to leave without Nora, so I suggested she stay with Mother too. I really hoped the girls behaved.

Jasim was the name of the landlord. He was tall with mixed black and gray hair, a thick moustache, and a beard. He adjusted his thick glasses on his dark eyes when Mandy introduced us by his front door. He didn't even smile back at us. It was hard to guess how old he was, fifty-five to sixty, I guessed. He didn't have many wrinkles, but he looked run down. I really hoped he wasn't cranky all the time. His name sounded Middle Eastern, but I decided not to inquire. His place from the outside was much smaller than Mandy's. Without saying a word, he left his house, locking it right away, and stalked toward a back entrance.

Having a separate entrance was awesome. He opened the front door, which led to a medium size room. A small kitchen was on one corner, right next to the entrance. The rest of the space was empty. I smiled when I saw the fireplace. That was an added bonus. I had always wanted to have a fireplace. The washroom was small but acceptable. And the bedroom was right across from the bathroom. It was a bit bigger than my current diminutive size space. I could imagine painting it with purple and white for Nora and maybe even buying her a fairy-tale bed, something similar to Tiffany's. I really wanted the owner to like me and for the rent to be affordable, cheap enough. Mandy's budget could be very expensive for me. I already loved the space.

Once we were done with the very short tour, Jasim invited us to have tea at his place to discuss the rent. He could probably sense my hesitation. He said in a friendlier tone than earlier, "Come on! When do I ever get the chance to sit with two beautiful women?"

Mandy rolled her eyes. I smiled lightly. Maybe he was hiding a sense of humor somewhere deep inside. I really didn't want to disappoint him, since I wished to be his tenant. After sitting around the kitchen table, which was right across from his backyard window, I offered to help with the tea. Jasim sat down across from Mandy after handing me the tea supplies and cups. After bringing tea for everyone, I sat down next to Mandy, across from Jasim, who glanced at me with a tight smile.

He said, "Good girl." He sipped some of his tea and added, "Okay, the rent is five hundred dollars a month plus half of the utilities, which comes up to about six hundred dollars."

I was quickly calculating in my head while I sipped some tea; I could afford it. It was going to be tough, but I could do it. I would have to cut down on some of Nora's indulgences and some unnecessary expenses. Maybe soon, I could land a better-paying job.

I heard him add, "But I have a suggestion for you. My last tenant used to help me clean around my house, do my laundry, and cook occasionally. She used to get credit back of one hundred dollars per week."

My eyes grew wide. That would be a steal! I could clean and do laundry to get some money back. That would be awesome. I cleared my throat and said tactfully, "That sounds good. I mean I can clean and do laundry." I didn't want to mention the cooking part.

"Can you cook too?"

I was hoping he wouldn't ask me about that. I pressed my lips tight and then frowned lightly and said, "I could try." I looked away, gazing at my tea. I didn't understand why I always had trouble cooking. I heard Jasim chuckle. I gaped at him, stunned; I didn't think he could do that.

He said in a low, deep voice, "I like you. You are honest."

I looked at him, smiling. Did that mean I was approved?

Jasim agreed to let me move in as soon as I could. He wasn't even going to charge me rent until the beginning of the month. I was glad there was still no snow on the ground. All my family, including the twins, helped me move my very few belongings. Mandy knew of someone who was selling his furniture at a cheap price because he was moving. I bought his sofa bed, his small TV set, and a small kitchen table. Mandy convinced me not to buy his bedroom set. She said there was another, much better bedroom at a much better price. In a few months, when I could afford it, I was going to buy Nora a fairy-tale bed.

A few days after I moved, Nora and I were sleeping on the sofa bed. One day, Mandy suggested that I give her the house's keys during the day when I went to work, since the man who was selling the bedroom suit could only bring it during the day when I was working.

That day, I came back home with Nora after picking up the key from Mandy. As soon as I walked into my little apartment, I noticed that the place reeked with a strong paint smell. That was strange. Nora ran to the bedroom. Then I heard her yell out.

I followed her. I gasped when I looked around me. The room was painted pink and white, just like Tiffany's room, and the bed was exactly the same as Tiffany's too, with a matching dresser and lamp tables. I felt tears on my cheeks when I saw Nora's reaction. She was so happy, jumping up and down. Then she ran to me and hugged me tight. I picked her up to carry her excited little body.

"Mommy, did you see that! I have a princess room! My very own princess room!"

I thought of Mandy's wonderful heart. I didn't know how to repay her. Then I briefly recalled Debra, my friend from the shelter, and the thousand dollars she gave me, which bought my freedom for a while. I knew at that moment that I shouldn't give up on my life because there were a few people, a very few, like Mandy and Debra still existing.

***

A couple of weeks passed, during which I cleaned Jasim's place on Saturday and Sunday, and did all his laundry. Jasim was a clean man; and his place was only a bit larger than Mother's, so his house was low maintenance. I noticed that sometimes he was a bit feisty and other times he was very calm and composed. He merely mentioned that he was from the Middle East, a first-generation Canadian from the age of ten, which explained his Middle-Eastern name; his English lacked any ethnic accent. He didn't seem to go to work, since his car was always there in the morning and still there when I came back from work. I wondered if he was retired. I just couldn't bring myself to ask him personal questions.

One Saturday morning, I was in Jasim's kitchen. I placed the simple breakfast, which consisted of boiled eggs and a slice of toast and cheese, on a small kitchen table that overlooked the backyard. The weather outside was way too gloomy. I decided I wasn't going anywhere; I could do my grocery shopping the next day. I was waiting for the tea to boil. Nora was watching a show, lazing around Jasim's comfortable brown-lined couch. The room was dark since the curtains were still closed. I moved the small round oak coffee table to the side, away from Nora, who kept on resting her legs on it. The room was like most of the rooms in the house, clean but plain, and lacked any life and a woman's touch. The only picture that I saw stood out, since it was the only decoration on the fireplace mantel shelf. I had seen the picture before as I dusted, but I was reluctant to ask Jasim if he ever had a daughter. That day was the first time I had allowed myself to examine it as I grabbed it in my hands. There was Jasim years younger. A woman a few years his junior was to his left side. I suspected she was his wife. She was pretty with her shoulder-length brown hair, dark skin, and big smile. A much younger girl, who seemed to be in her teens—maybe fifteen, I guessed—was to his right side. She really resembled the older woman. Could she have been their daughter? I didn't know why my heart sank. I almost jumped when I heard a low, firm voice behind me.

"Those two women were the loves of my life."

My hands started to tremble. I placed the picture back and turned to face Jasim's long face. I didn't know why I felt really sad all of a sudden. I really didn't wish to see sadness on his face. Until that moment, I really didn't think that I would ever really care for a man who was a stranger. Apart from my brothers, whom I loved a lot, and a few family members, I thought very little of men in general because of the males who shattered my life. I felt as if I was merely a shadow of a woman. I was afraid to feel happy because my happiness was always taken away from me by them.

I was quietly gazing at Jasim's face and was averse to asking him what had happened. But I didn't have to, because he continued, "A drunken foolish man stole my life from me—killed me along with them."

I wet my lips. The sound of a deadly accident didn't sit well with me. My chest tightened. I gulped hard.

"You are probably too young to understand how it feels." He turned to face the picture. "To lose someone you really love." He started to shed tears. I was never really that close to an older man who was crying. That was mesmerizing. I reached for the tissue paper and brought one close to him. He wouldn't take it; he was too busy shedding tears and scrutinizing the picture. I brought the tissue close to his face to wipe away his tears. I felt my heart sink further. Then I felt him hugging me tight, way too tight. He was almost suffocating me. He continued saying loudly in between his sobs, "It feels as if someone has broken into your rib cage, removed your heart, and sliced it into pieces."

I didn't want to cry, but I did. I couldn't stop my tears. I really didn't understand the feeling he described, but somehow, I could sense his pain. I didn't know men could be that vulnerable, sensitive, and weak. A few minutes later, his weeping calmed down. I noticed that the tea was already boiling; I had somehow tuned out the boiling sound when Jasim was sobbing, and I turned to look at Nora, who was watching us with big brown eyes. I had even forgotten she was in the same room.

Ten minutes later, Jasim, Nora, and I were sitting around the kitchen table. It was Jasim's idea to have breakfast together. He was smiling at the both of us for the very first time, which put me at ease. Ever since I had moved in, as part of the deal we had, I merely made breakfast, cleaned the house, and did the laundry as quickly as I could just so I didn't have to see the scowl on his face for long. He really made me feel unwelcome at first.

Nora and I were having cereal, which Jasim called junk food. He buttered his bread lightly, took a bite, and sipped his tea before he asked, "Are you not married?"

He looked at Nora, who was busy eating. I knew that Middle-Eastern men disapproved of single women bearing children. I didn't know if Mandy mentioned anything, but I wasn't going to mention anything in front of Nora.

After sipping some tea, I said, "I was married." My gaze traveled between Nora and him. He understood my message. As I sipped my tea, I wondered what had happened to him all of a sudden. Maybe he needed someone's company for the day. We spoke lightly. He was even speaking to Nora, asking questions about her school. Somehow, the conversation shifted to Nora's lead. She was speaking about her favorite subject—princesses. I was surprised to see Jasim attentively listening to her.

Later on that night, Nora was cuddled in bed downstairs in the basement. Jasim had suggested I use the indoor entrance that led to the basement through a stairway. He also asked me to join him for some tea. I kept the door open just in case Nora woke up. I was in the kitchen making tea for the both of us. I could hear noises coming from the living room. I looked outside the window and noticed that we had started to get freezing rain. I closed the kitchen blinds. I carried the two mugs to the living room where Jasim was waiting for me. The light was soft, yet welcoming, glowing tenderly from a table lamp in one corner. Then I noticed the log fire burning inside the large open grate. The room felt warm and cozy as the light created shadows over the walls and furniture, complemented by crunching sounds of oak logs as they gradually melted away.

Jasim had a tray of chestnuts and two long metal sticks with warm handles. I smiled. My heart squeezed. I didn't know how to interpret this new feeling I had just encountered. I placed the mugs close to him, next to the fireplace. I then sat on the floor, staring at the fire. Jasim sat next to me. He smiled warmly and handed me my chestnut stick. We were both silent, just watching our chestnuts roasting and sipping our tea.

We had almost finished eating our share of chestnuts when he asked me, "You are very quiet. How come?"

I pressed my lips together and took a deep breath. I was still gazing at the fire when I answered, "Sometimes, I don't know what to say, and I don't like to talk nonsense."

I could tell he was watching me when he said, "You seem a little too wise for someone as young as you are."

I turned to face him. "I am not too wise. I don't know what I am." My lips curled into a sad smile. Then I turned my gaze away. I really didn't want to reveal too much to him.

"Tell me more about you … whatever you want to say, no pressure."

I looked toward the empty wall and said, "I am a widow. My husband died in an accident. I would like to tell you one day." Then I took a deep breath and added, "But not today, if you don't mind." I smiled dimly at him.

He smiled back sincerely. I knew he was overwhelmed but was wise enough not to say much.

He said, "Take your time … as long as you want." He then got up and left the room, only to come back a few minutes later while I was still buried in my past reflection. He had a little box in his hand. He placed it on the couch and said, "We can play a game of backgammon. My father once taught me how to play it, and I taught Sofia." He sighed. "My daughter and I used to play on cold nights like this." I could tell he was holding back his tears when he looked at me again. "My wife, Nawal, used to watch."

My heart sank. I got up almost immediately and sat right across from him.

I smiled and said sincerely, "I hope you won't mind, but you have to teach me first."

He smiled faintly, right before he rolled the dice.

Chapter Seven

A WEEK BEFORE NEW YEAR'S, I got a call from Henry. I was surprised to hear his voice. It felt like the embarrassing club incident had happened ages ago. I wondered if Jasmine had given him my number.

"Hi, Henry! How are you?"

"I am doing fine! How are you?" I could tell he was hesitant. "I was thinking of you."

"Really?" *What is he thinking about?* I wondered. Maybe he was thinking how foolish I was.

"Yes, in fact, I was thinking maybe you would like to grab a coffee sometime."

I bit my lower lip, frowning. Was he asking me on a date? That was scary! Could I hang up right then and pretend that had never happened. I cleared my throat.

I was tongue-tied, but I managed to stutter, "H-H-Henry, coffee … um, let's see … um." I didn't know how to say no to him, recalling how he had let me rest my head on his shoulder for at least thirty minutes.

"Yes, coffee. Don't you have coffee sometimes? Don't worry; it's not a date." He sounded friendly and yet stern.

I breathed out. "Okay, I guess. I heard that you live a little too far away." Jasmine had filled me in on unnecessary details about him.

"Only half an hour away, not too far. Plus, I am going to be around your area tomorrow evening."

"I am babysitting tomorrow evening. I swear I am." I didn't know why I said it that way and felt foolish right after. I didn't know how to have a conversation with people of the male gender. I always felt uneasy.

I heard him giggle. How could he not?

"That's okay. You mean your daughter?" His tone was a bit sarcastic.

"My daughter and her friend. Her mother has a date, and I offered to babysit."

"She has a date, huh? How about if I treat you girls to Burger Land? They have food and coffee too!"

"Why? I mean, I don't want to trouble you. The girls are quite a handful."

"No trouble at all. I can pick you guys up."

My head was spinning. Why was he being so nice to me? That wasn't normal.

"No, that's okay." We were both silent for a few seconds. I stuttered, "I-I can meet you there, um … if you want. I mean there is a Burger Land not too far from us."

"Sounds good! Just tell me when and where and I will be there."

My mind went blank. What was I doing? I gave him the address and the approximate time. Right after I hung up with him, I examined my reflection in the mirror in front of me. I looked really anxious. The idea of sitting alone face-to-face with a man while sober was frightening still.

***

I was watching the girls play. I glanced at my watch. Henry hadn't shown up yet. Maybe he had forgotten; I really hoped so. I wasn't looking forward to being obnoxiously nervous. I went back to my book, sipping some coffee and nibbling on some fries. I was dressed casually in tight blue jeans and a loose blue sweater. My hair was long, loose, and wavy, and I wore minimal makeup. I heard someone calling my name.

"Hannah."

I turned to face him. He looked handsome. His hair was smooth and neatly brushed, and his complexion was clear under the bright light. He did have a boyish, round face. His eyes were light brown. His lips were thin but defined. As he smiled, he revealed a set of straight white teeth. He was dressed casually too, in jeans and a white shirt under his winter jacket. I smiled shyly at him, feeling nervous right away. I said hi back. He sat on the chair beside me. Right away, cautiously, I pulled my body a few inches away. He placed his hands on the table and looked toward me, smiling.

He said casually, "So, how are you?"

I smiled nervously. My body felt stiff. "I'm good. You?"

"Good. What would you like to eat?"

I looked at my unfinished fries and the girls' kids' meals and said, "Nothing, I had some fries. I'm okay."

"I will get you something. And how do you take your coffee?"

"I have a coffee. Um, don't worry about me, really!" I wondered if I sounded as awkward as I felt.

"I will be back."

I watched him order the food and then glanced at the girls playing and then at my book. I couldn't read anymore. I just couldn't concentrate. A few minutes later, he came back with a tray full of food.

I bit my lip, frowning lightly. "I, um, this is too much, Henry!"

"Don't worry. I'll finish the whole thing even if you don't touch anything." He then placed a coffee in front of me with cream and sugar on the side. I really didn't want another coffee, and I didn't want him to waste money on me, but then again, it would be impolite to refuse it.

"Thank you. You really shouldn't have," I said, while picking up the coffee he had bought me, adding one package of sugar and cream.

He looked around and said, "So, where are the girls?"

I pointed in their direction. They both had pink-and-white dresses on, and their hair was styled the same way, in a long ponytail, one blonde, one brunette.

He smiled. "I am assuming the brunette is your daughter."

Obviously, I thought as I smiled curtly.

"Yes. Nora." I sipped some coffee.

"She is so pretty, just like her mother."

I blushed.

He continued, "I heard from Jasmine that your husband passed away."

I looked away. I didn't wish to speak of him. "He did."

"He must have been young."

I wanted to ask him to stop with his inquiries, but I couldn't.

"He wasn't old," I replied.

"You don't want to talk about him, do you?"

I just shook my head. I breathed a sigh of relief when he changed the subject.

"What are you doing on New Year's?"

I didn't know what I was doing. Maybe I'd join Mother at her friends' house. They were her neighbors. Even Nora had plans. She was going to spend it with Tiffany at her grandmother's house; her housekeeper could look after them. Jasim was going to play poker with some of his old buddies.

"Maybe join Mother and her friend. I don't know yet."

He tilted his head slightly, smiling. "Nathan, Jasmine, and I are going to Travis's place. You should come too."

Jasmine had already mentioned it to me. I wasn't sure if I was going to join, so I told her maybe. I really wanted to be alone. That would be the best thing I could do for myself.

"I don't know about that, Henry. I don't go out much."

I didn't know why I said that, because he grinned.

"When was the last time you went out?"

I looked at him. I felt as if I were doing a job interview.

"I went out, like a few weeks ago," I lied. The only time and the last time I had gone out was last July.

"It's New Year's; come on. You are too young to bury yourself alive."

Had Jasmine been talking to him? Those were her words.

"I will see. Maybe I will come." I smiled. I just wanted to agree to his face and to avoid the subject altogether when we said good-bye to each other, maybe, I hoped, soon.

"Okay. I will let Travis know that you will be coming. You can either come with your sister, or I can even pick you up."

I looked at him silently. What was wrong with him? I didn't say I was going to come for sure. "I will speak to Jasmine." I drank some coffee and even took a bite of the chicken nuggets. I wanted to avoid his gaze. I heard Nora and Tiffany approach. They were both staring at Henry. I sat them on the chair and placed their food and drinks next to them.

Soon, they were both talking to me at the same time. Usually, that annoyed me, but just then, I didn't mind, since it took some of the tension I had with Henry away. Both the girls liked Henry. They were speaking with so much interest of a princess movie they had watched twenty times over. I even memorized all the songs they played, finding myself singing along while cleaning around the house.

Henry gave me and the girls a hug each before he left. I then got the girls in their snowsuits, getting them ready for the very chilly weather outside.

***

Two days before New Year's, Jasmine called me.

"Hey, Jasmine," I said happily. I noticed that I had missed her dearly.

"Hey, Sis, I can't wait till the New Year. That will be so much fun!" she said enthusiastically.

I scolded, "What do you mean? I am not going."

"What? But why? Henry told me you were coming. Come on, Sis! When was the last time you went out? Last decade?"

"It was on my birthday!" I said irritably.

"You need to get out more, really, Sis. Sometimes, I feel that you missed a whole lot in your life."

"Jasmine! I don't feel comfortable being in a party. Last time, I felt really awkward in front of your cool friends."

"That's because you don't see anyone. I don't think you could even get any of the new jokes."

I frowned, feeling angry with Jasmine and her pushiness in trying to get me out of my shell. Maybe she meant well, but I wished she could understand me. I was happier being alone and was miserable around people like her friends. I didn't belong with them. I didn't comprehend how Mandy tolerated our quiet coffee breaks when we had them at her place. She was the one who always took over the conversation. I was more than happy to listen.

"Nathan is picking me up from your place, where we will both get ready. I will bring you a sexy-mama dress."

My blood flushed irritably. I wanted to say no, but I couldn't. She was too stubborn for me. It was as if we had switched personalities and I was the weak one who had no say. What was going on with me? Was I always that frail?

Ever since Jasim had opened up to me about the family he had lost, he seemed happier, and I felt more settled in the humble apartment, which was my and Nora's new home. He even encouraged me to look for a better job. When Mother wasn't too busy at work, she cooked extra food for us, and after the cozy night Jasim and I had had, I made sure he was well looked after too. I convinced Mother to cook for all of us, and when she refused the money I gave her, I insisted on buying her shopping once a week. I knew Mother was proud but was struggling financially since she was still looking after the twins. I took Mandy, Tiffany, and Nora to a nice dinner, knowing that my gesture wouldn't repay even a fraction of Mandy's generosity. I bought stars that glowed in the dark and glued them to our bedroom ceiling. I covered Nora's wall with so many fairy-tale Disney princesses. As I cuddled next to her in bed every night, I could imagine myself being under the stars, in a fairy-tale land. It was magical. I didn't mind my life right then, and I didn't wish anyone to come and disturb my peaceful surroundings by making me go to parties and meet new people.

***

New Year's Eve, Jasmine showed up around 7:00 p.m. Nora was already at Mandy's mother's, since Mandy was spending New Year's with her new boyfriend, John.

First, we had some coffee and a couple of snacks. Then we got ready in the bedroom. Every time I looked at Nora's bed, I wondered how much money Mandy had spent. It was even a comfortable bed to sleep on, so the mattress must have been expensive too. When Nora had Tiffany over for the weekend, which was becoming frequent, I usually spent the night on the sofa bed in the living room.

At 9:00 p.m., we were both ready to go. We wore long, sleek, strapless dresses. Mine was navy blue; hers was red. With my makeup and hair done, I felt a little more confident.

Jasmine opened a bottle of champagne and gave me a glass. She tipped her drink to mine, saying, "Cheers!" We drank the sparkly sweet drink. I really liked it. I heard Jasmine adding, "I dreamed of nights like this, being with you, Sis. I was worried sick about you when you were gone."

I didn't want to cry. I didn't want to mess up the makeup. I didn't know that Jasmine had felt that way about me. I swallowed my tears.

She added while hugging me, "I love you, Hannah. You are my blood, my sister, and my friend."

My tears were running. *Crap!*

"I love you too, Jasmine. I should be the one giving you that speech. I am your oldest sister." I sobbed more. I could hear her crying too. We were both a pile of mess in beautiful gowns. After we dried our tears, Jasmine suggested that she fix my makeup. We had another glass of champagne each. Then she placed the rest in the fridge. I was glad I had agreed to come, at least for Jasmine's sake.

Nathan arrived at 10:00 p.m. I started to feel a little lightheaded. I liked the feeling. It was calming my nerves. I said to Nathan happily, "Hi, Jasmine's boyfriend, I mean Nathan." I giggled lightly. I liked myself better with a little buzz in my head.

"Hi, Jasmine's sister, I mean Hannah." He grinned too.

I liked him. He was cool and handsome. I really hoped he remained a good man and did not change his mask like Yusuf. I was all of a sudden angry with myself for even bringing Yusuf back into my mind. That night, I would enjoy myself.

Travis's house was something similar to Mandy's on the outside, but we went in a different entrance. I guessed the party was in his basement.

The basement was very spacious—more than three times the size of my place. It was dim. I guessed he reduced the light on purpose. I felt as if I were in the club once again. There was a pool table on the side. A few people were playing. There were at least thirty guests already, girls and guys of different colors and sizes. I even saw a bartender behind a medium-sized bar.

Nathan spotted Travis. We all walked toward him and handed him a couple of bottles of champagne. Travis gave Jasmine and me a hug, complimenting our looks. I spotted the bartender moving his hands swiftly to accommodate all the orders. We walked toward the bar. Nathan ordered us wine. I sipped some of it; it tasted bitter. I didn't like it. I decided quickly that I wouldn't be switching my drink because I didn't feel like getting drunk that night.

There was some music playing; it reminded me of the club music. We walked around. I noticed that there were snacks on the other side of the bar. There were some chips, vegetables, dips, crackers, cheese, and snack-sized hors d'oeuvres. I heard Henry's voice greeting Jasmine and Nathan. I turned to say hello. He had a wide smile. Soon, we all sat in one corner, but they were constantly being greeted by different people. They were popular, I guessed. I smiled politely at everyone. Travis came with Claire and sat next to us. I refused all the drinks that were offered. I really didn't want to be embarrassed again.

The music started to play. Nathan pulled Jasmine to dance. Travis was dancing with Claire. Henry and I were alone. He glanced at my flushed face a few times, and then without saying a word, he grabbed me gently by the arm and led me to the dance floor. I was a little less tense. At that moment, I decided to loosen up and try to have some fun. Henry started to twirl me around; I really didn't mind him too much.

He led me toward the bar, and as he did, I could tell that his eyes were wandering to a woman's behind in a tight, short skirt. I probably noticed this because I was sober. My memory traveled back in time, back to the beach, to when I was a teenager. I recalled Majeed's eyes wandering toward the two girls wearing bikini tops and shorts. I was then only thirteen years old, and Majeed was a man whom I met at one of our family beach trips. He was the first and only man I ever liked, maybe even loved. He was handsome and charming. Back then, I was too foolish to understand that he was also a player and merely wanted to take advantage of my vulnerability, but now, I knew better. Henry was indeed another player … *I shall not fall for him,* I decided.

When we got to the bar, he requested a couple of shots, which came in small plastic cups.

He told me, "I won't let you get drunk; I promise. This is the last one." He smiled.

I took it and gulped it. It was sweet. I liked it. Henry pulled me again to the dance floor. I was following his lead. Despite the fact that I had already made up my mind about Henry, I still liked him as a friend.

A few minutes before midnight, I sat alone since Henry went to get more alcohol and had been gone for a while. Jasmine and Nathan came to find me.

The countdown to the New Year was loud and fast. Friends were hugging each other, and lovers were kissing passionately. I gave Nathan and Jasmine their privacy after we hugged and wished each other "Happy New Year!" Fifteen minutes after midnight, I stood in one corner, not too far from Jasmine. I saw Henry walking toward me. He gave me a long, profound hug. I had to pull myself away from his embrace. I could tell he was already drunk. I smiled politely. He bent his head down. I froze, but he quickly shifted to kiss my cheek. That was when I breathed out.

Chapter Eight

WEEKS PASSED. IT WAS MONDAY morning and the first day on my new job. I made sure I bought myself a few sharp outfits, mostly dark skirts and white and cream-colored blouses. I wore comfortable, short high heels. And my dark-brown hair was styled long and wavy.

The elevator dropped me off at the twentieth floor. I was excited and scared at the same time. I had finally landed a better-paying employment with benefits at a big law firm; the only problem was it wasn't full-time.

A couple of months earlier, after Jasim had encouraged me to look for better-paying employment, I began going on many job interviews. Most of the jobs were far away for the same money I was currently earning. I refused a couple of the jobs when they were offered. I wanted to look for a job that offered benefits and security, and so I went on another interview. It was for a part-time receptionist in a law firm. I dressed really carefully for the interview, trying to look as professional as I could. During the interview, I learned that the tall older man who interviewed me was the firm manager. I would be replacing someone who had already resigned. I was glad when he mentioned that being French-English bilingual was going to be an asset. At least with effort, I could climb up. A few days later, I got a call. I got the job and would start in a couple of weeks since I gave my previous employer a two-week notice. The job came with full training, earned me the same even being only part-time, and on top of that, offered some benefits. I had also been advised that with time, I could move on to full-time with full benefits.

The weather was really cold that day. Snow covered the ground. But that didn't bother me. I felt that I was moving forward this year and had already made some progress.

As soon as I walked into the firm, I was greeted by Mary, a petite and pretty Chinese woman with long brown hair. She was probably a second- or third-generation Canadian. Her English lacked any ethnic accent. It was hard for me to guess her age, somewhere in her thirties. She looked flawless with her crisp, expensive clothes and immaculate makeup. Her eyebrows were perfectly shaped and defined, and her dark gaze looked sharp. I could tell she was studying me. I could've mistaken her for a lawyer. She was sitting right behind one of the three identical cherry desks. I guessed one of the empty desks was going to be mine. Large windows overlooked the space. The light-brown curtains were drawn to one side, allowing the light in to define the few paintings on the wall, which consisted merely of colors, shapes, and textures that matched the classy ambiance. There were a few leather couches around the large sitting area with a couple of small glass table lamps and a large glass coffee table. On both sides of the elevator stood a long, bright hallway that led to many offices.

Mary simply showed me around the supply room, the kitchen, and the printer room. Brandy, the full-time receptionist, came to the office a little later than usual. She was a large African American who seemed to be somewhere in her late forties or early fifties. She was very reserved. Brandy took over training me that day. We spoke about picking up and delivering items and how to operate the equipment and answer clients on the phone. By the end of the day, my head was spinning, and I was glad to be out of the office at 4:00 p.m. Mandy was going to watch Nora until I came back, which made me realize how lucky I was to have her.

***

A few days had passed. Brandy and I hardly conversed. When we did, we merely spoke of work and what was expected of me. I felt as if I were in school and Brandy was my strict teacher. Mary popped in a few times, sat at her desk without speaking to either of us, and walked away soon after. I could tell that Brandy didn't like Mary from the way she became stiff behind her computer. I didn't understand why. I decided to keep myself busy, hoping to do an amazing job. At home every night, after Nora went to bed, I was in front of my laptop learning what I could from my own notes that I had taken during the day or training myself more about computers from books that I had bought. I really wanted to be the best at my job.

After the first week, I started to feel a bit settled. I tried to remember the many lawyers' names. There was a lot to remember. I really hoped I could keep this job for a while. It would be nice to have an office and give orders around, just like the couple of female lawyers I had met, but I knew not to dream the impossible. Maybe eventually I could even become a legal assistant. I knew that they made more money than I did.

Slowly, faces were becoming familiar. I noticed that there were more men than women lawyers. I didn't realize how big the law firm was when I was first interviewed. It had extensive administrative and support staff at its disposal, which included legal administrators, legal secretaries, paralegals, and the list could still go on.

Everyone around the office was very formal. I heard that most of the shares belonged to two lawyers. They were brother and sister, Jason and Adrianna Miller, and the rest of the shares were distributed among the partners. The firm where I worked was the main branch with a couple of others around the city. The sibling partners' main offices were at the main branch. I just saw them in and out of the firm. They were both always preoccupied on their cell phones.

A couple of months had passed. One day, I was alone at my desk, working away. Brandy was working at another branch. Adrianna's tall body leaned against my desk. She asked about Mary, who had been around the office that day but left soon after she got there. I stuttered badly with my sentence when I had to explain that I didn't know where Mary was. There was a distinctive aura about her. Her dark-green eyes were piercing and sharp and looked right through me. I hated the way she studied me, with her narrowed, cold gaze, making me feel inferior. Her dark eyeliner defined her round green eyes. She pouted her thin, well-defined, shiny red lips as she spoke with a great authority. I had seen Adrianna a few times already, but that day, she looked pretty and really polished, as if she had spent her day at the spa. She was dressed carefully in a black, fitted short-sleeve, calf-length dress, as if she were about to take a snapshot for one of the magazines; she probably had a meeting with an important client. She glanced at her watch quickly, grabbed a card from her black Louis Vuitton purse, and handed it to me.

She said sternly, "I want you to call this number for this catering company. Make sure they have the list from Simon Miller's firm I just emailed and the address for tomorrow's event."

"No problem, Ms. Miller," I said politely.

She then swiftly walked away, swinging her hips from side to side. I watched her with stunned eyes. She really seemed different that day. I called the number right away. A few minutes later, Mary arrived while I was on the phone with the catering company, who assured me that they had received the list and everything was under control. Mary sighed.

She said, "I already called to confirm. Adrianna is being too fussy with this funeral. Mary, deliver flowers. Mary..." She stopped abruptly, probably just realizing that she was talking to me as I watched with wide eyes. We seldom exchanged words about anything, apart from work. She had never even once asked me a personal question about my life. We were strangers more than coworkers.

I cleared my throat. "Who died?" I asked.

"Some old client, his name is Neil Harris. He had a heart attack a couple of days ago."

I shrugged my shoulders. "He must have a big account with the firm."

She rolled her eyes and turned to her computer screen. I turned back to my screen too. It was none of my business. As long as I did my job right and kept it at the end of the day, I didn't care. Jason, Adrianna's brother and partner, emerged in our reception area. He always looked neat, with his combed black hair, tall figure, and fair complexion. His face and body were too thin, but overall, he was a good-looking man, especially with his polished smile. Since I had started working there, we had never exchanged words face-to-face. It was mostly on the phone.

He said politely, "Adrianna was checking. Did you call the catering company?"

I blushed from the way his eyes were studying me. "I did. I even emailed her the confirmation."

He smiled. "Okay, good." He looked at me for a bit longer. I smiled at him again, feeling puzzled. "Hannah, right?" he added.

"Yes." I was starting to feel nervous. *That was awkward,* I thought. I wasn't used to anyone being friendly around there, especially not the loaded partners.

"Nice to meet you. I mean, thank you for emailing the confirmation."

I smiled at him. Instantly, I felt my face was boiling; that was really unusual. He then left the office. I avoided Mary staring at me. What would she think?

She leaned against her desk and mumbled, "I think he likes you!"

I turned to her and stuttered, "M-me? Um … I don't think so." I really hoped not; plus, I couldn't see why, especially with the way I looked compared to all the rest of the elegant staff.

"Well, he is a player. Plus, Adrianna has a problem with lawyers dating receptionists." Was that a warning? But why? Maybe I should just avoid Jason altogether and be very formal. I really needed to keep this job.

***

I glanced at the clock. It was already the lunch hour. I wondered where the time had evaporated this morning at the office. I went to the kitchen and poured myself some coffee. I grabbed my homemade turkey sandwich from the fridge. I was going to eat my lunch sitting at my desk, as always. This way, I could organize my afternoon work. Brandy had moved to work full-time at a different branch. I took over her full-time hours, with full benefits, which was something I was happy about. I was working with a new part-time intern, Christine. She was about my age, short, with dark hair and a dark complexion. She was quiet and reserved, but she was always immaculate with her expensive-looking clothes and refined gestures. A few days ago, I saw her parking her sporty red Mercedes in our underground garage, but I couldn't bring myself to ask why she was working as a clerk. Christine was gone for the rest of the day. I was used to Mary just popping in whenever she wanted to, looking as immaculate as always. When I went back to my desk, I skimmed through the client list I was about to call on behalf of one of the lawyers' assistants while I sipped some coffee. I was about to unwrap my sandwich when I felt that someone's eyes were on me. I almost jumped out of my skin when I looked up to meet Jason's wide, pearly smile. I didn't understand what he was doing in there. I gave him a tight smile, feeling my face burn. I started to quiver lightly.

Ever since Mary's warning about Jason, which was about a month earlier, I had kept myself busy and out of trouble. I kept my desk neat and tried to be as swift as I could while keeping everything in perfect order. When I had learned my job perfectly and taken over Brandy's job a couple of weeks earlier, my salary changed accordingly to twenty-one-thousand-dollars a year; even after paying taxes, I was still able to indulge Nora and myself. I thought maybe one day I could start fixing my credit and purchase a better car, so I didn't mind doing extra work given to me by different assistants. I was always doing something. Most of the time, I even worked during my lunch hour just to make sure I pleased everyone. I tried to keep it formal with Jason and merely offered a smile when he occasionally said hello.

Now I felt my heart racing. I wished he would just leave me alone so I could keep this job.

He said sincerely, "Working on your lunch too? That's very impressive."

I smiled nervously. I didn't know how to reply to him, so I remained quiet.

He added, "Or maybe lonely."

I had no answer to that either. I was lonely too. I didn't know how to have a single conversation with anyone around. Everyone seemed arrogant, even Christine, so I gazed at him for a few seconds.

He added, "You can join me for coffee. My treat."

I hesitated, recalling Mary's warning. I cleared my throat, trying not to frown.

I said, "Mr. Miller, you don't have to do that." I smiled politely.

Jason said firmly, "I know I don't have to. I want to. There is a difference."

Why was he doing this?

"People around the office will talk and gossip." I felt my heart sprint.

"I want to give you a list of things to do, so this is a work-related meeting coffee break." He walked away from my desk and then turned to face me, adding, "Are you coming?"

I cleared my throat. "You mean now?" He smiled mockingly. I felt so foolish as I followed after grabbing my purse and light jacket.

I walked behind him to a nice upscale café located right across the large building. He ordered me a latte and a turkey sandwich. I sat right across from him. He sipped his latte and took a bite from his sandwich. I started sipping my latte quietly. I hated to admit it, but it was really good, probably one of the best gourmet coffees I had had so far. Jason broke the silence by saying.

"How do you like your job?"

I cleared my throat before answering, "I like it. I am still learning."

"From what I have heard, you are doing an excellent job."

I felt a bit happy about the news. Maybe I could keep this job and even climb up the ladder eventually.

I smiled contently. "I am trying. I never worked in a big firm before." I was still trying to figure out what I was doing having coffee with a big-time lawyer and firm partner.

"You will get used to it."

I smiled politely, grabbed my sandwich, and ate a little bite. All of a sudden, I felt self-conscious being around him.

He wiped his thin lips and asked, "Do you live far?"

"No, not too far. Twenty minutes away." I wondered when he was going to give me the work list.

"That's not too bad!"

"How long have you been a partner for?"

"Five years. My sister and I took over the firm when Father passed away."

I looked away and tried to breathe deeply. All of a sudden, I was searching my brain to find something smart to talk about, since I had never had coffee before with someone who held such a high-level job.

"You've never been at this café before?"

"No." I blushed shyly. I added, "It's really good. The best I've had so far."

"Yes, it's not too bad. Where do you normally go for lunch?"

I smiled hesitantly. I didn't want to say that I always brought my food from home because spending money on lunch every day was way out of my league.

"I usually bring salads from home. And sometimes, I buy sandwiches," I lied. "I'm still not familiar with the city."

"One day, I will take you to a nice Japanese place. You will like it."

That felt uncomfortable. I gave him a curt smile.

"Do you have a big family?"

"I do. I have a sister, three brothers, and a little girl."

His gazed widened. "You have a daughter? You seem too young."

"I was young." I smiled.

He sipped more coffee.

"How about you?" I added.

"I only have one twin sister."

I looked at him. Maybe they shared the same refined gestures, round eyes, and thin lips, but I wouldn't have guessed they were twins.

"I have twin brothers."

He just smiled. "Right." It was as if he was dismissing what I had said. "Were you married?"

My heart was once again racing with the mention of my marriage. Looking away, I said, "I was."

"So you are divorced?" He wiped his lips.

"He passed away." I sipped more latte.

"Oh! I am so sorry." He sounded sincere.

I took a deep breath. "That's okay."

"How did he die? If you don't mind me asking."

I took a deep breath, trying to dismiss the awful memories momentarily.

"An accident." I was getting tenser by the second.

"How old is your daughter?"

"She is almost six."

"Is she as pretty as you?" His eyes shone.

I blushed and then stumbled to find an answer to that.

I smiled politely and said, "She is much prettier!"

"That is sweet to say. Do you have a picture of her?"

The conversation was becoming more personal by the second, but what kind of a mother would I be if I didn't have a picture! I grabbed my purse and opened my wallet. I showed him the last picture we had taken together. She was wearing a pink dress. Her long brown hair was down to her midback, and she was hugging me tight as we both smiled.

"She is gorgeous, just like you."

That was an overstatement; I pulled my body back a bit, avoiding his gaze.

"Thank you," I mumbled.

There was a still, quiet moment before he broke it. "I was married once too. We got divorced a couple of years ago." He sipped more latte.

"Sorry to hear that." I saw a little grimace, but he didn't seem to be affected or hurt. "Were you married long?"

After wiping his lips with a napkin, he said, "Ten years."

I didn't know why I was interrogating him, but he didn't seem to mind.

"Do you have any children?" I asked after sipping some latte.

"No, we were both too busy. Plus, she had a couple of older children who graduated university from a previous marriage."

"Graduated university!"

Jason seemed to only be in his mid- to late thirties. Maybe his ex-wife was young when she married the first time. "She married young."

He gave me a curt smile. "No, she was much older than I."

"I see." This subject was getting interesting. "Did she have a good job?"

"She was a CEO at a big company. She was always busy. Our schedule was hectic."

A CEO! I tried to smile. All of a sudden, I felt as if I were an uneducated, chaotic woman with a horrific past. I wondered if I should ask him about the list for work, since he hadn't mentioned it yet.

"What did your husband do, before he passed away?"

I froze at this complicated question. I had to lie and make up an answer. I had no choice. I tried not to stutter as much when I answered, "He was, um, an electronic engineer." I had no idea what he was, but I briefly recalled all Yusuf's spying equipment. Well, that wasn't too far from the truth.

"Really!"

I just nodded. "I like the sandwich. It's good. Thank you for lunch." I really wanted to change the subject. I was wishing I had never asked about his personal life.

"I'm glad you liked it." He glanced at his watch. "I have a meeting in ten minutes."

"You never gave me the list you had mentioned."

He smiled. "That slipped my mind; that's okay. I will email it to you upstairs."

I got up right away. That was very awkward.

"We should do this again," he said.

I just nodded, picked up my purse and jacket, and followed him toward the large building.

When I came back to my desk, I tried to dismiss the coffee break with Jason since I didn't understand his motives and concentrate on my job.

Later on, Adrianna stood by my desk. With her dark-green gaze behind her reading glasses, she looked immaculate. I really wondered what she would want from me.

"Hannah, I need you to stay late. My assistant is home sick today, and I have some piled-up work."

I gulped my discomfort. I couldn't say no. I had to accept, even though I had promised Nora to watch a kids' show with her.

"Sure. Just let me know how long you will need me so I can arrange for someone to keep my daughter."

"I will let you know," she said brusquely, and then she walked away. There was no thank-you, nothing. Well, I did work for her. I supposed she shouldn't really appreciate my efforts.

I called Mandy and asked her to keep Nora until I was finished with work. She agreed. Mandy and I were becoming close, almost like family, especially since Tiffany almost always spent the weekend at my place. I was done at 7:00 that night. I had followed Adrianna's orders precisely. It was so hard to work with her, constantly watching her haughty expression. I followed Adrianna toward the parking lot. She walked toward a brand-new white BMW.

Right before she got into her car, I said, "Goodnight, Ms. Miller."

She didn't even answer me, maybe because she didn't hear me. I walked past her to my ten-year-old green Nissan.

Chapter Nine

It was on a spring Saturday morning. I woke up to the sound of the lawnmower. Nora was still sleeping next to me. We were both covered with a pink comforter. I hugged her little body tight. That day was a special day.

I whispered into her ear, "Happy birthday, Princess Nora."

I could tell she had heard me because she had a little smile at the corners of her lips, even though her eyes were still closed. A couple of minutes later, she pushed the comforter off of her, stretched her little hands out, and said happily, "My birthday is finally here!"

In a few seconds, she was jumping on the bed, repeating, "Today's my birthday! Today is my birthday!"

I was on my feet. I reached for my home slippers. I had to hold my balance because Nora decided to jump into my arms while repeating the same sentence. Nora was excited because for the first time, she was celebrating her birthday later in the afternoon at a local glow-in-the-dark kids' little golf place. I invited a few of her friends, including Tiffany, of course. Nora and I made the beds, changed our pajamas, and were on our way to make her birthday breakfast: a Mickey Mouse–shaped pancake. I hoped I could manage to do it right, since it was Nora's idea and I didn't wish to disappoint her on her birthday.

Jasim kept the door that separated the basement from main floor open all the time, since I always made our breakfast on the weekend and sometimes during the week too. He even suggested I use one of his two spare bedrooms for storage.

The backyard door was open, inviting the strong sun to powerfully illuminate the kitchen and the living room area. I glanced at the green garden outside. The signs of spring always filled my heart with joy, especially after this particularly long winter. The snow didn't start to melt before the end of March. We had even had a couple of snowstorms in April that year.

Nora ran to the living room to watch TV. She already wore a pink fluffy princess dress and a little toy tiara on her head. I found some flour, eggs, and baking soda. I glanced outside the window again. I finally located Jasim; he was working on his garden still, which had started to bloom.

Mother's little garden always blooms too, I ruminated.

I stepped outside into the backyard, breathing in the fresh smell of the garden. It was invigorating. I called Jasim and told him that the big breakfast would be ready soon. He just lifted his hand, his sign saying he heard me. I was getting used to his body language, his likes and dislikes, as if I had known him all my life. Then I heard the knock announcing my visitors' arrival. I really wanted Nora to feel special on her birthday, so I invited all my family.

An hour later, we were sitting around the table having breakfast. Mother and all my siblings joined us. I was glad Hady was able to join us as well. I hardly saw him since he worked most of the time. Mother prepared a traditional Middle-Eastern breakfast, which was fava beans crushed with lemon juice and olive oil. Jasim seemed to really enjoy himself, just like the rest of us. I tried not to mess up Nora's special pancake, but somehow, I did. I merely got Mickey Mouse's ears right; the head was weirdly shaped, but she didn't seem to mind. All of a sudden, my mind traveled to my father. I couldn't even remember once having a peaceful family gathering with him. I studied my family's faces, one at a time. I knew that deep inside they were all thinking the same way I was. I then glanced at Jasim, who seemed happy, but I knew his mind was probably traveling in time, to before he lost his family. *How ironic,* I thought. We were a family who never knew the love of my deceased father, and he was a father who would give away everything just to love his family once again. I smiled sulkily at this realization. Fate sometimes had an evil, revolting face.

Around noon, the twins left to meet up with some friends. Mother, Hady, and Jasim were in the backyard chatting. Nora was coloring. Jasmine and I were in the living room having coffee.

She said, "So, Sis, have you been on a date yet?"

I glanced at her. I knew she wanted to see me happy with a man, but I really wished she would leave me alone.

I sighed after sipping some coffee. "No, not yet."

"You need to go out more. I heard Henry is single again."

I laughed at the last sentence. It seemed to me that Henry changed girlfriends along with the season change.

I said sarcastically, "Good for him, now he can find him a new one."

Jasmine laughed too.

"I think he is still into you. That's what I think."

I scowled. "I think he is into girls in general. He has changed girlfriends twice from the time I met him," I said sarcastically.

After a moment of silence, she said, "Well, maybe he hasn't found the right one yet."

"Well, I hope he finds the right one soon. It won't be me. I can't even have a conversation with the guy," I snapped lightly.

"Are you telling me that you have conversations with different guys all the time, but you just can't have one with Henry?"

I squeezed my lips tight, frowning. She'd gotten me. I just lost my cool with men. I expected the worst out of them and became awkward all of a sudden. I recalled my last coffee and lunch with Jason. That was really agonizing. I was quietly sipping my coffee, since I didn't have an answer to that.

A couple of hours later, I drove Nora to her birthday party, which was at a big mall. Mother and Jasmine came along with me. I was looking for a parking space, when I noticed Mary by surprise. She was in the parking lot. From her gestures, she seemed frustrated and lost while looking around her. Did she need help? I wondered. I wavered at first but drove near her, rolled my window down, and called her name. She turned; her sunglasses were hiding her expression.

I said politely, "Mary, are you okay? Do you need any help?"

She was surprised to see me, because she paused at first and then said, "Well, my phone just died, while I was trying to call for someone to tow my car."

I reached for my cell phone and said, "You may use mine. We will be at the glow-in-the-dark kids' golf place. You can hand it over to me there."

She hesitated at first and then smiled, took my phone, and thanked me.

I added, "We will be there for a while. It's my daughter's birthday, so take your time."

She smiled politely. Once we were inside, we found our reserved table. A few of Nora's school friends were being dropped off by either their mother or father and sometimes both parents. Mandy had already mentioned that Tiffany's father was going to drop her off. He was handsome, of average height, and had fair skin; wavy, dirty-blond hair; and piercing blue eyes. Tiffany gave him a long hug right before she joined the rest of the kids.

The place was loud and full of kids' screams. Fifteen minutes later, I saw Mary. She walked in elegantly and found me right away. I was with Mother and Jasmine, and we were distributing pizza and pop to the loud kids.

She came closer and said, "Thank you, Hannah. I really appreciate it. I'm waiting for someone to tow my car."

I hung back at first, but I said, "You can wait here with us if you want, have some pizza. You can call the towing company and ask them to call my cell when they get here."

She looked around. Jasmine's and Mother's smiles were welcoming.

I added, "This way, you don't have to wait alone outside, as long as you don't mind some loud kids around you."

She smiled, looking around again. I introduced her to my family. Without a word, she reached for my phone, made a call, and took a seat next to us. She even helped herself to some pizza.

An hour later, I got a call. It was Mary's towing company. I was surprised to see a different side of her during the last hour. She was fun and was even joking around and bonding with my family. When she asked about Nora's father, Mother took her time to explain to her that he had died and how he died. I was running around with the kids, and I could hear bits and pieces. Unfortunately, I couldn't give Mother the hint to stop talking about me. I hated when she told my life story to strangers. Right before leaving, Mary said good-bye and even gave Nora a big hug. I smiled at that. She was a lot nicer than I had thought.

After I dropped Mother and Jasmine at their home, I glanced over at Nora. She didn't seem as happy as she should be after a long, happy day. I had tried to please her the best way I could, but I didn't know why I had still failed.

Finally, when I was lying in bed next to her at night, she asked me, "Why did Daddy die?"

I felt a strong squeeze in my chest. I didn't know how to answer that. I said tactfully, "Because daddies do die sometimes." I sighed.

"Are you going to die too?"

I took a deep breath. "I hope not." Then I turned and touched her hair lightly. "Why are you asking these questions, honey?"

She sighed. "You told me that your daddy died. My uncle Hisham told me a long time ago that his daddy died too."

"That's because we share the same father, sweetie. His father was mine—Jasmine's, Wissam's, and Hady's too. He was also your grandpa." It was sad that since we hardly spoke of my father, Nora didn't comprehend the relation he had with us, his kids.

"Oh." She was silent for a long time. She said, "My friend Tiffany has a daddy. He didn't die yet."

Now I got why Nora was gloomy that day. She had seen her best friend with her father. I swallowed my anguish. I knew what she was going through. I knew what she was yearning for, a father's love.

"Yes, I know."

"Do you think my daddy loved me?"

I was glad we were in the dark because she couldn't see my confounded expression.

Trying to keep my voice from wobbling, I said, "Yes, he did. How could he not when you are so special, beautiful, and smart?"

She sighed. "I love you, Mommy. I don't want you to ever die." She kissed my cheek lightly. My heart sank.

"I love you too. And guess what! You are my favorite girl in this whole wide world."

She sighed. We were both quiet for a few seconds, looking at the glowing plastic stars.

She mumbled, "Good night, Mommy," turning onto her side.

"Good night, my beautiful Nora." I moved her little body next to mine and hugged her tight. Then I buried my face in the softness of her long, flowery, fragranced soft hair.

***

A few weeks had passed. I was back at the office on a Monday morning. I placed my cup of tea on my desk, and started going through my list of work email. Since our lunch at the café, I had only seen Jason a few times. I was thankful he never asked me to join him again. Since then, I had kept a simple, fresh look with minimal makeup; my clothes were very professional and neat but conservative, and my hair was in a bun with simple side bangs most of the time. I was happy lately with the money I was making and decided to do whatever it took to keep my job—even if it meant drawing the minimal amount of attention to myself. Mary was around the office more often, and despite our one-time bonding during Nora's birthday, we still hardly talked to one another, but she smiled at me more often.

I was used to Adrianna, since she utilized me a few more times. She was different from her brother, who, despite his refined gestures, was still charming and friendly with a hint of humbleness. Adrianna was supercilious, abrupt, and fractious. I did precisely what I was told to do, not even expecting any gratitude since she never had any.

Nevertheless, I was getting better at my job. I was even helping lawyers around if their assistants weren't available. I called clients, typed letters, booked appointments, made reservations, arranged flights ...

***

Later on that day, I was having lunch at my desk when I saw Jason walking toward me. I immediately placed my bagel and cheese away and wiped my lips with some tissue. I knew that many lawyers and all the assistants and staff, including Christine, were going out for lunch to a big nearby restaurant.

"Hi, Hannah, how are you?" He smiled sincerely.

"Hi, Mr. Miller." I smiled back.

"As you know, some of our staff team is joining us for lunch. Sorry you couldn't come."

I smiled politely. I really didn't mind, especially since Adrianna would be attending.

I said, "That's okay."

"We are going to this Italian place. I can bring you something."

I cleared my throat. "I already had lunch. But thank you."

His eyes narrowed. "Are you sure?"

I said with confidence, "Of course."

"Next time, I will bring you with us."

I didn't know why he was worried about me. It was making me feel very uncomfortable.

"Sure. I mean, you don't have to." He didn't say another word; he just waved good-bye. Right after he left, I grabbed my half-eaten bagel back. I was trying to analyze his peculiar behavior. I didn't want to think of the possibility that someone in his position could be attracted to someone like me. Maybe it was because he felt bad since everyone else around the office was going, I decided. Well, he was much nicer than his sister. I couldn't comprehend why she wasn't fond of me, since she was nicer to Mary and everyone else around the office.

I was busy for the rest of the day. I didn't notice Jasmine's and Mother's missed call until I left the building. I was about to call Jasmine back when I got a call from Henry. I was surprised to hear from him. I wasn't afraid to answer him this time. I had gotten over the awkwardness of having a phone conversation since my job required it most of the day.

"Hi, Henry, how are you?" I said in friendly but firm tone.

He sounded pleasant. "Good, Hannah, long time no see or talk."

I sighed. "I know. How is life?"

"Could be better. You know what I heard today?"

"No, what?"

"Nathan proposed to Jasmine."

My eyes grew wide. I said breathlessly, "Really!"

"Really, I am surprised she didn't tell you yet."

"She called me a few times. I missed her calls."

"Damn! Don't tell her I told you. She probably wanted to tell you herself."

"How did you find out?"

"Travis told me."

I didn't know men were sentimental about engagements and weddings.

"Jasmine agreed?"

"Yes, she did." He sounded excited. My heart skipped. He laughed. "Again, you didn't hear it from me."

I rolled my eyes. "Okay, no worries, Henry. Maybe I should call you back after I call my sister."

"Yes, I will be waiting for your call."

"Sure thing." As soon as I hung up with Henry, I called Jasmine.

I said happily, "Hey, Sis."

She answered breathlessly, "Hi. Hold on. Hold on. Let me go to my room first."

A few seconds later, her voice came over the receiver. "I got engaged!" she squealed happily.

I had to sound surprised. "Really! Oh my gosh, I am so happy for you!" I hoped I sounded convincing.

"I am so happy, Hannah. You should see the way he proposed." She sounded really excited, just like a little child.

I gasped. "How?"

"Well, we went for lunch today. Since it was my day off, we went to this nice little restaurant. Nathan didn't say anything at all. We spoke of regular things, you know, nothing important." Jasmine's voice was becoming strangled. I could tell she was very emotional. She continued,

"After I got out of the restaurant with Nathan, I saw a white minivan driving so slow with red paint all over it. It said …" She started to cry. I could tell she was trying so hard to maintain herself. She continued with a cracking voice, "'Jasmine, will you marry me?'"

I felt tears in my eyes, especially after my sister started to sob again. I said after long seconds, "Then what happened?" I really wondered if Travis was the one driving the minivan since he was Nathan's good friend and partner.

She added, "People on the street were cheering. That was so embarrassing, Sis, and yet … *magical*. I can't explain to you."

I felt my chest squeeze. "Are you happy?"

"I am so happy!" Then she started to cry again.

I really wondered how a man's love and affection could make someone feel happy to the point of shedding tears, the way Jasmine had been for the last few minutes.

I said sincerely, "I am so happy for you. I really think you deserve to be happy." I parked at my home and got into my little apartment.

"I hope you find someone who makes you feel the same way."

I frowned, placing my keys on the kitchen counter. "I hope so." I sighed. Deep inside, I doubted it. "When are you going to tell Mother?"

"I already told her. I know she tried to call you to complain and couldn't get ahold of you. Nathan is coming to ask for my hand in marriage from her tonight." There was a silence. "Can you please be here when Nathan and his family come in a couple of hours?"

"Sure I can. How many beautiful sisters do I have? Only one crazy one, who finally found her match." I giggled and then stretched out on Nora's princess bed. I hung up soon with my sister and gazed at the princess pictures on the wall. *Maybe happy endings exists for some people*, I mused dreamily. Half an hour later, I got up off the bed hastily, interrupting my beautiful reverie—imagining Jasmine's future wedding reception. I had completely forgotten to pick up Nora from Mandy's house, and I had to be ready soon to go to Mother's house.

On my way to get Nora, Mother called me on the phone, complaining as I suspected. Once again, Jasmine was getting married to a non–Middle Eastern man. But after she snapped a few times on the phone, she decided that she wouldn't get involved. I could tell she was still not happy— worrying about what our community would say about the mixed marriage. After I hung up with Mother, I had an idea.

Later on that evening, I sat next to Mother, who was being friendly and looked really radiant. I was glad since I had been expecting her to look miserable with a long, formal face.

Nathan, who was from an Italian background, came with both his parents. His mother, Marge, sat next to Mother, and his father, Lucas, sat next to Jasim, whose presence smoothed out the whole atmosphere.

A little earlier, right after I picked up Nora from Mandy's, I convinced Jasim to come along with me. We needed a mature man, since Uncle Waleed was out of town. He had agreed right away and got ready quickly. I called Mother to tell her that I was bringing Jasim with me. She was silent at first and then snapped, complaining that I should have told her earlier.

After announcing their engagement, Nathan slipped the beautiful, shiny gold diamond engagement ring on Jasmine's finger.

I smiled, dismissing the memories of years earlier when I'd had to wear mine. I took a deep breath and hoped that Nathan was as genuine as he seemed right then.

Chapter Ten

Back on Monday a week later, I was about to have my packed lunch from home at my desk again. Christine was out for lunch as usual. As I was about to place the sandwich in my mouth, I heard someone clearing his throat. I hesitated slightly when I looked at Jason's dark-green gaze. His lips curled into a smile. I put my sandwich down.

I cleared my throat and said, "Hi, Mr. Miller."

"Hi, Hannah." He looked around him and then turned back to look at me adding, "I was going for lunch. I would like you to join me."

I looked blankly at him for a few seconds, trying to decide quickly what my answer was going to sound like. I didn't know how to refuse.

I heard myself say, "Are you sure?" I wet my lips, thinking of the best excuse to give him.

"Of course I am sure! You never went to any of our staff meetings. I need to fill you in."

Christine could fill me in, I thought while trying not to pout.

I gave him a curt smile and said, "We can always sit here." I pointed at the guest-seating area.

"We could, but I'm hungry too." He glanced at his watch and then turned back to face me. I really felt annoyed, especially since I had been put on the spot. I got up, quivering lightly. I straightened my dark pencil skirt and my long-sleeve light-cream blouse. I grabbed my purse and walked next to Jason toward the elevator. I followed him around the underground parking lot. We were going to take his car, since he suggested that it would be faster than me following him. He opened his black Porsche with a remote control. I sat next to him. I had never been inside a luxurious sports car like this before.

The car smelled brand new. He drove his car toward the garage exit. As soon as we were driving on the road; he turned to me and said, "I hope you like sushi."

I had never had sushi before either.

I said, "Sure." I took a deep breath. I felt really uptight, but I was trying not to show it. I mumbled, "Nice car."

He said proudly, "Thanks. I just got it last month." He then turned the music on, which was soft, like classical. The ride was very short, merely a few minutes. Once again, I followed him. We went inside the laid-back restaurant. We sat at one of the dark, round tables. I looked around in astonishment. Dark gray and black tones were the main colors of the furniture, floor, tables, and bar. The walls, however, were a light creamy color. The contrast of the two dark and light colors gave the restaurant an earthy, inviting ambiance.

***

A short older Japanese waiter came up to our table and bowed slightly. He wore a dark clean uniform and a black apron. He filled our glasses with water.

Jason said, "Give us green tea for each, a selection of the makimono platter, and two miso soups." As soon as the waiter was gone, Jason turned to me and said, "This place is remarkable. I come here at least twice a week."

I smiled politely. I had no clue what to say to that, since I had no idea what sushi tasted like.

I said, glancing around me, "The place looks beautiful and chic." I had nothing else to say, since I felt that I didn't fit there, especially after seeing a couple of fashionable women sitting across from us. I felt way too plain, with my minimal makeup and modest clothes.

"Yes, it is." The waiter came back with a pot of tea and two small white cups. He filled them. They were soon followed by the soups, which came in small classy white bowls.

I waited for Jason to start with his soup before I started with mine. I was a bit tense still. It had been ages since I had come to a nice, elegant restaurant. Yusuf had still been alive. I released his memory right away; I didn't need to feel even more stressed than I was. I liked the soup, and I wished it came in a bigger portion, because I finished it quickly. I really wanted to say something. But I couldn't think of anything. My mind was very blurry.

I was thinking about a sentence to say when I heard Jason mumble to my distress, "You are very quiet."

I wiped the side of my mouth and said, "I am … I am sorry."

I just didn't know what else to say to him. That man was my boss, who was really rich and acted sophisticated. I was afraid to open my mouth and say something incredibly foolish that could cost me my job. He grinned lightly.

"You don't have to be sorry."

"You … um … said that you are going to fill me in with some staff meeting information."

He gaped at me. "An excuse. I really didn't want to come here alone." He smiled at my blank face.

So was I his lunch companion? Or maybe he was a player, I thought, recalling Mary's warning. He hesitated a bit before he asked me, "If you don't mind me asking, how old are you?"

I cleared my throat.

"I will be turning twenty-five in July."

He smiled, and I smiled back nervously. "Too young to be a widow."

I nodded my head. I had heard this sentence one too many times already.

"Was your husband from Lebanon too?"

I froze. My back was pulled straight. I didn't know how to answer that complicated question. I didn't know where my husband came from. How could I explain that?

I cleared my throat and stuttered, "H-he was from the Middle East."

"Where?" He really wanted to know.

"He was …" I hesitated. I didn't want to lie to him. I looked hesitantly at him for a few long seconds, and then I decided I didn't want to raise suspicions as I had done in the past.

I said calmly, "I don't know where he came from." I breathed out, looking at my knotted fingers. I really didn't want to look at his shocked expression.

"Really," he said evenly. "How come?"

I cleared my throat. "He married me under a false name. He stole many identities in the past."

"Wow."

The food came. I looked at the big, colorful tray in front of me, which had many different-shaped filled rolls. The waiter placed an elegant square plate with a couple of metal chopsticks on the table; he then refilled both of our green teas. As soon as the waiter left, Jason took a sip of his tea.

He said, "You married a con."

I nodded. I tried not to stutter when I said, "I-I-I didn't know he was a con when I married him. I was very young and naïve."

"I see." With his chopsticks, he grabbed a couple of rolls of sushi. I just watched. I didn't know how to handle those chopsticks. I was probably going to drop food all over the table, making a mess. He placed a couple of sushi on my plate. I was put on the spot. I had to grab my dark metal chopsticks. I quickly studied the way he was holding his and tried to copy him. I dropped both of them on the floor almost as soon as I tried holding them. I bit my lower lip in despair.

I couldn't look at him when I mumbled, "Sorry." Then I bent down to pick them up, placing them on the side. There was no use in trying to embarrass myself again.

He was hiding a grin when he asked, "You've never used chopsticks before?"

I just shook my head. I sipped more of my green tea.

"I will ask the waiter to get you some cutlery." As soon as he spotted the waiter, he called him up to our table.

I didn't want to look at the waiter's gaze when Jason explained to him that I couldn't eat using chopsticks. A couple of minutes later, I was trying to cut the sushi with my fork and knife. I placed a small portion in my mouth. I tried to chew it for a long time. I didn't like sushi. Perhaps I was still not used to the way it tasted.

After a long few minutes of silence, he said, "Don't you want to find out your husband's true identity?"

I swallowed a tiny piece of rice from the sushi. Since Yusuf had passed away, I had tried to put the past with him behind me. Unfortunately, his recollection kept on coming back, especially lately, ever since I had found out that he had managed to ruin my credit entirely with all the credit cards he falsely used under my name. It was really hard shutting the door on his horrific memory.

I said, "Maybe, one day. We had a daughter together."

After a few seconds of studying me while chewing his food, he said, "I know some people who could help."

My eyes grew wide. That meant I had to tell him the details of my life with him. Would he know that the police had suspected me of being a partner in his scam? I didn't know what the astute thing to do was.

"How can they help?"

"We deal with different investigating services who can sometimes help locate people or a deceased person's origins."

"I know, but I really don't wish to take you away from your work. I mean those services are probably very costly." My head was going blurry. I had to decide if I wanted his help or not.

"Let's not worry about the money right now. I will inquire about it and will let you know what I can do."

I hesitated before saying, "If you don't mind, I don't want anyone to know of this."

"Don't worry, Hannah; our office is very professional, and all matters are usually kept confidential."

I could only pick the rice from the sushi. I could feel Jason's eyes on me—watching me silently. When I turned to look at him, he had a smile on his face. He said, "Remind me not to bring you to a sushi restaurant again."

I didn't know what that meant. Was he planning to bring me to more lunches? But why?

I bit my lower lip nervously. "I'm sorry. I tried to like it."

As soon as the waiter came to clear the table, he noticed that the platter was still half full. He asked politely if we would like the rest packed to-go. Jason smiled.

He said sternly, "The lovely lady would love to have it packed to go, for dinner."

I looked at him, staggered, right before he gave me a wink. I smiled back at him. Maybe he was hiding a sense of humor somewhere behind his cold expression. Jason placed an order for some chicken curry with rice. Somehow, the conversation shifted first to his type of work. Then he was elaborating on a few of the criminal law cases his office had to deal with. Since he already knew that my husband was a criminal, all of a sudden, I felt uneasy. I breathed a sigh of relief when I saw the waiter coming with the bill and the bag of takeout food. After signing the bill, Jason handed me the bag saying, "It's yours. Please don't tell me you don't like curry chicken."

I hesitated for a few seconds. I was overwhelmed by his nice gesture. I gave him a shy smile and thanked him. He looked intently at me and added, "Has anyone ever mentioned to you before that you have a gorgeous smile?"

I blushed instantly, thanking him again. He smiled sincerely, and then we both walked toward the restaurant's exit door.

***

It was on a Tuesday, a couple of weeks later, when Jason stopped by my desk and handed me an envelope with a document that required my signature. Jason always smiled when he passed me by, which made me feel uneasy, especially around either Christine or Mary. I read the file he gave me thoroughly; it was a legal release agreement. With my signature, I was giving the law firm my permission to look up my husband on my behalf. At that moment, I wished I had never opened my mouth to Jason, but then again, I didn't want to keep on hiding forever. Was finding Yusuf's identity the right thing to do? I knew at that point I had no choice but to sign the document. If I didn't sign, Jason would think that I was hiding something.

Henry called me during my lunch break. He insisted that I come with Jasmine and Nathan to his pool party on the weekend. I agreed since Jasmine and Nathan were coming too. I was getting used to speaking periodically to Henry on the phone since he called me about Jasmine's engagement. He was so easy to talk to, and at times, I found him really amusing.

***

A couple of hours later, I walked toward Jason's office. After knocking on the door, I staggered in. I had never been in his office before. It was like the rest of the offices, pristine, but it was much bigger, with the addition of a few more paintings around the wall, a large black L-shaped leather sofa, and a glass coffee table. I had the envelope in my hand. I placed it on his desk and then turned to leave.

When I reached the door, he said, "Do you sometimes go out with your friends?"

I shrugged. Was he going to ask me out? I wasn't ready for the answer. I turned to face him.

"Sometimes."

My mouth dried up all of a sudden. I smiled nervously. He opened a drawer, took out a small white envelope, and placed it on his desk.

"I have club guest passes."

I breathed out. So he wasn't asking me out. I liked Jason, but I found him way too out of my league and serious. Around him, I felt self-conscious most of the time. Plus, Mary's warning was always in the back of my mind.

"Thank you. I mean, I don't know what to say."

He thrust his back against his leather chair, and his eyes were still on me. "You don't have to say anything. You may use them; they are yours."

I smiled at that. I had only been to a club once before. I knew it would be impolite to refuse the guest passes, so I took the envelope from his desk.

"Just make sure the friends you bring act classy."

I tried not to frown.

On my way out, I heard him say evenly, "Maybe you will take me there one day soon." I managed to hide my discomfort. Was that an open invitation?

I cleared my throat and said, "Sure. I will?" I smiled, right before leaving the office.

Chapter Eleven

WE GATHERED AROUND A BIG rectangular table at a laid-back Italian restaurant. I immediately liked the casual atmosphere. The lights were bright, and the large place had a wide-open concept. All the tables around us were filled. People were loud, cheering and laughing. The table across from us was surrounded by a few waitresses singing a happy birthday song. I felt at ease, maybe because of the happy context or perhaps because everyone around me was content, including my family, Jasim, Nathan, and his parents.

Nathan invited both his family and ours to dinner to discuss the wedding. I asked Nathan if Jasim could join too. I didn't want him to be alone at home while we all had dinner as a family. I also noticed that he was looking younger, by at least five years. I was still reluctant to ask him about his age.

I didn't have time to change after work, so I still wore my modest clothes, no makeup, and hair smoothed in a bun. Hady and the twins were sitting next to each other at the end of one side of the table. They were busy talking about sports. My mother looked elegant and sat next to Nathan's mother, Marge, who was petite with a medium round body. She had short brown hair, and her makeup looked immaculate. They were speaking vociferously, each with a very thick ethnic accent. Nathan's father, Lucas, was also short. He had big, dark eyes and thinning hair. He was quietly just smiling away. Nathan had inherited his father's eyes, but I really wondered where he got his height from.

I glanced at both Jasmine and Nathan, who sat right across from me. They both looked good. I smiled sincerely at their blissful expressions. I really hoped Nathan was always going to be genuine toward my sister. They were whispering to each other. I wondered what they were talking about, because Jasmine kept on giggling lightly. Jasim sat to my left side. He was quietly looking around.

Nora sat to my right side. I was thankful she was still behaving herself. My contemplation was suddenly interrupted when the waitress came with our soups and salads.

After a few minutes, Nathan looked at Nora and asked her, "So, Nora, what do you want to be when you grow up?"

Nora stopped nibbling on some garlic bread. I knew she wouldn't be thinking about her answer too long.

"I want to be a princess."

I sighed and smiled. I hoped she wouldn't start with the princess subject.

And so we all waited for Nora to finish telling her story. Nathan, surprisingly, was listening intently while having his soup. He didn't even seem bored.

After the story, Jasim asked Nathan, "So, Nathan, what do you do for a living?"

After wiping his mouth with a clean cloth, he said, "I own a home renovation company with a partner." Then he added as a bonus, "I make a decent living. I have to take care of my woman right!" He then turned to look at Jasmine, who seemed so happy and proud. He placed his arm around her shoulders and tugged her closer to him.

My gaze traveled in between them. I felt happy, because they suited each other perfectly. Nathan appeared nice, and Jasmine seemed to really love him. Maybe love really existed, and it wasn't something beautiful that happened only in fairy tales. Nora's eyes were glancing in between Nathan and Jasmine, and she wore a big, bright smile.

Her eyes flickered when she asked enthusiastically, "Are you in love with my aunty or something?"

Jasim chuckled at the way Nora asked her question. Jasmine blushed away, and Nathan said while laughing, "Of course, I am. See, Jasmine is my princess."

Nora added excitedly, "Really!" She looked around her, stunned. "So you are a prince?"

"Yes, I am. My name is Prince Nathan."

Not again, I thought, while rolling my eyes. A few minutes later, I heard Nathan speaking to Jasim and his father about work. Later during the conversation, Jasim was speaking of his business.

"I owned a few dollar stores a while back. Now I rent a few properties."

I looked at him. I didn't know he had a few properties. He gave me a wink and added with a smile, "I feel younger now, ever since these two beautiful girls came to live with me."

I smiled; it was nice to see him happy. Jasim directed his conversation to Lucas, asking about his job.

Lucas said in a loud tone, "My brother and I owned a very good Italian restaurant for twenty-five years; now I don't work so hard no more." He chuckled lightly before he continued, "I worked hard enough for this boy to be so tall!" His thick Italian accent was mesmerizing. I loved it. We all laughed at the way he spoke.

I quickly glanced at Jasim. I wanted to know everything about him, but I was afraid to ask. I didn't want to bring back any sad memories for him. The food arrived on big square white plates. All of a sudden, the table was quiet, including Nora, who was enjoying her spaghetti and cheese. The food was superb and in big quantities.

The rest of the evening went well. We all said good-bye and parted. As soon as we got in the car, Nora fell asleep in the backseat.

Jasim was on the passenger seat. He glanced at me a couple of times before saying, "I hope one day soon you find a good man like Nathan."

I smiled. I was afraid to think about it. I knew I had some sort of a curse and the next man could be another abuser or a criminal. Debra's sad story zoomed right to my brain suddenly. I remembered how she ended up with a few abusive boyfriends after having a criminal father and an assaulter stepfather. But then again, Jasmine found Nathan after our abusive father and her abusive first husband. I didn't know anymore. I decided I'd rather not think about it.

I said, "Maybe one day. I don't think I am ready yet!"

He sighed, saying, "Hannah, I know you don't want to speak of your husband, but I think you need to let it out. Your mother told me some bits and pieces."

I peeped at him. Mother was speaking to Jasim behind my back!

He added, "You have to remember, not all men are the same, but next time you need to know him before you marry him, just like your sister is getting to know Nathan."

I giggled. "You are not like some Arabs, who believe in arranged marriages."

"Absolutely not. How can you put two strangers together and ask them to become husband and wife?" He shook his head.

"Jasim, I think you are very wise."

He said, "I think you are wise too, but you seem as if you shut down the doors on your past. And with that, you shut yourself up along with it."

We were both silent until we got home. I brought Nora to her bed. Then I came back upstairs. Jasim was sitting, staring at the wall in front of him.

I made us some green tea, placed it on the coffee table in front of us, sat next to him, and said calmly, "Once upon a time, in a faraway, warring land, I found myself being part of a dysfunctional family …" I spoke my heart out. I didn't leave anything out. I spoke of my father, Uncle Nader, Majeed, and then finally, my nameless husband. Jasim was silent. He didn't even say one word or ask a question until I was done. I merely cried right after I concluded the story with my husband's death. Jasim held me tight. I wept for a long time on his shoulder. After my cries calmed down, he looked deep into my eyes.

He said, "You are a survivor; you fought hard for your existence. You should be proud of what you have overcome already."

I just nodded my head.

He added sincerely, "Because I am so proud of you." Those last few words were coming from him, but I wished to hear them from my father, who was my own flesh and blood. "You are going to be okay. I promise you that."

I shook my head and smiled faintly.

"You are beautiful and smart. All you need is just a little confidence in yourself. Don't let your past drag you down."

All of a sudden, I felt calm and warm. Maybe Jasim was right. I was going to be okay one day.

I said in a wobbly voice, "Thank you, Jasim. Your words mean a lot to me."

He tapped on my shoulder. "You are a good girl."

We then played a game of backgammon, which had become our Friday and even Saturday night custom. I noticed that I smiled and laughed more than usual. I was even looking forward to Henry's pool party the following day. I felt like a kid again.

**

I woke up a little earlier the next day, feeling refreshed, I found a couple of my two-piece swimming costumes I'd owned from before. I'd worn them a few times last year when Jasmine suggested we tan in Mother's backyard. But as soon as I touched the material, flashes from the past came zooming back, and then I recalled Jasim's words, *"Don't let your past drag you down."* I right away took them and threw them in the trash and then placed the garbage back in Jasim's garage. If I had had more time, I would've just burned them. It was time for me to buy a new one anyway, with my own money, not with some other's people's hard-earned money stolen by my husband. I grabbed Nora and hit the mall. I could always buy her some ice cream on the way since the weather was beautiful and sunny.

I grabbed a one-piece white-and-pink costume from a discounted department store. I then stopped at the grocery store and bought a cheesecake for Henry. I couldn't go empty-handed.

Right after the mall, I dropped Nora at Mandy's. She was suntanning next to her pool; the two girls were delighted. I played and giggled with the both of them briefly. I was even laughing at their jokes.

Mandy got up from her long chair as I was leaving and told me, "Hannah, you look different today. What happened to you?"

I laughed lightly. "I think it's the weather. Nothing happened to me." I turned to leave, but then I stopped and turned back to face Mandy, saying happily, "Mandy, why don't we go out sometime? I mean, just the two of us, without the kids."

She lifted both her eyebrows and said, "Sure. I mean, that's what I suggested we do in the past, but I guess. Sure, why not?"

"Sounds good!" I said, grinning.

"Hannah!" she called me worriedly.

"Yes?" I turned back to face her again.

She mumbled, "Did you have any … um …" She hesitated before she continued, "… maybe some alcohol today?"

What? Why would she think that?

"Mandy, of course not! What makes you think so?"

"Never mind, Hannah. Have a wonderful time. I can see you are already in a party mood."

"Okay, see you soon." I smiled at her stunned expression.

I ran swiftly out of her backyard. I wondered what was wrong with Mandy that day. She didn't seem like herself. I drove back home and waited for Nathan to pick me up along with Jasmine.

***

Around 2:00 p.m. in the afternoon, I stood in front of the mirror, examining my look. Jasmine said that I should look casual for Henry's pool party.

I had my hair down, and I wore a simple yellow summer dress I had just bought myself for the occasion. I wore simple makeup. Oddly, that day, I really felt happier. I even looked more refreshed. Maybe because I had had a good night sleep for a change, I could even take a deep breath without feeling pain in my chest.

I was still studying the mirror when my cell rang. It was Jasmine. Nathan and she were waiting for me outside. I grabbed my things and was on my way out.

Nathan looked very casual with his knee-length navy-blue shorts and white shirt. Jasmine wore a small, short pink dress. Her hair was in a ponytail.

After settling into Nathan's car, I asked the both of them, "So what is the special occasion?"

While glancing at me in his car's rearview mirror, Nathan said, "I heard that Henry always has a party at his parents' house around this time. He takes advantage when they go to Italy for the summer, I suppose." He then chuckled, glancing at Jasmine. He added, "Can you imagine if his parents came back today?"

"Oh, so Henry is Italian like you?" I asked.

"He is. Why? Didn't he tell you?"

"Maybe he did, but I don't remember."

Jasmine turned to glance at me and said, "Hey, Sis, it's nice to see you look more alive today."

I shrugged lightly. I did notice something different in me this morning. Even Mandy mentioned it. I just didn't know why, but I felt happier.

"I think it's the weather. Have you noticed how beautiful the weather is today?"

"Yeah, well, it's been nice all week. Where have you been? In the north pole?"

I giggled. She really sounded funny. Soon, Nathan turned on the music. And I noticed myself singing along. I couldn't help it, since it was a happy tune.

Nathan turned toward a huge house. I was astonished to see how long the driveway was. Jasmine told me once that Henry's parents were rich, which reminded me of something.

"Oh, I forgot to mention that I have a few guest passes to some nightclub. I think we should use them soon."

"Sounds good," said Nathan. "Maybe we can go next week, on your birthday, right after dinner."

That was strange! Jasmine never mentioned anything about dinner; I had completely forgotten that my birthday was coming up soon.

Then I heard him say, "Ouch. What?" He glanced at Jasmine. He added, "Oh! Shoot."

She snapped lightly. "Thanks a lot, Nathan. That was supposed to be a surprise for Hannah."

He replied impetuously, "You never told me it was a surprise."

She replied, "Yes, I did … I told you in front of Travis. You can even ask him if you want."

I rolled my eyes. I said loudly over them, "That's okay. I am so glad I found out about it. I hate surprises."

She turned to give me a sad face. "Oh … I really wanted to make it a surprise. But Nathan here blew it."

I said quickly, "I don't mind really. Nathan, I am glad you blew it, and, Jasmine, this is not a big deal!" I took a deep breath. I really didn't want to them to start fighting over me. "Come on, Jasmine! How were you going to surprise me with dinner on my birthday? Do you think I am that dumb? I would have figured it out anyway." I looked over both of them. They were frowning when we got out of the car.

I said happily, "You both smile. We are here to have some fun. It's a beautiful day!"

They both had a stunned look on their faces when they looked at me.

I carried the cheesecake and my small bag, which had a towel, sunscreen, and some makeup.

We walked past a big, beautiful landscape—all different-colored flowers and a long row of identical shaped trees used as a fence to the back big backyard. The great backyard gate was open, and a large, clear-water swimming pool centered the huge space with slides and a diving board. Long, colorful chairs surrounded the pool. There was a large table that was set under a striped blue-and-white tent.

A few people had already arrived. Some were already walking around with their swimming costumes on. I saw Henry walking toward us. He looked very casual with his beach slippers, knee-length green shorts, and no shirt. His chest was flat, masculine, and tanned. He hid his eyes behind dark sunglasses and wore a big smile on his face when he greeted both Jasmine and me with a hug. He smelled like sunscreen lotion. He took the cake from me, thanking me sincerely. I should've gotten something more sophisticated like wine. I didn't know why I didn't think of that.

Nathan walked toward a big open cooler, which was full of ice, and placed the big box of beer he had in his hand next to it and then the beer bottles on the ice. Henry left so he could finish greeting more guests. I followed my sister, who greeted a couple of her acquaintances. There were so many faces. Most of them were in their twenties to early thirties.

A couple of big, tall men with hairy shoulders started to work on the barbecue. I was watching, astonished. It was as if my senses were working in a different way. I wasn't just watching. I was feeling without having any alcohol in my system yet. People were throwing jokes around me. I realized that Italian people had a different sense of humor. They were walking around with a drink in their hand, contently joking about themselves, about their own foolishness. They then chuckled ferociously. One second, they spoke to one another in an offensive way, and the next second, they tapped their drinks while cheering, which got me very confused. Jasmine was right. I needed to get out more often. I felt like an outcast, but that day, for some odd reason, I really wanted to fit in.

Nathan handed me a wine cooler. It tasted like sour berries. I liked it. I walked up to them, making a round around the swimming pool to meet Travis and Claire. We finally settled on one of the long beach chairs. Jasmine and I each placed a towel on the chair and lay down under the sun. Jasmine took off her dress. She was wearing a two-piece strapless dark-blue bikini. I hesitated for a second before I took off my dress. It had been a while since I wore a swimsuit in public. But then again, I was going to be one of the many girls around, who mostly were in two-piece suits.

Jasmine turned around and mumbled, "Why didn't you bring your two-piece? It suited you better!"

I frowned before replying, "I threw it in the garbage."

"Why?"

"Just because." I didn't want to bring up the Yusuf subject. I added, "What's wrong with this suit?"

"Nothing, Hannah, as long as you feel comfortable and happy."

I glanced at my suit and then quickly compared it to Jasmine's and those of the rest of the girls around. Suddenly, I didn't like mine anymore. I didn't want to be too modest. I wanted to fit in. I felt self-conscious. I shouldn't have bought my suit in haste.

"Do you happen to have an extra suit with you?" I knew the answer was going to be no. No one brought an extra suit anyway.

"I do. It's in my bag."

My brows lifted. I really didn't expect that answer.

"Weird. Why did you bring two suits?"

"I couldn't decide which one I wanted to wear." She sipped from her cooler. "So I brought the other one with me, just in case I changed my mind. But you are welcome to wear it if you want." She glanced at me, adding, "I will get it for you." She got up swiftly.

I put my sundress back on. My suit really looked old-fashioned. I followed Jasmine toward the tent, bringing my towel with me.

I glanced at myself in the mirror with Jasmine's black suit on. I frowned. If Mother saw us, she would kill us. I turned away from the mirror. Well, Mother wasn't there at the moment. What she didn't know wouldn't hurt her. Plus, why was I worrying about Mother? I was old enough with a child of my own to care for. I should try to be carefree just like Jasmine. I hesitated before I left the washroom, and then I placed my towel around me. I needed to adjust slowly to being this carefree woman.

I felt a little self-conscious as I stretched out next to Jasmine. I started sipping my berry drink. Half an hour later, I started to feel at ease. I had finished two bottles of berry coolers already, and we both lazily lay on our backs.

I glanced at her and said casually, "So where were you taking me for my surprise dinner party?"

She sighed and said, "To a nice Greek place. But since this is no longer a surprise, we can go first to the salon to style our hair, some grooming. It will be my treat."

"Jasmine, you don't need to spend your money on me. I work and make my own money."

"Well, Hannah, I wanted to do that as a thank-you, since you are going to be my maid of honor."

"I'm going to be your maid of honor?" I froze for a moment.

"Yes, you are going to help with invitation cards, booking appointments … You are going to be busy."

"Really!" I had just mulled over something we had never even discussed. "How was your first wedding?"

Jasmine sighed. "What wedding? We had a small party at my ex-husband's parents' house. The party was over by 8:00 p.m., since there were no guests, only parents and siblings."

I was glad that she didn't seem to be bothered by her past. I wondered if Father attended, but I decided not to inquire.

I said, "That's okay. This time around, it will be different. Nathan seems to really love you."

"I know. Listen, I can see Henry. He is on his way here. Sis, just be cool with him."

I looked up to glance at Henry. He was carrying three drinks in his hands.

He said gleefully, "Hey, girls, I want you to try my specialty drink," while handing a drink to Jasmine and me.

My head had already started to spin. I didn't need another drink, but I took the tall glass of red-orange-colored drink from Henry's hand. I thanked him shyly and placed it beside me on the ground.

A couple of minutes later, Henry brought a long beach chair closer to me. I glanced at Jasmine. She had a mischievous smile on her face. I grabbed my drink and slurped some of it nervously. I liked it. It was probably one of the tastiest drinks I'd had so far. Jasmine excused herself from beside me, stating that she had to find her fiancé.

Henry just lay lazily next to me for long minutes. I really felt like hiding myself. I was way too exposed for his wandering eyes.

Henry glanced over my side and said casually, "You look good."

"Thanks." My drink vanished soon after. Maybe I was a nervous drinker.

"We should go for a dip after, just you and me."

I sighed and said, "Sure."

"Do you like your drink?"

"Amazing."

"Do you want another one?"

"Why not? But I need to use the powder room first." I didn't know why I said that so fast because Henry leaped to his feet to get me another one and I was on my way to the restroom.

My head was whirling when I came back, and I felt really happy. He was already waiting for me. I was getting too hot, so I sat down hastily on the long chair and reached for my suntan lotion.

He placed the drink by my side. "I made it personally," he said impishly. "I added some of my special mixture."

"Okay," I said, grinning.

"Hey, why don't you let me put some sunscreen lotion on your back? You are getting too red."

I hesitated. But I didn't feel too nervous. I sipped some of the drink, noticing that it was even better than the first one. I took my time with my answer. I had almost forgotten how it felt to drink excessively, since it had been a year since my last embarrassing moment at the nightclub with him.

I objected, "I can do it myself."

He said playfully, "Hey, how are you going to reach your back?"

I hesitated. "Let me finish my drink first." Arguing was getting me restless, so I sipped my drink slowly. A few minutes later, I asked him, "What is this drink called?"

He grinned. "Do you really want to know?"

I said, giggling, "I do. This is an awesome drink."

"That is because it's called …" Then he muttered slowly, "Sex on the beach."

I burst out laughing. Maybe he was making a joke. He was Italian after all.

I said, between laughing, "That's funny!"

"It's not a joke … It's called sex on the beach. Or maybe you prefer it to be called sex around the swimming pool?"

I giggled again even louder. He sounded hilarious with the way he said it.

After I calmed down, I said, "I like the beach better." His eyebrows lifted, and he then bit on his lower lip, but I continued, "But not the sex."

I could still see his frown behind his sunglasses. "Why don't you like sex?"

I couldn't believe where the conversation was going. But I decided that I should answer him.

I sighed. "Sex is only for men to enjoy."

"Really!" He held up the sunscreen and moved closer. I sat on the beach long chair and turned my back to him. The lotion felt cool under his hands.

I shivered lightly. "I think you need to experience sex with the right man. I really don't mind being that man …"

I wanted to laugh at that sentence. I was surprised that I wasn't too shy. A few moments later, I wasn't listening to him anymore; but I could feel his hands massaging my shoulders, which was easing my muscles, to help me relax some more. I felt like I wanted to sleep. If only I could lay my head anywhere. I turned my gaze to him and asked, "Do you mind if I lie down?"

"No, not at all." I repositioned myself to lie down on the chair, facing down. Henry was massaging my shoulders, back, lower back … I didn't care where else because I felt so relaxed, so good …

Something cool splashed on my back. I shivered, turned quickly, and was looking at Jasmine's stare. I felt disoriented for a bit. Then I quickly remembered where I was.

"What happened, Sis? You came here to take a nap?"

"No." I looked around me. I then remembered that Henry was applying lotion on my back. "How long was I asleep for?"

"Like an hour. You need to eat something. Come on. I don't want to eat alone."

I was soon on my feet. I put my sundress on. I felt better being fully clothed. I glanced at the pool, noticing that many people were in the pool.

I grabbed a paper plate and followed Jasmine to the food table. There were hamburgers, hot dogs, and fries. I grabbed a hamburger and fries. I felt really hungry, remembering briefly that I hadn't eaten that day. We were almost done with our food when Nathan appeared out of nowhere and grabbed Jasmine's hand. In a second, she was been lifted like a sack of potatoes on his shoulder. She was screaming her lungs out. He then dropped both of them in the cool water. I watched the quick scene with big, stunned eyes. I was glad I wasn't Jasmine at that moment. The water must be so cool. I felt my body shiver at the thought. A moment later, I felt my hand was being pulled. I was being carried. Stunned, I turned to face Henry. What on earth was going on? I started calling out loudly, "No, no, no!" He wasn't listening. All of a sudden, I felt cold and was gasping for air since I was in the water too. I turned to face Henry. Angrily, I swam toward him; he was swimming away from me. I had to swim faster toward him. All of a sudden, he dived underwater and lifted me lightly. His hands were around my waist. Then I remembered that I was still wearing my dress. With difficulty, I turned to face him. With my fist, I hit him across his chest irritably. I didn't know what I was doing anymore. I was caught off guard. He was laughing out loud. I turned to look for Jasmine. She was swimming next to Nathan. Well, she didn't seem angry anymore.

I heard Henry mumble next to my ear, "Let me help you out of that." He was pulling my dress off.

"I will do it. You don't need to help me."

He wasn't listening and still helped me out of my dress. I felt nervous all of a sudden.

"I will put your dress in the dryer for you." He had a mischievous smile, adding, "If I don't find you in the pool when I come back, I promise you I'll repeat the throwing-you-in-the-pool episode."

My eyes grew wide. Was he threatening me? I glanced around as soon as he got out of the pool swiftly. There were at least seven people in the pool.

I swam toward my sister. I looked at Nathan and snapped, "You guys are crazy."

He grinned. "Oh, what happened to you? The water messed up your hairstyle!" he said mockingly.

Jasmine sprayed water across his face. Then she swam away from him, squealing. He grinned and followed her just to catch her and then throw her in the water again. They looked like two children having fun. I glanced toward the drink ice cooler, and I thought of something.

A few minutes later, I heard a loud splash behind me. It was Henry.

He said, "I was hoping you had disobeyed me, just so I could throw you in the water again."

"Henry, you are so funny, but how about this." I took out the bag of mixed ice and water I had been hiding in my hand for a couple of minutes and emptied it on his head. I burst into laughter at his stunned expression. I thought that was priceless. I cried out, "The joke is on you!"

He dipped in the water just so he could catch me and throw me again.

After almost an hour of playing like a couple of children, we lay lazily on the long chair. Henry was beside me. I glanced at him from behind my glasses. He was fun. I really liked him. He had brought me another sex on the beach drink.

He mumbled, after licking his lips. "I think you find me too warm and cozy; that's why you like to snuggle next to me …"

I grinned, recalling the first time I had slept on his shoulder and then the second time while he was applying lotion. I blushed.

"I think you like to get me drunk, giving me no choice but to snuggle next to you …"

He laughed.

"I don't usually need to get women drunk. They willingly beg to be able to snuggle next to me."

I frowned lightly. I said mystifyingly, "Is that so?"

"Do you want to bet?"

"Bet for what?"

He mumbled, in a low tone, "Bet that I can make you want to snuggle next to me."

I was silent. Our conversation was going in a different direction. All of a sudden, I didn't want to encourage it anymore. Henry was charming, handsome, rich, and, most important, a big-time player, I wanted to discontinue the flirting but without being abrupt. I smiled.

"Henry. I am not ready. Y-you know, after my husband …" I was stuttering. "I need more time."

"That's okay. Take your time. I am not in a rush." Then he leaped suddenly to his feet. "I am hungry now. Do you want to share some fries and a hamburger?"

I smiled faintly. And to my shock, he bent down and gave me a moist kiss on my lips. I was stunned. *What was that?* He had told me just a minute earlier to take my time. I looked around, hoping no one saw the embrace. Henry smiled mischievously at my stunned, blazing face right before he ran toward the food table.

At the end of the day, right before we said good night, Henry hugged me tight, kissing only the corner of my lip, right before I left with my sister and Nathan. I lay in the backseat of Nathan's SUV, half asleep. I glanced at the clock; it was almost 9:00 p.m. I had called Mandy earlier; she said that Nora was already fast asleep. I was going to miss Nora, but being all alone in a bed without being kicked left and right by her feet after an eventful day like that day was going to be priceless.

***

The Friday before my birthday weekend event, right after lunch, I managed to see Jason. I hadn't seen him since he gave me the guest passes. I had heard that he was on a business trip out of town. He greeted me casually at first, but then he turned back and walked toward my desk, smiling. No one else was around. I wanted to shy away. I knew why I had gotten his attention this time around.

***

A day after the pool party, I went shopping in hopes of changing my outfit to match my new happy attitude. I wanted to look pretty. That would probably boost my confidence. I even styled my hair differently and was wearing a bit more makeup. I felt that I needed some change. The fear of drawing attention around the office was no longer on my mind. *Maybe I should stop worrying about what people think of me; I need to be more like Jasmine—carefree.* Even Christine complimented my new look.

When I met Jasmine a couple of days after Henry's pool party, I handed her half the nightclub guest passes, keeping four. I was even looking forward to having some fun. Nathan could give them to Travis and Claire since he already knew of my surprise party, which Jasmine was planning. Mandy was going out of town with her boyfriend, John, so Nora was going to spend the night with Tiffany at Mandy's mother's place.

Jason was the one who gave me the passes. It was going to be awkward, but I decided, after thinking about it for a few days, that it was the right thing to do, to ask him if he would like to join me at the club, especially since he suggested that I take him with me one day soon. So what if he came along, which was unlikely anyway? I assured myself that he would certainly refuse. Someone like him would probably have to attend a few party events over the weekend. He would definitely feel uneasy if he found out I was going with my friends, so I texted him earlier that day, casually asking him if he would like to join me and my friends, without mentioning my birthday event.

He was now standing in front of me. All of a sudden, I felt that my white, short-sleeve shirt was too tight and was wishing that I had placed my hair in a ponytail or a bun, because Mary's warning was suddenly back in my head.

"Hi, Hannah!" He smiled.

"Hi, Mr. Miller," I replied hesitantly.

"You look bright today, different." He was scrutinizing me.

"It's probably my tan." My tan was still visible since Henry's pool party.

"Whatever it is, it suits you." His eyes flickered, and with the way he was looking at me, I blushed.

"Thanks," I muttered. Then I cleared my throat before I added, trying to sound casual, "About my text." He smiled right before I added, "I mean, I know you are always busy and all; you probably won't have time to—"

He interrupted me. "I have a party I have to attend that night." I breathed out. "But I don't mind joining you; however, that would be a bit after midnight. I can pick you up."

My heart sank. I was hoping he would refuse the invitation. I smiled nervously. *Great assumption,* I told myself.

"That's okay. I can meet you there. I'm going with a couple of friends." My mind went blank.

He then scratched his chin lightly. "Let me see how I am going to do this. I will text you if I can't make it." I smiled politely.

"Sure, um, I guess you already have my number."

"Okay. I will see you tomorrow." Right before he walked to his office, he added, "Hannah, call me by Jason when no one else is around."

I tried to smile and said, "Okay." I hoped Jason would keep this between us and wouldn't tell his sister about it. All of a sudden, I felt as if I had made a bad decision by asking him to join, *too late for that now.*

***

Right after Jason left, I got a call from Henry, which I ignored because I was busy with another call. Later, I noticed that he left me a voice mail. A couple of hours later, I listened to his message. He cheerfully thanked me for the pass to the club we were going to attend after dinner.

That was when I felt ill to my stomach while listening to the rest of the message.

He said that it was supposed to be a surprise, and he wanted to pick me up from my place.

Not only was Henry going to join us for dinner; he was also going to be at the nightclub too.

I rested my head briefly on the desk in front of me. My heart was pounding. What was I supposed to do with Jason? How did this happen to me?

***

Later on that evening, I called Jasmine to discuss my dilemma with her.

"Hey, Sis."

"Hey, Jasmine …" I hesitated. "Listen, do you think that there is a possibility that Henry won't come tomorrow evening to the club?"

"Of course not. That's all he has been talking about since we told him. Come on, Sis; you can't be that cruel."

I blushed.

"Why?" she added.

I snapped, "But I didn't invite him; you did." She sighed. "Is Henry expecting to be my date?"

"Knowing Henry, yes … I think so."

"Well, it can't be a date; I have another date."

She burst out, "What?"

"Yep, and guess who. My boss … He gave me the damn passes!"

"Crap! What are we going to do?"

"Maybe cancel the whole thing."

"Are you crazy? We're not canceling your birthday." She sighed. "Oh! Now I get it. Nathan wondered where you got those passes from. You know, they are worth, like, a lot of money."

I gasped. "Really?" I was shocked. "I thought each was around ten dollars," recalling briefly the only time I went to a nightclub.

"No. Nathan said that this club is more exclusive and very expensive to get in." She was silent for a bit. "You little weasel, how come you never told me about your boss?"

"There was nothing to tell. We went for coffee and then again for sushi. He said it was work-related."

"No, really! Sometimes, you startle me, Hannah. And most of the time, I don't get you."

We were both silent. I didn't know how to answer her. She continued, "You hardly go out, and then all of a sudden, you find yourself with two dates in one evening … one with my fiancé's friend and the other one with your boss."

"I didn't invite Henry," I said, irritated.

"I should've mentioned it to you. Well, the surprise birthday party was Henry's idea."

Crap, can this get any more awkward?

I snapped, "I thought it was your idea!"

"Well, we were having dinner with Henry and Travis when he mentioned you and how guilty he felt after giving you one too many drinks on your last birthday; then soon I got a text from him suggesting we throw you a surprise party this year."

I felt my heart racing—a whole lot of dilemmas could've been avoided if Jasmine had told me about all this earlier. I said, frustrated, "Great, that's just great!"

Jasmine added in a defensive tone, "But you guys looked so into each other playing in the pool like two lovers."

I snapped, "I wasn't playing with him like a lover. We were just having fun." I felt terrible all of a sudden. It was my fault. I had led Henry on. The whole time at the pool party, I didn't feel too awkward; for the first time in as long as I could remember, I really enjoyed myself, and what did I make out of it? A big pile of mess, and soon after, I made a terrible decision by inviting Jason along. My attempt at getting out of my shell into the world, hoping to gain some confidence, was a terrible idea. I was still not ready. I wished I could turn back time. All of a sudden, I felt hopeless again. "Jasmine, don't add to my agony."

"You never even indicated to me about your boss. How come? I thought we were sisters and friends."

I sighed. "Jasmine, it's a story that wasn't worth mentioning, I swear." It was hard to explain the way Jason had convinced me that both the coffee and sushi lunch were work-related. She wouldn't believe me.

Jasmine mumbled, "I am sorry, Sis." There was a silence. "What time did your boss say he was coming?"

"After midnight." I sighed.

"I don't know what you are going to do. Maybe you should be honest with Henry. Or I could ask my friend Jessica to come. Henry had a crush on her once."

"I think Henry has a crush on every woman he meets and doesn't seem to give up on women he can't have. I have three more guest passes. You can invite three different girls."

"I don't know what happened to Jessica and Henry. They exchanged phone numbers, and Henry never called her, or she never replied. I don't know."

"I don't care. They will probably hit it off once they see each other again."

"I thought you liked Henry."

"I don't know. I do like him, but after spending time with him on Saturday, I think I like him more as a friend. Plus, he is a player."

"Hannah, some men are players till they find the right woman." She sighed again. "I don't want you to end up in tears on your birthday."

"I am not going to cry over any man, Jasmine. Trust me. I just don't want to lose Henry's friendship or Nathan's respect, and I don't want to lose my job. That's all."

"Wow, that's a short list you got. I can't promise miracles, but let me see what I can do. Henry said that he can get in the club without a pass. Travis is going to give it to Claire. You know what? I can ask Claire's if her sister Pat could join, so I may need an extra pass. I just remembered that Jessica is out of town; I'm meeting Nathan tonight, I can pick it up soon."

"You can have all three passes." I wouldn't need them anyways.

"Listen, seriously now. Tomorrow, we get ready and hope to have fun. And whatever happens happens."

"Okay. Fine," I said breathlessly and then decided not to think about the event until the time came.

Chapter Twelve

The next morning, I woke up earlier than usual. After breakfast, Jasim, Nora, and I were sitting in the backyard, enjoying the sun and the garden view. I knew Jasim loved nature, just like Mother. I was thinking about the upcoming convoluted nightclub event while sipping my tea when Nora broke my train of thought.

She said happily, "I have something for you."

I smiled, pretending to be stunned. "For me?"

"Yes." She ran inside for few minutes, and then she came back. I could tell she was hiding something behind her back.

"What is it, Nora? What are you hiding?"

She glanced quickly at Jasim with a mischievous smile and then placed a card in front of me. I gasped excitedly. There was a pink heart with many colors and hearts. My heart sank. And in big, uneven writing, it said, "Happy Birthday, Mommy!" I looked at her with a big grin on my face. I then pulled her close to me and hugged her tight. I had tears in my eyes.

I mumbled happily, "Thank you, sweetie. It's so beautiful."

She said, grinning, "You are welcome, Mommy."

I said in between kissing her cheek, "I love you so much, my baby girl."

"I love you too." She pulled back from my embrace and said, "Can I watch TV now?"

"Sure." My eyes followed her until she disappeared inside Jasim's house.

I heard a low, firm voice. "My turn."

Then I saw an envelope right next to me. I looked at Jasim's kind face. I smiled. All of a sudden, I felt a flow of excitement. I had never felt that special before. I really didn't want to cry again. With shaky hands, I opened the envelope. It was a prepaid Visa, with one hundred dollars. I got off my seat and hugged him tightly. I was trying to contain my tears.

He said, "There is still something left in the envelope."

I looked at him, puzzled, since that was too much already. I reached for the envelope and noticed that there was a necklace. I looked at the simple white-gold half-moon-shaped pendant necklace. I felt hot tears on my cheek. I loved it. Right away, I put it on. My hands were shaky, but I managed. I brought my chair up next to him.

Wiping away my tears, I said, "I love it. It's beautiful. I will cherish it forever."

All of a sudden, I felt something. There was a squeeze deep inside my chest and my stomach at the same time. It wasn't a painful or uncomfortable feeling. I held his hands and said through my tears, "I love you, Jasim. Thank you."

"I love you too, my dear."

I touched the moon pendant. Could Jasim really love me? I felt very special. I hoped nothing would change in my life at that moment. It was perfect just the way it was.

***

Right after, I dropped Nora at Mandy's mother's and thanked her for looking after her. She said that it was her pleasure, especially since Tiffany behaved a lot better when Nora was around.

***

I met up with my sister at an upscale hair salon and spa. She was already waiting for me. I handed her the iced-coffee that I had brought with me. Then I sat next to her, waiting for our names to be called, sipping my own iced-coffee. She glanced at me.

"I think you should highlight your hair with a little blonde. It would look good on you."

"Okay. I am open to suggestions."

A girl called my name and then my sister's name. I got up instantly. We walked toward a back room. An Asian girl wearing a front-buttoned white simple dress emerged. I glanced at Jasmine; she grinned.

She said mockingly, "I thought your eyebrows need some work too. I mean, you need to look spectacular for your two dates tonight." I gave her a curt smile right before stretching out on a bendable chair under a bright lamp.

Two hours later, we finally got out of the salon, looking so different from the way we went in. My hair was sleek with a few blonde highlights. My eyebrows were shaped professionally for the very first time in my life. I even got a manicure and a pedicure done. I felt like a changed woman. However, I was afraid to ask Jasmine about the small fortune she had paid at the salon. I felt spoiled by all the gifts that I had received—Nora's special birthday card, Jasim's necklace and gift card, Mother's and my brothers' gift of another hundred-dollar gift card, Jason's club passes, Jasmine's generous gift, and Mandy's present of the latest top-model cell phone; and when I objected, afraid to learn the price she paid, she exclaimed that I always babysat Tiffany on the weekend.

I convinced Jasmine to stop by a small café for some lunch as my treat. We both sat on the patio outside, under a large umbrella, hiding our gazes behind our sunglasses, since the sun was beaming across from us.

A couple of men sat at a table across from us, having lunch. They were grinning while glancing at us periodically. We both ignored them as we tried to enjoy our grilled chicken and salads. A few minutes later, a waitress came with two drinks. She said that they had already been purchased by a customer. I looked across the table. The two men held their glasses over their heads. I didn't know what to do. I turned to Jasmine.

She said quickly, almost whispering, "If we accept the drinks, they will come and sit with us."

I ignored their gaze for a few long minutes.

The waitress emerged on the patio again. Jasmine called to her. She told her in a low tone, "Please take the drinks back and tell those two men … thank you, but we are not single."

I smiled wickedly at Jasmine and added, "You may not be single, but I am still looking for someone to ruin my perfect life."

She sipped her drink. Then she snapped quietly, "You kill me with your negativity, Sis. What is wrong with you?"

I added pessimistically, "I am scared. I mean, I just discovered this morning that I love my life just the way it is right now."

"You say that now, because you haven't met the right man."

"How did you feel when you first met Nathan? Did you know right away that he was the right man?"

She sighed dreamily. "No, at first, I thought he was gorgeous but a bit annoying. But for some reason, I just couldn't keep him off my mind, no matter how hard I tried."

I hesitated before I said, "Did he ever make you feel inferior to him, you know, since he's got money …?"

She finished my sentence. "And I don't!"

I knew I shouldn't put her down like this, too late for that. Yusuf's degrading poems still affected my self-esteem; I would never forget how he loved insulting my poor, uneducated background.

"I know it sucks to come from a family like ours, but Nathan made me feel equal right away. I met a couple of his friends on our second date, and since then, he has been showering me with gifts. Never once has he made me feel inferior to him. He knows if he ever said one word to put me down, I would then just pack all his gifts and give them back to him."

I recalled Yusuf's generous purchase, only to make up for that purchase many times over, ruining my credit with over twelve thousand dollars in unpaid credit cards. I wished then I had the ability to give him everything and walk away. He wouldn't even let me do that … I was stuck.

"Sorry, Jasmine, I want you to be happy." I sipped some water. "Speaking of gifts, I feel as if I was showered with gifts today." I smiled.

"You deserve it, Sis."

"Tell me, how were you showered with gifts?"

Jasmine's face lit up. She told me about the jewelry, the iPad, the cell phone, the gym membership, and many more gifts and the fact he wouldn't take no for an answer. Mandy was always speaking of how her boyfriend spoiled her, but then again, she was already rich. Maybe few good men did exist, and they were hard to find. All of a sudden, I recalled my past again. A long time ago, I merely had one simple wish: to live a peaceful, modest life with a humble, caring man. I didn't want any gifts or money. I shook the ugly memories and wished I could erase my past from my head.

"One day, someone will come and spoil you even better, you will see. You need to open up your heart."

I felt my chest squeeze. I doubted it.

"I don't know about that. I mean, I've lost my trust in men." I gave her a sad smile. "Before Yusuf, there was Majeed. Unfortunately, only a certain type of man is attracted to me, the ones who want to take advantage and destroy me."

"Who's Majeed?"

I smiled cynically at his memory. Jasmine probably didn't remember his name. "Majeed was someone gorgeous I knew a long, long time ago." I lingered for few seconds, and then I continued, "You know him too; he was the one who hit me with the beach canoe."

Jasmine's gaze was lost; she was probably trying to recall Majeed. She mumbled, "I remember him, you have to tell me what happened. You can't hide anything."

I smiled lightly. I wasn't going to hide anything. Jasmine was wiser and stronger than I was in so many different ways. Maybe I could learn a couple of things from her. A soft breeze came to caress my beautifully styled hair. I closed my eyes and took a deep breath. I could still remember as if it were yesterday—the tangy, salty odor; the soothing sound of the waves slap-lapping the seashore; the golden, glittering bright sand under the sizzling sunlight, and the majestic deep blue sea ...

"It was summertime at the beach back in Lebanon. I was then almost fourteen years old ... minding my own business, swimming with my eyes closed, in the middle of a beautiful daydream, when something hit me all of a sudden, pushing me underwater. The man who carried me to the shore was Majeed …" Jasmine, for the first time, was listening attentively to me. I must have been talking for a while, because I noticed when I was done that the two men across from us were already gone and another couple had taken over their spot.

Jasmine said, stunned, "Wow, Sis. That is terrible. I am sorry you had to go through that."

"That's okay. That's why sometimes I feel scared to be infatuated with men. I am afraid to get hurt again."

Jasmine's soft, freshly polished hand touched my soft, polished hand.

She said, "Not all men are bad. Just because you had bad luck with Majeed, your nameless husband, and you know who …"

I knew she meant Nader.

I shrugged and muttered, "I am afraid to get hurt again." I thought briefly about Henry and Jason. I had a feeling that Henry was a player. He would probably keep on jumping from one girl to the next one. He didn't have to settle down since he was already too spoiled by his parents and still lived as if he were a teenage boy and not a grown man in his late twenties. Jason, however, seemed nice but too refined compared to my humble self, and there was always his sister, who seemed to hate me. I would definitely feel discomfited being around his sophisticated friends. That explained why I had felt inept the couple of times we had met for lunch.

"Don't dwell on the negative. Be a little hopeful."

A few minutes later, the waitress brought me the chicken-and-rice meal that came with a salad I had ordered for Jasim's early dinner. I hoped he would enjoy it. Soon after, we were on our way back to my apartment after she dropped her car at Mother's house, where we were supposed to get ready before we got picked up by Nathan. I was glad I had already called Henry this morning and declined his offer to pick me up from home.

Back at home, I met with Jasim, who was sitting on his patio. Right away, he noticed my new look and praised me. I was so happy, feeling a boost of confidence. I brought his takeout food and placed it next to him. He smiled delightedly. I pulled out a chair and sat close to him while he picked up his fork. A few minutes later, Jasim and I were having a small conversation when I heard Jasmine's voice from behind me. I immediately remembered that she was waiting for me just so we could start getting ready. I got up right away and bent to kiss Jasim's temple, excusing myself.

Jasmine brought me a small sleek red dress. I wore it and was pleased with the way it fit. It was a few inches above my knees, showing off my tanned, well-shaped legs, but I frowned when I noticed that it was showing more cleavage than I liked. I tried to pull it up, but it was no use. I couldn't even place a pin in it because it would ruin the way the dress looked. I decided I wasn't going to show Jasim my revealing little outfit. He would probably disapprove and be disappointed in me, and I didn't want that.

Jasmine applied an excessive amount of makeup to my face. I didn't look at myself in the mirror during the process. I was afraid I'd look like a clown after all the layers of different cream, foundations, and powder she applied. But I felt delighted when I saw myself. I cocked my head in different directions. I didn't expect to look as good as I did.

Her voice came from behind me. "Remember, don't touch your face and eyes every second, the way you usually do."

I giggled and said sarcastically, "Yes, Mommy."

She then pulled me up, saying with a sigh, "You look gorgeous, Sis. I hope your two dates won't end up in a big battle over you tonight."

"Jasmine, do you have to remind me every second about my two dates. I have to worry about them after midnight. Right now, I only want to have fun and not think of the awkward, upcoming event." I glanced at myself again in the mirror. I added, "There is still a possibility that Jason won't show up. Don't forget he has another party to go to."

"Let's hope. Plus, the good news is that Claire's sister Pat is coming tonight." I was delighted by that news. A few minutes later, her cell phone rang. Nathan was waiting for us outside. I glanced at Jasmine. She always looked gorgeous. She had on a deep-purple, open-back sleek dress with small, fitted shoulder straps. It fell a few inches above her knees. Her hair was freshly highlighted in red. Her makeup was obviously immaculate.

"Ready, Sis?"

"Ready," I said, following her to the front door.

***

I felt a homey but vibrant atmosphere when we entered this Greek restaurant. The owner welcomed us with a big smile and then walked us to our beautifully set-up table. A dark-blue tablecloth was on top of a white one. The two-color combination reminded me of the beach, the deep blue sea and waves covered with white foam. The walls were white with a gravelly texture, and the floor was plain stone, adding a special effect of the Greek ethnicity. I didn't know why, but at that moment, I remembered my old country, Lebanon, especially the beach. Surprisingly, for the first time, I felt my heart sink.

A few minutes later, we were sitting around the table. Henry walked in wearing his usual charming hyper attitude. He looked really handsome with his dark hair neatly styled and brushed, giving him a sharp and semicasual air. He wore crisp black pants and a gray shirt. His eyes shone when he looked at me.

He greeted Jasmine and Nathan, and then he squeezed me in a tight embrace, whispering in my ear, "Hi, gorgeous!"

I had to break from his tight hug. I smiled slightly, blushing. At that moment, I hated the idea of having to break his heart at the end of the night. I hoped the girl who was coming soon could manage to distract him away from me. A few minutes later, Travis walked in with Claire and a pretty brunette—Pat, I assumed. I noticed that they somewhat looked alike despite their different hair colors. Right away, I noticed Henry staring at her. I tried so hard not to roll my eyes; I knew that would happen.

A few baskets of warm, fresh bread, covered with a nice, white warm cloth were set on the table, followed by two big bottles of red wine. Small plates of spicy stuffed peppers with feta cheese and a few small plates of different-colored dips had been evenly distributed around our table.

Jasmine was sitting by my side and was constantly giggling at Nathan's jokes. I wished she had been sitting across from me so she would notice Henry's flirty, shimmery eyes looking toward Pat, who was sending him back a lustful look. I probably noticed the flirting because I made a point to do so.

Unexpectedly, I felt a bit annoyed. It was probably my female ego, which I had just started to discover in myself. What if I had regarded this as a date! But I pretended I didn't notice and looked the other way each time Henry looked my way. I sipped my wine leisurely and tried a bit of each of the dips. They were all delightful and refreshing.

Henry was having a smooth conversation and sharing funny jokes with Travis and occasionally with Claire and Pat, who was giggling constantly. I found myself grinning at the jokes too, deciding to have fun.

I couldn't visualize Henry as a husband; if he ever got married, he would probably start cheating right after the honeymoon or possibly during, if the right pretty girl came along. Majeed's memory came back briefly; he was engaged while he led me on. It was so hard to find someone loyal these days. The main entrée came along with a marinated tomato, black olive, and feta cheese salad. There were four oval-shaped white plates. One had marinated chicken kebabs, the second marinated beef kebabs, the third lamb chops, and the last one, which was right in the middle, was just plain lemon rice. I was stressed about the upcoming club event; I merely nibbled on some chicken and rice.

I glanced at my watch. It was already past 9:00 p.m. Right after the waitresses cleared the table, I heard the faint voices of people singing along, which was getting louder, but then I noticed that the owner was carrying a cake, followed by a few waitresses. They were singing a happy birthday song for me. I glanced around me. Everyone was singing along. I spluttered heavily. That was awkward. I forced a smile. I didn't know how to be the center of attention, since I hardly ever had been in the past. Then the champagne was opened.

I glanced at Henry. He had a wide smile on his face; he only gave me a light hug, and soon, I found myself hugging everyone at the table, including a couple of the waitresses and the owner of the restaurant himself. Everyone was kind, trying to make me feel special, but that didn't help with my awkwardness. Travis and Nathan split the huge bill. I felt bad. I didn't wish to cost anyone a fortune. Jasmine said she was going to the powder room. I followed her.

After reapplying some makeup, I turned to Jasmine to tell her of Henry's flirty traits, but I had to stop because I heard a couple of familiar giggles, which belonged to Claire and Pat. I smiled lightly, glancing at them. When I was happy again with the way I looked, I followed Jasmine to the restaurant.

The guys were ready to leave. Henry held my hand, squeezed it lightly, and kissed the corner of my mouth. He then glanced toward the washroom and withdrew quickly. I took a deep breath; I feared he was going to kiss me some more. *How embarrassing.* I decided I had to speak to him very soon, about not showing affection in public. When I glanced to where Henry was secretly glancing, I noticed that Claire and Pat were walking toward us, which explained Henry's sudden withdrawal from me. At that moment, I hoped his heart got broken before the end of the night, but then again, a man like Henry would be cured in a couple of hours or at the sight of another pretty girl.

I followed Jasmine and Nathan. We were on our way to that club, which was around forty-five minutes away, where I was supposed to meet Jason in a couple of hours. My heart sank. I sighed lightly. As soon as Nathan got out of the car, Jasmine placed something on my head.

I gasped. "What are you doing?"

Jasmine said calmly, "This is a little fancy tiara. Don't worry; I didn't get it from a kids' store."

I snapped, "No way! Are you out of your mind?"

She sighed. "No keep it, it looks so cute on you; it just says, 'Birthday Girl.'"

I grumbled, "Take it off! What am I, two years old?"

"Don't worry; it's not obvious at all. Plus, it will be too dark inside. No one will see." She added, "Trust me." I hesitated for a bit. She grabbed a mirror from her purse. I glanced at it. She was right. It did look cute and fancy; the letters were too small to be obvious.

I sighed and murmured, "Okay, you win. I will wear it, just for you!"

Jasmine then handed me two of the leftover guest passes, since I had given her the rest of mine.

"Your leftover passes, they are yours; you may need them again."

I didn't care to have them back, but then again I didn't want to argue with her. I took from her and placed them in my purse.

***

Once inside the nightclub, I noticed that it was very dim and not as crowded as the only other club I had gone to with Jasmine. There were a few bars, and the lights were ongoing. The DJ was playing top-forty music. Despite that, it wasn't exceedingly crowded. The atmosphere was high energy, and the fashion was both trendy and swanky.

I followed Nathan and Jasmine toward the bar. I wondered how much a drink would cost here. I was afraid to ask the waiter. I was supposed to be classy, recalling that Jason stressed the idea of being classy. A few minutes later, Henry came from behind me. In a firm tone, he ordered a bottle of champagne. I was hoping he hadn't ordered it for my birthday. I really didn't want him to spend money because of me.

I saw him paying with a credit card. The bartender placed a few champagne glasses on the bar and was even chatting with him. I took one with a shaky hand. I sipped the first and then the second glass leisurely after tapping it with everyone around me again. Acting classy was always in the back of my mind. I looked around; I wondered where Travis went with Claire and Pat.

As soon as everyone was done drinking the champagne bottle, I pulled closer to the bar after making sure that Jasmine and Nathan were busy talking. I asked the bartender for the same champagne. I did have a one-hundred-dollar Visa card from Jasim and another hundred in cash. I could do this. I really didn't wish to owe Henry anything.

"Two hundred fifty dollars," the tall Caucasian bartender said evenly. I blinked twice, trying so hard not to choke.

After giving him both the credit card and the cash, I asked in a low voice, "Can you take the rest on debit?" I could tell that the bartender wasn't too pleased, even after I gave him a whole ten dollars as a tip. He didn't even fill the glasses the way he did for Henry.

Henry was too busy joking with Nathan and Jasmine when I tapped him lightly on his shoulder and whispered in his ear, "I bought some champagne for everyone."

He turned an angry gaze toward me. He said disappointedly, "No, you didn't."

"I did. It's here." I so wanted to add, "And it already made me broke." I saw the same disappointed stare from both Nathan and Jasmine. Oh well, too late to turn back time and undo the $250 damage that went down the drain. This time around, we had to fill our own glasses. I avoided the bartender's stare.

Henry pulled me by my hand to the dance floor. I almost knocked over a tall waitress wearing a shiny outfit. I knew I shouldn't drink anymore. Henry pulled me too close. I pulled myself away slightly. It was about 11:30 p.m. I was thankful that Jasmine came after me to save me. Henry danced with the both of us for a bit and then excused himself. I breathed out. The music was a mix of hip-hop music. A few minutes passed, and I had a sudden urge to visit the restroom. I whispered into Jasmine's ear that I wanted to use the ladies' room. She said she had seen it somewhere and to follow her. I almost got knocked over by another waitress and stumbled upon a small table. I had to act classier than this. What if Jason saw me right then? I heard Jasmine yell in my ear. Her speech sounded slurry. I giggled at that.

"Oh, Sis, I think Henry is sooo … into you."

"Jasmine, stop. Henry is so …" I just couldn't think of the word to describe him. My mind was fuzzy. I added something that came all of a sudden into my mind. "Debra, my um … stripper friend said once—"

Jasmine's eyes grew wide. "Your friend was a stripper?"

"Yes. Debra. I like her."

"What did she tell you?"

We found the restroom finally.

I breathed out while dashing toward the toilet. I was thinking about what Debra had told me a long time ago. "Oh yes. Don't … you …" I forgot suddenly what Debra had told me. I had to think again, and then

I remembered. "I should now kiss the boys and make them ... cry." I felt much more relaxed. Then I remembered something else.

"Where are Travis and the girls?"

I got up and flushed the toilet. I brought my dress down while I opened the bathroom door at the same time. I squeaked suddenly. There was a man in front of me. I closed the restroom door in his face quickly. Where did Jasmine go? What was going on? I sat on the toilet again. I was trembling. At that moment, I felt more alert. I said, "You can't be here ... in a women's restroom."

I heard him say in a deep and husky tone, "Well, the last time I checked, it said 'men' on the door."

Did I see some door signs? I just realized that I didn't, but Jasmine did. She was leading the way.

I cleared my throat and said confidently, "My sister was here too. I mean, I don't think that we ... both went to the wrong place." I was trying not to sound too drunk.

He said sarcastically, "So the girl who froze suddenly and then ran out a second later was your sister?"

Was he kidding me? *Jasmine left!* Without warning me! I squeezed my lips tight. I stuttered, maybe even implored, "C-can you please leave?"

"I think you will be safe with me," he said in a firm tone.

I didn't hear his steps leaving. *Just breathe,* I told myself. I slowly opened the door, without looking at him. I was on my way to the exit door when I remembered something. I turned back toward the sink. I didn't want this stranger to think that I was both stupid and filthy.

I could feel his stare on me, even though I avoided looking at his tall, masculine frame. I heard him say, "Happy birthday!"

I froze suddenly. *Crap, my little tiara ...* How did he notice the little words? I quickly reached to remove it from my hair. I cursed faintly, "Damn you, Jasmine, and your silly idea." Was my tiara stuck? It wouldn't come off! I stopped and breathed deeply, and then I tried again. What did Jasmine do? Tangle it with my hair?

I stomped my feet, feeling angry and frustrated. I didn't need this. I was already stressed out. I cried out loud, "Damn!" Then I remembered the man, whose gaze was following me. My face felt so hot. I was acting like a foolish, temperamental kid, as opposed to the classy woman I wanted to be.

He said appealingly, "Let me help you." He had a big grin on his face. "Before you rip your hair off your head …" Without waiting for my answer, he moved behind me, facing the restroom mirror and started gently separating my oversprayed hair, which was tangled with the tiara. I was praying that no one else came in. While I was looking around, my body shivered when I saw the urinal. This was indeed a men's restroom!

My hands were unsteady. Suddenly, I was aware of him behind me, and he was touching my hair. My heart was beating so fast. I saw my face in the mirror; it was red. But I wasn't afraid. It was something different … something I'd never experienced before.

I looked at our reflections. He was dark, as if he had been under the sun all day. I noticed that he was tall with a strong build and stunning features—deep, dark eyes; thick, black, well-shaped eyebrows; and a strong jaw. His mouth looked too sexy, too sensual, especially the way he was smiling with his straight, pearly white teeth. My stomach felt like a knot. All of a sudden, I wanted to know what he thought of me. I then frowned lightly. He was probably mocking me. How could he not? I was a grown woman, wearing a tiara, and stomping my feet angrily, while cursing. Maybe I shouldn't think about what he thought of me. His hair was thick and jet-black, and he wore it brushed to the back. He was a mixture of sex and class combined. The contrast of his white shirt against his dark skin was mesmerizing; I was wondering how his skin would feel on mine. *I could only imagine.* That crazy whimsy made my bones feel like some sort of liquid. Maybe it was the alcohol. I couldn't say anything.

"So, how old are you, birthday girl?" he asked. His hands were still in my hair; he was taking his sweet time.

I said with a shaky voice, "Twenty-five." I tried not to peep at him, but I couldn't help it, something about him felt gripping. I hoped he didn't notice me glancing at him periodically. He untangled the tiara from my hair. I should have felt relieved, but I didn't.

"There," he said. He handed the tiara to me. Our hands touched and eyes locked. I placed the tiara quickly in my little purse. I knew I had to leave right away before I made a fool out of myself. He was looking deep into my eyes, as if he knew me from before.

Then I stuttered lightly, "Th-thank you ... for your help." I was on my way out, and then I remembered something. I turned back to look into his eyes again before continuing, "Could you wait like two minutes before you get out of here?" I was no longer drunk.

His grin disappeared; he was looking serious, and then he opened his mouth to say something, but I didn't give him a chance. I ran out.

I spotted Jasmine right after I left the washroom. She looked worried when she turned to me and said, "What happened? I was waiting for over five minutes."

"My tiara got stuck. It's a long story." Then we started walking away from the restroom. I added, "What happened to you, Jasmine? You leave me in the men's restroom with a stranger?"

"Oh! I'm so sorry ... As soon as I saw him, I got scared, and then I found myself outside." We were close to the bar. Travis, Claire, and Pat were there. Travis seemed to be in the middle of a conversation with Nathan, and Henry was on another side speaking with both the girls.

"Jasmine, let's leave them alone and dance. I think Henry is into Pat."

She grumbled, "But I want to check on Nathan."

I pulled her hand toward the dance floor.

"Just give me ten minutes."

While walking toward the dance floor, I spotted the handsome man from the men's restroom incident. I felt a tight knot in my stomach again. I looked away from him.

I heard Jasmine say, "Well, what happened with this guy in the washroom?"

I shrugged.

"He is cute!" she added.

I snapped lightly, "Your silly tiara got stuck in my hair. He helped me untangle it."

"He did?" she said, stunned. We started dancing lightly to soft R&B music.

Then we both turned when someone said, "May I have this dance with the birthday girl?"

I glanced over at Jasmine. She had an astounded smile on her face. Without a word, she walked away. I couldn't even speak. I didn't reply, but somehow, I was already in his arms. We started to dance slowly to a smooth song. But the music soon ended. Another song started to play; it was a song I loved, "Breathe Again." It was romantic and smooth. He drew me closer. He was dancing slowly, nice and steady. He smelled incredible. Maybe it was his aftershave, or it could have been his cologne or his body smell. I inhaled his scent deep into my lungs. Little shivers traveled around my body. I closed my eyes, feeling utterly lost.

He drew me closer. My lips were almost touching his neck. I swallowed my strange, erotic desires and then wet my lips with my tongue. I had a sudden urge to place my lips on his neck, to kiss his dark, glowing skin. Was I still too drunk? Maybe I was. I just loved that feeling. At the same time, I feared it. That wasn't like me. I could only take short, interrupted breaths.

He drew me even closer. I closed my eyes tight again. The urge of really wishing I could run my lips across his neck was starting to bother me. I could feel his lips touching the top of my hair and his sweet, warm breath. Both his hands held my waist even tighter. His lips were now traveling to my temple. I let go of a sigh. *What on earth?* That was insane. Only one thing mattered to me at that moment. Where were his warm, tingly lips moving so slowly? They felt so soft, so good. I gasped one more time when they landed on my cheek. I wondered if he felt my racing heartbeat. He whispered close to my ear, "Your skin is so warm and soft."

My body was on fire instantly, listening to his sexy whispers in my ear.

His lips were again on my hair. I wanted to look up and glance at his face once again. My hands were wrapped up tighter around his lean body, as if I were afraid to lose him.

"May I dance with my girl now?" Henry's voice came like thunder, waking me up from a beautiful dream. The man unwrapped his hands from around me, and I felt cold all of a sudden. I started to feel panicky. Then I saw him taking off without saying even a word. I couldn't see him anymore, disappearing into the crowd.

I didn't even look at Henry. I walked away from him. I didn't know where I was going—just walking around feeling despondent all of a sudden. I wasn't even a bit drunk; I was fully awake. I didn't know how much time had passed, maybe only few minutes, but I felt hands grabbing me lightly by my arm.

"What happened to you, Hannah?" Henry snapped.

"Nothing happened to me … Why don't you go back to your girl, Pat, and leave me alone?" I pulled my arm from his hand angrily.

"Is that why you decided to make out with a total stranger, here in the middle of the dance floor?"

"Henry, I wasn't making out with him." I wondered how pathetic we must look. Right that moment, Jason came to my mind. I wondered what time it was. "Plus, you are not my boyfriend. Why should you care?"

"I think you are drunk. That's why that man took advantage of you." He hesitated before he continued, "Pat means nothing to me."

"No, I am not drunk! And that man didn't take advantage of me."

His tone was calmer when he said, "I promise you that I will pay attention to you only. Pat merely came tonight with a plan to distract my attention from you."

Wasn't he listening to me? What kind of a lame excuse was that! And how foolish did he think I was, watching him while his eyes were on her during the whole dinner?

"No, Henry, don't give me that bullshit. I'm not stupid. Okay?" I didn't know what had happened to me. I was filled up with rage. He stared at me for a few seconds and then took off. I felt a sudden headache.

***

"So how did the dance go?" my sister said as soon as she spotted me a few minutes later.

I looked away and mumbled, "I don't want to talk, Jasmine." I felt like I was going to burst into tears.

"Why? What happened?" she said, looking somewhat disappointed.

I couldn't speak. I looked around and noticed that Henry, Travis, and the sister were gone.

Jasmine was probably watching my searching gaze. She said, "Henry left."

I asked mockingly, "With Pat?"

"Travis, Henry, and the girls left together. I don't know. Henry looked pissed."

My shoulders slumped.

"Where is Nathan?"

"He is by the bar, speaking to someone about business." She added after a few seconds, "Look on the bright side; it's a little after midnight, and you succeeded in getting rid of your first date. What happened? Why was he pissed?"

I frowned. "I'll tell you later."

All of a sudden, my phone beeped. My heart sank. I glanced at the message from Jason. He asked me first if my friends were still there. With shaky fingers, I replied with a simple no. Then I was in the middle of sending him another message, stating that my sister and her fiancé were still there, when his reply came right after with "I'm here," so I deleted the message. I could tell him face-to-face, I supposed.

That night was a total mess. I couldn't even think clearly. I was terrible at planning and making assumptions. I went to the powder room. I glanced at my face in the mirror, and then I saw a man's face. It was dark and gorgeous with a sexy smile. I shook my head. I should just forget about him. I took my time before I went to meet Jason. I needed to recover some strength.

My cell phone beeped. It was Jason. He was waiting for me at the bar by the entrance. I took a deep breath and then went out to meet him. I hoped this night wouldn't get any stranger.

As I approached the bar, I could see Jason's slim frame sitting on the long bar chair. He looked dapper as usual. He got up as soon as he saw me and gave me a hug. He then invited me to sit next to him, which I did.

He asked me politely, "What would you like to drink?"

I didn't really care. "Wine is good." I could drink it slowly, since I wasn't fond of it. I was glad that a different bartender from earlier served us, handing me a glass of red. I wondered how much it was. Thirty dollars a glass? I didn't know why I felt cynical and irritated.

Jason asked politely, "How do you like this club?"

"It's beautiful obviously. And the drinks are pretty … good." I was going to say "expensive."

"You should try the lemon martini; it's to die for."

I tried not to roll my eyes. Maybe I should go for the martini. I felt a sudden stiffness and anger. I was afraid I would snap soon.

Examining me intently, his eyes shining, Jason said, "I'm glad you met me at this bar."

I felt annoyed but faked a smile. "Why?"

"You look really different, chic and lovely. It would have been really hard to locate you."

I blushed.

"Thank you." I wanted to change this awkward subject. "My sister and fiancé are here too. We came together."

"Really?"

"Yes, they are my ride back."

He seemed serious when he said, "I didn't know you came with your family." I bit my lip fretfully. I never mentioned my family coming to the club, only my friends. He added, "I can always drive you back."

Crap! Nothing was going right that night. I smiled politely, thinking that I would rather walk home, but I thanked him.

A few minutes passed. He asked, "Do you want to dance?"

The idea of dancing with someone else right then was scary.

I answered tentatively, "I am not a good dancer."

"Neither am I." I smiled tightly. I was glad. I really didn't want to dance for the rest of the night.

Then to my distress, he said, "Shall we dance then?"

"You want to dance? But you said you are not a good dancer," I said timidly.

"I'm not. Neither are you. This way, we won't look odd when we dance."

I tried to hide my frown and smiled lightly. Latin music was playing. He drew me closer. I tried to keep my distance. He smelled good too. But I wasn't interested in inhaling his scent deep into my lungs. He spun me around, and then, all of a sudden, he was holding my waist while I had to place my arms around him. He was drawing me closer to him, too close for my comfort, I thought. I couldn't stand his nearness; it was agonizing, after my dance with some stranger. I was thinking of the best way I could keep him far away.

Then I whispered in his ear, "I need to visit the powder room."

He stopped. "Sure, I will meet you at the bar." He pulled his body away from me.

I breathed, and then I found myself running toward the restroom. As soon as I was alone, I texted my sister, who had told me earlier that she was going to give me my privacy with Jason and to text her when I was ready to leave. I found out where she was around the club. Jasmine and I didn't discuss Nathan—whether to mention my second date to him or not; in fact, it was hard to plan for anything with the short notice we had, but I decided to mention my second date for the night. This could be the only way I could keep the distance between me and Jason, and so I asked her to meet me with Nathan at the bar, where Jason was waiting for me. Later, I could explain my decision to her.

Jason hid his frown well when I introduced him to Jasmine and Nathan. I could tell that he was disappointed. I didn't know what he expected from meeting me that night.

I avoided Nathan's stare. What would he think of me after this night? I had a date with his friend before midnight and then had a date with my boss after midnight. A few minutes later, we were sitting by one of the comfortable couches. Nathan offered to buy me more drinks. I declined. I didn't think I could fit another drink in without making a fool out of myself. The one thing I really liked about Nathan was he could talk about anything. He was soon conversing with Jason, while Jasmine and I listened. That was perfect. I was hoping we could just call it a night soon.

Half an hour later, Jason got up. He said good-bye to Jasmine and Nathan.

Jason hugged me and whispered into my ear, "We should do this again, just you and I."

"Sure." I faked a smile.

As soon we were out of the club, in the mild, cool night, I felt a faint squeeze in my chest, recalling my dance with the man I briefly met at the restroom. I would remember him as my handsome stranger. *What a night!* I then let go of a long, frustrated sigh.

Chapter Thirteen

I drove to meet Jasmine at the bridal shop. I struggled to control my fretfulness. As I parked my car, I tried so hard to kick all the dark memories that emerged suddenly in my head.

As soon as I walked in, I felt a bit shaky. The room was beautifully laid out. There were a few platforms and a mirror right across. I couldn't ignore the images that I saw—a reflection of myself years back—a hopeless teenager trying three of Yusuf's favorite dresses, while picking the perfect gown to wear on the day that marked the beginning of my black calendar for years to come. I turned away. Jasmine was already inside trying on her gown. I sat on the one comfortable white leather couch waiting for her to come out from the fitting room. I hoped she did soon.

***

The next couple of weeks after my birthday dragged. I noticed that I was getting annoyed by little things that didn't bother me before, like when Nora left a pile of mess behind for no reason. I started yelling at her more often, sending her to more time-outs. I really did spoil her and shelter her way too much while growing up. She thought she could do whatever she wanted without getting punished for it. At work, I found myself taking off for lunch to stay in the privacy of my car. I didn't know why I felt so easily annoyed and short-tempered.

A few days after my birthday, I heard from Jasmine that Henry had started to date Pat, just to prove my point. I felt vindictive about the news, not because I was jealous, but because to him, girls were easily disposed of and replaceable. Jasmine could right then see why I didn't want to give him a chance to ruin my already disturbed life.

Jason was out of town on business. I was hoping he would give up on me the way Henry did. I was hopeless after all. I just couldn't pretend to like either Henry or Jason, and on my birthday, I couldn't hide a weird sensation I felt toward a stranger. What was wrong with me?

***

After work, I was getting really busy, helping Jasmine plan for her wedding. However, I felt apprehensive about that wedding dress fitting, troubled to see what I had just seen, a flashback of my past.

She emerged from the fitting room, moving very slowly. I was speechless. She looked so beautiful, so innocent, like a beautiful white flower. The tight strapless dress had satin around the bust, half covered with well-designed beading, and poofed up slightly from the waist down. Her veil was simple with an embroidered edge. I held back my tears.

I approached her and said, "Jasmine, you look incredible!"

"I'm glad you like it too." She was still looking at herself. I had to ask her the next question. I just had to.

"Can you now picture Nathan next to you?" Those flashbacks, reminded me that I couldn't then picture Yusuf next to me.

She sighed happily with a wide smile, and without any hesitation, she said proudly, "I can."

I came closer and gave her a tight hug. I was glad she had finally found someone who would make her happy. She mumbled, "I hope to see you soon as a happy bride."

My lips curled into a faint smile. I didn't want to tell her that this was an impossible dream.

***

One day, I found Jason leaning against my desk. He had just come back from out of town. It had been three weeks since my birthday. I looked bright with my fresh makeup and my new short-sleeve purple blouse and tight pencil skirt. My hair was wavy and loose.

He said casually, "Would you like to join me for lunch?"

I smiled politely. I was quiet for a few seconds. He gave me no choice but to accept. He added lightly, "Don't worry; we won't go for sushi today. I was thinking maybe Greek? I know Lebanese food is similar."

I said shyly, "I like Greek."

"Good. I like Greek too. We finally found some common ground."

I could only speculate about what he meant.

Our ride was quiet, filled with classical music. I started to relax around him. I noticed that he pulled his car toward a familiar restaurant, where my birthday dinner was held. Right after we both got out of the car and began walking toward the restaurant entrance, he said, "An old friend of mine recommended this place."

"I tried it the other day with couple of my friends. It's actually good." I was glad he had brought me here. At least I knew what to order.

"In that case, maybe you can order for me."

"Sure," I said, and to my surprise, he drew me to him while walking toward the restaurant.

I felt at ease, since the place was familiar. We found a seat next to a window. It was a nice, sunny day outside. I glanced at my watch.

"I hope we won't be late. Thirty minutes has passed since my lunch hour."

"Don't worry; I can always notify Mary or Christine to cover your desk until you come back." I smiled nervously. Mary was around that day. I wished it was only Christine, since she always minded her own business. I wondered what she would say when I came back. "I will tell her that you are running errands for me." I didn't know what to say to that. I knew that the excuse he was going to give her wouldn't fix my discomfiture; it would, in fact, add to it. The waitress came to bring our drinks. I had tap water, and Jason ordered Perrier. I glanced away from his drink. *Yusuf had loved his Perrier too.* I then placed our food order, which was something I was familiar with. I ordered some dips and warm bread for an appetizer, chicken and beef kebabs with rice, and a salad for an entrée.

A few minutes after our food order arrived, the owner himself came to greet us. I remembered his middle-aged short, bulky body, shaved head, and fair complexion.

"Hey! I remember you!"

I smiled shyly. I was hoping he wouldn't remember me. I nodded.

"You were the birthday girl! Am I right?"

I cleared my throat. "Yes. It's me."

I glanced at Jason. He was watching the both of us with a small smile.

I added timidly, "The food here is very good."

He turned to Jason and said, "Good, good, that's what I like to hear."

"How are you, sir? How is everything?"

Jason wiped his mouth and said firmly, "Good. Thanks."

The owner turned to me and said, "Good to see you again. Enjoy." He then turned away and left.

Jason turned to me and said, "Well, I must admit. The food is good here." There were a few long seconds of silence. "Do you have lot of friends?"

"A few. Nathan, my soon-to-be brother-in-law, knows a lot of Italian people."

"I see." We spoke of mostly his life, his travels, and his girlfriends, who didn't seem as sophisticated as his CEO ex-wife. I wondered when he had the chance to have that many since he was married for ten years and only divorced for two. He also mentioned his old friend whose life had been turned upside down because of a poor junky girl.

Jason was careful not to mention names; even his ex-girlfriends' names were hidden. He was just telling me stories, adding that he felt at ease speaking to me and he didn't know why. Well, I didn't know why either. All I did was listen to his conversation, just asking a few questions, trying to learn how his kind of people lived. I figured that Jason was fed up with his marriage way before the divorce. I recalled Mary's words; she had called him a player. I gathered that his ex-wife was obviously much older, filthy rich but cold. I was startled by Jason's honesty and talkative personality, which didn't match his sophisticated exterior appearance. Half an hour had passed, and the table was still full of food.

I said apologetically, "I am sorry. I didn't know the food would come in this quantity."

He smiled. "No worries." The waitress came to collect the dishes.

***

Mary was on the phone when I came back almost forty-five minutes late. I was hoping she wouldn't mention my delay. As soon as she placed the phone down, she said, annoyed, "I heard you were busy running some errands for Jason."

I cleared my throat. "Yes."

She said sternly, "You need to know that Jason has been in and out of a relationship with Katie from the time he was still married. The last receptionist had quit because of him. She couldn't handle the pressure when he dumped her to go back with Katie." She paused for few seconds before she added in a calmer tone, "Hannah, please keep this between us."

Why was she telling me this? And where did she get all this information? I wished Jason would leave me alone; at the same time, I didn't want to lose my job.

"He invited me to lunch. I was being polite."

She turned away. "Learn to make excuses. I really don't want you to get burned."

Was she concerned about me? No, why should she be? Trying to solve this mystery was impossible, so I turned to my screen, avoiding her for the rest of the day.

***

Later on that day, Adrianna asked me to stay late. She was her usual demanding self. I didn't understand why she was in such a bad mood. I even smelled alcohol on her breath when she was speaking to me. I didn't leave home until after 7:30 p.m. I had to cancel with my sister, who was supposed to meet me at a bakery for her wedding cake. She called Mother to be with her instead. I hoped I didn't have to stay late at work until after my sister got married, which was in a couple of weeks.

I was exhausted when I went back home. Later on at night, I made tea for Jasim and me and felt much better after speaking freely about the trouble that I had had with Adrianna; however, I avoided speaking of Jason and the lunch we had had together and Mary's interference and warnings. Despite the fact that I had totally opened up to him about my past, I still felt embarrassed telling him about the man trouble I was currently facing.

***

I was bustling around, helping Jasmine with her wedding preparation. I was at Mother's house one day, trying to put the finishing touches on Nora's dress. I examined it and decided that it looked perfect. Nora wanted some pink in her white fluffy dress I had bought her, so I pinned a few pink flowers around the bottom of the dress as an extra touch. Nora would be pleased. She was going to be a gorgeous little flower girl at the wedding. Jasmine had a chart with the seating arrangements laid out.

She was having a real wedding this time. I tried not to compare it to my awful wedding day. I heard the phone ring. Nora was watching TV in Mother's living room since the twins were out of the house. Mother was probably in the backyard. It didn't seem like Jasmine was going to move an inch while examining the chart. I supposed I was the only one who could answer. I ran to the phone.

"Hello," I said, panting.

A male voice said, "Hello, Jasmine."

"No, it's Hannah, her sister."

That wasn't the first time someone had mistaken me for Jasmine, since we almost had the same voice.

"Oh, hi, Hannah. Finally, I get to speak to my sister-in-law."

I shrugged. "Nathan!" That was strange; he didn't sound like Nathan.

His tone was irritated when he said, "Who's Nathan?"

"Who is this?"

"It's Mike, Jasmine's husband."

"You mean Jasmine's ex-husband."

"Whatever. Who is Nathan?" His tone was rude and intimidating.

"Why do you want to know?" I said, annoyed.

He tried to moderate his tone when he asked, "Is Jasmine there? I really have to speak to her."

I said calmly, "Why is that? I don't think she wants to speak to you."

"Oh, yes, she does. You can even ask her."

I sighed. "Hold on." I ran to Jasmine's bedroom. As soon as I told her that her ex-husband was on the other line, she looked as if she had seen a ghost. I asked if she minded if I told him that Nathan was her fiancé. She said she didn't care. I ran back downstairs.

I took a deep breath before I said, "Mike, I told Jasmine you were on the phone, and you know what she said?"

"What?"

I sighed. "Nothing. She just looked as if she had seen a ghost. You should see the look on her face!"

"I need to speak to her. Tell her it's urgent," he said loudly. He was obviously getting really impatient.

I said in a composed tone, "Mike, please, there is no reason to be rude to me. It's not my fault." I was trying to maintain my composure. "You have to understand. Jasmine is super busy right now. Do you know why?" I could hear him breathing hard, about to explode. He didn't answer. I said in friendly, breathy tone, "Well, I will tell you anyway. She is getting married to this awesome man. My new bother-in-law, Nathan, who won't abuse her and make her miserable like my ex-brother-in-law Mike." Then I heard the hang-up click on his side announcing the end of our conversation. I frowned. Mike had hung up on me! What a shame, I was starting to enjoy my conversation with him. *That's okay; I won't hold that against him,* I thought with a sudden surge of energy.

Chapter Fourteen

Nora looked so pretty in her poufy dress. She was twirling around in front of the mirror for over half an hour already. We had just come back from the hairdresser and were waiting for the limo to pick us up. My gown was long, sleek, off-the-shoulder, and baby blue. My hair looked exquisite in a loose side bun. My sister looked striking. Her hair was in a bun. She wore a little tiara that complemented her red highlighted hair. Mother wore a long, sleek red dress. That day, she seemed ten years younger, pretty, and, most important, *happy*.

My brothers were sharp but uncomfortable wearing tuxes for the first time in their lives. Jasim looked particularly handsome wearing his elegant dark suit. I made sure to pin a little white boutonniere on his top jacket.

The limo ride was fun. It was my and my family's first such experience. My brothers couldn't stop joking and laughing the whole time. Jasmine seemed a little nervous. She wanted the wedding to go according to the plan. I remembered briefly my wedding. I didn't have a say about anything. I didn't care if it went according to any plan. I was terrified of the night ahead, alone with Yusuf. Those same happy faces were sad then, as if they were going to a funeral. Maybe it was a sign that Jasmine was going to be happily married. I closed my eyes. I should learn to let go of my past. Why was I allowing it to flood back into my brain?

When the limo stopped, the door was opened up by the limo driver. A videographer was videotaping the whole event. After the wedding ceremony, Jasmine went into Nathan's limo.

We finally made it to the wedding hall. We arrived before the bride and groom. I had seen the hall before that day with Jasmine and her wedding planner. As soon as we made our way to the entrance, I noticed a few men wearing tuxes had started to play the violin. Champagne was being distributed to the guests, even before they made their way to the hall, which looked fabulous with all the flower arrangements, the many semibright chandeliers, and the large hardwood dance floor that had a little stand for the DJ.

I met up with Mandy, John, and Tiffany. I had introduced Jasmine to Mandy months earlier. Well, they did have so much in common. Mandy invited her and Nathan over for dinner at her place. Nathan and John got along right away. They found some similarity, especially with their type of work, which dealt with home construction and renovation. We had all become friends.

Tiffany had a dress similar to Nora's. We were hoping to avoid any anguish during the party between the girls. Staff started guiding people to their exquisitely set-up tables. Once almost everyone was seated, I was able to spot my uncle Waleed, his wife, and his three children. My grandmother Amina looked different that day, since she wore some makeup. Uncle Wael was there with his fiancée. I felt happy. Finally, the family was celebrating a good event. If Father was still alive, would he have come?

The wedding planner was moving swiftly, making sure everything was running smoothly and according to the plan. She had to make sure the newlywed couple's entrance was spectacular, just the way I had imagined it to be. I heard the loud drumming noises. My heart skipped; this was it. I made sure all the ladies around me knew what to do. Young, sharp-looking men formed a straight line, each holding a tambourine. They all started to move them swiftly, making music along with the violinists. I could see the drummer and the belly dancer, and memories of the first wedding I ever attended came back. I told the ladies to reach for their baskets and to start gently throwing those dry rice and red flower petals on the newlyweds. I couldn't help it; my tears fell down my cheeks. I looked over at Mother. She had tears too. Nora and Tiffany were just excitedly jumping and throwing away. The couple moved slowly to sit at the head table. Nathan looked so handsome. I smiled at the both of them. They seemed ecstatic to finally tie the knot between them.

I sat next to the head table, along with Jasmine's bridesmaids. I could see Henry sitting at a table not too far from me. He sat with his family and guy friends. I wondered what had happened to Pat. Was she another one of his many exes? Jasmine had been too busy lately to fill me in on the details. Soft background music was playing. I scanned the guests quickly. I found Nora, sitting next to Tiffany. I could see them counting the pink flowers pinned on their dresses. I smiled; I was glad she was busy doing something. My family's table, which also included Jasim, was only one table across, just like Nathan's family table. I requested that Mandy's table was not too far away either. I wanted to keep an eye on Nora. Guests were still greeting each other. Jasmine and Nathan were receiving continuous greetings from guests. I recalled briefly Farah's wedding, which was the first happy event I had witnessed. That day was another happy event. I smiled lightly. I remembered the once-dreamy teenager I had been before I was transformed into a realistic, shattered woman. Behind a smile, I was hiding the dark shadows of my past that obscured my mind unexpectedly. I refused to visualize having a wedding like that anymore. I was terrified of my reverie, which transformed within seconds into dark nightmares. I sipped more of my champagne. I needed to be happy that day. I had to keep my memories off my mind.

Food started to arrive at the tables, carried by many sharp-looking staff members. Salad was followed by seafood, pasta, chicken, and steak, and drinks were filled periodically. I glanced at Nora, thankful she was being careful with her food. I knew she didn't want to mess up her poufy dress. The open dessert table was set. I smiled when I saw the chocolate fountain. I was glad Jasmine had added it to her dessert menu requests. I wanted her to have all the things I once dreamed of. That day, at least, I could feel it through her.

***

Later on that night, Travis got up to give his speech, holding a microphone. I started quivering, because my speech came next. I was not a public speaker. I was hoping I could just read it without stammering much. Travis's speech was fun. He managed to make the crowd laugh. People clapped their hands right before he sat down. I didn't want it to end, but then it did.

I stood up, smiling. Travis gave me the microphone. I wished at this moment I hadn't had all the champagne that I did. I dropped the microphone on the table, but I grabbed it right away. My voice quivered when I said, "Sorry. I am so clumsy. Um …" I lifted the piece of paper that I had written my speech on in front of me. I was too nervous to start reading. Then I thought of a joke. "Speaking of clumsy, that's how I felt when I married once." I sighed, looking around at the still faces. "I couldn't see the deep hole, and I fell in it. It took me years to climb out of that damn hole, just to be here today." People were looking at me with big eyes. I took a deep breath. I didn't know what I was saying. "My beautiful sister, Jasmine, is walking a straight line today. I know she won't fall into any scary holes. And that's because she is walking next to Nathan." I sighed heavily. "I know that he is going to be the man Jasmine deserves, a caring, loving, hardworking man … to always protect and cherish her. And she will be what he deserves, a beautiful, kind, smart, full-of-life woman … to complete him." Then I lifted my glass to Jasmine and Nathan. I was shocked to see Jasmine in tears. I had thought my speech was terrible, since it wasn't really planned. "Here is to the new couple, and, Nathan, welcome to our family." Then I heard a clap. People were cheering. The room was very loud. I felt my face go red. I sat down; I guessed my speech didn't go so badly after all.

Nathan's father spoke next. It was a very quick mixed Italian-English speech.

The DJ started with the music next. Nathan grabbed Jasmine and led her to the large dance floor, followed by his parents. Travis walked me to the dance floor and danced with me first, since we were the best man and maid of honor. Soon, the dance floor was filled with people. Travis went to find Claire to dance with her a few minutes later.

I saw Jasmine dancing with Jasim. I knew deep inside he was in pain, wishing he was dancing with his daughter on her wedding day. As soon as we finished a couple of songs, I walked swiftly to Nora, who was looking around with big brown eyes. She had a big smile when she saw me. I held her hand and then Tiffany's and said excitedly, "Girls, let's dance!" At that moment, I hoped for one thing: that one day, Nora could have a big wedding like that, dancing with her husband, whom she loved and cherished. Even my brothers, my uncles, and my family hit the dance floor.

A few hours had passed. People didn't stop dancing. The DJ was playing a mixture of Italian, Arabic, top-forty, and Latino songs. Henry and I happened to bump into each other on the dance floor. We just said hi, keeping our distance. I didn't want to hold a grudge toward him during my sister's wedding. But all of a sudden, I heard a song, "Breathe Again." It had been playing in my head like a nonstop melody since my birthday. I felt a squeeze in my chest. His face came crawling down my mind like a beautiful picture. His whisper was in my ear, telling me how soft my skin was, while dancing too close to me. I felt tingly recalling his hands around me, hugging me tight. I had to sit down right away. I had promised myself since I was teenager that I wouldn't dream. But I couldn't help but close my eyes for a few seconds and fancy that the handsome stranger was dancing with me again.

***

A few days later, on a Saturday morning, Mandy called me. She sounded depressed, asking me to join her at a local bar. Our conversation was brief and tense. I wondered what had happened between her and her boyfriend, John.

During our car ride, she confessed to me that she and John had had a huge fight. She had found out through a friend of hers that he went to a party when she was out of town at her family's cottage without even telling her. I really didn't see the big deal, but Mandy did. He was either cheating or wanting to end the relationship, she insisted.

She said, "Men are sneaky."

I sighed, and then I asked, "Are you going to tell him that we are going to the bar?"

She snapped, "Of course not! Are you crazy?"

I rolled my eyes. I didn't get Mandy one bit.

"Can't you see that you are contradicting yourself?"

She was quiet for a few long seconds.

"I think it's over anyway. I know it."

I sighed.

Right outside the bar, I reached for my wallet to grab my ID. Then two guest passes fell from my purse. I glanced at them for a moment and asked Mandy, "Do you want to go to a more exclusive bar?" They were the last two passes left after the other night. Mandy agreed; she just wanted to talk. A classier atmosphere would definitely help cool her down.

Mandy drove her car there. It was over forty-five-minute-long ride, during which she was complaining about her and John. He was insensitive, self-centered, forgetful, and arrogant ... I was glad Mandy and I had gotten ready at her place after dropping our daughters off at the babysitter. My hair was in a loose side bun, similar to the style I had worn at my sister's wedding. And my dress was something I had bought months earlier. It was black and simple yet elegant. Mandy had her long blonde hair loose, and she wore a sleek dark-brown dress.

As soon as we got in, Mandy mentioned to me that she used to come to that club with her ex-husband.

I whispered into her ear, "Whatever you do, don't buy the bottle of champagne, unless you want to mortgage your house."

She giggled lightly. "You make me laugh, Hannah. What do you want to drink? It's my treat."

"Nothing."

"Come on. I am sure it won't be that bad. I mean I never paid for drinks here. It was always on Josh's tab." We stood next to the bar. I suggested we order two martinis, *Jason's recommendation,* I recalled. I looked around periodically.

Mandy whispered, "I hope I won't see my ex here."

A tall lady with a familiar voice ordered a couple of drinks. My heart started to race. At that moment, I was glad I was standing on the other side of Mandy. At least I was hidden from her sight. I tried to keep my head tilted away from Mandy. I just didn't want to be seen. A couple of minutes passed. I breathed out. She was gone after picking up a couple of drinks. Mandy noticed my strange behavior. "Who were you hiding from?" she asked.

"Adrianna, the lady who was right beside you getting a couple of drinks."

"Oh! So that's your boss?"

I frowned. I said, annoyed, "Yep, that's my boss."

She sounded astonished when she said, "She is young and pretty."

"And super rich." I sipped some of my martini. "Did I mention that she is a bitch?"

"You did."

I had forgotten how many times in the past I grumbled to Mandy about Adrianna's horrific attitude.

She sighed, adding, "Do you want to dance after this?"

"Sure, whatever you say." I didn't know why seeing Adrianna put me off completely. "I wonder if her brother Jason is here too."

Mandy already knew about Jason too. "Why don't you go where she is sitting and say hello?"

"Are you kidding? How many times I told you that this woman looks at me as if I were an inferior bug."

As she twirled her drink, she asked, "That's because she can sense your anxiety, don't be afraid of her?"

I knitted my brows. "I'm not afraid! She just terrifies me. There is something about her; she has this evil stare." Mandy giggled. I giggled too, because I just realized that my defense didn't make any sense even to me.

"Hannah, you can't let those people make you feel substandard, just because they have more money." I shook my head. Mandy wouldn't get it, since making her living didn't depend on Adrianna.

Mandy followed me to the dance floor, which wasn't too crowded yet. We danced for almost half an hour and then went back to the bar. I ordered us a twenty-dollar martini each and found an empty couch to sit on. Mandy and I spoke for thirty minutes. John was texting her. I excused myself to go to the washroom to give her more privacy. I was sitting on the toilet when I heard someone's phone ring. Then I heard Adrianna's voice. I wasn't paying attention at first to what she was saying, but the next line rang in my ears. She said, snapping, "I think he's still hooked on his trailer trash." She laughed wickedly. "Meet me in an hour. We need to talk. New place, 1649 Kartar Drive." *Trailer trash!* I wondered whom she was referring to. Soon after, I heard the door swing shut, announcing her exit from the washroom. I breathed out, thinking how abrupt and efficient her short conversation was. For some reason, the last part was still ringing in my ear.

When I went back to where Mandy was, she said happily, "Ready to go? John is waiting for me." My eyes grew wide—a few minutes' of a text conversation and Mandy and John's problem was solved. She admitted that she was taking the trivial matter way too seriously. I wondered if I could ever experience that jealous feeling with anyone.

On the way back, Mandy was speaking of John's good qualities. He was sincere, charming, and handsome. I was speechless. How could someone flip from cold to hot in a couple of hours? I was quieter than usual, feeling a little distressed since I had left the nightclub. There was a big possibility that I would never see the handsome stranger again.

***

A couple of weeks passed. It was during my lunch when my cell phone rang. It was Jason.

He said, "Do you have time for a little meeting?" The last few times he had invited me for lunch I had made an excuse. I didn't need any complications, with either Katie or Adrianna, especially after Mary's second warning.

"What for?"

"I wanted to give you an update about your husband's police psychiatrist report. You can come by my office."

I said hesitantly, "Sure. When is the best time for you?"

After a few seconds of silence he replied, "Come to my office now." His tone was icy firm.

I hung up the phone and walked toward his office. When I sat across from him, he seemed a little distressed, maybe because I had refused his last few lunch dates. He had a coffee on his desk. He said evenly, "You are avoiding me, Hannah. How come?"

I took a deep breath and decided not to mention Mary's warning or my knowledge of his girlfriend Katie; she *did* ask me to keep it between us. I stammered, not prepared to answer, "Jason, um, I'm …" My mind went blank.

He looked away. "Hannah, no need to explain. I get it."

I wondered if he was hurt. His usually composed expression seemed angry for the very first time; he swung his chair to the side to face the window.

I said calmly, "You said you have information about my husband."

He turned and gaped at me for a moment, sending shivers through my body, but his face became calmer. He sounded like a lawyer when he said, "I was able to obtain some of your husband's psychiatric report from his time in jail, after stating that he had a daughter and she wanted to know his country of origin." He sipped from his coffee. "Thankfully, the court didn't seize this information after his death. The report isn't long. It shows here that he was fearless; he insisted that he was just like his father he never knew, since his American mother raised him. The only fact he knew of his father was that he was from the Middle East."

I interrupted him, "His mother was an American?"

My heart was racing. He continued, "He said he has one brother. He hated his mother; she kicked him out when he was a teenager. She kept stating that he came from nowhere, and since then, he never came back home."

"But my husband was a con, he lied about everything. Why not these reports?"

He stared at my flushed face for a long moment and then said, "Even criminals have rights. His psychiatrist didn't find your husband harmful during his therapy; therefore, his mental report wasn't disclosed to the police investigation. I am not saying that those reports are a hundred percent true. He could have made them up. I don't know."

My head was spinning. I wished I had never come to know anything at that moment. He hated his mother. Would that be the reason behind the way he treated me? I felt a sharp headache.

I asked hesitantly, "What else do you know?"

"He was never married before you, and he merely mentioned his daughter, Nora."

I frowned. "Are you sure that there was no rich ex-wife anywhere?"

"According to the report, yes, I'm sure."

I said tactfully, "Did he mention anywhere why he chose me?" He hesitated for a few seconds. "You can tell me." I took a deep breath.

He sighed. "Well, you are not going to like this. He found you almost as damaged as he was. He thought he had found in you his soul mate."

I said irritably, "What? That doesn't make any sense!"

"I have dealt with a few people like your husband in my career. Your husband was probably so disturbed by his past life he was looking for revenge. And since he found you so shattered, he probably assumed that he could make you into someone like him. I know this because I was comparing the medical report with the police investigation." He sank his back toward his leather chair. "In the victim's statement, they also referred to you as his soul mate."

I snapped, annoyed, "What? That can't be … I hated him from the beginning. He forced me to deal with those people he called friends. I had no choice. I hardly talked to them; plus, I didn't know what was going on behind my back." I was running out of breath, while trembling hard. I recalled my talk with the detective. That was why I was part of their investigation. Yusuf's plan was to raise suspicion around me, just so I didn't have anyone to turn to. My being isolated and scared gave

Yusuf the ultimate power to utterly control and disturb me. But his plan failed. He went to jail, and I went to the shelter, where I met Debra ...

He interrupted my bewildered past reflection with a calm, composed tone. "I was reading in between the lines. Your husband loved you, but he never spoke of how you felt about him. He probably knew that you despised him. I think he was careful not to raise the psychiatrist's suspicion."

The suspicion that we was planning to kill me? I thought.

I said, "He ruined my credit when we first got married. He also tried to scam me of all my savings right before the accident."

"Of course, his biggest nightmare was for you to become strong. And having good credit and some extra money is some sort of strength."

My stomach felt too tight. I felt cheated by my disturbed destiny. I tried to control my tears by taking a deep breath and swallowing my pain.

I said while trying to keep my voice from wobbling, "Thank you for all the trouble."

He hesitated before saying, "No problem, those investigations aren't free, but don't worry about it."

I took a deep breath before I asked, "How much do they cost? I mean, I can pay slowly." I wished I had never agreed to his help in the first place.

"We are not going to speak of money right now."

"Does Adrianna know?"

"She does," he said casually.

"But you said that this matter was confidential."

"It's still confidential, within our firm."

I felt my body go rigid. I despised the idea that Adrianna knew so much about me. Adrianna already regarded me as someone inferior; I wondered if she knew that her brother had an interest in me. I recalled the conversation I had overheard at the exclusive club restroom. *Trailer trash*, was she referring to me? Since I had moved around with my husband in a stolen motor home, I didn't feel like talking anymore. My head was throbbing, and I wished I could just go home and hide under the covers.

"But you still don't know what my husband's true identity is?"

"No, not yet. This could cost even more money and time. I really don't mind." He looked at me. His gaze traveled to my tight red shirt, and then my skirt. I felt my chest go tight. Unconsciously, I pulled on my knee-length skirt that had ridden up a few inches, revealing part of my thighs, down. Was he giving me a lustful look? I really couldn't comprehend it. He leaped off his seat, walked toward the window, and looked out. Had I just been dismissed? I got up too and cleared my throat.

I said cautiously, "Thank you, Jason." I hesitated. "Could you please stop with those investigations? My husband is someone I want to forget, and, um, I really think I should pay for all the time you've invested already."

He turned around and strolled toward me. I froze. What was on his mind? I was thankful he stood a few feet away. His face seemed stressed, as if he was containing himself.

His tone was thick when he said, "Don't worry about it for now."

I hated owing him; I would rather pay him and get it over with. I was slowly accumulating some money to use toward a new car, but I could pay him first. I thanked him again right before leaving his office. I felt as if I had swallowed a whole apple.

When I came back to my desk, Mary was there. I was surprised by her presence. I was glad she had already warned me about Jason. I must have looked gloomy because she asked me, "Are you okay?"

My brief meeting with Jason brought my past back to my mind. Out of nowhere, I started to cry.

She came closer. "What happened?" she said in a sincere tone.

"I'm glad you warned me about Jason." She was quiet. "His sister thinks so lowly of me, and he thinks that by helping me with his expert law services, he could …" I couldn't continue. I was weeping. What a mess I made out of myself! She sighed. I said to her in a clipped, wobbly voice, "I mean, I just want to live in peace and raise my daughter, but every step that I take leads me to more trouble."

Mary glanced at me and said, "You may leave early today. I don't mind covering for you."

I looked at her. She had a scowl on her face.

She added, "If you have to pay off Jason for any services his law firm has provided you, I could help you with money. Don't owe him anything."

I wiped my tears away, shocked to hear this from Mary. I would never have guessed she had such a kind heart.

She continued while handing me a tissue, "As long as you keep it between us."

I nodded, thanking her sincerely, deciding to send an email to Jason and request a bill. I could even ask Jasim or Mandy to land me some money.

A few minutes later, I was on my way outside the office. I got into my car and was exiting the underground parking garage when I saw a black BMW whose driver reminded me of someone. He was entering the underground parking lot at my office building. It was a glimpse. My first instinct was to go after him and see where he was going. I parked my car outside, overwhelmed for a few minutes, making a decision.

As I drove on the highway, I was thinking of that night at the club. I was probably still seeing things. I worked in a big building where hundreds of cars used the underground parking garage. The chance of finding him was almost nonexistent. *It was not him,* I told myself. It was all in my head.

Chapter Fifteen

It was on a Friday, at the beginning of December. I woke to a huge headache. Nora whined all morning. She was being more than fussy. When I finally got into my car to drive her to school, I found out that my battery was dead. I must have left the lights on during the night. I was, however, thankful for Jasim's help with recharging my car battery, but then I was late for both Nora's school and work. When I finally got to the office, Adrianna had sent me a very long list of running around to do on her behalf.

That day, the office only opened for a few hours in the morning. By noon, everyone, except for me, was sent back home to get ready for the firm's holiday evening party. Mary told me that I had to attend, especially since Christine was granted a whole month's worth of vacation, as I suspected her father was one of the smaller firm partners.

Lately, Mary and I were getting closer. Somehow, we clicked. She asked me to join her for a lunch break a few times; I had even opened up to her about my past with Yusuf. Jason had kept his distance ever since our last meeting. He never even replied to my email I had sent him requesting the bill.

After picking up Nora from Mandy's, I drove her to Jasmine's house where I unenthusiastically got ready for the party. Jasmine noticed my glum expression, and to cheer me up, she helped me style my hair and applied my makeup. She was going to take Nora with her to the grocery store after, so we were both leaving her house at the same time. I was wearing a long jacket over my newly bought fitted, deep-purple, knee-length strap dress, and my shoes felt too slippery on her icy, lightly snow-covered driveway. I was realizing in agony that cold and ice had arrived a bit too early this year. Right before I got into the car, after I'd cleared the snow off my car, Jasmine called me.

She said, "Can I borrow your snow brush? Nathan took mine because his was broken."

I replied, "Yes. Sure."

"Wait for me. I will clean the car and then give it back to you. I heard that we were supposed to have more snow or freezing rain this evening."

I faltered for a moment and then said, "I have to go home first anyway. I need to bring my matching purse. I know Jasim has a couple of snow brushes. I will borrow one from him."

"Thanks, Sis. I owe you."

I smiled sincerely. "Are you kidding me? I am the one who owes you. Thanks for looking after Nora for me."

"Have a good time."

I tried not to frown. "I will try."

I drove back home and grabbed my purse. I then had a phone call from Adrianna. She wanted me to run some errands for her before we met at the hall. This week, we hardly had work to do around the office, since it was a very slow time of the year. To keep me busy, Adrianna had me running around for her, so I picked up her dry cleaning, booked her spa appointment, bought cases of alcohol for when she held parties at her place, brought her lunches … I was practically her temporary personal assistant.

It was after 8:00 p.m. when I finally got to the reception hall. I was carrying a box of specially requested bottles of champagne when it started to snow. I almost fell because of my long, high-heeled slippery shoes. Once inside, I noticed that one of my shoe heels had shattered, and it was hard for me to walk. I didn't want it to break completely.

One of the venue staff members, who was waiting for the alcohol to arrive, carried the box over. I went to the washroom to check on my looks and place a fake smile on my face before walking carefully toward the large reception hall, which was beautifully decorated with a holiday theme, and a bright, colorful Christmas tree that stood tall and large in one corner. The lights were dim, and the setting was classy.

All those around me were looking elegant with their dresses and suits. They were in small groups speaking to each other. There was a man wearing a suit playing the piano, which filled the background with soft, mellow music. Waiters were swiftly walking around with medium-sized trays filled with either alcohol or hors d'oeuvres.

I found myself standing in one corner, sipping leisurely on a glass of champagne. I scanned the room, hoping to see Mary. Then I sent a message to Adrianna, stating that I was around if she needed me. I wished I could just go home. I didn't feel like charming any clients that night. An old gray-haired man walked toward me; he recognized me right away. His name was Brad. He was a client of ours. I had seen him a couple of times since I started working. He held a glass of red wine.

He said in a deep, rough voice, "Happy holidays, Hannah. You look so lovely today. What are you doing here all alone?"

I smiled. I wasn't going to reveal to him my shoe dysfunction.

I said cautiously, "Hi, Brad. Happy holidays to you too. I am just taking a break from all this." I sipped more champagne.

"If you are looking for your colleagues, I saw a few by the bar." He looked around and added, "This is a beautiful place."

"I know. Jason chose it. I heard from Mary that the firm has held its holiday parties here for a few years now." Soon, I had been speaking to Brad for over fifteen minutes; he spoke of his grandchildren and his many houses around the world. I knew that most of the guests at that party were rich.

I was afraid to move from my spot. My movements had just become unreliable because of my shattered heel. Adrianna came up right behind Brad. She looked pretty that night, with her thin straps and knee-length blue satin dress. Her shoulder-length hair was wavy. She had a big, charming smile on her face, and she looked nothing like the Adrianna I knew at the office. All of the sudden, I felt graceless, and I hoped she wouldn't give me another task to do. How was I going to explain to her that I couldn't move much?

Brad complimented her, saying, "Looking lovely as always."

She smiled and said sincerely, "Thank you, Brad." She then gave him a hug and a kiss on his cheek and asked him casually about his family.

I smiled at her weird transformation, reminding me of someone I wanted to forget, *Yusuf.* Brad moved away to greet more people. A few minutes later, Adrianna moved closer to me, and my heart sank.

She whispered in my ear, "I want you to walk around and make sure everyone is having a good time."

I started to walk, but my heel was getting really disconnected from my shoe. With difficulty, I walked up close to Adrianna again. She was glancing at her watch nervously; she noticed my discomfort.

After looking around her, she snapped quietly, "What's wrong now?"

My heart was pounding. I felt like a little child in trouble and was afraid of her reaction. "I can't walk around. My heel is broken." She sighed and then smiled. I tried not to frown but bit my tongue instead.

She came closer, and keeping her smile on, her voice low and daunting, she said, "Then in this case, you can go home. I don't need you to embarrass me at this party."

I was hurt, but then again, I had been relieved of my duties. "I can go now?" I just had to make sure she really had her way to completely intimidate me.

"Of course now." She then glanced at her watch again. It took me a long time to walk to the exit door after fetching my jacket. I was wearing my jacket when I saw a familiar face from the corner of my eye. He even stopped to look at me, but when I turned, I couldn't see him anymore. I sighed. Maybe I was dreaming again. What was happening to me? I had to get rid of my reveries. I walked toward the exit door. Once I was outside, I noticed that it had stopped snowing but a thin layer of icy snow covered the ground. I sighed grumpily. I had hoped I wouldn't fall down and break a leg. That would definitely add more rubbish to my chaotic, murky day.

I was finally by my car, which was covered with snow mixed with ice. I opened the trunk to reach for my snow brush. I couldn't find it. I then searched my car. All of a sudden, it came back to me. Jasmine had it. I was supposed to borrow Jasim's brush, but I had gotten distracted by Adrianna's call. I completely forgot. I slammed the passenger door angrily. From the front seat, I grabbed a CD and a roll of paper towels. I had no choice but to improvise. I put my gloves on and then started with my tedious job, clearing the snow and ice with the CD while moving around with difficulty. I couldn't wait until I made it home and hid under the covers. I even decided that I wouldn't pick up Nora from my sister's.

"Do you need help?" a deep male voice came from behind me.

"I think I am okay, thank you!" I wasn't going to accept any man's help that night.

He said, "The birthday girl can be stubborn too, I see!"

I froze. Where had I heard that voice before? Of course! Could it be? I was so afraid to turn around, afraid to be in the middle of one of my reveries again, but he came around the side, swiftly clearing the snow and ice off my car using a brush.

I slowly looked at him. He was the man from the exclusive club, and he was wearing a long jacket and gloves.

I stared at him for a long moment. This felt unreal. Was I in a dream? Did I drive home and fall asleep and was dreaming all this? I blinked a few times. Just in case I was dreaming, I even pinched myself lightly. I was glad that I didn't wake up.

When he was done, he turned to face me with the features I couldn't erase from my mind, no matter how hard I tried.

He said, "You do owe me for cleaning your car. I will, however, settle for coffee. I know of a place you can follow me if you want." His tone was a sweet order.

I stuttered, as if were under the influence of alcohol, when I had only had half a glass of champagne. "How, um, is it far?"

He sounded serious when he said, "Nope." I wet my lips. "I will need your phone number."

"Um, sure, it's …" I gave him my number, and he called it right away. I noticed that his phone was the same model as mine. I smiled, pleased with Mandy's gift. My cell ring tone sounded like a beautiful melody. I saved his number with shaky hands.

He left me then and got into his black BMW. My heart raced. I wasn't crazy when I saw him the first time! *It was him!* He was driving to my office building's underground garage.

I drove my car behind him. My heart sprinted faster. I had to grab ahold of myself. I was no longer a virgin teenager. In fact, I had gone through hell and back. *I should be stronger than this.*

I quickly checked my reflection in my rearview mirror. My eyes looked bright, and my cheeks were tomato red. My lips could, however, use a bit more plum lip gloss. I reached for my purse and quickly applied a glossy thin layer without overdoing it.

He parked his car in front of a small café. I pulled in behind him. He waited for me, so I could walk toward him with difficulty. He must have noticed my trouble because he came toward me and held my hand.

I said hesitantly, "My shoe heel broke."

He grinned and held on to my arm, just so I didn't fall.

He said evenly, "Tonight isn't your night." I turned to him, smiling. Was he kidding me? That night was my ultimate night. We entered a classy but laid-back café. The lights were dim. He knew where he was going because he led me right in front of an electric fireplace, which was surrounded by two small, comfy-looking cream-colored couches and a small brown round table. I felt warm and snug right away. I noticed that there were only a few more customers sitting around. A young waitress came to take our order. He turned to me and said, "The latte is good here."

I nodded. He ordered the two lattes with some cake. I got up to take my jacket off. I was getting hot. He did the same. He was a lot lighter than I remembered. Maybe he was suntanned the first time that I had met him. Well, to me, he looked handsome either way. He wore a suit—he probably was one of my firm's guests. After all, he found me next to my car. I thought I saw him inside from the corner of my eye as I was leaving. He stopped and came after me. I felt tickled at that thought. What a small, amazing world! His eyes were on mine right after I sat down. I felt tingly all over. He said in a firm but playful tone, "I need to know the name of that stubborn, temperamental birthday girl who wants to kiss the boys and make them cry."

I tried not to frown. Debra's advice, I recalled. I even forgot what I had said that night. I hoped I didn't say anything else, but I could feel myself spluttering. I smiled warily, recalling the night when I met him. The memory of him in front of the restroom woke me up from my drunkenness.

I looked at him and replied in a soft tone, "You can call me, Hannah. And yours?"

He said, "You can call me Aiden." He smiled, showing some amazingly straight teeth. He added, "Hannah, Hannah, what a surprise!"

My hand started to shake. I stared back at him and smiled. I just couldn't take my eyes off him.

"What were you doing in the parking lot?" I asked.

"I was waiting for you to come out. I had a feeling you were going to need some help … again." His tone was impish. My heart skipped fast. I was hoping and wishing I would not wake up right then, finding myself in bed in the morning.

"I thought you said it was a surprise," I mumbled.

"It was … an out-of-this-world kind of surprise."

Was it really? Did he mean what he said?

Hoping I could hide my nervousness, I asked casually, "Are you one of the firm's guests?"

After a few seconds, he said, "Yes."

I looked around me. "What a small world! I work for the firm hosting the party."

Tonelessly, he said, "Really." His eyes narrowed. "What is your job title?"

I blushed and hesitated. "My title isn't a lawyer."

He said almost immediately, "I could've guessed that … You are too young to be a lawyer, unless you graduated and got a job immediately in a big firm, which is unlikely."

My heart sank. I wondered what he meant by that.

He must know Jason and Adrianna. They knew all about me and my husband. Our lattes arrived in beautiful white cappuccino mugs along with a chocolate mousse cake for each of us.

"What is your last name?" I asked, recalling Yusuf's unknown identity.

"Harris, Aiden Harris."

His last name sounded familiar. I tried to search my brain. Where had I heard it before?

He interrupted my train of thought by saying tightly, "What happened to your friend at the club?"

Henry! I'd totally forgotten about him.

I stammered, "Henry was … a friend, only a friend."

He shook his head lightly. I heard his cell phone ring. He glanced at the number, frowned, and then placed the phone back in his pocket.

"My friends at the party are probably wondering what happened to me."

I felt my heart squeeze lightly.

"So Henry is a jealous friend?" he added.

I bit my lip anxiously. How was I going to explain that? I sighed. "Henry thought we were on a date that night, but in reality, it wasn't a real date." I just realized that I wasn't making sense at all, because he looked baffled, so I continued, "I mean, Henry is a flirt. I think his goal is to date as many women as he can. He wants to hit some sort of a record."

He started to laugh loudly. "You are amusing." He stared at me for a few seconds. He seemed serious when he said, "What is your idea of a perfect date? Maybe I should say a real date?"

I blinked twice. I wasn't a dating expert; in fact, I had no clue. I couldn't describe to him the lunches and coffee I went to with Jason; to me, they were strictly work lunch dates. Nor did I tell him about when he met me at the club. My mind then was fuzzy thinking of him. Yusuf came zooming into my head again, but I kicked him right out. He was the last person I wanted to think of. I had seen movies in the past where couples went for dates; plus, Jasmine told me about her first date with Nathan. Those could be good examples of real dates.

I looked at him dreamily. "Okay, a man knocks on the woman's door, flowers in his hands. He then drives both of them to a nice restaurant."

He laughed. I tried not to frown at that.

He said, "How often have you gone on dates?"

I shrugged, with no answer; I hated how callow I seemed.

"Beautiful girl like you, how come?"

He thought I was beautiful? My head went fuzzy. I was silent for a few seconds, and then I remembered the dating subject.

"I was too busy to date." I sipped from my latte.

"Were you in school?" I shook my head. He sipped some latte.

"No, I was raising my daughter."

He was silent for a few seconds. "You have a daughter?"

I nodded. I wondered if this new discovery of me being a single mother would change his assessment of me.

"Nora. She is six."

He glanced at my finger, maybe looking for a ring, wondering if I was still married. He was probably reluctant to ask.

"I am not married anymore. He passed away." I took a deep breath.

"Sorry to hear that." His eyes seemed sincere. "How long ago?"

I looked away. I hated placing Yusuf back in my head.

"Two years ago."

His cell rang again. He glanced at it, frowning again.

"Are you single?" I held my breath.

He stared at me for a few long seconds. "Yes."

I breathed out. I hesitated. "Were you married before?" His gaze went dark all of a sudden. He then looked away. His tone was thick. "I was engaged." He then sipped some latte.

"So are you a client at our firm?"

His lips curved into a smile. "You can say that. My father always dealt with Simon Miller's firm." I must have looked confused because he added, "He passed away not too long ago."

I suddenly remembered his name. Adrianna wanted a caterer for his father's funeral. I even called the catering company myself to confirm. I recalled when even Mary was complaining about how fussy she was about planning his funeral. I didn't want to mention that day; it could be painful for him still.

"You know the twin partners then?"

He nodded, glancing away from me. My heart sank. He must know Adrianna very well, since she was fussing about his father's funeral.

"What do you do at the firm?"

I loathed answering that question. Adrianna thought so little of me, and Jason wanted to date me, probably behind his sister's back. They both had my life record in front of them.

I knotted my fingers and mumbled tentatively, "I do clerical work. I answer client calls and fill in wherever they need me. I probably answered your calls and took messages on your behalf."

I stared at my knotted fingers. I wondered what he thought of me. I was nobody at that firm, with the lowest job description, highly replaceable indeed.

"Then I would've recognized your voice. You know, I have a good memory."

I smiled politely. I felt tickled by his confession. He remembered my voice, and he also remembered my foolishness, talking nonsense while wearing that silly tiara, and my bad temper when I stomped my feet like a child.

He continued, "Try the cake. I think you are going to love it."

We talked casually for a few more minutes. He mentioned that he was turning thirty-seven years old in the spring. He was half Greek and half Spanish, with other nationalities in his family. His grandpa, from his father's side, was half Lebanese. At least we had some distant common ground.

We ate the chocolate mousse. Aiden was right; it was tasty. He had a little chocolate on the side of his sexy lips. I glanced at him. I was about to tell him when I heard him say in a smoky, husky tone, "Your eyes are dangerous. You can get in trouble one day … with me."

My eyes grew wide. Shivers traveled around my whole body in a split second. What was that feeling?

I cleared my throat. I said, stuttering, "Y-y-you have something on the side of your lips … from the chocolate cake." I blushed while smiling shyly, looking away briefly. He probably just realized that he had misjudged me. *I was defiantly not giving him a lustful look,* I reassured myself.

He grinned while wiping his lip slowly with a tissue. I found myself watching him intently, feeling my blood steaming. Suddenly, erotic fantasies zipped through my head; I wished my tongue could take his tissue's job. I became angry with myself. What was wrong with me? My delusions were never naughty before! *Ever!* I wet my lips with my tongue, feeling hot all over. My dangerous reveries were interrupted when he said, "How long have you been working for the firm?"

I sighed. "Since last winter." I asked tactfully, "How well do you know the twin partners?"

He seemed a bit annoyed. "They were old friends, family friends. We went to the same university and then Law school." My heart sank. "I lived away for a while, so we kind of drifted apart."

"So you are a lawyer?"

"I studied law. I didn't practice it." He stared at me. "You are not going back to the party tonight?" Would he want me to go back with him? Then I quickly imagined what Adrianna's and Jason's reactions would be, maybe terrifying. But the idea of him being around Adrianna, who looked pretty, was petrifying too. I had to shake these thoughts away. Was I being jealous already?

I said casually, "No, my heel broke, so I was sent back home since I couldn't entertain guests or help around."

"Entertain guests?" he asked. His eyes narrowed.

I said, clarifying, "You know, talk to them, make them feel comfortable. Adrianna wants happy guests, and it's part of my job."

He frowned. I wondered if I had said something wrong. "Well, I am glad you were sent back home early."

I said teasingly, "Well, I would've met you there anyway, and since I had to entertain all the guests …" I smiled. He didn't smile. Had I said something wrong again? I continued stuttering, "I-I mean, I would've greeted you." I should just stop talking, because he didn't seem amused.

"Are you close to your coworkers, your bosses? Are they nice to you?"

To me, Mary was more than a coworker, perhaps even a friend. For some odd reason, she seemed to really care about me, and apart from Jason, thinking of Adrianna, Christine, and all the other extensive staff and lawyers, I found them arrogant, making it hard to socialize with any of them. But I wasn't going to elaborate on how I felt about each and every one.

I said cautiously, "My coworker Mary is the only one I associate with." I continued, as his expression was impassive, "Unfortunately, she works part-time."

He said tonelessly, "I see."

I wondered about his interest in my job and environment. Was that because he cared?

"Do you come to the firm sometimes?" I asked as I recalled his BMW driving into the garage.

"Hardly, and the last time I was there, you were not."

I smiled; at least he was telling the truth.

"I have to go back." My heart sank when he leaped up, standing about six feet tall on his feet. He was tall, like Yusuf, whom I had to stop thinking of. He was nothing like Yusuf.

He helped me get into my jacket. He even helped with the buttons. I felt like a little girl; compared to him, I was small and fragile.

We were walking toward our parked cars. I was walking very slowly. He held on to me until I got to my car. He then asked me to wait. He ran to his black BMW, only to come back with a snow brush.

"A CD is only for playing music. Text me when you make it inside your home safely with that broken heel."

"Yes, sir."

His eyes narrowed.

I protested by saying playfully, "You are still a client."

He smirked, and my heart raced.

He held my hot face with his big, cool hands and said firmly, "To you, I am only Aiden. Understand?" Wow! Right then, he seemed to be like the man in charge. I didn't know what to make out of that. Yusuf was domineering and had his way with me too, but the two men couldn't be compared.

"Yes, Aiden."

He then bent. I licked my lips quickly to moisten them. I stared at his firm, semifull, soft lips and shook lightly, waiting for him to pull me to him and kiss me the way I wanted to be kissed—the way I had been playing it in my head over and over again, since I saw him that night. But instead, he kissed my cheek. He then placed his arms around me and hugged me tight. I placed my head on his shoulder for a few seconds. I wanted his embrace to last forever. I felt cold all of a sudden, right after he released me. I stared at him. I didn't want to hide anymore the way I felt. It didn't matter if my facial expression showed how much I wanted him, how much he aroused me all over. He stared back at me. His eyes were mysterious. I could feel him. He didn't want to let go either. It was as if the world had stopped spinning around. It was intense, and I was afraid to move.

    He suddenly broke it off and said, "I will call you, um, tomorrow." He touched my face with his finger, right before he walked away.

Chapter Sixteen

I was driving back home, feeling refreshed. I was listening to loud music and singing along. I could go for a long run with my broken heel and would still have some energy left in me. As soon as I got home, I texted Aiden saying, "I'm safe at home. Hannah☺."

I got a message right after that said, "Sweet dreams, my sweet Hannah☺."

I got up in the morning, feeling so refreshed. The first thing I did was send Aiden a quick message that said, "Good Morning☺."

I was even in a great mood to clean. I turned the music on loud and started tidying up until everything was spotless. I even made Jasim a big breakfast and was very talkative. I tidied his place after until it was spotless too, periodically glancing at my phone for any reply. I picked up Nora from my sister before the big storm.

When I got home, with a late lunch I had picked up from Mother's house, I placed it on the kitchen table and called Jasim to come down and eat. I noticed a heavy blizzard from the open kitchen window. Then I remembered my cell, which I had left in my purse. When I fished for it, I found a missed call from Aiden. *Crap!* I called him back, but I got his voice mail. I decided quickly that I wasn't going to leave a message.

After our lunch, I got a message from Aiden that said, "Please tell me that you are not using your broom and dust pan as snow shoveling material."

I giggled when I read it. Aiden must have already thought I was hopeless, so I replied, "For your information, I do own a big shovel, and I am not afraid to use it, lol."

Then he replied, "Hannah, that could be scary, if only you were a foot taller and a 150 lbs heavier, but I can still recall how petite you are!"

"Aiden, I am a lot tougher than I look; *trust me*!"

"Well, I can't wait till I listen to you telling me about how tough you are while I am enjoying my steak dinner with you."

"Sounds good." I started skipping to that message as if I were a little child.

"I will pick you up this Saturday, 6:00 p.m. Just send me your address."

As soon as I found out that I had an official date, I had a quick flood of energy. I turned the music on and said to Nora, "Come on, honey; let's dance and have a little fun," laughingly, while taking her by her little hand and twirling her around.

"Mommy! Stop! I am too tired to dance …" she said crankily.

That put an end to our very short happy dance, but all of a sudden, I had a better idea.

"How about we watch a fairy-tale movie? We can watch a couple of them if you want, with some popcorn."

"Really?" She started jumping up and down. I usually hated watching those fairly-tale movies. I always ended up getting distracted, finding something else to do instead, but that day, I was in the mood for an enchanted romance.

We even ordered pizza and convinced Jasim to watch *Cinderella* with us. Right after Nora went to bed, Jasim and I played our backgammon. Right then, I just wanted to please, because I was so happy …

***

Aiden and I talked on the phone a few times throughout the week. He told me that he owned a car dealership and many other investments. He was constantly busy working. He also mentioned that he was selling his business back in Victoria, British Columbia, since his father had passed away, to settle in Ontario. Until then, he was going to be always traveling in between. When he asked casually about my family, my reply was tentative and brief. I didn't want to have to mention my past to him. I wasn't sure how he was going to perceive me, if he ever knew of Yusuf's criminal background. I would mention it only when the right time arose.

I convinced myself never to dream again and tried to dismiss the fact that he was too out of my league. Aiden was wealthy and well educated. I didn't want to feel self-conscious, but then I did.

As I got closer to Saturday, my heart filled with soothing hopes, but my brain was overflowing with scary doubts. Could he be like Jason and Adrianna? I decided to ignore my mind and listen to my heart. I would look forward to my date with him. Soon, he would introduce me to his other close friends. I hoped he would stay away from the twin partners. After all, their friendship had kind of faded, as he mentioned.

***

Saturday finally came. I had felt anxious since morning. I asked my sister to babysit Nora since Mandy and John were out of town at his parents' place, and then I got ready at her place while Nora was busy watching a movie on TV with Nathan. My chest tightened, seeing them together. I knew Nora needed some sort of a father figure. My mind drifted to Aiden once again.

I was in Jasmine's master bedroom. It was late in the afternoon. After styling my hair in the latest trend—long and wavy, bangs styled and brushed to the side—she was applying my makeup. I told her to give me a sophisticated, older look. I didn't want to pass for a teenager as I did most of the time. I was happy with the end result. I could now see myself walking next to Aiden. I was in a black, top-fitted, long-sleeve semi-short dress. *Too short*, I realized.

"Sis, you look smart and very sexy."

I smiled. That was the look I had been aiming for.

"Remember, no means no," she added.

I knew what she was referring to. I blushed. He was too irresistible. I had to keep on reminding myself that no meant no, not fulfilling all the erotic fantasies.

I turned to her and said, "Pinch me please. I feel that I am dreaming still. This doesn't feel true."

She said warningly, "This better be true. You are wearing my favorite shoes. And I want them back."

We both giggled. Her black high-heeled shoes fit perfectly.

"Don't worry; they will be safe and sound. I feel that I am showing too much cleavage. I am drawing so much attention," I said, glancing at my new mirror reflection.

"You look beautiful. A little attention won't hurt, Sis. You look classy, not trashy. There is a difference."

I smiled. I still felt disconcerted. I sighed, no turning back.

"I have to leave soon. Aiden is picking me up from home in an hour," I said hurriedly, while picking up my purse and heading toward the front door. "Don't feed Nora any chocolate, or she won't go to bed early."

I hesitated first, but I texted Aiden to knock on the side door entrance of my basement apartment. At that moment, I wondered if Aiden would think less of me. He was rich, surrounding himself with rich people. I recalled briefly Yusuf's constant degrading of my poor background.

Aiden arrived right on time. When I heard his knock, I checked my reflection quickly. My cheeks were boiling hot. I opened the door and right away felt nervous. He was tall, masculine, and staggeringly handsome. I let go of a little sigh and smiled at him, inviting him in. He had both his hands behind his back. When I saw his hands, I gasped. He was carrying a bouquet of flowers. They were beautiful. I didn't know what to say; I wasn't expecting that.

I mumbled, "You shouldn't have. Thank you."

"I hope this confirms to you that this is a real date." He smiled mystifyingly.

Was he mocking me? I recalled the conversation we had had at the café. I didn't reply; instead, I reached shyly to take the bouquet from him with very shaky hands. Our hands touched, and I felt instant electrical shocks. He walked in and was looking around with a smile. I didn't want to look at his reaction. I knew my place was very small, but I made sure it looked immaculate.

He exclaimed, "Nice place!"

I smiled and replied politely, "Thank you."

He stood in the little space that separated the living room from my kitchen. I went to find a vase. From the corner of my eye, I could tell that his gaze was on me. I tried to control my shaky hands, so I didn't drop the vase. He glanced at the picture of Nora that I had hung on the wall. It was the same picture I had showed Jason a while back. I loved it because it captured the happy moment we had at that time.

"Your daughter?"

I looked toward where he was looking. "Yes."

He said sincerely, "She is gorgeous, just like a little princess." He added, "She looks like you."

"Thank you. I think Nora thinks she is a real princess."

He smiled.

The little vase was blooming with the colorful flowers. I turned to Aiden, whose gaze was on me. His expression was impenetrable. He then smiled and came closer. He grasped my chin with two long fingers.

His voice was low. "You look so beautiful."

My lips shook. I took a deep breath. I said tremulously, "You … um … look good too."

He didn't smile. He just brought his lips to kiss my temple gently and then turned his gaze away.

"Ready to go?"

"Yes." And on that note, I put on my new expensive long coat, grabbed my purse, and walked with him toward my front entrance.

Once in his car, I looked around me; it had spotless, dark leather and was obviously fully loaded—just as I had imagined. I glanced at him a few times. His big hands seemed powerful. Long fingers wrapped around the steering wheel. I could imagine those hands touching me. I felt my blood flood into my face once again. I had to stop doing that. My mind traveled in time, over a decade earlier, when I first met

Majeed, who was the reason I had shut myself off from feeling anything again, up until Aiden came along.

Aiden wore a long, elegant winter coat. His hair was short and brushed neatly. I felt like reaching out to touch it. He seemed powerful and sophisticated. I frowned lightly, realizing he was too sophisticated for my modest self. He didn't have to try hard, the way I was struggling to seem like someone refined—someone I was not. He was already there. It was, after all, his environment. He was probably born that way. I breathed thoroughly. I should be able to relax. He was nothing like Jason, who, according to Mary, was a player. He held my hand lightly. I was glad I had let my sister do my manicure.

"Relax," he said lightly. Could he tell that I was a nervous wreck? "I am taking you somewhere special. I think you are going to love the food." I remained quiet. "I was thinking tomorrow, we can catch a movie, maybe in the afternoon."

My eyes grew wide. He was already setting up the next date. I cleared my throat.

"Sure. I love movies." I stared at my small hand wrapped in his. That felt good.

Thirty minutes later, he parked in front of a large, castle-like building. I turned to face him. Where were we?

As if he had read my mind, he said, "This is a restaurant. I know it's hard to tell from the outside."

I smiled and then said, "Is it exclusive?" I briefly recalled the exclusive nightclub.

"No, it's not."

I said nervously, "I can't wait to try it." I couldn't hide all my fears.

The entrance was grand. The ceiling was high; a glowing chandelier gave the area a majestic look. We were greeted right away by an older man who wore a tux. Aiden's arm was around me. We walked a few feet away and were greeted by a couple more men wearing suits. One of them asked me if I needed to put my coat away. Aiden removed his hand from around my shoulder to take off his coat, and I too removed mine. I was shaking hard. I glanced at Aiden, who was wearing sleek, dark-gray pants and a semiformal white shirt under a semicasual dark-blue suit jacket. He looked very comfortable. He placed his arms around me again, drawing me closer to his body.

"Mason, I want you to give me the best available spot, preferably next to a fireplace."

Aiden was apparently a regular at this restaurant. He must have brought girls by the dozen here, placing his arm around their shoulders, as he had mine. He was after all too comfortable and relaxed, because he'd done this one too many times. Was I being jealous again? What was going on with me?

We walked toward a square table, right next to a fireplace.

After we sat down, I said, "I feel that we are alone in this restaurant."

His lips curled into a smile. "We are not alone. There are probably over one hundred guests already scattered around."

"Really! How come I can't see anyone around?"

"This is a more private spot." He smiled and continued playfully, "If you really want to see the rest of the guests, I can take you on a tour next."

I sighed. I felt a little too silly.

"No, that's okay. I am sure they would rather have their privacy."

Right away, another man in a tux greeted us.

Aiden asked me, "What would you like to drink?"

I looked blankly at him.

"I don't know. Whatever you think isn't too strong, maybe a little on the sweet side, and tastes fruity."

He was hiding a giggle. Maybe because he finally apprehended that I was undeveloped and absurd.

He said, "Give us a bottle of your flavored champagne." He then turned to me, while I was still glancing around. I felt as if I were playing a part in a fairy tale.

"Do you like this place?"

I smiled shyly.

"I love it." I hesitated at first. "Do you come here a lot? You seem like a regular."

"Enough, usually in between my traveling. I like the way it's laid out. I come here when I feel like clearing my mind."

I tried not to frown. "Do you feel like you want to clear your mind today?"

He stared at me for a moment.

He said evenly, "No. My mind is pretty clear today." He was very tactical with his answer. I wanted to know if he came with other women often, and I got nowhere near an answer.

"How long were you married for?"

My throat felt dry all of a sudden. "Five years."

The champagne arrived quickly. The waiter opened it and gave me a little taste. Aiden was watching me intently. I sipped a little of the sparkly liquid, and then I looked at Aiden shyly. That was an amazing drink. I wondered how much it cost, recalling the $250 champagne at the club.

"Do you like it?"

"Yes. It's tastes really good." The waiter filled my tall skinny shiny glass with the cold, tasty drink.

"Cheers," Aiden said. We tipped our glasses. "You may take a look at the menu if you like, or I can order for the both of us. I've already tried everything here," he said firmly. At that moment, he sounded like Jason.

"You can order. I think I can trust you."

He grinned lightly. "You think!" he said, narrowing his eyes.

I smiled and said cautiously, "I don't know you well enough to know if I can fully trust you yet." Again, I was being ridiculously foolish. What was going on with me? It was as if I was pushing him away. "I mean, I want to trust you." I should just stop talking altogether. I sipped more champagne, looking away, trying to ease my tensed muscles.

He started to laugh. I knew I had to smile, so I offered a tiny one. The waiter came back. Aiden ordered the food while I looked at him. I needed to loosen up. I was way too nervous. He reached for my hand and began playing lightly with my fingers. His touch was dangerous. I could feel it all over my body, making my knees feel weak.

"Relax. One day, you will know me well enough to trust me."

I smiled. Was he just saying that? Or did he mean what he was saying? Why was I all of a sudden skeptical about everything happening around me? All week, I had been waiting for this moment, and now my tense muscles were causing me to say foolish things. I had to grab hold of myself.

"How come you haven't married yet?"

He sighed, looking away. He then sipped some of his champagne before saying tonelessly, "Marriage is a big commitment and must be with only the right woman."

My heart raced. I recalled Jameel, the man I had wanted to marry before Yusuf just to get out of my parents' house. I wasn't then thinking of the right man. I was thinking—any man would do.

"Or maybe because you have high expectations." I tried to sound casual.

I sipped more champagne and a waiter brought a basket of warm bread and fluffy butter on the side. He then filled my almost empty champagne glass.

"My expectations are realistic. Do you have high expectations?"

I wanted to laugh at that question, recalling that once upon a time, I had merely one expectation—being away from my father.

I replied tautly, "No, not really."

"Good. That means I may have a chance."

I smiled. I was starting to understand his sense of humor. He was fit to be any woman's dream man, and yet he was pretending to be humble, just pretending. He reached for the bread basket, grabbed a piece, and buttered it. He then brought it to my lips to take a bite. At first, I pulled my head back unexpectedly, and then I took a little bite. He brought the bitten side of the piece of bread to his lips, which I found sensual. I blushed heavily.

"I am surprised to see a woman who was once married blush the way you do."

I didn't know how to answer that. I felt as if I were a virgin all over again.

"Maybe it's because of my culture."

"I don't think so."

How did he know?

"Have you dated a Middle-Eastern girl before?"

"Yes," he said casually.

I tried not to frown at this vexing news. "What happened to her?"

"It didn't work out with them."

Them! How many were there?

I said tentatively, "Did she ... I mean *they* become your girlfriends after?"

His tone was casual. "Different stories, different reasons why some of my relationships didn't work out."

Perhaps he didn't even remember, which to me didn't sound so good. He sipped more champagne. Our salad arrived. It was a wild mushroom salad. I had a couple of bites; it was indeed divine.

"Have you had anyone in your life since your husband?" he asked right before placing a forkful of mushrooms and lettuce into his mouth.

I tried not to react to his question. "No. I was busy working, raising my daughter."

"Do you go to the clubs often?"

"No, only a couple of times. Do you?"

"I hardly go to clubs, even though some of my friends convinced me to become a member at the club we met at." He smiled. "I still can't believe how both you and your sister misread the restroom sign."

I turned my uncomfortable gaze away. "Alcohol did it. I don't usually drink much." I sipped more champagne.

"I think I will have to escort you to the proper restroom, later on."

I couldn't believe he said that.

I said, "Don't worry. I am not that hopeless." My lips curled into a smile. "You said you didn't go to clubs. What were you doing that night then?"

"I was supposed to meet up with an old friend. He insisted that I come since his date came with some of her friends. I was glad I was early." He sipped some champagne and continued in a playful tone, "I had this feeling I was going to find a birthday girl lost in the men's restroom ... and I helped fix her dilemma."

I giggled. My head was spinning lightly. "Did you meet-up with your friend after?"

"No, I left early, but then he left me a message after midnight saying that his date's friends had already left, no need for me to come, since he needed his privacy with her." He paused before he continued, "I guessed he didn't know that I was already there and gone."

I stared at him. My face was frozen while my heart raced. Could he be speaking of Jason? They were old buddies? No, that couldn't be, so I decided to dismiss this terrifying possible conclusion. I really didn't want to think of that night anymore or feel flattered that he could've left early because of Henry, not after what I just heard.

"Did you stay long after?" he asked.

Now I had to be careful with my answer. "Henry left right after you left. I stayed for another hour with my sister and her fiancé." I turned my gaze away. The waiter came back; this time, he pushed a small workstation with a little stove, a pan, and a few dressings on the side. He first turned on the flame and then heated some sort of sauce that he later on placed on the two exquisite-looking plates of lamb chops with roasted mini potatoes and vegetables.

That was spectacular, I thought. I almost wanted to clap my hands at the end of the presentation since I already felt lightheaded. I never knew a restaurant offered such services. He placed the plates neatly in front of us, and then he filled my champagne once again. Aiden refused his drink refill.

He said jokingly to the waiter, "Someone needs to drive this lovely lady back home."

Our conversation continued. I felt at ease with him. He spoke of his mother, who was from Spain, and his hobbies—tennis, waterskiing, and traveling. He also expressed his love for sports, especially hockey. I felt as if I had known him for a while.

"I will take you to a real hockey game. After that, you are going to love watching the game with me."

I recalled Jasim, who loved watching his sports as well. I was never interested in sitting with him and watching any games.

"We'll see." *That could be interesting,* I guessed.

After dinner, he ordered a couple of small portions of cheesecake. I refused the coffee he offered, because I couldn't place anything else in my stomach. I was sad when the waiter came to collect his bill. This fairy-tale dinner was over. He held my hand on our way out, while walking toward his car.

He said, "So, is tomorrow evening at five a good time to pick you up?"

I smiled, delighted I was going to see him again the next day.

"Sure. What are we watching?"

He said playfully, "Whatever you want. No chick flick or horror."

"No chick flick, no horror."

He grasped my hand in his. I breathed deeply. I hoped he liked me a fraction as much as I liked him. I knew that wasn't the alcohol. It was true feelings.

He parked a few feet away from Jasim's driveway, as per my request. He turned to face me.

I said nervously, "That was a lovely night. Thank you." I wasn't sure what else to say.

He wasn't smiling, just staring at me silently. I couldn't read his eyes. Was he going to kiss me now? I stopped breathing when he finally bent down slowly and placed his warm, soft lips on my cheek. I gasped when his lips then moved quickly to my lips, which had been patiently and eagerly waiting for his kiss. His kiss was gentle at first but got deeper and more passionate by the second. I was flying. My body felt alive, as if it had been awakened from a long sleep, as if I had never been kissed before. His lips went to my cheeks and then to my neck, only to claim my lips once again. I found my arms around his neck. I didn't remember when I placed them there, but somehow, I did. When our lips met again, I was kissing him back with the same eagerness. My lips were discovering his lips, just like his were discovering mine. I heard myself sighing gently. He smelled divine, a mixture of aftershave and cologne.

He stopped all of a sudden, held my face in his hands, looked at my hot skin, and said in a husky, thick voice, "Hannah, if we continue like this, then I won't be able to stop myself." He sat back, his breathing uneven.

I looked away, feeling a bit embarrassed. What had happened to me? I was not acting like a lady at all; I was acting like someone I didn't know. Who was I? What would Aiden think of me?

I mumbled, "I should go." I was still reluctant to leave, as if I were glued to the car seat. He glanced at me quickly. I was breathless when he grabbed me and claimed my lips again. His kiss didn't start as gently, but he wasn't harsh either. It was a deep, sensual kiss. He was spinning my head around. I didn't know what I was doing, but I was just kissing him back. My lips were on his cheek, his neck, and then his lips. My actions were possessed by my desires, which were untamed.

He stopped again, this time with a growl. He held my shoulders and gaped at my flushed face. His face was red too. He felt sweaty; right away, my mind traveled to his groin area, thinking, *How aroused is he?*

He scowled. "What are you doing to me? God, in my wildest dreams, I didn't imagine this!"

I felt tickled; knowing that I was able to arouse him was making me feel like a powerful woman in control. It was a weird and yet beautiful feeling I had never encountered before. He sat up straight and held the steering wheel tightly. He looked like he was holding in a loud growl.

I bit my lower lip; I had to leave immediately. "I will see you tomorrow!" I said, while opening the car door.

"At five," he said, without even looking at me. When I opened my house door, I noticed that his car had taken off in the dark, and then I felt sad and empty on the inside to see him go.

***

The next day, at noon, I had coffee at Jasmine's. I mentioned to her that she needed to babysit again, since I had another date that night. She was so delighted. We then went to the mall. I needed to buy new outfits, and her vast experience with shopping was what I needed. I bought knee-high boots, a couple of skirts, and new fitted sweaters, and of course, I had to buy Nora a few things. I also treated Jasmine to lunch; hundreds of dollars later, we were on our way back home. Jasmine recommended the casual look—tight jeans, my new boots, a nice red fitted sweater, and a tight brown belt. My hair was long and wavy. Jasmine gave me a bouncy style. I was really glad that I was benefiting from her expert hairdressing technique. I wanted to keep my makeup light and fresh, but Jasmine insisted on adding the smoky eyes as an extra touch. She said it would complement the casual look.

He was only a few minutes late. He didn't come in this time. Instead, he texted me when he was waiting outside. My heart raced as soon as I saw him. I was recalling the passionate kiss from the night before.

He said sincerely, "You look stunning, as usual."

I replied timidly, "You look good too." Why couldn't I sound more confident?

I avoided his gaze. He *did* look very handsome and casual, with his blue jeans and black jacket over a white T-shirt.

"You are making me feel old."

I raised my brows.

He continued, "You look too young and fresh. I feel I want to hide you away."

I grinned lightly, feeling tongue tied. I managed to say nervously, "You don't look old at all … I don't know what you are talking about."

"Thank you for your compliment. I feel better now," he answered sarcastically with a grin.

I wondered what he meant by that statement, but I decided not to answer.

I leaped out of his car as soon as we made it to the theater. He reached out to hold my hand.

After buying a large popcorn and pop, he told me, "I haven't been to the theater for over a year now."

I laughed lightly and said, "I have only seen kids' movies in the theater, ever since Nora was born."

"Didn't you and your husband go on dates after she was born?"

I hesitated. "No, not really."

He drew me closer to him. I was thankful he didn't ask more questions. When the movie started, Aiden's hand left my hand to rest on my hair. His hand then traveled to the back of my neck. At that moment, I stopped paying attention to the movie. I concentrated on Aiden's fingers instead. They were giving my neck a sensual massage. I let out a sigh. I couldn't even eat the popcorn in front of me. His fingers then lightly moved to my face. His touch was light, like a feather. I was battling the urge to throw away the popcorn between us, sit on his lap, and kiss him passionately, right there in the theater. But all I could do was gasp for air once every few seconds.

I was glad Aiden didn't ask me what I thought of the movie, because I had no clue how it ended. It was, after all, his fault, since his fingers were playing with my skin as if it was a musical instrument. All I was hearing was my own heartbeat and my breathing, and my head was playing a very erotic movie, with Aiden and me cast as the leads.

I walked to his car feeling drunk on pop. He didn't touch me after he got behind his steering wheel. It was a very short ride. When he stopped, he said, "I am going out of town tomorrow. I will be gone for a few days."

My heart sank. "Where are you going?"

"Victoria. I will be traveling in between for a few months unfortunately."

At that moment, doubt zipped into my mind.

"Do you have a house there?"

He looked in front of him and answered casually, "Yes, I am selling it."

I said thickly, "Okay. I will see you after you come back, I guess." I opened the door. He held my hand.

"I will text you from there. You can text me or call me whenever you want."

I didn't know why I felt so sad. Was he really going to keep in touch? Or was he going to forget about me? I wondered if he had another woman back in Victoria waiting for him. I turned just so he didn't see my sad eyes.

I said nervously, "I will, and have a good flight."

He sighed. "I won't let you go if you don't give me a smile."

I swallowed my heartache, turned to him, and smiled painfully. He pulled me closer and placed a light kiss on my lips. The pain that I had felt overwhelmed my emotions. His gaze was unexplained when he said good-bye. I walked toward my front door, and when I turned, his car was gone …

Chapter Seventeen

BACK IN THE OFFICE, IT was Friday morning. Adrianna had recently made me her personal assistant, and the workload seemed less these days, as many lawyers were already taking a holiday vacation. I was catering to her demands all day—booking hair appointments, picking up her dry cleaning, buying her coffee …

In the morning, she came by my desk and asked, "Hannah, I am so pressed today; before you pick up my dry cleaning, I want you to go online and book me three tickets to this resort." She then gave me all the details and the dates during which she wanted to book it, right before rushing for her hair appointment. I was used to booking hotels, flights, and resorts for many of the lawyers who couldn't find the time to do so. After all, it was part of my job. But I couldn't help but think of Aiden, who was coming back that night from Victoria.

The last few days dragged, but I was delighted when I heard back from him before the end of the week. We merely communicated using text messages.

Aiden and I were supposed to go to a hockey game soon, as he mentioned in his last text message.

I needed to keep Aiden off my mind and concentrate on booking these resort tickets. When I went online, I saw pictures of the exquisite resort in Cancun. I started daydreaming of Aiden and me together in a beautiful, exclusive paradise next to the beach. That would be so delightful!

I noticed that the third ticket belonged to a girl by the name of Katherine Johns. Katherine is a nickname for Katie—Jason's Katie, I assumed sulkily. I was glad I had refused to go to any more lunches with him. Mary was right about him. Jason, Henry—this world was overfilled with players. I was momentarily overwhelmed by that disturbing realization but had to shake it off to go back to booking the tickets.

Adrianna called a few times throughout the day to remind me that she needed those spots as soon as I could get them.

I breathed out when I got the booking for the resort. That should put Adrianna at ease and get her off my back. She was probably having a dinner meeting that night with some important clients, I supposed, which explained the reason behind her fussiness that day.

When I finally went back home, after picking up a parcel, I wondered what Aiden was doing. I texted him casually. "Busy tonight?"

He replied almost immediately, "Yes," but he wouldn't explain what he was busy with.

"You must have a pile of work!"

"I do, and I'm meeting a few people over dinner, some business associates."

I was glad he couldn't see my frown. "Have fun," I said.

"I will try. Have you received a parcel yet? We are going tomorrow to see the game."

I smiled. I was finally going to see him soon. He added to the message, "Do you like the shirt?"

"The shirt?"

"A petite hockey shirt, your size."

I opened the parcel only to find a long T-shirt. I sighed. That could be fun, I guessed. Our texting continued for a bit, and then he told me that he had to go. I was babysitting Tiffany, who was spending the night. I decided to take them to Burger Land. It was better than being at home feeling anxious, I had assumed, but I was wrong. The whole time at Burger Land, I was thinking about Aiden. Who were his business associates? Were they ladies or men? I didn't know that liking a man could tangle my mind with scary doubts.

The next day, I woke up feeling refreshed. I got breakfast ready for the girls and Jasim and picked around my small living room and bedroom, annoyed. Those girls were like a trashing machine. I tried to finish up my chores early in the morning. I wanted to take the girls to a kids' movie at noon, just so I could bring them back happy to Mandy's. It was her turn to babysit. I felt a surge of excitement thinking of the evening ahead.

Getting ready was easy. I slipped on a pair of tight blue jeans. I wore the hockey T-shirt, styled my hair into a ponytail, and finally put on some light makeup. I scowled at my image, thinking it was too casual. Aiden texted me when he arrived to pick me up. His car was waiting by my house. I grabbed my newly bought casual jacket, put on my tennis shoes, and then ran outside. When I approached the car, I noticed that he was wearing a casual blue insulated jacket over a hockey shirt, which was a copy of mine, a matching hat, and faded blue jeans. He looked really different, very humble and down to earth. As soon as I got in the car, he gave me a matching hat to wear too. I put it on after restyling my ponytail.

He said enthusiastically, "Ready for some fun?"

"Ready." I tried to sound cheerful, since I had no idea what to expect.

He glanced at me saying, "I missed you."

"You did? I mean, I missed you too." That was awkward, but I felt my heart racing rapidly.

"Did you?"

"Yes, I did" He held my hand. I took a deep breath before I asked him, "How was your dinner last night?"

He looked away, as if he didn't like my query about the dinner. "Long and boring. I wanted to cancel, but I promised a few people I'd be there." He sighed.

I wanted to ask more questions, but I felt reluctant. I didn't want to sound like an interrogator. We then spoke casually about my day and his day, which he told me was spent working. He seemed to be stressed and overloaded with work.

I glanced around. We were at the arena. I was amazed by how many people attended the hockey game. During the game, people were loud and cheered periodically. I noticed that we had one of the best seats available, right in the VIP box. Everyone looked casual. Most wore hats too. At first, Aiden had to explain the game to me. Once I got the hang of it, I cheered loudly along with him. I found that the whole experience was a lot of fun. I could scream, and people didn't care that I was screaming. That whole process was a good stress reliever. We ate hot dogs and drank pop.

The game was over, and Aiden's team had won. I got off my seat, cheering loudly along with Aiden, who soon after hugged me and kissed me. At first, I was shy, but I kissed him with the same passion he had for me. When he peeled me away, I looked around, feeling embarrassed, but I was glad that people were still too busy cheering away.

He took my hand, led me to the exit door toward his car, and said, "Did you have fun?"

"Yes, that was fun. I wouldn't mind coming again."

I was still feeling the swell of excitement from the game.

He said excitedly, "Good."

During the car ride, I took off my hat and placed it beside me. I had seen another side of Aiden, the casual and modest. But at that moment, I could feel some strange tension in the air. Aiden put some Latin music on, and I started to relax a bit. It was a quiet ride.

When we got to my home, I turned to him. I tried to sound casual when I said, "I had a good time. Thank you." He stared at me for a few seconds.

He mumbled, "I had a good time too." He then reached over and gave me a long kiss that left me breathless after.

When he pulled back, I said thickly, "Okay, I will see you soon, right?"

He turned to look straight ahead. I was kind of disappointed. I was hoping he would kiss me again; plus, he didn't even reply to my question. I took my time fiddling with my house key. I then turned to him and said, "Good night."

He replied with a simple good night; that was strange—I thought he had fun. I walked slowly toward my home. My heart sank further when I heard his car leave. I went inside, trying not to feel worried about Aiden's sudden mood change. Right after I took off my jacket, I heard a knock at the door. I felt a rush of excitement that traveled in seconds through my body. I dashed to open it; it was Aiden at the front door. He was tall and so sexy. Our eyes locked for a few long seconds. My feet felt completely numb, and my stomach felt as if it were a home for a flock of butterflies. His eyes were even darker, and his face was flushed. I knew what he had come back for. Jasmine's sentence came back to me: "No means no." I dismissed it. To me, it was a *yes* …

He said, almost whispering, "You forgot your hat."

My eyes narrowed slightly. With shaky hands, I took the hat from him and placed it on the kitchen counter.

I said breathlessly, "It's funny; I was thinking about that hat too." It never crossed my mind.

I don't remember how it happened, but we started kissing passionately as he hastily took off his jacket. We were still in the kitchen when his hands went under my long, baggy shirt and fondled my bare skin. My hands trailed down under his shirt. Slowly and softly, I stroked his smooth abs and slightly hairy chest. With my finger, I traced a line right around his belt. I felt his muscles tighten under my touch, and then I heard him sigh.

His arms lifted me to sit me on the kitchen counter. He took off my shirt and then his shirt. I was glad I had worn a sexy pink, lacy bra. I looked lustily at his round arms and firm stomach, which was mesmerizing. He then released my hair from the ponytail to fall around my face. He found my lips again, right after his fingers undid my bra, which landed on the kitchen floor.

I froze suddenly, recalling Yusuf and his first attack. I closed my eyes tightly. My arms were around my bare chest, hiding my breasts from Aiden's gaze. I didn't know how I seemed to him right at that moment. I hoped not as frightened as I felt. His finger moved my chin up to look at him.

I stuttered, "I-i-it has been a long time since …" I didn't want to mention Yusuf's name.

"I can stop. We don't have to," he said in a very thick, clipped, breathless tone.

I knew he was containing himself with difficulty. I took a deep breath. What was I doing? I wanted this. I had been fantasizing about this moment. I slowly removed my arms from around my chest. Aiden's gaze traveled where my arms had been. I bit my lip lightly. I was a bit more at ease. I had to remind myself that he was nothing like Yusuf, who would've already bruised my lips and hurt my body from both his ruthless lips and cruel hands.

Aiden's lips came to claim mine, while his hands traveled over my bare skin. His touch wasn't too tender but not too rough either; it was perfect. Soon, I was on fire once again and tried not to shy away from his hungry gaze.

I sucked lightly and slowly right below his jaw. My hand played with his soft, thick hair.

He whispered breathlessly, "I want you now. I don't think I can wait anymore." He then carried me toward the only bedroom. I felt the cool covers under my hot skin. All of a sudden, I felt my jeans being peeled off. Soon, I was naked. I hid quickly under the pink covers. He followed me after taking off his pants and boxers. His skin was hot, firm, and round under my touch. His hands touched a place that used to belong to Yusuf; I dismissed him from my head once again. Aiden was nothing like him. I had to remind myself once more. I wanted Aiden to make love to me. With Yusuf, my body was shut down and cold. Yusuf caused me to dismiss the meaning of feelings, just so I wouldn't feel pain. With Aiden, I was sensitive to the slightest touch.

Aiden traced kisses around my whole body. I quivered, shying away at first, but then I gave in once again to this crazy moment. I heard myself sighing loudly.

He brought his face close to mine, stared at me, and whispered, "I want you right now."

I said thickly, "Yes, please, please. Just don't stop. Aiden, I want you more." And on that note, I felt him. It was different from what I remembered. It was pure pleasure, with no pain. What ladylike manners? What traditional conduct? Nothing mattered at that moment because my body was calling for his in a loud cry. It was something I was just experiencing for the very first time in my life.

***

I was lying next to him in bed, thinking about that beautiful dream, or was it a reality? I never imagined that sex could be so pleasurable. He was looking around him, with stunned eyes. The faint light from the kitchen gently illuminated the very girly room we were in, with its pink and white walls, pictures of the many Disney princess characters, and the faintly glowing ceiling stars.

He mumbled, "I feel like I am in an enchanted Disney movie, which is so inspiring."

I said softly, "Inspiring? To do what?" I was now tracing a line slowly with my finger, from his neck toward his chest.

"To tell you a bedtime story."

I grinned and then mumbled softly, "I love stories."

He took a deep breath. "Okay then, you need to listen." He cleared his throat. "Once upon a time, in faraway land, lived a prince."

I glanced at him. With interest, I said, "Was he good-looking?"

"Some people say he was."

"What was his name?"

"Let's call him Aiden."

I tried to hide my giggle. I added, "Prince Aiden? I've heard of him. He's really handsome and strong." My finger was tracing a line over his abs.

He said proudly, "Yep, very strong. One day, he heard a cry for help. He ran, only to find a girl who was lost, wearing a little crown."

My lips curled into a smile. "I think it was a silly tiara. She didn't cry for help. Strong, handsome Prince Aiden volunteered."

He added, "Shhh." As he placed his finger on my lips, he said, "You are ruining my story."

My finger was tracing around his lower stomach area.

He held my hand to stop it from going any further and added, "She was young and beautiful and full of surprises …" In a split second, I removed the blanket covering us and was sitting on top of his groin area, my legs around him.

I muttered, "Did you say she was full of surprises?" I could feel his breathing was getting harder and more uneven by the second. "What happened next? I want to hear more."

I could feel his arousal.

"She is … She was …" He wasn't making sense anymore. My lips came down on his, and in a split second, he flipped me. He growled, "Did I mention that she was way too naughty …"

I wrapped my legs around him. I felt really wild and was only thinking about pleasing him and myself.

"Only with Prince Aiden …" His lips covered mine to shut me up.

***

Sometime later, we were sitting around my small kitchen table. I was sipping tea and watching Aiden's round, tanned muscles and flat stomach. His faded jeans looked so sexy on his lean hips; he was shirtless since I was wearing his hockey shirt, which covered most of my thighs. At that moment, I wished he belonged to me.

He interrupted my deep, tingly whims by saying, "You ruined it for me, Hannah. The next hockey game, I will be imagining you with this shirt on. I won't be able to concentrate."

I blushed, turning my gaze away from his.

He sipped more tea while looking for my shy gaze. "I love the way you blush. You kind of look innocent now; you have these multiple personalities. One is sweet and very shy, and the other one is sexy, naughty, and eager to please."

I looked at him. The "multiple personalities" part didn't sit well with me. God, when would those flashbacks stop happening. I was quiet and suddenly afraid to look at him.

He continued, "You are different from all the girls I have gone out with." As he reached for my hand, all of a sudden I felt jealous of whoever he knew before me.

I tried to sound casual when I said, "Are you telling me that you have trails of girlfriends?"

"I dated a lot. I am not going to lie." Was he merely dating me? Was I just another girl? Did he think that I was way too easy? Naughty and eager to please?

Touching my cheek, he said, "Did I say something wrong? You went pale all of a sudden."

"No, you didn't. When was the last time you were single?"

He turned away. He said after a sigh, "Ages ago."

I tried not to show the anxiousness that I felt. Was he another Henry? "That long, huh? How about your ex-fiancée? Do you still see her sometimes?" I sighed before the next question, because Aiden didn't answer. "Why did you guys break up?"

He froze and turned his gaze away. I didn't know why I asked this question. I just really wanted to know him better. "I'm sorry, Aiden … You don't have to answer."

To my surprise, he drew me closer and said, "You are different and beautiful …" He started placing trails of kisses on my neck, my cheek, and my lips, and my bad deliberations evaporated all of a sudden. I was once again full of craving for him. Aiden left soon after midnight. I felt cold and sad when I took his hockey shirt off. He couldn't leave shirtless, I supposed. I watched the closed door after he left for at least an hour. I just couldn't go back to my empty bed.

Chapter Eighteen

A FEW DAYS LATER, AIDEN went back to Victoria. I learned that he was going to be away until after the New Year. We spoke on the phone periodically. He was trying to convince me to take some time off work in a few weeks. When I asked why, he said that he wanted to take me somewhere special. I hoped he wouldn't start spoiling me too soon. I wondered if I was ready to be treated exceptionally by a man. Jasmine wasn't ready, and she got used to it because Nathan regarded her as his equal. Would Aiden regard me as equal? I didn't want gifts. I just didn't wish to feel inferior to him.

When I tried to take some time off, I was advised by Adrianna that I couldn't book my vacation sooner than the end of winter.

I accepted Travis's invitation to spend New Year's at his place, along with Jasmine and Nathan. I knew that Henry was going to be there, and I wasn't looking forward to his company. Right then, I had an excuse. I was dating Aiden. Nora and Tiffany spent time together again. This time, Mandy hired a retired nanny to watch them at her place. At least the girls only needed each other for company over the New Year.

We arrived at Travis's place soon after 10:00 p.m. Fifteen minutes later, Henry came to greet me. I gave him a light hug. He stood too close to me. I moved a few inches away. When we sat on Travis's couch, Henry once again sat close to me. I moved away. I wanted to start a conversation with him so I could tell him that I was dating and for him to keep away from me. Nathan pulled Jasmine to the dance floor. Henry pulled closer to me.

I asked him casually, "Henry, how is your dating life these days?"

He sighed. "I am single right now." He gave me sad puppy eyes.

I hid my grin away and tried to sound composed when I said, "Again, Henry?" I was trying not to roll my eyes. "Why is that?"

"Not the right girls, I guess."

I recalled Aiden's dating history. He was also looking for the right girl. Was he possibly like Henry? I felt annoyed with that possibility. I really hoped not.

He asked, "How about you?"

I answered almost immediately, "I am dating."

"But you are still single until you are in a relationship."

I was quiet. At that moment, I didn't like the word *single*. I wanted to be in a relationship. I wanted to belong to Aiden.

"I think we are getting serious." We were; after the steamy night we had had, we *had* to be serious. How could we not? But then again, he could be the kind of man who jumped from one girl to the next, just like Henry. How would I know?

He looked at me for a few seconds and said, "Good for you. I am happy for you."

At that moment, I hoped I wouldn't end up in tears over Aiden! What if he changed his mind about me?

He continued, "Where is he? He shouldn't leave you all alone on New Year's Eve!"

I shrugged and said, looking away, "He is out of town … on business."

A few moments later, he said, "Do you want to dance?"

"Maybe later." At that moment, I felt that dancing close to Henry was almost like cheating on Aiden. Could I be at the beginning of a messy road? Later on, Henry gave up on me and found a pretty redheaded girl to dance with. I danced with Jasmine, Nathan, and couple of girls I had met at the party. Right after the countdown, I had a call. I answered while people cheered around me. I heard Aiden's voice at the end of the line. The world stopped suddenly.

He said, "Happy New Year!"

I replied happily, "Happy New Year!"

"Are you at a party?"

"Yes, with Jasmine and her husband, Nathan, at their friend's house."

"Promise me not to overdrink."

I giggled lightly. Was he being overprotective? But why? *Maybe because he cares about me,* I told myself. "I promise."

"Drink as much as you want only when you are around me. This way, I don't have to worry about you … doing the wrong things."

I was glad he couldn't see my frowns. Was he real? "What wrong things?"

He was silent for a few seconds. He said, "Mistaking a door sign, dancing too close to a man, turning him on …" He was silent, as if he were restraining himself from saying more. "There are so many wrong things."

I laughed, as I tried to dismiss Yusuf from my head.

He asked, "Is your friend Henry there?"

I said defensively, "He is, but he already found a girl to dance with."

After a few seconds of silence, he said, "I should've been with you." Was he jealous?

"You should have." I asked him, "Are you going to a New Year's party too?"

"Yes, with my buddies."

"You mean male buddies?"

He laughed. *I have the right to ask questions too,* I thought.

"Hannah, I will let you go back to your friends."

What? He had ignored my question about the male buddies.

"They are too busy cheering … Okay then, I will call you in three hours, to wish you a happy New Year too!"

"Okay, Hannah. Please promise me that you won't overdrink."

I rolled my eyes. I wished he could just stop; this conversation was bringing some ugly memories back. *Aiden is different,* I assured myself.

"I promise you, Aiden. I will be sober."

"Fine, I …" There was a silence. "I will talk to you later."

I froze. Was he going to say what I thought he was going to say? Maybe it was only in my head. "Okay."

I hung up, feeling refreshed and empty at the same time. Everyone was still cheering and drinking away. Maybe I should join them and wish them all a happy New Year. Henry was handing everyone fruity shots. I gulped mine. It tasted sourly sweet. After a few more shots, I felt dizzy. I didn't think that those shots would have that effect. I found myself dancing with Jasmine and Nathan. I glanced at my watch. It was 2:00 a.m. Another half hour had passed. I could see that Henry was approaching us again. His eyes already looked red. I wondered how drunk he was. I moved away from him. I felt a couple of hands turning me.

"One dance won't hurt." Henry's face was way too close to mine.

"Henry, I think you are way too drunk," I said, turning my face away from him.

"Nope, I am not drunk at all." He then held me tight.

I sighed and pulled away. I said irritably, "If you want to dance, we dance far away, not too close to each other."

He laughed sarcastically. "That's because you prefer to dance way too close with men you just met."

I flushed and walked away. Who did he think he was, judging me that way? I sat alone in the dark, hiding away and glancing at my phone periodically. Maybe I could call Aiden from the powder room, which was the only place with peace and quiet. Why was Aiden the only man I felt safe around? I recalled our passionate night together. I couldn't imagine myself being with anyone else, only with him. Why was that?

At exactly 3:00 a.m., I called Aiden from Travis's powder room. He picked up right away. I could hear loud noises in the background. I wished him a happy New Year, and then he asked me when I was going home, because he wanted to call me when I got there. At that moment, I wished I had come in my own car so I could leave immediately.

I was thankful Nathan called it a night as soon as I got out of the bathroom. Aiden called me as soon as I got home.

"Where are you?" he asked.

"I'm lying under the stars, thinking of you."

He was silent for a few seconds, and then I heard music, which brought me back months earlier to when we danced the first time—when he was hugging me tight. I felt my stomach tighten. "Do you remember that song?" he mumbled.

I said breathlessly, "How can I forget? That's our song."

"You know what I feel like doing right now?"

"Yes, I do." I murmured.

"Do you?" His voice was more like a whisper.

I couldn't even take a deep breath.

"I want to feel you next to me. Even thinking about it, I am already turned on," he said.

I closed my eyes and imagined him next to me in bed. "How turned on … are you?"

He laughed tensely and answered in a low tone, "Really, really turned on, and can only think of you."

I said breathlessly, "This is no good; I mean, what are you going to do about your little dilemma?"

"A cold shower, what else can I do?"

I felt hot, excited. I said in a low whisper, "I can rub your … um …" I was silent for a few seconds. I could hear him breathing hard. "Back, if you want. I know you won't be able to reach it."

He growled, "You are killing me, Hannah."

I didn't know that conversations like this could bring tons of excitement and fun.

"I don't want to kill you. I want to revive you. I want you breathing next to me." I didn't know I could say that. Where was this coming from?

"You can't do that to me … thousands of miles away …" I heard a knock at the door. "I have to go. I am calling you from the bathroom, and someone apparently wants to use it now. Damn people," he said irritably.

I laughed, recalling that I had to call him from Travis's bathroom.

I stared at my ceiling for hours after I hung up with him, replaying our lovemaking over and over again in my mind.

***

Aiden was delayed in Victoria for another week, during which I spoke to him regularly on the phone. However, our conversations were brief, since he was always busy.

Mary was spending less time at the office. I found myself missing her.

One day, I was reading something off of my screen at work when I saw Adrianna approaching my desk. She was apparently back from out of town, I haven't seen her since before New Years; I noticed, however, that she was looking paler than usual.

"Hello, Ms. Miller," I said casually.

"Hi." Her lips curled into a smile. "I need you to take the rest of the afternoon off."

I looked blankly at her.

"Why?"

"I need you to come with me to pick up a few things, if that's okay with you."

What had happened all of a sudden with her? This was the nicest she had been to me.

"Sure. I mean, who's going to answer the calls?"

"I told Christine to come after lunch. She is going to start full-time shifts as of next week, and a young intern by the name of Madison will be starting that day too."

Did they just replace me? "I don't understand. I mean, what am I supposed to do?" I felt my heart race.

She smiled and said calmly, "You are going to do a different type of work. I will need you to be my personal assistant, and your job is very secure." I tried not to frown. Being her assistant would be a nightmare. I wondered what had happened to her assistant. My desk phone rang.

She said, "You better get that." She then turned away toward her office, leaving me puzzled. I couldn't lose that job, since my spending had doubled ever since last month. *Impressing Aiden came with a price tag*, I thought, annoyed.

Later on in the afternoon, I reluctantly followed Adrianna to her BMW, whose interior was identical to Aiden's, except for the white color of the leather seats. During the car ride, I took notes about her upcoming schedule, but she was always being interrupted by her phone calls. The last phone call she had had was with a friend, I assumed, since her tone was very friendly. I turned away, thinking how boring that was and wishing I could go back to the office instead. She really didn't need me. Her conversation, however, caught my attention. She was speaking about her previous relationship. That could be interesting, so I tried to listen.

"We are still friends. I know he spoiled me rotten. Well, I didn't ask for all the expensive gifts he gave me. So you think I should return my watch, necklaces, and rings?"

I turned away. That didn't sound like Adrianna. I glanced over her hand at her watch, which was in a square, white-gold case with a brown-leather bracelet material. It looked kind of expensive. She had a couple of stunning diamond rings and a necklace with a square-shaped diamond pendent. It looked really classy and pricey. Her ex must have been loaded. How come I never paid attention to her jewelry before? Then I went back to listening. "It was my idea to take a break from each other. I just need some time. He understands. We're meeting over coffee on the weekend …" I didn't want to listen anymore. I wasn't interested in her anyway. She always sounded arrogant and spoiled, and now she was being ignorant and selfish. If she broke up with a man, she should at least return his expensive gifts—well, that was my opinion anyway.

***

Aiden arrived back on Friday night. On Saturday morning, he texted me that he wanted to take me out for dinner. Before I accepted, I briefly remembered Majeed, who wanted to hide me. Aiden was, however, different. Could he want to do the same? I was suddenly afraid. Right after breakfast, I spoke to Jasim casually about Aiden, while keeping all the intimacy we had shared strictly to myself.

He said, "Why don't you bring him over for dinner? I would like to meet him."

My eyes grew wide. If Aiden refused to come and insisted on seeing me privately, then I would have to step on my heart and break it off with him. After Jasim left the house to meet up with some of his friends, I called Aiden.

"Hi, Hannah."

"Hi, Aiden, I can't find a babysitter for tonight," I lied. "I was thinking maybe you would like to come over for dinner here instead. Jasim, my landlord, is like a father to me." My heart squeezed at the last sentence, as if I just realized how much Jasim meant to me. I continued, "He would love to have you over, if you'd like." There was a long silence during which I stopped breathing, waiting for an excuse.

He said, "What time?"

I breathed deeply. "Any time after six."

He said firmly, "I will be there. I hope your Jasim won't restrain me from seeing you after."

I giggled, feeling so relieved. "On the contrary, I think he is going to tell me that you are too good for me."

He was silent for a moment. His tone was low. "Is that what you think?"

I took a deep breath. "Yes."

He said, "I think it's the other way around. I sometimes ask myself, 'How did I get so lucky?' You are all I need."

I felt a tight squeeze in my chest. Was I dreaming all this? Did he mean what he said? I was silent; somehow, I felt that my mind was blank.

He said, "I will see you in the evening. I can't wait till I meet little Princess Nora."

I smiled happily. "Aiden." I didn't know why I called his name. He was silent. "I really miss you."

"I miss you too."

He then hung up. I twirled around the room. Aiden could've refused, but he didn't.

As soon as I was done cleaning, I called Mother. She mentioned that she was cooking. I convinced her to cook extra food and requested a couple of her famous, delicious dishes. When she complained, I told her that I would do all her shopping and help her cook.

I bought a car's worth of groceries. It was already past noon when Nora and I arrived at Mother's place.

"Who are you and Jasim entertaining?" she asked when she saw all the food I brought to her front door. Nora was right behind me.

"Just a few friends."

She said, "Do I know them?"

My eyes narrowed. What was wrong with her suspicious tone?

I said cautiously, "No, but Jasim does."

That lie won't hurt anyone, I decided.

"What's the occasion?"

Was she on a quest to find out why she wasn't invited?

"Jasim invited his buddies over to watch some hockey game. I promised him that I would take care of the food."

"You? Since when?"

I frowned. Carefully hiding my annoyance, I said, "Since yesterday, Mother." She puckered her brows.

Her tone was thick. "Tell Jasim that I have guests coming during the evening too, my friends." What happened to Mother all of a sudden? Was she angry with me or Jasim for having to cook? I thought she agreed when I asked her earlier. She always volunteered to cook for us.

I sighed, annoyed. "I can always cook for those men if you want me too."

She didn't answer. She seemed to be thinking about what I had just told her. Her reaction to not being invited seemed kind of odd. Well, there was no way I could invite her. How could I explain Aiden to her? I added tentatively, "Last time I cooked some beef and rice, I think it came out so dry, because Jasim choked." *A little exaggeration won't kill anyone.*

My mother's eyes softened. "Jasim choked? When?"

"Just the other day." I looked away.

She sighed. "Fine! I don't want those men to choke and blame my own daughter for it. I will cook if you can help me clean around my home."

I smiled, came closer, and kissed her cheek. How could I refuse a deal like that? "Deal."

I walked around the living room and said hello to my twin brothers. They were too busy watching TV. They didn't even reply. I glanced at Nora, who skipped to the living room and then jumped in between the twins. I left the room quickly, but I could still hear the twins' tetchy protests in the background. Nora was probably annoying them with wanting to switch the TV channel. Then I heard Hisham say to her that he would only play a game with her if she let them watch their show in peace. I was thankful to see she behaved after.

A couple of hours later, I was already exhausted from all the cleaning I had to do for one day. I supposed that was the price I had to pay for being a below-average cook. Nora and the twins got along well. There were no clashes or battles. The food was packed and Mother's house—including the kitchen—shined. I carried the platter of rice, cooked chicken kebabs, marinated beef, parsley and tomato salad, and dips to the car. I sighed happily when I placed the food in the fridge. I simply had to heat and serve. But first, I needed to get Nora and myself ready.

I was dressed in a casual, short-sleeve, blue dress. I styled my hair straight and left it loose. My makeup was simple and fresh. The table was set, and the food was heating in the oven. Nora looked cute in her purple dress. Her long brown hair was in a ponytail. Jasim wore crisp black dress pants and a gray and white shirt. His hair was neat, especially after his new haircut. He even shaved his long beard and looked much younger. *Wow,* he really looked sharp, and handsome! What a transformation a shave and a haircut could make. I couldn't stop looking at him.

I came closer, gave him a hug, and said sincerely, "Jasim, you look so handsome today, just like a superstar."

He grinned. "Of course. I didn't want your rich friend to think that he was better than me."

I laughed. "Jasim, no one can come close to thinking they are better than you. To me, you are the best." I breathed in. I meant what I had said. I had hardly complimented any men in the past or spoken of my true emotions. I was changing in many ways, I realized.

He came close to me and tucked a stray strand of hair that was close to my face behind my ear. I smiled.

He then placed his hand on my face and said, "I'm happy when you're happy."

I felt really special. Those few simple words were worth more than all the expensive diamonds and gifts combined. There was a knock on the door. I glanced at the mirror quickly. I heard Jasim say, "You look stunning, as always."

I smiled right before I dashed to open Jasim's front entrance.

Aidan stood tall in a long, classy black coat and smart gray pants. His dark hair was brushed to the back, sleek and sexy. He carried a bouquet of flowers and a white box with shiny bow ties. Some sort of sweet, I presumed.

From behind me, Jasim said in a firm, welcoming tone, "Aiden, come on in."

I took the flowers. Jasim took the white box and placed it on a small corner table. My heart was racing. Aiden took his coat off. Jasim hung it for him. He wore a casual, blue-and-white-striped shirt, under a navy-blue semiformal jacket. When I came back, Jasim and Aiden were sitting in the living room across from each other. Nora sat by Aiden's side. She was already speaking freely about herself, while the two men listened interestedly. I smiled contently. Nora was being her supercute, girly self again. I sat next to Jasim, who placed his arm around me.

He said, "Hannah is like my daughter, Nora like my granddaughter. Who said family is only connected by blood?" He smiled.

I glanced at Aiden. He looked at the both of us sincerely.

He said, "Hannah did say that she wanted me to meet the man who was like a father to her."

Jasim's arm tightened around my shoulder. "Whatever hurts Hannah and Nora hurts me. Remember that."

"Yes, sir," he said and grinned.

I blushed. But at the same time, I felt relaxed, because Jasim was by my side. I cleared my throat and then went to check on the food that was being reheated in the oven. A few minutes later, I said, "Dinner is ready."

We all walked to the nicely set up dinner table in Jasim's medium-size dining room. Nora sat next to me. Aiden and Jasim sat across from us. The two men spoke of work and properties. I realized that Jasim was very smart; he was discussing business with deep knowledge, and when Aiden discussed the many properties he owned, Jasim spoke of a couple his own rental properties. I kept quiet most of the time. It was a habit I had developed when I was married to Yusuf; I was not to speak when men were speaking.

Aiden was impressed with the food. He looked at me and said, "Did you cook all this food?"

I glanced over at Jasim, who turned his gaze to his plate. Nora was listening with interest.

I said casually, "Mother helped me a little."

Nora said proudly, "Grandma is the best cook ever."

Aiden turned to her and grinned. "Really! Your mom must be good too!"

She just shook her head and turned to face her plate. Jasim chuckled lightly. He knew of my unsuccessful attempts to make a decent dinner, which at times, had ended up in the garbage. I blushed, looking away.

"That's okay. I can live with that."

"I am not that bad!" I protested. "I make a good pasta and cheese dinner." This was the only dish I had so far managed not to wreck.

"Good, my favorite dish too!" Aiden said. He then gave me a wink. I giggled lightly as I recalled Yusuf's past constant degrading of my cooking. The conversation shifted to my work. Jasim was telling Aiden how hard I had worked and that I most of the time stayed late in the office helping Adrianna, who seemed to be always behind on her work.

I turned red and then added, "Adrianna has been nicer to me lately." I wished to know how close their friendship was. "Aiden knows some of the lawyers at the firm I work for."

Aiden looked away.

"This is how you guys met?" Jasim asked.

I found Aiden's gaze and smiled shyly. We shouldn't mention to Jasim where we really met. That was way too embarrassing. I said, "We met at the firm's holiday party."

"It was my lucky day," Aiden said and smiled. I blushed. He turned to Jasim and said casually, "I was going to suggest to Hannah to work for me. I have an amazing job position available."

I froze, recalling Yusuf's offer to get me a job at his car rental place. It was a joke of a job; it was his way to control me.

"I like working for the firm."

Aiden's gaze was mystifying. I looked away. I didn't want to show him the discomfort that I felt.

Jasim cleared his throat, adding, "As long as Hannah is happy; I mean she really works hard."

The rest of the evening went very well. The sweets Aiden had brought were Middle-Eastern pastries—Jasim's favorite. Aiden stood up to leave. After he had fetched his jacket, Jasim, Nora, and I followed him to the front door. I smiled contently. I just couldn't wait until Jasim told me what he thought of him.

"I like him. I think he cares about you. I can sense it."

I grinned. "Really?" I asked happily, feeling a sudden charge of energy. I hoped he was right.

Chapter Nineteen

It was an evening a few days later, after dinner; I had just finished taking a shower and drying my hair. Nora was wearing her pink pajamas. She had scattered the living room area with her books, dolls, and crayons. I sighed. I had to be stricter with her when it came to tidiness. I went to gather the laundry from the bedroom and place them in my overflowing basket. Last weekend, I had no time to finish my laundry. Lately I hadn't had the time to do any of my chores properly; Aiden was distracting me, even when he wasn't around. My cell rung, cutting my train of thoughts. It was Aiden. Suddenly, laundry was no longer on my mind.

"Hi, Aiden."

"Hi, Hannah."

I was used to speaking to Aiden almost daily. Our conversation, however, was always cut short because of Nora's constant demand for my attention. I glanced at Nora quickly; luckily, she was busy at the moment. Quietly, I went to my bedroom and closed the door. I needed my peace and quiet.

"How was your day at work?" he asked. Lately, he had asked me regularly about my work, ever since Jasim declared to him that I had had to stay late in the past.

"Good, and yours?"

He said evenly, "Good. You know, Hannah, bear in mind that if you are not happy with your job, I can hook you up with a better one."

Not again! Something inside of me refused the idea immediately.

"I will bear it in mind."

"I do miss you." He almost hissed the last few words, sending electrical shots all over my body. I knew what he was implying, recalling briefly Yusuf's rough approach to sex. I was his; he could do whatever he wanted to do with my body, leaving me bruised each and every time. I had to dismiss him. I hated when he came into my head uninvited. Aiden was different. I should stop comparing the two men.

"I miss you too," I confessed. The night we spent together was the only thing on my mind when I went to bed at night. There was a long, tense silence. I could hear his breathing.

"Is Nora around you?"

"Nope, I am alone, lying on top of a pink bed."

He sighed, and I felt my stomach knot.

"Where is she?"

"Busy, coloring in the living room."

"Is Jasim upstairs?"

"He is out with some of his buddies."

"What are you wearing right now?"

I took a deep breath. I then stretched my body on the bed and said in a very low tone, almost hissing, "I am wearing pink satin shorts and a matching little tight lacy camisole." I didn't know what it was about him; I was always in the mood to be naughty. I recalled briefly our erotic conversation right after New Year's.

"That's it—no bra, no panties?"

I sighed, hiding my giggles deep inside my throat. "Nope."

"Don't do that to me."

I giggled lightly.

"I can imagine you. You probably look too exposed."

I giggled and said softly, "Maybe."

"I am closing my eyes. I can picture your long strands of hair, loose and free. Pink shorts and small, tight camisole."

My hair was in a bun. I got off the bed, took my hair tie off, and stood in front of the mirror, fixing my hair with my free hand. I was glad I had dried my hair, while adding some hair product. It looked long and wavy and even neat.

He continued, "I just opened my eyes. And guess what. I found myself in front of your door." I froze. He added, "May I come in?" My eyes grew wide.

Was he kidding? My heart raced; that couldn't be. I said agitatedly, "Aiden, you are joking, right?" I heard a knock at the door and Nora's running steps toward the front entrance. My heart jumped. His phone went dead. I heard Nora scream, "Mom, your friend is here!"

I glanced at my warm pajamas with Winnie the Pooh printed all over them. I never even owned pink satin shorts or a tiny camisole. My current pajamas would be a turn-off even for a deprived homeless man. I quickly glanced at myself in the mirror and put on some blush and lip gloss. Apart from that, my face was bare of any makeup. I took off my oversized slippers with the same print as my pajamas. I had gotten both of them on sale as a set. Then I put them back; I forgot to paint my toes after I removed my nail polish. *Crap,* I was suddenly breathing hard. Nora burst my room door open while I was looking for something else to wear. At that moment, I regretted placing most of my clothes in Jasim's spare bedroom; my current closet I shared with Nora only carried more of my silly pajamas and a basket full of dirty laundry.

"Mommy! Look what I got!" She was carrying something in her hand. *An iPad,* I narrowed my eyes.

"Who gave it to you?"

She said enthusiastically while jumping, "Your friend gave it to me. Tiffany has the same! I can't wait until I show her." Aiden was starting to spoil Nora! I would have to tell him to stop. Nora would get used to it in no time. I realized that I shouldn't let Aiden wait any longer; I had no choice but to come out looking like the total opposite of the sexy woman I was trying to portray.

I sighed, annoyed, and left the room. I tried not to look at Aiden's gaze. I said hesitantly, "Hi, Aiden, what a surprise!"

Nora was still in the bedroom. He came closer. Slowly, I turned my gaze to him. He was scrutinizing me, from top to bottom, wearing a big grin on his face. How could he not? I looked more than funny, maybe even hilarious.

His tone was playful. "Looking good, Hannah. Someone could have a hard time identifying the mother from the child."

I felt my blood surge. "Funny, very funny."

I tried not to roll my eyes. I froze in front of him, not knowing what to do. I felt lost.

His tone was playful but firm. "When you told me you were wearing some skimpy little outfit and exposing too much skin, I was really concerned."

"Why is that?" I said calmly, blushing from embarrassment.

"I didn't want to you to catch a cold."

I gave him a curt smile. "Don't worry yourself, Aiden. With these slippers, I will never catch a cold."

"Good." I felt horrified when I noticed the living room. It was filled with children's books, crayons, and toys. I started to tidy up quickly.

"I was in the neighborhood. I thought I could stop here for some tea," he said as he came closer. He was too close.

I stuttered while looking at him. "I-I have tea and cupcakes."

"I love the way you look right now. So innocent … just the way I pictured you would be." He then placed a quick kiss on my cheek.

I smiled at that compliment, even though I knew it was a lie. I stopped tidying up at Aiden's request. Instead, I went to the kitchen to make the tea.

He stood near me; he even opened the fridge.

"Are you hungry? I can make you something quickly."

"I was in meetings all day, too busy to think of food. As soon as I was done, I found myself outside your door."

I felt really flattered, but I wished he hadn't surprised me the way he did; at least I could've wore something less funny. I came close and gave him a light kiss on his lips.

"I will make you something." I hesitated before I added, "Something good." Nora came back from the bedroom, wearing one of her dresses. I took a deep, angry breath. She probably made a mess in the bedroom too.

"Nora, why did you change your pajamas? You are going to bed soon!"

"Mommy, I had to. Your friend came to visit." I heard Aiden's laugh.

I turned to the fridge. I didn't want to argue in front of Aiden Then I remembered something. I turned to Aiden and whispered, "Aiden, you really shouldn't spoil Nora; she already thinks she's a princess."

He grinned and strolled to sit next to her, surrounded by her pile of mess. *How embarrassing.* He said addressing Nora, "Nora is a princess, right, Nora?"

I heard her positive answer in the background.

Great! I thought irritably. *As if Nora wasn't spoiled enough already!*

I heated some okra and meat stew with rice on the side, which was something Mother gave me the night before. I made a spinach-and-cheese omelet and a quick garden salad and opened a couple of cans of mushroom soup. I didn't know how hungry Aiden was. I wanted to make sure to prepare enough food. I glanced over at both of them. I noticed that Nora had already brought all our picture albums out to show Aiden. I shook my head, annoyed. I was thinking about the mess she had to have made to be able to find those albums.

We all sat by the small table. Aiden looked around and said, "That looks amazing. Thank you."

"Sorry, Aiden, if I knew you were coming, I would've been more prepared." *With some takeout,* I thought.

"This is perfect." He started digging his fork into the rice and okra dish. Nora had already had her dinner but still enjoyed a couple of bites of rice and omelet. I looked around me. Despite my disordered surroundings, I felt calm. Would I ever be let down?

***

The next day, I got a call from Mandy inviting Nora and me to Sunday brunch. She mentioned that she had already invited Jasmine and Nathan. I hesitated at first, but then I called Aiden and he answered right away.

"Aiden, a friend of mine invited us to a Sunday brunch at her house. Would you like to come?"

"When?"

"This Sunday before noon."

He paused for a moment and then said, "I can make it."

My heart skipped. "Really?"

"Of course."

All of a sudden, I thought of something; he had never suggested that I come with him to visit his friends. "What are you doing this Saturday?"

He was silent. "I have a couple of meetings and a fundraiser event I promised to attend on Mother's behalf from a month earlier."

I didn't want to seem whiney or pushy, so I just said, "Okay, have fun at your event."

I knew that those events were some sort of gatherings or parties. I wondered why he couldn't at least suggest that I come along with him. He was silent.

"Hannah, my offer for the job still stands. I think you are working way too hard at that firm." Why this constant mentioning of my job? I didn't wish to be controlled the way I had been in the past. With my degree, I was aware that no job was going to match my current pay and benefits.

"I like working for this firm. Really, Adrianna is no trouble at all lately. She even made me her personal assistant."

His tone was serious. "When did that happen?"

"Like a week ago. I mean, I still do some reception from time to time, but my workload is much lighter now"—and less needed, and I wasn't going to mention how much I hated it. There was a long silence before he said that he had to go suddenly.

***

Sunday at 10:30 a.m., Aiden knocked on my door. He looked casual but smart. I wore a new outfit: a fitted red shirt; a semishort black skirt, and my knee-high black boots. My hair was wavy and long, with smooth bangs over my eyes. Aiden helped me bring the salad I had made that morning to his car. Nora was busy playing a game, Aiden's gift to her.

Once we settled in the car, I noticed that he had gotten some sweets. *How classy of him!* I thought happily.

We were the first couple to arrive. I never thought about what to introduce Aiden as—a friend? My boyfriend? John and Mandy immediately took my salad and Aiden's wrapped sweets. Nora ran after Tiffany toward her playroom.

When John came back, I introduced them, "Aiden, this is Mandy and her boyfriend, John."

"Fiancé," Mandy corrected, showing off her big, shiny stone. "John proposed this morning."

I smiled happily while hugging her tight. "Congratulations! I am so happy for the both of you." John placed his arm around Mandy. Then he reached to shake Aiden's hand.

"Aiden, Hannah's boyfriend." Mandy's eyes grew wide. She was speechless.

So it is official. I am in a relationship … I wanted to skip happily, just like a child.

He then placed his arm around me and added, "Congratulations to the both of you."

We settled in Mandy's big guest sitting room. Outside, it was a cold, sunny day, but the warm sun settled on one part of a rich beige-colored wall. Aiden looked very comfortable while he started a conversation with John. John was as tall and masculine as Aiden. He was, however, fair with light-brown hair, compared to Aiden's olive complexion and dark hair. I knew how crazy Mandy was about John. He was after all a good-looking man. His strong jaw and firm, athletic body, along with his classy attitude, gave the impression that he was a politician more than the owner of a construction company who specialized in building private homes. I glanced over at Aiden, realizing dreamily that no one was better-looking.

I followed Mandy to the kitchen. I was still under the effect of being officially in a relationship. Mandy's table was already set.

She turned to me and said, "Sexy! Where on earth did you find him?"

I blushed. "You don't want to know."

She gasped. "I do want to know. In fact, I am dying to know. Do tell."

The bell rang at that moment. It was probably Jasmine and Nathan. Once again, I introduced my sister and my brother-in-law to Aiden. Jasmine followed Mandy and me to the kitchen. Mandy was still insisting on hearing my embarrassing story of how I met Aiden. I took a deep breath and started with when Jasmine led me by mistake into a men's restroom and left me there with a handsome stranger.

When we sat around the table, I felt Aiden's hand on my thigh. I reached to hold his hand under the table. I felt so tingly. All of a sudden, the colorful food wasn't appealing anymore. I was craving Aiden, craving his love.

John was speaking of a resort he and Mandy were going to visit at the end of winter. Nathan also mentioned the vacation he and my sister were taking in a few weeks. Soon, talk about vacations began. I recalled the vacation I booked for Adrianna, Jason, and Katie at an exquisite resort. I felt as if I couldn't participate in this type of conversation. I had gone places with Yusuf, but because I was running away with him, even our honeymoon vacation was awful. I dismissed those memories quickly.

Then I heard Aiden saying, "I'm going on a vacation to a nice resort next week."

My eyes grew wide. I felt my stomach tighten. I couldn't say anything. I was feeling foolish since I had just heard the news.

"Where will you be going?" John asked.

Aiden said, "Royal Cancun." *I had heard this name somewhere before.*

John said, "I've heard of it; it's a really beautiful resort."

Mandy was glancing at me, as was Jasmine. I looked away. There was a long silence around the table.

Aiden cleared his throat and said casually, "George, one of my father's old business associates, prebooked it for me. We are going as a group with his kids and their families."

I felt as if he was explaining himself too much. Why was that?

"I just remembered …" He was addressing his conversation to John. "George Melisso wants to build a house for each of his children. Do you mind if I forward him your business card?"

John replied, "George Melisso? I know him through my father. He even came to my parents' fortieth anniversary. Sure, you can give him my business card. We are in our slow season right now."

I tried not to roll my eyes, thinking that was how the rich got richer—they all knew each other.

Aiden said, "He is a good guy, shrewd and fair in business with tons of connections." He sipped some orange juice. "But he could be annoying at times and short-tempered."

John said to me, "I also heard he likes to have fun thinking he is still in his thirties. He always surrounds himself with much younger girls." He then giggled.

I wondered what that meant.

Aiden said defensively, "He is not that bad." He placed his arms around me. "I told Hannah to come with me, but she can't take time off work."

I shrugged and hid my annoyance by chewing slowly on some bread.

John said to me, "I would go if I were you."

Mandy suggested, "Ask your boss again for time off."

I said, annoyed, "I already did. My next vacation time is the end of winter."

John snapped his fingers, addressing everyone at the table. "Why don't you guys come with us? We are going to Cancun at that time."

Nathan said, "That would've been awesome, but we are taking a vacation soon. We already booked ours in Italy."

I was quiet. I knew how expensive those vacations were, so I replied, "I don't think so. I mean, where am I supposed to leave Nora?"

Aiden said, "We can take her with us." He was addressing John and Mandy. "Are you guys taking Tiffany with you?"

Mandy said, "Yes, we are. That's a great idea. I will book the vacation tomorrow."

Aiden's tone was firm and a bit bossy when he said, "Do that. I will leave you with my credit card number before I go."

I frowned; it was as if I had no say.

I cleared my throat and added, "Wait a minute. I may not be able to go." I didn't want to say why. "I mean I don't want to take Nora out of school."

Mandy said, "Come on, Hannah, as if she were graduating this year."

My mind was occupied with Aiden's vacation, which was going to be spent with an old man who surrounded himself with young girls.

Aiden said, placing his arms around me, "I will convince her; book the three seats for now."

Soon, the conversation shifted away from vacations and resorts. The men were speaking of work. Slowly, I started to feel at ease about the vacation possibility. My reverie came back again to the day I was booking the resort vacation for Adrianna. I recalled the beautiful pictures, the white sandy beach, lying next to Aiden. That sounded really good. Then I felt Aiden's hand on my thigh again. I sighed, thinking, *Not again!* while feeling a flow of excitement traveling through my body.

A couple of hours later, the two other couples were in the guest sitting room. I could hear their laughter in the background. Nora was still playing with Tiffany. Aiden and I sat in the living room, too close to each other.

He mumbled, "That's why I offered you a job in my company; this way, you can travel with me whenever you want."

I said tightly, "Maybe in the future; I don't want to leave the firm yet." I held his hand that was on my thigh. "You never mentioned you were going on a vacation before today."

He hesitated at first. "I was going to mention it to you. But then I forgot."

I frowned lightly. He forgot to mention going on an exclusive vacation! Maybe it was because vacations like that didn't mean much to him.

He continued, "At first, I didn't want to accept George's offer to pay for my vacation."

"Why did you accept?" I was hoping that I didn't sound like an investigator.

"I am in the middle of buying one of his businesses. I lowered the offer price, so we are in the middle of negotiating it."

"Negotiating it in a resort full of pretty ... beaches?" I was going to say "girls," but I changed my mind at the last second. He giggled. "I'm just trying to understand how business works."

He said firmly, "Everyone works differently. I have known George since I was a kid. He was one of my father's close friends."

Was he implying that George worked better in a resort with half-naked women? I was quiet.

He stared at me for several long seconds and continued, "I could be around so many pretty ... beaches, but I am attracted to only one." Then his soft, moist lips suckled my neck slowly. I wished he didn't have this magical way with me, weakening my knees and disabling my disturbed thoughts.

I mumbled softly, "I'm not a beach ... I am just a ..." I forgot what I was about to say. He was nibbling on my earlobe. I hated it, but I loved what he was doing to me. His kisses were so sensual and dangerous. I said breathlessly, "I think you like to tease me. Why do you do that?"

He sighed, his warm breath on my neck. "I like to tease you. Your eyes widen ... You then look wild and sexy and ready for my love."

My blood streamed all over my body. I mumbled, "I am only wild with you."

"Do you want to know how wild I feel right now?" he said breathlessly. He then placed my hand right beside his arousal. Blood traveled to my head while I glanced around. I was thankful we were alone still. I licked my lips.

He whispered, "Only wild with you." I knew that this was a white lie, considering all the girls he had been with, but all of a sudden, I was merely thinking about one thing. I stared at where my hand was, close to his groin. Through his pants, I could tell how aroused he was.

I mumbled, "Really?" while feeling goose bumps all over. I was starting to feel sweaty. God, what kind of a sex freak was I becoming?

I peeled my stare away from his groin area, breathing hard, to look at his dark gaze. He was watching my reaction intently.

"Trust me!" His voice was low.

I glanced at his sensual lips. I wanted to kiss him so badly right then. I said softly, "What do you want to do?"

My hand was moving slowly to touch his inner thigh. I heard him sigh. He said breathlessly, "Maybe we can make an excuse and leave right away. I want you … now!"

"I have to see if Mandy can keep Nora." My body was feeling overheated all of a sudden.

"Do that."

I remembered that my cell wasn't around.

"I don't know where my cell is."

He reached over to give me his. There was a password. He whispered it to me while placing sensual kisses on my neck. With shaky fingers, I texted Mandy. I knew her number by heart.

"Mandy, it's Hannah texting you from Aiden's phone. I have to go with him. He wants to grab something from somewhere. Can you please, please keep Nora for a bit?" I couldn't even think clearly. My brain felt occupied by some crazy desires. I sent her the message. Aiden's lips were on my cheek when I heard a message beep.

And it said, "Grab all you want. We will still be here."

"Tell my sister it was an emergency."

"Emergency it is …" I didn't remember how I walked out the door with Aiden, heading toward his car. We didn't even bother with our coats. He stopped the car right across a deserted field. He moved his seat to the back and grabbed me to sit me on top of him with my legs around his thighs. I kissed his soft, moist lips and tasted his sweet sweat off his cheek and neck. His hands were under my skirt. It was too tight, so I went back to my seat and took it off. I was wearing only my thigh-high pantyhose and panties. I was glad that Aiden's windows were lightly tinted. We were in the middle of nowhere anyway. I could feel that he had already slid his pants off when I got back on top of him. He cupped my chest under my fitted shirt. I didn't care about the material. I didn't care for anything at that moment except the weird sensation that was about to explode. I forgot I had my panties on. I was getting frustrated.

And so I told him, while gasping, "Rip it off. Just get rid of it … just … I don't care."

I panted as I felt his strong hands ripping the delicate material. They were removed in a split second. I had to keep half my cries in. I breathed heavily. I could feel him, just the way I had been fantasizing each and every night for a while. He held my face, and his lips found mine. I was moving with him, while we both sighed at the same time.

Less than ten minutes later, I was sitting on the passenger side. My skirt was back on. Aiden's pants were back on too. I felt delusional. What had just happened?

I snapped lightly, "You are a crazy, naughty man, Aiden."

He grinned before saying, "And I finally found my match." He bent to kiss my boiling cheek. "You are just perfect." At that moment, I wondered what he thought of the naughtiness that I had just discovered in myself. "I don't like my woman to be cold," he added right before he put his car in gear.

His woman? Did that mean he owned me? Yusuf believed I was his; he could do whatever he wanted to do with me. I glanced at my ripped panties. I picked them up quickly. The scene of Yusuf and me making out in the cab right after we left the strip club emerged back in my head. I also remembered what he told me when we went back to the hotel room. I felt then as if I were his unwilling sex slave. With Aiden, I was willingly and blindly following my wild desires. I was being someone I didn't recognize. *No,* Aiden was nothing like Yusuf, whose persistent memory wouldn't abandon my mind lately.

He stopped by a nice bakery and turned to me.

"We have to bring something with us." I followed him inside and went straight to the restroom. I needed to freshen up. A few minutes later, I was staring at a large chocolate and vanilla cake that read, "Congrats to John and Mandy."

Good thinking! I thought. What a great excuse for our sudden absence. He was so smart.

Mandy and Jasmine were in the kitchen when I carried the cake over. Mandy smiled wickedly and then whispered in my ear, "How did it go?"

I then opened the box of cake; she stared at it with big blue eyes. "Seriously!"

I blushed. I hid a grin while I said, "What did you think we went to grab?"

"Not a cake for sure."

I smiled mysteriously.

She added, "I guess I have a twisted, sick mind."

I sighed. "That's okay, Mandy. Sometimes, that's what I love about you: your twisted, sick mind …"

She smiled gratefully. "You guys really shouldn't have. The cake looks awesome."

I hoped my smile didn't look as naughty as I felt. Maybe one day, I would tell her, but not then. For the time being, that was Aiden's and my little secret.

Chapter Twenty

On Monday, only one day before Aiden left for his vacation, I was sent by Adrianna on a mission with a list. I hated being her assistant. I really detested the way she treated me, as if she owned me. I bought her groceries and alcohol; and transferred them into her car, while she watched. I carried her shopping and bags and parked her car in the middle of the busy downtown and court area—just so she didn't have to walk. I waited for her at the spa, hair appointments, and while she shopped for clothes; I found myself bringing a book, since I felt bored with nothing much to do. I really didn't find myself useful or deserving of the salary I was making. I hoped I could go back to my original job.

While grabbing her beach necessities, which included suntan lotions and beach towels, I was thinking about the odds of Aiden, Adrianna, Jason and Katie leaving the same day. Was it a coincidence? I wanted to speak to Aiden, but he was so pressed with meetings, he simply replied by saying that he was going to call me back when he had time. When I finally came back to the office, I discovered Christine had had an emergency and had to go home, so I got Adrianna's permission to cover for her.

I went quickly through my computer's history; out of curiosity, I wanted to check the name of the resort Adrianna was going to, since it had already slipped my mind. My heart raced when I saw "Royal Cancun." That was strange. Were they all going together? With that disturbing possibility, I couldn't concentrate for the rest of the day. I was lost, and Aiden's lack of reply was causing me some agony. I even called Mandy and Jasmine to ask casually which resort Aiden was going to. Mandy said it was either "The Regal Cancun" or "Royal Cancun." She wasn't sure, and my sister hadn't really been paying attention to the name. During the last two hours of my shift, I was constantly on the phone with other clients. Aiden called me a couple of times during that time when I didn't answer. I was finally out of the office. I could finally call Aiden, and when I did, he didn't pick up. I felt frustrated, so I wanted to place the phone angrily in my purse. Instead, it landed on the ground. My heart plunged. *Crap!* That was a big drop. I picked it up only to realize that the phone stopped working. I wanted to scream in agony. How was I supposed to call Aiden?

I took the phone straight to a cell-phone repair store. I waited for over an hour to hear that the phone should be ready by the next day. I came back home feeling distressed after bringing Nora home. I didn't even feel like having dinner or chatting with Jasim, especially after calling Aiden from Jasim's phone with no reply. This time, I left him a message explaining what had happened to my phone and asked him to call me at Jasim's phone instead. The night passed without a word from Aiden. My skepticisms were weighing me down. Was he playing me? I really hoped he was different from all the men who had come into my life. I couldn't bear another disappointment.

The next day, I brought Nora along with me after coming back from work to pick up my cell phone. After paying the huge bill, I turned the phone on and checked to see if there were any text messages from Aiden, since he never left any voice messages. There was one, and it said, "Hannah! I hate playing phone tag. Sorry I was so busy today. I will be leaving early tomorrow morning. I will try to call you after I land. Will be missing you … Aiden."

I couldn't feel happy even after the message. I was still doubtful.

I was making some dinner, which consisted of frozen chicken breast, salad, and mashed potatoes for both Nora and Jasim when I got a call from Aiden. I couldn't pick up the phone fast enough. It was from his cell.

"Hi, Hannah! Finally, we talk," he said. His voice wasn't very clear. I could tell that the reception was awful.

"Hi, my phone fell and broke yesterday. I had to repair it." I just couldn't help it, and I heard myself posing this question, "What is the name of that resort you are staying at?"

There was a long silence. He said, "Why?"

I wasn't going to tell him about my suspicions.

"I don't know. I want to look it up. I want to know where you are staying." I loathed the way my trembling voice revealed my suspicion.

He said something I couldn't hear. I was getting too frustrated.

"I can't hear you, Aiden. Say that again."

He said something again, and then the phone went dead.

I was about to shed tears at the disturbance that I felt. I spent the next half an hour dropping the salad on the floor and burning the potatoes. I was a mess, and I couldn't do anything right.

The phone rang again; it was Aiden.

"I can hear you now, much better." I tried to sound cheerful. What if he was innocent?

"What were you saying, Hannah?"

I repeated my last question.

He said abruptly, "It's called Sandaqua."

I frowned, since I remembered what I had heard during our brunch.

"Sandaqua?" I repeated; that didn't make sense. There was a long silence.

"Yes, Sandaqua." There was an awkward calmness in his voice. "George did the booking. I forgot the resort's name." I pressed my lips together hard and stared at the void I was looking at. I wanted to make sense out of it.

"How many people does your group consist of?" I didn't care if I sounded like an annoying girlfriend.

"A few, mostly families. When I come back, I want to take you to see Mother. I was speaking of you to her last night, since she is back from Spain now."

I swallowed my suspicion, hoping to digest it somehow. Maybe there was nothing to worry about; it was probably all in my head. Since I was constantly comparing him to Yusuf, I should just stop.

"That sounds good. I can't wait." I knew that my cheerful tone sounded fake. "I will let you go. You are on a vacation, and I have hungry people to feed."

"Okay, babe, I will be in touch." Yusuf's voice and tone passed through my head, he used to call me babe too, when he happened to be in a good mood.

"Yes, we will." My tone was cold. I just couldn't help it.

"Hannah, I will miss you."

"I'll miss you too, bye." I hung up soon after, not waiting for him to hang up first as I usually did. I didn't know why, but I started to cry out of nowhere. I felt self-pity. I hated feeling that way. I sensed that he was hiding something, recalling Yusuf's many talents in lying and deceiving.

Later on that night, I breathed out in relief after looking up and finding the Sandaqua resort. I was afraid to find that Sandaqua didn't exist. It was a few hours away from Royal Cancun and as exquisite. I lay down next to Nora, under the fake stars. Maybe I should just get rid of all my awful conjectures. I loved how his arms felt around me; the way he looked at me with his sexy, dreamy eyes; and his lips when he kissed me. Why would someone like Aiden want to lie to me when he could have any girl he wanted with only a single wish? And yet, he wanted to be with someone like me, who was shattered by her destiny. I decided to try my best to hide my suspicions caused by my past. I should also stop focusing on his faults, comparing them to Yusuf's, because I just realized that ... I really loved him.

***

I tried to occupy myself for the rest of the week. I joined a gym. I cleaned constantly. I even tried a couple of new dishes, which weren't a complete disaster, since Mother had been working long hours lately. We all finished the overbaked dry roast and mushy lasagna that I made. I was thankful Jasim didn't even complain.

Thinking was driving me insane, so I tried to kick my brain cells on a temporary holiday and concentrated instead on getting perfect abs and strong legs by exercising extra hard. Mandy joined too, since we were able to place the girls with some babysitting services provided by the gym.

***

Back at the office after the weekend, Christine was still off since her grandfather had passed away. Mary even bought me a latte from across the street. I thanked her and said politely, "You shouldn't have, Mary. Let me at least pay for it."

"Don't mention it."

"Thank you," I said, sipping the delicious latte. I really wondered what exactly Mary did around the office; that was something we never talked about.

I heard her say, "If Adrianna asks how the party at my place was, tell her that you were going to come but your daughter was sick."

I frowned. That was strange.

"What party?" I scowled.

"There was a party. Adrianna wanted me to host it since she is out of town." I was hurt and couldn't hide my frowns. I thought Mary liked me. She was my only friend around the office. Why didn't she want me to be at her party? I wouldn't have come, but it was nice to be invited. She sighed. "Hannah, that party wasn't suitable for you, tons of drinking and people usually act weird after."

I frowned. Was she hiding something from Adrianna? She added, "A little advice, only between us; if you ever get invited to parties around here, only go with your boyfriend … if you have one." I wondered if that was her way of finding out if I had a boyfriend.

But I said instead, because I couldn't hide my suspicion, "That sounds odd, Mary. I mean, I thought that people around here are professionals and really take care of their images."

"They do; trust me. Just worry about yourself and your image."

What was she implying? Maybe I should discuss this with Mandy. She had more experience when it came to parties, and images. I faltered for a bit, and then I said, "Well, I can always tell Adrianna that I only go to parties with my boyfriend and that he was out of town. I hate lying."

She stared at me for a few seconds, as if she was thinking intently. "It's up to you." She glanced at me a couple of times and added, "So you do have a boyfriend? You never mentioned him before."

I had to decide quickly whether to tell her about Aiden, who was a client at the firm, or not. I recalled her warning about Jason. At that moment, I got worried. What if she added more speculations to my mind about Aiden? I was already dealing with tons of my own doubts, which I was constantly trying to dismiss. I said, "Yes, because we started dating not too long ago."

"Where did you meet him?" She was looking for my gaze.

I answered quickly, "At a nightclub," which wasn't a lie.

"Oh, so he is not a client or part of this firm?" Her eyes narrowed skeptically.

"No, he is not." I wondered about this interrogation. I looked away, and then I turned to her after a long minute. I said in a heated tone, "There is something strange about Adrianna. I mean, why make me her assistant when she still has one? I feel as if I'm her servant or bodyguard or something. That wasn't the job I signed up for."

"Hannah, I really don't know what to tell you." She looked away; she seemed baffled too.

I didn't see Mary for the rest of the day. When I picked up Nora from Mandy's, I mentioned my conversation with Mary. She was puzzled by the weird, erratic personalities around the office, and she advised me only to go to parties with Aiden. Just like me, she sensed that something was really sketchy, especially after I told her about all Mary's warnings in the past. I really should start looking for another job soon, I decided.

***

Jason called the office on Tuesday morning from his house phone. That was strange. I was the one who booked the tickets; he shouldn't have been back yet. But I was reluctant to ask even Mary; a lot of things were not making sense around me anyway.

Aiden should have been back already. I found myself glancing at my phone periodically. I was still waiting to hear from him. It was

Wednesday afternoon. Adrianna was back from her vacation. I was even booking her next appointments. Christine was also back and claimed her full-time hours; the part-time intern, Madison was also around. I hated when I found myself with nothing much to do. I would much rather be productive.

I got a massage on my cell. I hurried to check it. I gasped, since it was from Aiden. It said, "Hey, babe. I just wanted to let you know that I'm still at the resort, and I miss you."

I frowned. "But you said that your vacation was only for one week!"

"George delayed it for another week."

"Damn you, George." I cursed under my breath.

"When are you coming back now?"

"The middle of next week, I will call you sometime. I miss hearing your voice."

"I miss you too. Call me after my work." I hesitated for a few seconds, and then I texted, "Did I mention that Adrianna went to Cancun too, same day as you did? … What a coincidence, huh?" I needed to kick some of my suspicions off my head—just so I could sleep at night.

"Really?"

"Yes, a place called Royal Cancun."

He ignored the message and replied with, "Hannah, I want you to take care of yourself. For me."

That was unusual and out of the blue. "Sure."

"Good. When I come back, I will try to cut my travels and keep them only during the weekdays."

"Okay." That was a relief. He then went back to the resort subject.

"The resort Mandy booked is amazing … You are going to love it."

I couldn't even smile. "Can't wait. I am already working on my abs …" We texted for a while; then he said that he had to go. I was feeling much better. Adrianna couldn't have been with him; otherwise, she would've delayed her stay too, since she didn't have any court dates or important appointments coming up. Later on that day, Aiden called me from a strange number stating that he didn't have good cell reception. I looked up the number's area code right away. When I found out that it was a number from Mexico, I breathed freely …

On Thursday, I saw Adrianna coming in. She was on her cell phone as usual. I noticed that she already looked stressed, just like she had the day she took off for the resort. The only difference was she was a few shades darker. A few minutes later, I picked up a call from her, but I was startled by her calm voice. She wanted me to join her and Mary for a coffee across the street. I wondered why she was not inviting her other assistant too. My new job when she was around was to only cater to her needs—and a lot of times listen to her talk on the phone about work, her spoiled life, and her ex who was still friends with her. He was apparently on a mission to get her back, at any cost. I didn't want to think of how degraded I felt when I was around her. It just made me want to quit my job immediately—but that was something I couldn't afford to do at that moment. After tucking myself in my warm jacket, I walked across the street and waited for them.

After ordering light sandwiches and lattes, we sat in a comfortable booth. Adrianna had her sunglasses on. I guessed maybe because the windows were open, inviting some sun in. I sipped some latte, waiting to see what the meeting was all about. Adrianna started with her talk, referring to a few issues with some mix-ups of clients' appointments. We needed to address them with both Christine and Madison. But soon, Adrianna shifted the conversation to her vacation. Mary seemed to be listening with interest, which was odd. I realized that there was something up with her. I watched her intently. Was she pretending to be interested?

As Adrianna described the beautiful resort and the exquisite service, my heart sank, recalling Aiden's vacation, which happened at the same time. I dismissed it. I couldn't believe how skeptical I was about Adrianna joining Aiden on his vacation. I really needed to learn to trust again. My vacation was coming up soon. Maybe I should concentrate on that, instead of letting my mind travel those erratic, rough, scary roads. Adrianna shifted to designer clothes and jewelry. I heard her say to Mary, while looking at her Da Vinci watch.

"I didn't pay for it; it was a gift from my boyfriend." She sighed. "Before we broke up." I tried not to frown. Having grown up poor, I was not familiar with designer jewelry, clothes, or shoes. I could merely distinguish expensive from cheap. I recognized very few designer names. I noticed the Louis Vuitton handbags Adrianna and Mary had in their hands only because Mandy had one. I recalled Adrianna's many phone conversations, when I had no choice but to listen to her; I felt irritated all of a sudden.

"Lucky you!" Mary exclaimed.

Adrianna said defensively, "Not that I can't afford some twenty-thousand-dollar watch myself."

What? Twenty-thousand-dollar watch! That was insane! I wouldn't have guessed that. I was careful not to roll my eyes at her indulgence. She got a call, excused herself, and got up from her seat. She began walking toward the front door to speak privately outside. I glanced around. Mary was being quiet all of a sudden.

I asked her, "What is this meeting all about?" I didn't know why I wanted to leave immediately. I felt my chest tighten.

"There was some mix-up with some appointments."

I tried not to frown. Was that even real? What happened to Mary all of a sudden? She avoided my gaze by checking her phone.

I said irritably, "If Adrianna's watch is worth over twenty thousand dollars, how much is her jewelry worth, you think?" I didn't know why I asked that, as if I need to feel more anguish.

"More than her watch, obviously. She only wears designer jewelry. Don't forget she is loaded." She narrowed her gaze adding, "Why?"

"Just a question." I sipped more latte. I could only nibble on a couple of bites of my sandwich—I had no appetite. "Most of her jewelry pieces are gifts, I suppose."

I was jealous of an eerie possibility. I dismissed it. That couldn't be.

Mary gave me the sign to stay silent, looking around her. Adrianna wasn't around us. Why should we worry? I felt a sudden nuisance.

"Let's not forget what the meeting is all about, Hannah, and you need to really address those issues with Christine when you go back to the office. We are a big practice, and our clients are very vital to our firm."

Mary then excused herself to go to the office. Right before we parted, after giving me a list of things to do for the rest of the afternoon, Adrianna turned to me as if she remembered something.

She asked, "How was the party?"

I froze, recalling May's warning. I placed my sunglasses on and said quickly, "Mary asked me to come, but my daughter had a fever, so I had to cancel." I turned away; I really didn't wish to be in the middle of this mess.

"Wait!" She called out. I turned to face her again. "I am hosting this party at my place this Friday. You should come. I could use some help with hosting."

I tried not to show the discomfort that I felt. I stammered, "I-I, um, I don't like to go to parties without my boyfriend. I know he won't like me going without him." I hoped she left me alone. She was silent for a moment.

"You may come with your boyfriend then."

I felt stunned, if only Aiden wasn't out of town in a beautiful resort.

I decided quickly not to volunteer any more information about Aiden being out of town. "I will try to come. If I can secure a babysitter for my daughter, I can however help you with all the preparty setup." I wanted to conclude this weird conversation graciously. I smiled at her and said good-bye.

I was relieved when I went back to my desk. I felt really uneasy with her and even Mary, whom I really liked. Then I recalled the clients' appointment issue, so I addressed those issues with both Christine and Madison. I hoped to see Mary alone soon, just so I could speak to her in private.

Right before I left for the day, I got a text from a blocked sender, it said, "Don't wait and try and solve your questionable perplexing surroundings. At that point, you may just want to pack up and leave before it's too late."

I frowned. I had never received a message from a blocked sender before, and that message sounded odd. Who could it be from, or was it just a random message sent around?

***

Aiden looked so dark and striking when I saw him after his holiday, and at the sight of him, all my skepticism evaporated. There had to be some sort of explanation. There *had* to be!

We spent the next few days going to dinners and movies. He even took me to his home to meet his mother, as he had promised. I learned from him that she constantly traveled between Canada and Spain, which was her home country. I was very nervous about the meeting. What if she didn't like me? She could find me unsuitable for her educated, handsome rich son. I even asked Jasmine about her experience with meeting her mother-in-law for the first time, and her tips were helpful. I dressed with care, trying to look as classy as I could. After all, the first impression was the most important one. The meeting was on a cold, snowy day. I wore crisp black pants, a half-sleeve flowing white blouse, and black shiny boots. My hair was styled in a long, wavy simple hairstyle. I wore a minimum amount of makeup, looking as usual much younger than my twenty-five years of age. Jasmine told me that I shouldn't look as if I were trying so hard to impress. I should still look like myself. I was putting on my long, black classy coat when Aiden called me to inform me that he was waiting for me outside.

I must have looked really nervous in the car because he said, "Relax! Mother is going to love you."

I took a deep breath. I really wanted to believe him. During the car ride, I recalled Mary. What had happened to her? She hadn't shown up since we had the coffee meeting with Adrianna. She never even answered my calls or replied to my messages, as if she had disappeared suddenly. And when I asked around the office, I was told by both Adrianna and Christine that Mary moved out of town. I was hurt; Mary didn't even say goodbye before she left. The odd message that was sent to me that day, was it from her? Was that another warning? Lately, I started to look for another job and even went for a couple of interviews, but unfortunately, those two jobs offered less than my current salary. I really didn't wish to climb down the ladder. Well, I was not desperate for a job yet; plus, I heard that if I worked for two years at a big firm, I would have a good chance of landing a job with better pay in the future.

Aiden parked right outside a massive house, which sat on a vast snow-covered land. I wondered how beautiful the garden would look in the spring. I sat in the car, just gaping at it. I was afraid to get out. I felt really self-conscious, especially after driving through a majestic, long, wrought-iron gated entrance. He got out of the car and turned to open my passenger door. Gently, he reached for my frozen hand to help me out of the car. I felt lost and disoriented.

"Relax," he whispered into my ear. He could tell that I was still a wreck, I guessed.

I carefully stepped onto the stone driveway and walked with him, hand in hand. He opened the grand front entrance door. After walking down the large well-lit up and furnished open hallway, I found myself standing in a large, spacious, high-ceilinged living room. The colors of the furniture were warm and subtle. A couple of large, beige couches sat around the magnificent fireplace, and a large wood coffee table stood on a Persian rug. I looked away from the fancy paintings, and the two curved stairways. At that moment, my throat felt dry.

He said, "Make yourself comfortable. I will call Mother." He then disappeared. How could I be comfortable when I couldn't even breathe thoroughly? I felt as if I were in the middle of a luxury home show. That wasn't me. I sat on the edge of one of the couches feeling utterly anxious. I heard a few steps. I got up to greet a medium-height, fair-complexioned, classy-looking woman. She smiled widely at my nervous smile. Aiden introduced us.

"Mother, this is Hannah. Hannah, Mother Elaina."

With my quivering hand, I reached to shake hers, but to my surprise, she placed her arms around me and hugged me lightly. I placed my arms around her awkwardly.

She said sincerely, "Nice to meet you, Hannah. You are so lovely."

I sighed, looking at her. "Nice to meet you too. Now I know where Aiden got his good looks from."

"Oh, you are so sweet. Aiden looks like both his father and I, my dear. He's a good man like my dear husband, Neil."

I breathed lightly, smiling. I felt a little more at ease.

"You have a lovely home," I said, following her toward a smaller sunroom. The wall of windows led to a yard that was covered with snow. She thanked me with a warm smile. The furniture's vivid colors added to the brightness of the room. Despite the simple elegance that surrounded me, the room had a hint of humbleness. I was glad she led me to this room. On the round glass table, I noticed a teapot and colorful minicakes on a square crystal glass tray. I sat across from her. Aiden sat on a chair, keeping the same distance between the two of us.

"Hannah, Aiden told me so much about you already, but I don't mind hearing again."

At first, I hesitated, but her bright smile reminded me of Aiden's smile, which put me at ease. I found myself politely speaking about myself. I was thankful she didn't ask many questions about my past. I tried to focus on my present. I was hoping she didn't find me way out of her son's league. Later on, during our conversation, Elaina spoke of Aiden's father, whom she met in Spain. Her eyes filled with tears at his memory; she spoke of his kindness and his looks, and she also spoke of Spain …

The sweets we had were tasty. Elaina enjoyed her baking and gardening. She reminded me of my mother. I bet they could get along one day. I sighed at that beautiful fantasy. Aiden was quiet most of the time. He was always being interrupted by his business phone calls, which caused him to leave the room periodically.

"A woman must understand and be patient with her man. Some men like Aiden and his father don't like to be controlled or told what to do."

I was careful not to frown. I wondered what she meant by that. I said tactfully, "Some men can be very controlling … dominating without any reasoning." My heart raced; at that moment, I recalled Yusuf, and my fears from Aiden's ways of trying to control me.

She stared at me for a moment. After sipping from her tea, she said, "Not my Aiden. He is fair and kind ... but occasionally ill-tempered. After all, he's got some hot Mediterranean blood in him."

I giggled lightly. I recalled Aiden's blood mixture—Spanish, Greek, and Lebanese.

She asked, "Tell me; what is your ideal relationship between a man and woman?"

My eyes widened. I could tell her what my worst idea of a relationship was. I had to think about the answer while I took a deep breath. "I think a good relationship is a fair compromise and a good balance between a man and a woman. Each should understand that perfection doesn't exist and try to make the best out of their lives, which are always going to be full of ups and downs." I glanced at her. She was smiling. "They both should be able to complete each other."

She sighed. "I am glad Aiden brought you here, my dear. I can see why he is fond of you."

I gasped and swallowed a happy sob. "I'm glad Aiden brought me. I really feel special."

"That's because you are special." Then I heard Aiden entering the room again.

He said hurriedly, "Mother, I have to go to the office soon. I have an urgent meeting."

Elaina smiled and said, "Sure." I got up right away; she stood up too. I hugged her lightly. She even kissed my warm cheek. I knew she wasn't faking her fondness of me.

Once in the car, Aiden said, "Mother likes you. I can tell."

I smiled and said, "I like her too." I wondered how many women he had brought to meet his mother before me.

As if he were reading my mind, he said, "Mother doesn't usually meet the girls I date, unless they are family friends." My heart skipped.

"How about your ex-fiancée?" He glanced at me.

After a long silence, he replied, "She met her, of course."

"What happened between you two? Why did you break up?" I remembered when he flouted this same question the last time I asked him.

He glanced at me blankly. "It's a long story. We were both young, in Law school, and maybe she wasn't ready to commit."

She wasn't ready to commit with him? I found that absurd. Was she out of her mind? "I bet she is stunning."

He looked away and said, "Not as stunning as you are."

My lips curled into a smile. I knew he was being overly charming. "Did you love her?" He looked really annoyed. I breathed deeply before asking the rest of the question. "Maybe that's why you've never had a steady girlfriend since her."

"Working in a law firm is causing you to ask questions like a lawyer," he said, obviously irritated. His hands were tight around the steering wheel.

I frowned. "You don't have to answer that question."

He ran his long fingers through his hair nervously. "I did love her. It was a long time ago, and I don't want to speak of her right now."

I could tell he was keeping his composed tone from shaking. Was he still in love with her? My heart was racing rapidly. I felt confused. It would be best if I didn't ask any more questions, I decided. He said calmly, "I don't want to bring up some memory I already buried. One day, I promise to open up and tell you everything."

His lips curved into a faint smile. I turned to look in front of me, feeling lost.

Chapter Twenty-One

THE WEATHER WAS COLD. SNOW was still on the ground, even though we were approaching the end of winter. I was only a couple of weeks away from my holiday with Aiden. Mother's birthday was on Saturday. Jasmine had decided to have a surprise birthday party for her. She was going to have it at her house. We were going to invite Mother's friends and a few people that we knew. Jasmine invited Mandy and John. I hesitated but decided to invite Aiden, who was in town every weekend as he promised. After all, he was my boyfriend, and then I decided to try to explain to him about my strict family custom during our phone conversation on Tuesday night.

"There is something you need to know about my mother."

"Sure, babe."

"My mother is a lovely woman and kind, but she is old-fashioned."

He said evenly, "I see."

I cleared my throat. "She, um, she even made a fuss about Nathan at first, but she loves him dearly, you know, because of the different culture and all." He was silent. "When I introduce you to Mother, I can't present you as my boyfriend." I held on to my breath.

His tone was low and tense. "I see."

I added, "Mother only met Nathan when he proposed to Jasmine." I didn't know what I was saying. His lack of interaction during this awkward conversation was not making it any easier.

After a long, awkward silence, he said, "Now I am afraid to meet your mother. Would she make a scene if she found out that you are only my girlfriend?" I was silent, but he added, "I'm teasing you. I have a couple of old-fashioned Middle-Eastern friends. My father once was strict too." My heart sank. Maybe I wasn't fiancée material, just like his ex, whom he probably still loved and refused to speak of. Well, I couldn't complain much because I avoided speaking of Yusuf too. "I can be Nathan's friend; would that work for your lovely mother?"

I had to clear my throat and swallow my disappointment before I answered. "That would work, and thanks for understanding."

"When the party ends, you go back to being my girl, right?"

His temporary girl? I dismissed that awful assumption too.

"Right," I mumbled. There were several seconds of stillness.

"What do you do when I'm out of town?"

I sighed. My life was boring, and it merely got exciting when he was around, lately only on the weekend, but I wasn't going to tell him that.

"I meet my friends … Sometimes we go out." I hesitated. "You never asked me to meet your friends." During his second date, Nathan introduced Jasmine to couple of his friends. All of a sudden, I felt unworthy.

"I don't have a lot of friends here, business associates mostly, and trust me, when I'm in town, I work constantly." I was silent. "I only have fun when I'm with you."

I remembered the office's memo, an invite to the firm's staff cocktail party this coming Friday. Adrianna had mentioned to me that my boyfriend is welcome to join. "My firm is hosting this cocktail party, and you're welcome to come." I hoped he came. Jason was out of town, and seeing Aiden and Adrianna in one place, I could read their body language; maybe then my crazy speculation would evaporate.

He was awkwardly silent at first and then said, "When?"

"This Friday. We can make it since you are coming back on Thursday morning."

"I was going to ask you if you wanted to join me and Mother for dinner; we are going to a Mexican restaurant." My heart sank. "You can bring Nora."

"I will send an email saying I can't come."

He sighed. His tone was cold when he asked, "Did you get invited before or since we started dating?"

My heart raced. Why did he want to know?

"Adrianna invited me to a party to help her host it, I suppose." It was another awkward silence. "She then also suggested you come along too. She didn't know you were on a vacation; it doesn't matter anyway. I didn't end up going." I didn't know why I felt as if I had to explain myself.

"It's odd for someone like Adrianna to want to invite her staff to a party." Was he referring to the social gap between me and her? I was quiet, feeling a squeeze in my chest.

I tried to keep a cool tone when I said, "Aiden, don't forget that I'm her assistant now."

"Hannah, don't take this the wrong way! I mean, even Jasim mentioned how she used to be despicable to you at first, and I still can't grasp that idea."

She is still despicable, I thought. After another few seconds of silence, I wanted to feel happy that he cared, but I couldn't. Our conversation continued for a few more minutes, during which I tried to fake a cheerful tone.

***

Saturday morning, I went to my sister's along with Nora to help her decorate. Aiden, Jasim, Mandy, and the rest of the guests were coming later. I felt nervous about the meeting between Mother and Aiden. Jasmine ordered takeout dinner from a Lebanese restaurant. We couldn't expect Mother to cook on her birthday too. My uncle's family was out of town on a trip.

Guests started to arrive. As soon as I saw Aiden, I realized how much I'd missed him, despite the fact that I had become skeptical about the whole relationship idea and everything around me. He was some sort of craving I had developed. What was going on with me? Why was I slowly becoming this obedient, hassle-free woman? I was a prisoner of his love. Aiden didn't need to force it on me. I liberally built that invisible wall around me. Was he honest with me? Was he a loyal boyfriend? I wanted to believe so. Around him, I became powerless and could only think of one thing: how to keep him happy and in my life.

Soon, everyone was there except for Mother and the twins, who were being driven by Hady. While we were waiting for her to arrive, I grabbed Aiden by the hand and led him to Jasmine's large dining room. I then went on my tiptoes, grabbed his face, and kissed him passionately, since I knew that I couldn't do that in front of anyone around. We got carried away for a few seconds. He stopped it abruptly.

"Are you out of your mind? Your mother will kick my ass!"

I blushed. I was acting irrationally. I was thankful that one of us was still wise. When I was leaving the room, he grabbed me for another embrace. He then growled, "Next time, don't start something you can't finish. You know how long it's been?"

I grinned as I recalled the last time we had had a few minutes of quick pleasure in his car.

"Lately, you have become this gentleman," I teased him. Ever since he came back from his vacation, we didn't get to spend time alone. Nora came with us to most of our dinners, and when Aiden was at my place, he spent time sometimes with Jasim watching sports on TV.

"I just realized that the gentleman role doesn't suit me." He sighed. "I didn't want you to think that sex was the only reason I wanted to be with you." *Impressive!* He had been restraining himself lately.

I said naughtily, "Too bad, I was starting to enjoy the new role you were playing."

I drew myself closer to his lean body.

I heard him say breathlessly, "Do you think your sister will lend us one of her rooms upstairs, before your Mother arrives?" I frowned at him. "I am kidding. I can wait."

Could he really wait? I wondered how he would act on his temptation when he was alone thousands of miles away from me. Would he resist, or would he find a random girl who could momentarily satisfy his needs and desires?

My sister called us. Apparently, Mother was arriving in just a few minutes. We had to hide around her big open-concept living room and kitchen. She turned the light off. Nora was next to me. She was talking nonstop. I had to close her mouth with my hand. And that still didn't work; in the dark, I could merely hear Nora's and Tiffany's giggles. Mother switched the lights on. We all screamed, "Surprise!"

She had a stunned look on her face. It took Mother at least ten minutes to recuperate from her shock. I was very proud of how Mother looked; she had on full makeup, and her hair looked professionally styled. She wore a knee-length burgundy, short-sleeve dress. She knew she was coming to a dinner party, not realizing until then that it was her own birthday party. She then started to greet guests. When she finally got to Aiden, she scrutinized him for a bit longer. But then she smiled politely and turned away. That was when I relaxed.

Aiden was chatting to my brothers, Nathan, and other guests; he seemed to be enjoying himself. I watched him from afar, simply wishing that one day, he would belong to my family. I was thankful my sister listened to me and only invited Travis and not Henry. Henry and Aiden in the same room again would've been a horrific scene.

A few hours later, the party concluded. Mandy insisted on taking Nora with her. Aiden was still around when she left.

I made a quick decision. I missed Aiden, but there was something other than yearning. I was afraid to lose him, so afraid I wanted to give him what he wanted from me—well, what he wanted was want I wanted anyway. I was at the same time wondering if I could be ovulating. I hoped not. A couple of days ago, I couldn't find the birth control pills that I had started taking soon after my first date with Aiden.

I texted him right after saying, "I just remembered something. You never finished the story you started, about Prince Aiden."

His reply came quickly. "I was thinking the same thing."

"You can finish the story tonight, if you want."

"I can't; the story won't end tonight. I can only tell you the next chapter."

"Next chapter it is." I smiled. "But first you have to bring something with you, from the drugstore."

"What?"

I thought he was smarter than this. I blushed when I wrote, "Protection." I just couldn't write the word *condom*.

"I'll see you soon."

A few minutes later, I helped Jasmine clean quickly. Aiden said to call him when I was on my way.

When I got home, I heard a light knock on the door. It was Aiden! I jumped on him as soon as he walked in. My legs were around his strong hips and my arms around his neck, and his lips were on mine instantly—and that was how he carried me to my enchanted bedroom.

***

In the morning, I stretched in bed. I blushed as I recalled the night before. It was sensational. Love … I had never guessed that this type of love existed until I met Aiden. A few times last night, I wanted to scream that I loved him during our lovemaking, but I couldn't. What if he didn't feel that way toward me? I would then feel let down, maybe even destroyed.

I sighed. Aiden had forgotten to stop by the drugstore. I wanted our night to be memorable but not too memorable. But then again, having Aiden's baby wouldn't be such a bad thing, but what if he refused to marry me after?

I got up to use the washroom and found an envelope by my lamp dresser; it had a gift card to one of the nearby shopping malls. I was stunned when I saw the amount of two thousand dollars. That was insane! I couldn't take his money yet, knowing that with his wealth, he could make that much money in no time. I was about to call him and tell him that when my phone rang. Could it be him? My heart pounded as soon as the voice on the receiver said hello back to me. I started shaking. Could it be? No, it couldn't be.

"Is this Ms. Hannah Shaheen?" His voice was familiar.

All of a sudden, I recalled the deadly accident. *Yusuf is dead! He is dead!*

I said tentatively, "Who is this?"

"I am calling you with a great offer."

I glanced again at the number display on my cell phone. It was a blocked number.

"Are you a telemarketer?"

He was silent for a few seconds. "Yes, ma'am." His tone was similar too! A lady telemarketer had called my cell a few days earlier but from a toll-free number. My heart was about to jump out of my chest. Yusuf's image landed in my brain. This time, I couldn't dismiss it. I closed my eyes. "Maybe I can call some other time."

"Wait!" I yelled out. It was too late; he had already hung up.

The police recommended that I didn't see Yusuf's corpse. But I had insisted and then wished that I didn't. Nightmares of that day shattered my nights for at least a year after. Yusuf was dead. Why was I all of the sudden alarmed? Voices could be similar. When I used to live with Jasmine at Mother's house, people used to confuse me with Jasmine, because I sounded just like her on the phone. I breathed out. I would have to stop feeling skeptical, if I ever wanted to live in peace for once.

Chapter Twenty-Two

The sun broke through the wall of windows. I opened my eyes to the sight of the beach. I leaped up and ran to the balcony. I breathed the salty air in deeply. *Finally next to the beach,* I thought ecstatically. Palm trees were expertly laid out around, with gardens, flowers, and exotic plants. I glanced further down to where the shimmering sunlight caused the sand to sparkle. I moved my sight even further to where the sand touched the majestic, never-ending deep blue sea, the white foam from the waves caressing the wet sand. I closed my eyes and shivers traveled around my body. I couldn't wait until the cool, salty water touched my skin. I went back to the room where Nora was still sleeping. Aiden settled in the next room. All night I was thinking about walking in on him while he was sleeping and surprising him with steamy midnight sex. But I knew I couldn't. What if Nora woke up? I felt energetic and full of life. I recalled my argument with Aiden over the two-thousand-dollar gift card he gave me. He was really angry when I said I wasn't going to touch the money. A couple of hours later, I called him back, but he was still angry. I thanked him sincerely, saying that I was going to buy the whole mall. Since he was going out of town the next day, I didn't want him to leave while still annoyed with me. I just noticed that lately I cared how a man perceived me, but this time around, it was out of love and not out of fear. That day, I bought a couple of nice two-piece bikinis for me and Nora, and then we went on a shopping spree and bought all we wished to buy and couldn't since we were always on a small budget.

I ran to the dresser. I had already unpacked the night before, since I barely slept knowing that Aiden was merely a few feet away and I couldn't have him. I found the two bikinis; one was baby blue, and the other one was black and white. I hesitated before I chose the baby-blue one. I got ready quickly in the second bathroom. I dawdled before I knocked on Aiden's door. He didn't answer, so I entered his room slowly. I felt a tight knot in my stomach when I saw his bare back. He slept on his stomach. I came closer. His big dark eyes were closed, and his lips were semiopen. His strong jaw seemed relaxed. I gently shook his arm. He turned. His hair was messy. I had never seen his hair messy before since the only time he had slept over, he woke before me and left me the gift card before he took off. He looked gorgeous even with spiky, chaotic hair. I sat closer to him. He yawned.

"I like your hair like that. I think it suits you better." He looked at me with sleepy eyes. "How can you sleep through this beauty?"

"I can. It's too early still." I then recalled that he had been on a vacation not too long ago. He yawned and sat on the bed half asleep.

"You never showed me pictures of your last trip."

"I didn't take any pictures; with you, however, I will take pictures."

I smiled, reached to him, and hugged him. He was very sweet. His lips were on my cheek, and then he kissed my lips. I sighed right away. I hadn't kissed him passionately since the night he spent at my place. He pulled back.

"Nora—she could come in at any moment."

I pulled back; he was right. I walked around his room. It was as spacious as ours. It had walls of windows and opened to a beautiful balcony, overlooking the breathtaking scenery. "Are we going to be leaving soon? I just can't wait." I knew I sounded childish.

"Soon. Let me take a shower first." He then got up, wearing brown boxers. I looked away. I could tell that he was in the mood for something naughty. I really didn't feel like getting in trouble this morning.

I said breathlessly, "I will wait for you outside."

His tone was playful. "Unless you want to help me undress … then help me shower. There is an area I can't reach."

Seriously! I had to catch my breath.

"Aiden, I don't want to get in trouble, and you are pushing my naughty buttons one at a time. I am waiting for you outside." I could hear his laugh right before I closed the door. *What a man!* I thought dreamily …

Nora awoke as soon as I walked into our room. She leaped out of bed and ran to the balcony to look at the beach. I got her ready right away.

After a quick breakfast, we all walked to the beach. Mandy, John, Tiffany, and Nora were in their swimsuits, running toward the warm water. *Nora is in good hands,* I decided. I watched as the waves slapped the sand gently. A large, vast sea lay behind. I almost forgot the soothing sound of the waves, while the gentle breeze played softly with my hair. I breathed in, filling my lungs with salty air. I glanced at Aiden. He looked sexy already with his green swim trunks. His flat chest was still bronze from the last vacation he took. All of a sudden, I felt jealous. Two weeks with George, a flirt, in a beautiful place like this, where many women either walked around half naked or even topless. How could he not get tempted? I shook my head. I should stop agonizing again.

I hesitated at first, but I slowly took my white sundress off, knowing in advance that I looked a bit too revealing. Endless hours at the gym had given me some amazing results. I could feel Aiden's gaze on me. He didn't move an inch. He was also too silent at first, but then he said hesitantly, "Do you … um … have you seen yourself in the mirror?"

I looked at him. "Yes, why?"

"And you are okay with this?" That sounded more like a statement than a question. I glanced at him; he furrowed his brows.

I said stammering, "Y-you are not okay with it?"

"No, I am not. It's up to you, though. I won't force you." He snapped. That was the first time I realized that Aiden had a snappy side to him. I recalled his mother's words. "He is fair and gentle … occasionally ill-tempered."

Did I want to submit to Aiden's oppressing ways? At that moment, Yusuf landed on my head; lately, I had even been having nightmares about him, ever since that telemarketer had called me about an offer. I had even seen his ghost on couple of men's faces. I really hoped I wasn't going crazy. I took a deep breath and glanced quickly at my revealing suit, realizing how pathetic I looked. I put my sundress back on.

I said in a shaky voice, "I will change. I will go now." I grabbed the magnetic key from my beach purse and was on my way when I noticed that Aiden was walking beside me.

He said abruptly, "I'll come with you. I don't want you to get lost."

I was silent. His tone was clipped. I wondered if he came to fight with me, the way Yusuf did every time he believed that I had done something foolish. My heart started to pound. I recalled when I bought the two bikinis. One was a little too flashy, and one was more modest. Aiden was certainly an open-minded man—or so I had assumed; and I wanted to give him the impression that I was also a carefree, open-minded woman. Once again I was terrible at making assumptions and decision. I recalled long ago when Yusuf bought me a couple of bikinis for the first time and forced me to wear them, only to cover me up months later with a hijab and then again decide to allow me to wear what I wanted. After we landed in Las Vegas, after Nora was born, he bought me a few flashy bikinis, without even consulting me. I could never understand his erratic behavior. I was always and still confused with men.

Aiden was behind me when I entered our resort suite, and then again behind me when I went into the bedroom. I grabbed the very decent white-and-black suit and was on my way to change.

"Not so fast." He grabbed my arm.

Without thinking, I pulled back right away. I was about to cover my face, fearing a smack across it. I stopped myself. I didn't know why, but at that moment, I recalled Yusuf, and for a split second, I thought I needed to defend myself from him. I didn't know how that happened.

His eyes narrowed. "What happened to you? Do you think I am about to hurt you?" My heart was racing. "I would never hurt you, never."

I mumbled, "I know." He sat on the bed.

"I didn't mean to snap at you, the way I did, I'm sorry." he said calmly.

"I think you are being irrational. Mandy is even wearing a suit similar to mine." I didn't remember what she was wearing, but I decided that that was a good defensive line.

"Hannah, it's your body, and I shouldn't control you, but—"

I interrupted him by saying, "I'm going to change anyway. I don't want to argue." I was trying to keep a calm tone.

His frown vanished from his face. "Listen; please don't be angry at a pathetic jealous man."

Was he really jealous? Or was he another controlling man? But, If he wanted to hurt me, he could've already, I told myself. After all, we were alone. A couple of minutes had passed. There was a long silence, during which I had to chase Yusuf and my fears of Aiden out of my head.

I said calmly, "So you like it?"

He said breathlessly, "Yes … a lot."

I smiled and turned to leave Nora's room, carrying the other bikini with me. I went to Aiden's room. He followed me. I took off my dress slowly. I then glanced at my own reflection. What was I thinking? The bottom was okay, but the top was way too small and the baby-blue color and material were going to leave nothing to the imagination as soon as I got in the water.

"Aiden, I want you to do me a favor."

"Anything you want."

I turned and walked closer to him, and then I whispered close to his ear, "I want you to help me undress … then help me shower. There is an area I can't reach."

"That would be my pleasure, my little master," he said right before he closed his lips on mine.

***

My head was on his shoulder. His heartbeat became steadier. I pulled my head up lightly. He was looking at me with a light frown, and his gaze was lost as if he was thinking.

"What are you thinking about?"

He sighed at first and said, "Sometimes you startle me, Hannah. Not too long ago, you looked at me as if I were about to hurt you."

I shook lightly and turned to place my head on the pillow instead.

He continued, "See, you are pulling back now." He sounded annoyed.

"I don't know where you got that from. I know you are not going to hurt me." My tone wasn't as convincing as I intended it to be.

He was silent.

"You never spoke of your husband. I didn't even see one picture of him in your family album when Nora showed it to me."

I was hoping we would never speak of this. "I didn't want to think of him; that's why."

"But why? When Father passed away, my mother was devastated but didn't bury his pictures and memory with him too."

I was quiet. "Everyone grieves in a different way, I suppose." I didn't know what Aiden's view of being with someone with a terrible past would be, someone who was being investigated by the cops for being part of her nameless husband's scheme. What would Elaina say? She would find me really unsuitable for her son and probably encourage him to leave me. "You are very secretive about your life too!"

"What do you mean?"

I hesitated at first. I knew I promised myself not to open the subject during our vacation, but I couldn't help it.

"You know what I mean. How many times have you gotten me involved with your friends? Not once, and when I ask you questions about your past, you say, 'It's a long story.'" I tried not to show the anger I felt.

He sighed, looking away.

I continued, "Just because I don't complain, doesn't mean I don't see what's going on … It's as if you want to hide me away."

The last sentence that I said really did hurt. I recalled Majeed briefly and then Yusuf, Henry, and Jason. They all did the same thing. Majeed only wanted to take advantage of my naïveté, Yusuf completely isolated me, Henry wished to add me to his long list, and Jason wanted an employee with benefits, someone he could pass some fun time with, and now Aiden.

He sighed again and then turned to face me. I was watching him intently. "Hannah …" His gaze was hiding something. I knew it. "Men sometimes can feel weak, maybe even scared."

I stared at him. What was that supposed to mean? Was he not sure about me? Was he scared for me to meet his rich society friends?

"Plus, I told you already that I don't have a lot of friends here. I left soon after …" He stopped, as if he were making up an answer in his head. He sat on the bed. He was staring at the void ahead. "I left after my Law school and made new friends. Some of them live in Victoria." He smoothed his hair with his fingers. "In Ontario, I only have acquaintances, business associates, and a few of my old friends. I didn't lie to you when I told you the first time." I was quiet. "Listen, I want you to believe me when I say that I care about you."

Should I believe him right that moment? Or was he just dismissing the subject altogether? There was a long moment of silence.

"… the way I never cared for anyone before, and I mean it; that's why it's so hard."

What about his ex-fiancée? I wondered.

"I will settle in Ontario permanently in less than a couple of months. Things will be different then, I promise."

I said calmly, "Does this have to do with our social gap?"

He shook his head. I felt tense all of a sudden.

"No, I swear; this has nothing to do with money." He was hiding something, the same way I was hiding my past. I wondered what he had to go through.

"Aiden, it's okay … You don't have to tell me now."

Was he hiding a painful past as well? Maybe if I opened up about myself, he would then open up too.

"Listen. Lately, I've been getting some weird feeling about your job. I'm constantly thinking about you."

"What do you mean?" My heart raced. It was as if he knew about Adrianna's erratic and menacing character and Mary's warning and sudden departure. Or was he on a mission to become my employer? That was something I couldn't bear.

He sighed. "I've been looking forward to this holiday with you. I don't want to miss out on one beautiful moment." Maybe I should go back to being a shallow, obedient girlfriend. I just couldn't abide the idea of losing him. It was so painful to think. He shifted to lie right next to me.

He whispered, "Close your eyes."

It was so hard for me, but I did what I was told. I felt his lips kissing each of my closed eyelids. I shivered lightly. He then pulled me closer, wrapped his arms around me, and placed my head on his shoulder. I could feel his heartbeat. It was soothing, just like a beautiful, classical melody. Why did I have to love him so much? If it wasn't for my love for him, I would've been fleeing the room immediately with my belongings. He was still puzzling me. Since he had come into my life, I had become more skeptical. Nothing made sense to me. A big part of me was afraid of his powerful trait and the way he could easily control me, worried about the way he hid his past. Perhaps, that was the reason I was constantly comparing him to Yusuf; yet another part of me wanted to give in blindly to him. I wanted to believe him that there could be a valid explanation and possibly a future for us. At that moment, I wanted to believe that miracles existed.

***

A few more days had passed. I was lying on a long chair, painting in my head the picture of the blue beach that lay in front of me. I wanted to memorize every corner of it, while sipping a delicious blue martini, wearing one of the new navy-blue two-piece bikinis Aiden had bought me. I wore oversize sunglasses, and my hair was loose and wavy under a large navy-blue beach hat with a little pink bow, matching the couple of pink bows on my bikini top.

I sighed contently. Life was good. I wished I never had to go back to reality—if only we could stay there forever. I glanced over at Aiden. My heart squeezed at the sight of him. He lay lazily on his stomach.

He looked tanned, just like me. Nora was already under the care of Mandy and John. She suggested she give us some alone time by taking care of both Nora and Tiffany, as a payback since Tiffany had stayed with us last evening. The last few days were like heaven and eventful, since Aiden kept me busy with many of the resort's tours. That day was going to be a lazy day. We were not going to do anything, since the next day evening we went back to reality. I wasn't looking forward to that. Yusuf's memory didn't come as often to dilute my happy moments, and I was thankful Aiden didn't ask me any questions to interrupt the peace in my head.

Thinking of the night ahead was electrifying.

Alone with Aiden … the thought was very erotic and stimulating. I dismissed my erotic thoughts, because Aiden just woke up from his lazy sleep and turned to his back. He then reached to hold my hand and kissed my palm, sending shivers all around.

He mumbled, "Just you and I tonight. I can't wait."

I smiled. He stared at me. I said teasingly, "Wait for what?"

"Wait to love you. Come here." He pointed to his chest.

I said laughingly, "Do you want your chair to break in half? He didn't listen; instead, he pulled me gently by my arm, to lie awkwardly on top of him. I kissed his shoulder and neck. He tasted like a mixture of salty water and sunscreen.

The world stopped when I heard him say, "I love you, Hannah. I love you so much."

I froze. A single tear escaped from my eye to land on his chest, and then a few more tears followed.

I mumbled stutteringly, "I l-l-love you too. I love you, Aiden."

I felt his lips on mine and then kissing me passionately all over my face. I bet he could taste my falling tears. He then sighed. I lay on top of him for long minutes, feeling as if I were flying, right before he gently moved me away, just so he could leap up from his seat and then carry me and run toward the beach.

***

I stood in front of the mirror, taking my time with my hair and makeup. I needed to look my best. I wanted to make Aiden proud to be around me. I was almost done when Aiden walked into the bedroom. He glanced at me, smiling. I hoped he liked what I wore. I wore a long white-and-pink strapless semicasual dress and high-heeled pink sandals. I spent at least an hour on my hair and makeup.

He looked at my chest and my necklace. He said, "The moon needs a star." He then opened a jewelry box he had been hiding. My jaw dropped when I saw the necklace, white gold with a diamond star pendent. I was speechless and contained my tears. He placed the necklace around my neck. It was breathtaking. I then tuned to him and gave him a long kiss.

We walked hand in hand toward the resort's nightclub. It was a very dark room with moving spotlights. The Latino music was loud and stirring. We sat by one of the round tables, sipping a lemon martini. Half an hour later, Aiden went to use the washroom and I went to get us a couple of other drinks. I noticed that a tall man sitting by the bar was examining me from top to bottom, as if he were undressing me with his eyes. I could see him from the corner of my eye. I heard him say, "Hey, beautiful." I ignored him. "Do you want to dance?"

I turned to say that I was with my boyfriend. As soon as I looked at him, my mouth dried up and my heart started to race. I had already had three drinks. Was I seeing things again? What was going on with me? This man in front of me also resembled Yusuf. I recalled couple of other similar incidents the last couple of weeks. Why was I lately seeing Yusuf's face everywhere? My words were stuck in my throat. I was shaking. I felt an arm holding mine. I turned to see Aiden's face. I breathed out, feeling safe. I hugged him tight.

"Are you okay? Did that man say anything to you?"

"Aiden, let's just go back to our seat."

He turned to face the man who resembled Yusuf and said spitefully, "She is my girl. Get your own." I pulled Aiden's hand away. I didn't want him to end up in a fight. I didn't know he could be that fierce!

I whispered worriedly in his ear while walking away, "He just asked me if I wanted to dance."

He said, irritated, "And that's why you are shaking?"

I held his hand. "Don't worry about it. Let it go."

"No, tell me." I could tell from his tone that he wasn't going to let it go.

"He reminded me of my husband. He looks like him. That's all."

He sighed. I could tell that he was frowning under the dim light.

After a long moment, he said, "I am going to let it go for now, but I still think this bastard said something to disturb you."

I added faintly, "Just let it go! Please." He held me tight.

A few minutes later, I started to calm down. Later on that evening, Yusuf's face disappeared after I had another martini. I was giggling loudly when we got back to the resort suite. I had to hold on to Aiden most of the way. Right at the door, he carried me over his shoulder and bounced me onto the bed. Soon after, I felt him lying right next to me. I felt tipsy and little too wild, lying next to sexy Aiden, so I did what my instincts were telling me to do. I reached for him, drew him close, and whispered, "You need to read me another chapter of the story."

He grinned and brought me on top of him. "I know exactly what to read. I bet it will be your favorite chapter so far." His lips covered mine, while my hands started to unbutton his shirt.

I woke up feeling Aiden's arms around me. I was glad he was holding me tight. I didn't know why I felt scared. The sun hadn't risen yet. I had scary nightmares. I drew my body closer to his, where I felt so calm and safe.

I heard him mumble, "Are you okay?"

I didn't know he was awake.

"Yes. Why?"

"You've been talking in your sleep."

"Was I?" That was strange. I didn't know I talked in my sleep. "What was I saying?" He sighed.

"You were mumbling, *'Not real. Don't. Nora ...'* That was all I could understand."

"Oh!" Then I remembered my nightmares. Yusuf was in all of them, chasing me away in the dark. That was terrifying. Soon, we both drifted back to sleep.

***

Hours later, I lay next to him around the swimming pool. Nora and Tiffany were under the shaded umbrella playing with her electronic game. Aiden was sipping fresh juice. I noticed all the beautiful girls around us, wearing skimpy, colorful bikinis. I watched his gaze. He didn't seem to be glancing at any of the girls around him. I recalled Henry. He would've examined every girl around and probably tried to date at least half of them.

I said to him, "You must have had tons of girls."

He sighed. "I never said I was a saint."

"What bothered you about some of the girls you went out with in the past?"

He sighed again, apparently annoyed. "You don't tell me anything about you, and yet you want to know me inside out. Fine." He sipped more of his juice. "I hate spoiled whiney rich women. I also hate cheaters and women who would do anything for money." His tone was slightly heated. Did his ex-fiancée cheated on him, or was she the spoiled rich woman? Or maybe she was someone who would do anything for money. That was really confusing. He glanced at me and said in a calmer tone, "I really respect how hard you work and try to balance everything. I bet it's not easy to raise a child on your own." Would he respect me if he knew of my credit situation? I wanted to ask him questions about his ex-fiancée, but I was reluctant. I knew he was going to sack the subject. What was the point? He said abruptly, "My turn to ask questions now. How did you meet your husband?"

I pressed my lips together. Why did I have to keep on asking him questions about his previous women?

"I was a waitress. He was a customer."

His gaze was on mine; I looked away.

"Was he handsome?"

"You can say that."

"Was he rich?"

I tried not to giggle sarcastically at this question. What could I answer to that? *A phony rich con.*

"No, he wasn't."

"You don't like to speak of him, do you?"

I snapped, "That's because he is dead!" I looked at him. His gaze was impassive. I added calmly, "It's different."

"Wow, Hannah, you snapped! I'm impressed."

I hardly ever snapped in front of him; in fact, this was probably the first time.

"I know you like me perfect and quiet, and d ... trouble-less." I was going to say doubtless, but I changed my mind.

"What's wrong with perfection? You are perfect. It's always peaceful with you. Sometimes I feel that you are too good to be true." He grinned.

I wanted to laugh, realizing that maybe I was sugarcoating myself way too much—my temper, complaints, doubts, and many other things were tucked deep inside. I wondered for how long. "What I'm looking for is peace of mind. I am dealing with a big pile of mess at work."

My God, men in general are selfish creatures, I realized irritably. I needed to find my strength. What had happened to me? I shouldn't allow anyone to oppress me after Yusuf, even Aiden. But instead of fighting back, I heard myself say.

"I'm not perfect, Aiden."

"You are to me."

I glanced at him and smiled, deciding to change the subject, since there were only a few hours left in paradise.

Chapter Twenty-Three

A FEW DAYS LATER, WE were in Canada, back to work again. Aiden took me to one of his car dealerships. *BMW, wow, all these cars!* I tried to smile.

Walking around, I saw a white BMW copy of Adrianna's car parked next to a black BMW, Aiden's car. I glanced away from it, as if the sight of it was painful for my eyes, because all of a sudden, my ugly doubts came back to soak my brain.

On Monday morning, Aiden called me and suggested we go for lunch to a nice Greek restaurant, since he was flying to Victoria that same evening and was coming back on Thursday. But instead of having Greek food, I insisted we go across the street for a latte and light lunch. I decided I should slowly stop being so obedient. I needed to rebuild my shattered spine—to regain my strength; plus I wasn't going to hide him anymore, and if his old friends wanted to open up about my painful past, I would then know if he really loved me as he said. He should know that his dream perfect woman didn't exist.

At first, he was reluctant but decided to follow my lead in picking the place to eat for the first time. He called me when he was on his way over. Right before I took off for lunch, I glanced over at Christine; lately, she had always been working away, nonstop, as if nothing else existed in the room but her work. At that moment I thought of Mary. I felt my heart sink—I had missed her dearly. I still didn't understand why she didn't reply to my calls and messages; but I really hoped she was okay.

I asked Christine casually, "Have you heard from Mary?"

She glanced at me quickly and said, "Nope." She looked back at her screen.

I couldn't even make a simple conversation with Christine. I took a deep breath and asked her, "Did Mary tell you herself that she was going out of town?"

She replied without even looking at me, "Nope, Adrianna did."

I looked away, something wasn't making any sense.

After ordering our latte and chicken sandwiches, I sat by the window across from him. The sparkling rays from the sun penetrated the wide, classy room to illuminate the round black table we were sitting at. I noticed that Aiden wasn't himself. He seemed a little too stressed, glancing at the door periodically. When I asked him what was wrong with him, he said that he was having a stressful day at work.

I wondered when it would be a good time to tell him that Jason and I went on couple of dates. Maybe I should open up soon about my past, about Yusuf, and about the mess he left behind. But then he would think that I was after his money. There was a possibility that he wouldn't believe me at all. He did hate when women would do anything for money; he told me himself. I really didn't want to lose him over my past. All of a sudden, I felt dissuaded.

I said good-bye to him by his car. He told me he loved, to take care of myself and urged me to keep in touch with him at all times. He was acting strange again. I sensed a hint of concern in his voice. Was it because he loved me?—I really wanted to think so.

***

A month later, on a Friday, Adrianna called me to tell me, "I'm ordering takeout. I want you to join me in the meeting room. We have to discuss a few things."

I left my desk reluctantly. I had been off work for the last three weeks. One was my second week of vacation entitlement, and the other two weeks were granted to me with no pay. Adrianna was stressing me out completely, especially since Mary had moved out of town. I really wondered if I was her assistant or her stress-relief punching bag.

She was constantly in a bad mood and always had something negative to say about my work performance. During my time off, I got busy searching for a job and going to interviews. Then one night, when I was at Jasmine's house, Nathan mentioned that he was going to hire someone for his office since his office manager was resigning soon because she was moving to a different province in a few months. To me, that was amazing news. After working for the firm and the treatment I got from Adrianna, I would much rather be working for family.

Aiden and I met only on the weekend, during which we went to a few dinners with Nathan, John, Jasmine, and Mandy. Aiden assured me that within a few weeks his life would be back to normal.

Maybe during the meeting, I decided, I should try to ignore Adrianna's odd sarcasm and shift my mind to that night instead. I had been planning Aiden's birthday, which had already passed a couple of days ago. He had already arrived from Victoria and was picking me up right after work, to stay the weekend at his place for the first time since Elaina was out of town. He was to pick me up from Jasmine's house, since she was keeping Nora.

When I entered the meeting room with my bottle of water in my hand, Adrianna was already sitting at the table, a coffee mug next to her. She looked elegant as usual. Her expression was blank, and her eyes were frozen. She merely gave me a curt smile. I sat across from her on one of the many leather chairs. Even the sun coming from the windows couldn't lighten up the obscurity that surrounded Adrianna. I wanted to ask about Mary, her sudden departure was still bothering me; but I couldn't bring myself to do that. All of a sudden, I found myself frowning lightly. The room was immaculate, just like the rest of the firm, dark cherry wood with beautiful paintings.

Adrianna said, "I hope you like Chinese." I nodded. "Have you been to any good restaurants lately?"

I smiled, recalling the few restaurants I had gone to so far with Aiden. I told her about the one we visited on my first date with him. She was listening carefully, which was surprising to me. She was usually the one talking with me listening. "I know this restaurant. My ex and I went there a few times. It's all right, I guess."

Damn her ex, I thought irritably. I wished she would just stop speaking of him altogether. Maybe I should find the nerve and mention his name to her and watch her reaction intently.

She added, "It's expensive. I'm guessing your boyfriend is wealthy."

I bit my lip lightly. I said, "He's done well for himself, I guess." My throat suddenly went dry; I sipped some water from my bottle.

Adrianna added sneeringly, "He should maybe buy you a new car. I mean yours is very, very old and rusty."

I looked away. Why was she getting involved in my business? At that moment, I had to dismiss the irony that Aiden owned a car dealership and I was driving a very old rusty car, as Adrianna had said, but I never thought of that before that moment. I was glad he didn't offer. I would then have to refuse, but then again, why didn't he offer? I hated how Adrianna was suddenly playing with my head.

"I will buy myself a car, one day soon. I mean, just because he's my boyfriend doesn't mean he is responsible for me financially." I felt that I needed to defend my broken position as a woman. After all, her ex-boyfriend seemed to have spoiled her rotten. I took a deep breath and added, "Aiden spoiled me with a very expensive vacation and gave me a gift card to use for all the things that I needed for the trip and even bought me this necklace." I breathed out. I was planning to exaggerate, but I couldn't. I glanced at her reaction—which remained impassive.

She said casually. "How long have you been dating Aiden for?"

"Since December of last year."

She stared at me as she sipped more coffee. She hid a giggle. Was she mocking me?

"I know Aiden. He is very well off. His net inheritance from his father alone was over one hundred million dollars."

What! Suddenly I couldn't think straight. Why did she just tell me this? I tried to contain myself from blowing in her face. Was she indirectly telling me that Aiden wasn't taking care of me right? Adrianna fiddled with her Da Vinci watch, as if she were reminding me of her very expensive gift. Twenty thousand dollars was more than my current net salary, and he spent it just like that on one watch. That was absurd. But then again, that amount of money was a pocket change to Adrianna, and also *Aiden*; my heart bled at that thought.

"Does your ex-boyfriend visit your firm?" I asked.

Adrianna sipped more coffee. "He used to come, but lately, he has been so busy."

I didn't know why at that moment, I recalled seeing Aiden's car on his way to park in the firm's garage. "I wonder why Aiden seems to only watch his spending with you; he usually spoils his women rotten." She sighed.

Was she on a mission to destroy me, to make me feel unworthy and inferior? Up until now, I really believed that Aiden had spoiled me with what he had given me so far.

My tone was arctic. "How do you know that about him?"

Her stare was enigmatic. "We went to university and Law school together. I've known Aiden all my life; I knew his ex-fiancée, and few of his ex-girlfriends."

I wanted to ask her directly if she was his ex too, but the words wouldn't come out. I was afraid all of a sudden. Instead, keeping my wobbly voice as even as I could, I said, "I'm happy the way things are. Aiden loves me, and he told me so. That means more to me than being spoiled rotten."

She laughed and then sipped more coffee. I felt flushed. Were we meeting solely to humiliate me?

I mumbled, "If you don't mind, I would like to go back to my desk. I have a severe headache." I heard a knock at the door. Madison informed us that the food had arrived. My headache wasn't that severe. Lately, I hadn't felt like myself. I was even a bit concerned since my period was very light the previous month and was already late this month; I was also feeling a bit nauseous from time to time. I was afraid even to think of the scary possibility behind my messed up period, and being in the same room with Adrianna was adding to the pressure that I felt.

Her tone was low and intimidating. "No, we finish the meeting first."

Reluctantly, I took my plate. I had no appetite. I took a couple of bites from the chicken fried rice, and then I decided not to force myself.

She could fire me for not eating; I didn't care anymore. I just sipped some water, feeling my heart race. A few minutes later, I grabbed my purse and looked at her. I had made a decision.

"I can't do this anymore. You'll have to find someone else who can tolerate you, Ms. Miller." I took a deep breath and added, "I quit!" Then I stormed out of the meeting room to my desk where I gathered all my belongings. I knew I would regret my decision later, but right at that moment, I felt liberated from Adrianna.

***

I spent three hours sitting at a coffee shop. I didn't even call Aiden until it was time for me to pick up Nora from school. I really wanted to cancel with him I just couldn't be cruel and ruin his birthday, even though I was suddenly feeling insignificant and piteous; Adrianna's hurtful words were constantly playing in my head. He wouldn't listen to me and insisted on picking me up from my sister's place when I wished to drive myself to his house.

***

I felt tense when we entered the large gated entrance, thinking of the weekend ahead. Thanks to Adrianna, I now had an idea of how much money Aiden was worth. My speculations were weighing me down. I turned to face Aiden when he parked his car. I wanted to tell him that his wish came true, that I had just quit. I wanted to speak to him about my doubts. I decided that the time wasn't right. First, I had my little confession to make.

As soon as I stepped into the house, I felt overwhelmed again. And it got worse after Aiden gave me a tour. I was hoping to get a map to this place. I had a feeling I was going to get lost. I tried to take notes of where the exquisite kitchen with the top-of-the-line appliances, spacious living room, dining room, and sunroom were. I had already lost track of how many rooms we visited—the three oversized master bedrooms with living area and large, luxurious en-suite bathrooms, which could've been mistaken for a large living room, and an office on each floor.

Everything was flawless, not a single inequitable piece of furniture, painting, or decoration.

That was insane! Who lived like that? I wondered what Aiden thought when he saw my small living area and Nora's mess. The last and only time I came there to visit his mother, I felt more at ease toward the end of my visit. This time, I was staying for the weekend.

We settled in the large living room; I made sure to keep a few feet between us.

"Do you like it?" His eyes shone as he watched my facial expression.

I hesitated. "Yes, I do; it's beautiful and grand." I felt out of breath. "Did this place belong to your dad?"

"Yes." He gave me a murky smile.

He must miss his father.

"I am sorry. It must be hard to lose a father."

"It is. You lost a father too. You know how it feels." I pressed my lips together hard and nodded while looking around.

"Do you plan to live here?"

"Of course, this is the home I grew up in."

"You father was really rich!" I said, recalling briefly the unfortunate way we were raised. Sometimes, we didn't even have food to eat. Not in a million years did I dream of even entering a house like that. I couldn't share this with Aiden. He wouldn't understand what deprivation, hunger, war, abuse, need, and growing up always feeling inferior meant. At that moment, I wished I never came to know about his approximate net worth.

"He was always rich. He inherited money from his father, and he grew it."

"I see." The effect of my earlier meeting with Adrianna was still on my mind; I couldn't help but feel dejected.

"What did your father do, before he passed away?"

I wanted to laugh; that was a complicated question. I twisted the truth. "He had a degree in accounting." At that moment, I felt as if I was inside a fairy tale and he was my make-believe boyfriend. Our social class gap suddenly seemed huge, and it stood right there in front of me. Aiden would get tired of me very soon, and I would spend the rest of my life crying over him. For months, I had been polishing my every move around him. I was even watching my grammar and language. I tried to hide most of my displeasures and fears. I was merely myself during our lovemaking. I was the way he loved me, wild and free, but I knew I couldn't hide forever.

"How come you are an only child?"

He stretched his legs in front of him; I couldn't even move an inch. He said, "I heard that Mother couldn't bear children after me. I must have ruined something in her."

I had to giggle at that.

"Your mom thinks you are a good man."

He moved closer to me, and I froze. "That's because Mother doesn't know how naughty I can be. So, Hannah, please, this is our secret."

I didn't know why I felt awkward all of a sudden. I was more at ease being at my little place, making love to him under the fake glowing stars. I wished we were at my place right then.

"Aiden, um … why don't we spend the weekend at my place? I mean, I would hate not to be able to find you in the middle of the night." He laughed. I smiled lightly. It would be a miracle if he agreed.

"Don't worry; I will find you." He then grabbed me, placing me on his lap. I didn't know how his birthday present that I planned out for him was going to happen there. I was feeling way too tense.

"I'm hungry. Are you hungry?" I said nervously.

He sighed. "I can order us takeout." He got up and reached for his phone.

I didn't move. I bet he was clueless about how I felt right then. He suggested that I make myself comfortable. I grinned tensely when he disappeared, glancing around me. How could I manage to feel comfortable there?

I went to Aiden's bedroom, opened his closet, and then closed it. I decided not to use his closet. I could keep my belongings in my luggage bag. I hesitated, because all of a sudden, his birthday present seemed silly. I could give him the expensive cologne I bought him and forget the silly surprise. I glanced at his many expensive colognes, which sat perfectly on his dresser. My gift wouldn't even stand out after all.

Timidly, I reached for my luggage to find Aiden's surprise birthday present.

I heard him calling me. I had been sitting in his sitting area for at least fifteen minutes, watching the wall, trying so hard to chase away Adrianna from my head. I got up and placed a smile on my face. I was wearing a satin robe.

"The food is ready."

He was standing next to his bed; I came closer and stuttered, "I-I am not hungry anymore. I have ... I want to do something for you." That wasn't the sexy way I was planning in my head. He stared at me. "Close your eyes." He grinned and then followed my order. He knew I was full of surprises. I hoped that this one wouldn't be the worst he'd had so far. I turned off the lights. Only a very faint light came from a night-light. "Take off your clothes, but keep your boxers on."

"Seriously!" he started right away. I wanted to help him but quickly changed my mind. My hands were shaking, so I watched him as he hastily threw his clothes across the room to land on the expensive rug. I said firmly, "No peeking." I started to get back some confidence; I liked this room better in the dark.

He said, amused, "Yes, ma'am."

I removed the comforters. I had already placed towels over the bedsheets.

I said firmly, "Lay on your stomach."

His tone was serious. "Hannah, I may be naughty, but I am not kinky naughty."

I sighed. "Aiden, your naughtiness right now won't be necessary, because I am here to do a job." I said as I took off my own robe.

"What on earth!" He was about to turn, but I pushed him back to lay flat still. "Little miss bossy ha! Where did that came from?" He was quiet for a few long seconds. "I like that!"

"My name is Hannah Shaheen. I will be your massage therapist. I was hired by a company I work for to give you a special massage on your birthday." I could hear him giggle quietly. My plan to turn him on had failed. He probably already thought I was funny. What if he saw my outfit? He would then assume I was switching my job to become a comedian. I was wearing a short, white front dress, with a plunging collar, to show my pushed-up chest. I had even hastily placed a white cap on my head; right after Aiden lay in bed, to complete the ridiculous uniform I had bought at a costume store. "And, Mr. Harris, just so you know, this is strictly business." I placed some massage oil on his bare back and started to work away. I didn't hear him giggle after. I could even hear him sigh profoundly. I was using all the techniques that I had learned many years ago. I just wanted to impress him. I was moving my fingers, enjoying every moment of it, because I could feel that he liked it.

At least ten minutes passed, and he mumbled, "Where did you learn to massage like this?"

I was silent for a few seconds and then said, "It's my job, or did you forget?"

"Right." He turned to face me and then turned on the bright nightlight by the bed.

I immediately leaped and stood in front of him, trying not to giggle at my foolishness. I could tell he was hiding a chuckle.

He said, "At first, I thought you were joking, but with this outfit on …" His eyes examined me from top to bottom. "I now trust that you are indeed a brilliant massage therapist." He got up and pulled me closer. "Bossing me around on my birthday! Who do you think you are?" He frowned. "Now I am in charge, and I say it's your turn." I didn't know how, but I was facing the pillow. And slowly, my skimpy outfit was being peeled off.

"Can you turn off the lights at least?"

He grumbled as he said, "No. I don't like to work in the dark." I could feel the oil on my bare back. I felt goose bumps.

"It's not my birthday. I don't deserve a massage." I felt way too tense. No one had given me a sensual full-body massage before. I recalled at that moment Yusuf's ruthless, painful strokes and grips.

"Stop arguing." He flipped me to my back and then said in between kissing me. "Are you going to do what I say?"

I stuttered, "I-is what you are about to say going to cause me pain?" I didn't know why I said that. It just came out.

His gaze was dark. "I am not that kinky. I won't cause you pain. I promise." He kissed my neck in between his words. "Because I won't enjoy it. Your pain will be my pain, and your ultimate pleasure would be mine." Then he emptied a large amount of oil on my stomach.

***

Sometime later, we were sitting on his bed after covering the expensive linens once again with clean towels while eating chicken and rice—Aiden's idea. Food really tasted good. I glanced at Aiden while he held the chicken with his bare fingers, recalling briefly Jason's refined gestures; they were very different. Then I had to dismiss his sister Adrianna once again.

While we ate, he filled his large built-in Jacuzzi. Soon after, I finally started feeling at ease.

As soon as we were done eating, I changed the dirty linens. I was wearing Aiden's shirt. When I went to his bathroom, Aiden was already waiting for me in his huge round tub. I took off his shirt and slid into the warm water next to him and then into his arms.

At night, I slipped under the covers and cuddled with him, and surprisingly, I had a dreamless night.

During breakfast the next morning, I watched him as he sipped his coffee and flipped his newspaper. I sighed before deciding to tell him my little confession.

"Aiden, there is something I didn't tell you."

He turned to face me. I stuttered, "J-Jason, your old friend and I went on a date." His gaze narrowed. "Nothing happened, I swear."

His face was still. He pushed the newspaper away.

"Why didn't you tell me before today?"

"It was irrelevant. I mean, we merely went on a couple of dates. One was the day we met at the club. He was the one who gave me the passes, so I asked him to join me and my friends. The other one was at some Greek restaurant." It was no use. He seemed pissed. I added, "We never even kissed." I breathed out. It was out of my system. I could tell him next that I quit.

"And you decided to tell me that now?" He looked away. "How about Henry? You had two dates in one night! Or maybe you didn't know."

I was silent, but my heart was galloping rapidly. I was seeing Aiden's fierce, sarcastic side.

"Now is better than never. I mean, don't you have anything to tell me too? How about Adrianna?"

He pushed his chair back and got to his feet, dismissing my last sentence. I continued, "Aiden, please, I need to know. I'm not stupid."

He said abruptly, "I have work to do. I'll be in my office."

I frowned. That didn't go too well.

An hour later, I walked around the house. I wished I could just go home. I wondered if Aiden was still angry. Was he going to tell me if he was hiding something from me? Why did all the men I had encountered end up being mysterious? I was back in his bedroom. I glanced at his many expensive colognes, which reminded me I had to add his other gift and his birthday card. I reached for it from my small suitcase. It was an expensive cologne wrapped in a shiny gray gift wrap. At that moment, I recalled Adrianna's words, *"I wonder why Aiden seems to only watch his spending with you; he usually spoils his women rotten."* I went to his large walk-in closet, which was bigger than my kitchen. Nothing was out of place. I recalled my tiny closet at home, which held both my and Nora's clothes. I was grateful that Jasim told me to place all my extra clothes and storage in one of his two spare bedrooms upstairs. I recalled the squished motor home I once lived in. At that moment, Aiden seemed more a stranger than a boyfriend.

I opened a few drawers from his red cedar dresser. I studied his neatly folded clothes, and then I noticed a small box. I opened it. There were a few expensive watches, and my heart started to race. I already knew that Rolex was a brand name watch and then TAG Heuer … My eyes narrowed as I saw the next watch, the square white-gold case, brown-leather bracelet material—I read the next brand watch: Da Vinci. I froze. It was as if Aiden and Adrianna had bought them together, his and hers. His black BMW, her white BMW, that wasn't a coincidence. *No*, I refused to believe it. I felt my heart sink. I turned around. I ran downstairs, still lost, and walked into the kitchen. I found Aiden's cell phone. It was on the kitchen table. I hurried toward it.

I was almost out of breath when I reached for it. I carried it to the bathroom. I didn't wish for Aiden to surprise me while I snooped through his cell.

I remembered him giving me his password the day I texted Mandy from his cell. I entered it. He still kept the same password. I quickly went through his missed calls. My heart raced when I saw Adrianna's number a couple of days ago. Adrianna specialized in divorce cases, not in business transactions. I noticed that there were a few of them in his missed-call history, *but why?* Old friends didn't need to call each other that often, unless ... she was more than an old friend. I checked his incoming and outgoing calls. He never really called her back. I breathed out. But then again, that didn't mean he didn't get in touch with her. I went through his messages. I could only find my messages and many others. A couple of messages were from a blocked sender. I was tempted to open them but decided to ignore them. I should only concentrate on finding Adrianna's, but there were none. He could've just erased everything and forgotten to get to his missed calls. Was he hiding me from her? Or hiding her from me? I just couldn't think of his innocence as a possibility right at that moment. If he was hiding me from her, he would've erased my messages and calls, but he didn't. I closed my eyes. I hated when things didn't make sense. I almost jumped out of my skin when his phone rang. It was her, Adrianna. I hesitated, and then I decided to answer.

I said in a shaky tone, "Hello?"

There was silence, and then her voice came, sending ugly shivers through my body. "Who's this?"

As if she couldn't recognize my voice! I said, "Hannah."

"Hannah, why are you answering Aiden's phone? Is he not around?"

I decided to say that he wasn't around. We needed to resolve some traumatizing issues.

"He's not here right now. He forgot his phone with me. Can I take a message?"

"I will call him later. We are always in touch."

I said thickly, "Is Aiden your ex-boyfriend; the one you always talk about?"

"Yes, he is. Did he tell you?"

Her phone conversations about an ex-boyfriend zoomed back to me. I recalled her speaking of her designer watch, diamond rings, necklaces, and possibly a white BMW; they were still friends, and he was on a mission to get her back, at any cost. I was jealous. It was agonizing, but I didn't want to admit that. "I figured it out." I could hardly breathe thoroughly.

"I'm glad you finally got it." Her tone was menacing.

I closed my eyes. How foolish was I? The truth was right there in front of me. I turned the other way, just so I didn't have to look at it. Once again in my life, I was afraid to grasp the ugly truth.

Something told me to fight back, so I said, "Aiden is your ex-boyfriend now, but he's my current boyfriend."

"I think you are forgetting who you are and where you came from. Your temporary rebound status is getting to your empty head."

Rebound, what did she mean by that?

"What do you want from me?" I said breathlessly.

She laughed. "Nothing really, but it's a delightful feeling, knowing the sight of your hope with Aiden is finally slipping away."

I felt as if someone was strangling me when I said, "What makes you think that it's slipping away?"

She laughed again. "I have many reasons. You had the lowest job at my firm ... a personal assistant of mine. Now you are jobless. You live in a basement apartment. You drive a broken-down car. Your credit history is horrific. You are a single mother, whose criminal dead husband is nameless. I have sources that indicate that you were possibly his scam partner." She sighed. I felt the room spinning, but I held my head up. "Should I continue?"

"Was that why you made me your assistant? And suggested I come to your parties with Aiden?" *Just to degrade me,* I had just realized.

"You know what they say. Keep your friends close, but your enemy closer." She sighed again. "But that's okay, you were just a pass-time for

Aiden. You were going to be the same for Jason." How did she know about Jason?

"Jason meant nothing to me."

She sighed profoundly. "You never meant anything to either of them. Why do you think Aiden never showed up with you to the firm's party, deciding to come on his own?"

Did he go to the party after our Mexican dinner with his mother? We were done before 10:00 p.m. He could still have gone. When we went to the café across from the firm, he looked stressed and kept on looking toward the door.

"He didn't want me to find out; he didn't want to lose the possibility of us getting back together."

My head was throbbing. Now it all made sense.

She continued, "You probably remind Aiden of someone from his past. She ruined his life." Then I recalled Jason at the Greek restaurant, *when he mentioned about his old friend whose life turned upside down because of a poor junky girl.* I was silent. I couldn't even get myself to speak, while feeling my heartbeat speeding up. "She was a poor slut. She used him for his money, and on top of that, she cheated on him. I think all Aiden wanted was to find someone like her, fill her up with false hope … to purposely destroy her."

I hung up. I wanted to scream, but I contained myself. Quickly, I went to the bedroom and gathered my belongings, placing them hastily in my luggage bag. I then placed the necklace he gave me right next to his Da Vinci watch. I recalled when Aiden said himself, *"I hate spoiled whiney rich women. I also hate cheaters and women who would do anything for money."* Adrianna was right. Aiden was seeking revenge. After all, he was good at lying and getting himself out of an awkward situation; I recalled the day he took me to the bakery to buy Mandy and John an engagement cake to excuse our sudden absence. And oddly enough, a few times, Adrianna stated that she had dinner arrangements the same day Aiden also mentioned that he had business dinners to attend, and never once he suggested I came along. His interest in my job and environment wasn't because he cared; it was because he wanted to know if I would mention anything about our relationship to my coworkers. I couldn't believe his speech when he claimed he loved. *All men are liars!* I thought sullenly, *every single one of them.*

I went to the living room to grab my cell phone; I needed to call a cab. I was carrying my luggage bag while dialing the number when Aiden found me.

He sounded stunned when he said, "Where are you going?"

I snapped, "Out of here." I didn't even look at him.

"What happened? Hannah?" His tone was calm when he added, "Listen, I'm sorry I was angry about Jason, but you can't blame me; he is my friend. The message he left me after midnight that night asking me not to come indicated that—"

I interrupted him. "You think I'm a fool; because you don't think I know what's going on around me," I said loudly.

He seemed frightened all of a sudden; he said calmly, "Can you at least explain to me what happened to you all of a sudden?"

I tried to calm down; as if he didn't know what was going on already. Maybe I should enlighten him—his mask was revealed; I also needed to get all the tucked in pain off my chest, before I walked away for good from his life. "You're worried about Jason, with whom I merely had a couple of insignificant dates, and you forgot to mention Adrianna, your ex, your lover, your friend, your everything!"

He frowned. "Is that what Adrianna told you?" He came really close to face me. "What else did she tell you?" he asked in a very composed tone.

I took a few steps back and said, "She told me enough, giving me plenty of hints. I really didn't want to believe it at first. The car you gave her, her expensive Da Vinci watch, which is a copy of yours, and all the other gifts, and oh, the vacation that I booked for her at the Royal Cancun! Now I'm sure you guys met there!"

"She is lying to you. That's because she wants to break us up."

He turned away, facing the wall, and said in a slightly heated tone, "I knew that there was something weird going on, ever since she made you her assistant. Why do you think I wanted you to leave your damn job?"

"Aiden, I am not buying your lies anymore. The only reason you wanted me to quit was just so I didn't find out about you both. She was your ex—"

He interrupted. "Maybe at first. She was always stalking me after I suddenly withdrew myself from her. There is nothing between us. She was just a one-time mistake."

Adrianna's cruel words were playing in my head like a horrific symphony.

"You buy a super-expensive car and a twenty-some-thousand-dollar watch for a one-time mistake? What do you mean a mistake?"

He hesitated and then said irately, "We had sex once, right before we started dating. Are you happy now?" He walked away toward the fireplace and said in a calmer tone, "It was meaningless. She caught me off guard after a long, stressful day."

I turned away, feeling disgusted.

He continued, "I didn't buy her a car, just a watch. She even picked it out. I didn't pick it for her, because her firm helped me with a lot of legal advice when Father passed away, and she refused to get paid for it. I didn't want to have to owe her—"

I didn't care to hear the detailed explanation, so I interrupted him, "You guys had meaningless sex. She chose to buy an identical watch with your money, and I believed her that there were other designer gifts from you. You were spoiling someone you call a mistake? … Are you even listening to yourself?" I was restraining myself from blowing up. "Why don't you admit that you used me as a rebound and that I mean nothing to you? While you were trying to get back with her, you even refused to come to the law firm's party only to show up without me."

"That's a lie."

I didn't care to listen. "I was someone who reminded you of an underprivileged cheater, a slutty gold digger, someone you wanted to destroy," I said in a strangled tone. "I wasn't after your money." I looked around. "I don't care about any of this." I shook my head.

He walked toward me. He then stopped, as if he remembered something. "You have to listen; I got a couple of weird warning texts. They are starting to make sense now."

I thought only a few men like Yusuf existed, but I was wrong; they were all over the place.

He placed his hands to cover his face for a moment and then walked over to the side lamp table, grabbed the expensive vase, and threw it toward the fireplace, making a crashing sound. Glass shattered all over. His gesture didn't scare me. I was expecting his worst right then. All men who came into my life were the same!

"Adrianna is an evil snake." He cocked his head to the back.

"A snake you befriended, had sex with, and spoiled rotten." His jaw tightened. "Jason and I didn't even kiss, and that was before I even met you. You were angry when you found out, when you had no right; my life before you was none of your damn business." I turned to face him. "You guys went to the same resort while we were together. Can you deny it?"

He seemed distressed when he said, "When I found out she was coming too, I took off to Victoria on the same day. I didn't want to tell you the hideous details then, so I admit that I lied to you about staying in Sandaqua."

I gave him a murky smile.

He added, "You don't understand."

"You are wrong, Aiden. Now I do understand clearly, but I was the wrong person to want to destroy." I swallowed my tears. Yusuf, I recalled him the first time he met me at the restaurant. I was vulnerable, young, and easily manipulated. Aiden found me silly, amusing, easy to please, and callow compared to his sophisticated friends. "You realized I was inferior and foolish that night we met. I remind you of her. For some reason, you couldn't destroy her but thought you could destroy me instead," I said resentfully.

I knew he was at that moment seeing a different side of me, the fighter, the mad and unpleasant side. He turned to sit on the couch; his face was pale.

He said, "Someone dangerous is twisting things around." His eyes were looking into space, as if he were lost. We were both silent.

I didn't care to listen to him. I said calmly, "I lied when I said I liked your place … The truth is, I hate it." I glanced around and continued loudly, "Who needs seven or eight bedrooms and six washrooms? You need to print a guide map, the same thing they give you when you visit a museum." I laughed nervously. I could see that his jaw looked tense as he turned to look at me. "You said you want to know more about me. I will tell you." I breathed in deeply, trying to swallow my tears. I said in a wobbly voice, "I'm very happy living in my small basement apartment, which to me is like heaven compared to what I lived through before. I can't even rent a regular apartment because my credit is ruined. My criminal husband—I still don't know his real name—wrecked it for me." Yusuf, along with his degrading poems, was back in my head. I couldn't dismiss him anymore. My tears started to roll down my cheeks. I yelled out the next sentence while shaking, "At least I was lucky to be alive, not dead like him in a deadly accident when his aim was to get me killed. Just like you, he was selfish, a control freak; he lied to me, hid me away, and only aimed to hurt me." He closed his eyes, as if he were in pain, another one of his acts for sure. "Adrianna must've told you already. She probably even referred to me as 'trailer trash,' since my husband made me move around with him in a stolen motor home for a few months. They have my life report in front of them; most likely Adrianna already shared it with you." He froze, as if I had said something terrifying. "Someone rich with a golden spoon in his mouth like you and Adrianna wouldn't understand; you guys label poverty a sin." He just stared at me, blankly, as if he were seeing a ghost. Perhaps I looked like a crazy ghost. I continued, "I was trying to be what you want me to be. I was afraid to lose you. That's why I hid my crazy past, my doubts about you, and my battered identity."

I looked around again. "Living in a place like this, to me, was only a dream, a fantasy, because I was so poor. Sometimes my siblings and I didn't even have food to eat on the table." I tried to swallow my falling tears, looking away from his dark gaze. I didn't care how he perceived me anymore. "I dreamed that I would be a refined and cultured woman one day, like your Adrianna." I wiped my tears. My heart was suddenly throbbing hard, as if I were going through an attack. I screamed the last sentence in between my tight breaths. "Not anymore … I realized that … you and your old cultured friends are snakes … hiding behind fine-looking masks ... You think it's okay to play with people's hearts and lives as ..." I couldn't continue anymore. I felt the room spinning. All of a sudden, I blacked out.

***

I opened my eyes to see Aiden's face. What just happened to me? I got up and felt my head throbbing. I lay back on a couch.

"Hannah, are you okay?" he asked worriedly. "The ambulance is on its way."

"What happened to me?" Then I remembered our fight suddenly. I pulled myself away. I didn't want him near me. He felt my discomfort. He brought a glass of water and placed it close to my lips, I couldn't drink anything. I felt weak all of a sudden. I turned away, too tired to even cry.

"Aiden, please no need for an ambulance; just take me back home." He got up from beside me and sat on the next couch. I hid my face in my arms and turned away from him. A few minutes later, the door rang. Paramedics walked in with a stretcher. I felt my body being shifted and lifted. I couldn't resist. I just felt weak and broken.

***

At the hospital, I was advised to see a doctor since I was bleeding heavily. Aiden arrived right after I was dropped off. For the very first time since I had met him, I really didn't wish to see him.

During the time I was being examined, I looked blankly around me. I just couldn't think clearly. My head was continuously repeating the same symphony, *Aiden. Why did I love you the way I did? Why? When you are just like the rest of them* ... I was waiting once again. The doctor finally came to see me. I just nodded when he asked if he could speak in front of Aiden, who was sitting across from me. I didn't wish to fight right then. We hadn't spoken to each other since he came into the room. I was looking blankly still at the wall in front of me.

The doctor spoke in a cheerful tone at first. "I'm glad that you are okay. I could see that you were experiencing some sort of nervous breakdown." I just stared at him. His tone then switched to low and apologetic. "I'm sorry to tell you that you miscarried your baby."

My eyes widened. My baby! I had had this weird feeling for the last few weeks, ever since my very light period, and I was afraid to know. I shook my head.

"I think you were early on in your pregnancy …"

I stopped listening. I just closed my eyes, curled my body tight, and started to cry. I had lost Aiden's baby … a part of him. He was a liar, a player, and he wanted to destroy me. I shouldn't want that baby, so why was it so agonizing to lose it? *Why?* I felt Aiden's arm hugging me. I didn't have any energy to fight back, to push him away. He even brought his face next to mine, which felt wet.

I heard him say, "I'm sorry."

Did he have tears in his eyes? I would have never guessed that a man like him was capable of shedding one tear. Was he upset because the baby that I had lost was his?

He mumbled in a clipped tone, "You should've told me you were pregnant." He was silent for a few seconds before he continued, "I'm the reason why you lost our baby."

I wiped away my tears. It was no use. It was over, everything that I had built up for myself was right on the ground. All my dreams and faint hopes were replaced by a total blackout. I pulled myself away from his embrace.

My tone was husky but calm when I said, "Aiden, it will be best if I take a cab back to my sister's." He knew what I meant. He moved from beside me and left the room. I needed to be alone in my misery.

***

As the cab drove away, I felt as if a whole apple was stuck inside my throat. It was so hard for me to breathe or swallow. I recalled a similar feeling of despair I'd had when Yusuf was around me, but then I hated him.

In my experience, I knew that there were many reasons for death—accident, disease, war, old age—but could someone die from a broken heart? Right that moment, I felt as if I were dying ... but slowly.

I glanced outside the window in front of me. Clear blue skies, *what a myth!* I thought. The brilliant silky blue cloudless color was just a thin layer of fantasy that hid an enormous space of nothingness, obscurity, and darkness, which was the same as the dark feelings that lay deep inside my heart. *What happiness! What life!* It was all just an enormous fib ...

I recalled Yusuf's accident. Death felt like a relief right then ... a relief from this lie called life. I closed my eyes. Her hair smelled like flowers lying next me in bed ... Nora. I recalled her sentence.

"I love you, Mommy. I don't want you to ever die," she said before she kissed my cheek. She was the only reason left for me to want to live.

Chapter Twenty-Four

A FEW DAYS LATER, I was at home. Nora was still with Jasmine. I came to gather a few things before I went back to her place. All of a sudden, I felt drained. I lay on the pink bed, staring at the glowing plastic stars. I wished I could snatch them off the ceiling. I hated the memories that lay beneath them. I recalled Aiden along with all the events that hit me all over again. Was his plan to tear me up emotionally and then move on to be with someone else like Adrianna? I started to cry again. I couldn't sleep there anymore. I ran to the living room and stood in the middle of it. My hands covered my face. My cries were sounding more like weeping. I heard a knock. My weeping stopped, and then I froze. Could that be Aiden? The knock came again. I decided not to answer, just in case it was him. I lay on the sofa bed outside my living room, looking at my small, congested space, comparing it to Aiden's house. I wondered how long it would take me to get over him. Would I ever get over him? Long minutes passed, and I heard a knock on the door that connected my living space to Jasim's. I got up after the third knock. Maybe Jasim wanted to check on me.

His eyes narrowed when he looked at me. "What happened to you? Are you okay?"

My voice was raspy. "I'm fine; I just have a headache."

He frowned lightly. "Hannah, you can always talk to me about anything. Remember that."

"Thanks, Jasim." I then moved close to him. I hugged him tight. I needed his shoulder to cry on.

"Should I tell the man who came and asked about you to come back some other time?"

"What man?"

The person who knocked earlier wasn't Aiden. I didn't know why my heart sank that second.

"A man, his name is Ryan. He said it's urgent that he speak to you."

"Urgent! But why?"

"He wouldn't tell me. He seems nice. I will be by your side, my dear."

"Let me wash up first. I will be right up."

I quickly washed my face and freshened up. My eyes were still a bit red. I brushed my hair hurriedly. I merely put some lip gloss on my otherwise makeup-free weary face. As I approached Jasim's living room, I heard a couple of voices. I froze and then slowly walked while shaking. Ryan's voice was familiar.

As soon as I saw him, I screamed out loud. I was on my knees. I hid my face in my own arms.

"No! No!" I felt as if my heart was about to escape my chest. I felt a couple of arms around me. I was quivering frantically. Ryan's eyes looked so familiar … I saw the accident, his face, his dead body … I saw Yusuf.

I screamed, "Yusuf is dead!" I glared at him. "Who are you?" Then I heard myself repeat that same sentence a couple of times. I felt my body being led toward the couch. I lay down and then felt a damp cloth on my temple.

Jasim said worriedly, "Calm down." Then I heard him say to Ryan, "Who are you? What brings you here?" There was a long silence.

"I am Joseph's brother, who was her husband." I turned to face him. I shook my head in disbelief. My body was tense. His eyes … Yusuf's eyes. He was tall and fair, just like him. Yusuf's brother! Then I recalled the picture that I had found in Yusuf's office, a young teenage boy who resembled Yusuf carrying a boy toddler. Was the toddler Ryan?

I heard Jasim say, "I think you need to come back later. Hannah is not in the right state of mind to receive any disturbing information."

There was a long silence, and then I heard Ryan say, "Okay, I can come back later when she calms down." I could hear his step heading toward the front door.

I cried out, "Wait! Don't go please." I heard him coming back to sit next to me. My throat felt dry as a bone when I swallowed. "Did you say that his name was Joseph! His real name was Joseph!"

"Yes. Joseph Stanly. Mother always called him Joe."

My tone was mellow when I repeated after him, "Joseph Stanly." His name sounded common, as if I had heard it many times before. Joseph Stanly. Joseph was the English equivalent to Yusuf. So Yusuf was after all his Middle-Eastern name. "He wasn't Middle Eastern."

"Half, his father was from the Middle East. Mother was an American."

"You didn't share the same father?"

"No, we didn't."

I was taking little breaths, as it was painful to breathe fully. My lips were dry.

He continued, "Joe never knew his father. Mother couldn't find him after getting pregnant by him." That explained his non-Middle-Eastern last name.

I said evenly, "Yusuf is dead."

"I know that already. I have been looking for him since Mother passed away; it's been four years now."

I was still not believing that this was happening to me. Was he the telemarketer who called me a while back? He did have Yusuf's voice.

"Did you find his other wife?"

"I couldn't find anyone else but you. It was a long journey."

I offered a murky smile. "I bet." I glanced over at Jasim. His expression was kind; he was only looking at me, as if he were afraid of me having another nervous breakdown. I was now lost, confused, and shocked.

Ryan asked, "Where is your daughter?"

I was still lost in space and ignored his question.

I asked him, "Wait a minute. How did you find me?"

He sighed. "I hired a private investigator. They looked all over the state. He then found a police report in Arizona over a motor home theft. The police had his driver's license picture, which matched Joe's description."

I didn't want to trash Yusuf's description to him yet. Could I even trust him? After all, he was his brother; he could share the same crazy genes.

I said tightly, "What do you want from me?" I had to look away; he even had Yusuf's scowl.

His tone was hesitant. "At first, I wanted to find Yusuf, but then I found out that he passed away. I really wanted to know the brother I never knew."

Did he really want to know the monster who was once my husband? I wondered how much he knew of him.

"After Mother passed away, I felt the need to find my lost brother, especially since it was Mother's will before she died."

"Don't you have any other family members?"

"Far cousins, Father was from Palestine, and his family lived all over the world. My mother was adopted."

"You didn't tell me yet what you want from me."

"I just wanted to know you, know my niece. I would like to be there for you both if I may."

"How about your father?"

"He passed too, a few years before Mother passed away."

It was so much for me to take in. I felt exhausted, as if I had been running for months or even years, and all of a sudden, I just stopped—but I was nowhere near a comfortable place to lay my bushed body. I could see his scrutinizing gaze on me.

He asked tentatively, "Will it be okay to see my niece?"

I quivered, glancing over at Jasim.

Jasim said to Ryan, "Hannah is very tired right now. I think she needs to rest." He smiled at me sincerely. "Hannah and Nora have a good family, which includes me; she is not alone."

His tone was more of a warning than a statement. I breathed in, and then I glanced at Ryan, who frowned lightly.

"I understand that my brother put you guys through hell. I am not defending his actions, nor can I undo what he's done." He got up and handed me two cards, one was with his name and number and the other one had a hotel address.

"I will be in town for another week. Call me when you decide to arrange a meeting for me to see Nora, at your convenience."

I was avoiding looking at his face. Yusuf and Ryan must have looked more like their mother than their fathers. They had identical eyes. Ryan seemed to be in his late thirties. His lips were thinner, and his hairline was also thinner. He also had a rounder face. He was, however, as tall with the same square jaw and almost the same physical form; only Ryan was thinner. It was as if I were looking at Yusuf but years younger.

He added, "I would also like to change his gravestone, to reflect his real name."

I shook lightly as I recalled Yusuf's grave. I nodded.

Jasim walked him to the front door. He came back, sat close to me, and squeezed my hand tight.

I wasn't crying anymore. I just felt frozen. I knew I wasn't in a good state to drive to my sister's. I said, "I can't sleep downstairs tonight."

He tapped on my shoulder. "You can always sleep here; there is plenty of room."

I felt safe next to him. "Thank you for everything."

"Don't thank me; it is my duty to be there for you. You are just like my daughter."

As if someone had washed my bleeding heart with cool water, I felt better, more relaxed.

"What do you want me to say if Aiden calls or shows up?" He was too smart. It seemed as if he knew already what had happened.

"I don't think he will call or show up, but if he does, tell him I'm not here."

"Just relax. A good night's sleep can help. You will see how you feel in the morning."

I couldn't sleep; it was useless to try again.

"You know what will help me?"

"What?"

"If I win a game of backgammon."

He smiled and said, "Do you want to bet on it?"

I curled a smile, "Let's bet. But first, let me make a phone call to Jasmine." I didn't feel safe that I wasn't around my daughter. I let her know briefly of Nora's newfound uncle and to keep her safe. I was glad I played a couple of games of backgammon; it helped me forget momentarily my awful week. Hours later, I still lay awake snuggled under the light-green covers, looking around the medium-size room at the white dresser, glancing at the window's sheer green blind. The darkness transformed slowly to gray and then pale peach. That was when I fell asleep.

***

I was awakened by Jasim, creeping in and placing a tray on my side lamp dresser. I got up and rubbed my eyes. It was 10:00 a.m. I glanced over at the tray and noticed a cup of tea, a couple of slices of toast, cheese, and some fried eggs—breakfast in bed, which was my first. Then I recalled the dinner Aiden and I had had sitting on his oversized bed, after the love we had made. I felt a squeeze in my chest. I should've known that happy moments were always short-lived with me, recalling all the male faces I had seen in my life so far. At least when I got to Jasim's face, he was smiling at me, soothing my heart. I reached for the cup of tea and sipped some of it. I didn't want to let him down, after making all that effort.

I didn't do much that day at home. For the first time ever, I lazed around the living room and watched some old shows with Jasim. I was briefly thinking of Ryan. I had tons of questions to ask him then, and at the same time, I feared to know the answers.

I told Jasim briefly about what happened with Aiden—keeping our intimacy to myself. He tapped on my shoulder lightly. He didn't even try to defend him, but he said that sometimes, jealous people can take the role of a snake, separating two people. I knew that Adrianna was a snake, but Aiden used me as a rebound, he was also a skilful actor; he played his part well at the hospital—as if he really cared. I felt lost and wished I could erase the last few months from my life. Aiden's love confession to me once, under the clear blue skies, didn't mean he meant it. Yusuf also said he loved me—in his selfish, dominating, killer love. That perception was excoriating, causing pinches in my chest. Aiden lied—Adrianna was definitely not just a mistake—she *was* his ex-girlfriend—possibly his girlfriend now since Aiden and I broke up. I came from a different class. He was afraid that I was going to be a gold digger, like his poor slutty ex-fiancée, but not Adrianna; she was already rich with a better social rank. He wasn't afraid to spoil her rotten. *There was no better explanation,* I thought sullenly.

***

The next day, my mind drifted to Ryan, Yusuf's brother. Was he going to cause me trouble? I wondered if he was dangerous too. He could be hiding himself behind a sincere mask just like his brother. I was grateful, however, that I had Jasim's backing. I recalled his words. *"Hannah and Nora have a good family, which includes me; she is not alone."* I felt a slight soothing feeling, but then again, it was interrupted when Aiden landed back in my head, only to fill it with agony.

Being out of work gave me all day to think of my current messed-up life. My past, a hideous, long, scary path—somehow, I found myself walking on it again. Jasim was aware of my job situation. He reassured me that I would never starve or live on the streets, since he was going to be there for me. I forced a smile. I didn't know how to thank that man who wanted to protect me, as if I were his real daughter. I recalled my father's selfishness in the past, and Yusuf wasn't much better of a father to Nora. That made me wonder about fatherhood and common blood relations. Somehow, that subject didn't make any sense.

I decided to look for any job, until the job at Nathan's office became available.

A couple of days had passed, I came across Ryan's card. He was the CEO at a security computer system company. I hesitated, and then I called his number. What if he wasn't a bad person? He didn't really try to connect with me after he left that night. Maybe he wasn't as awful as his brother.

He answered almost immediately. I felt a shock in my chest. It felt as if I were speaking to Yusuf, whose tone transformed from nasty to kind with a composed timbre. Our conversation was quick. I told him that he was welcome to come and visit Nora, who was going to be at Mother's house. I wanted to be surrounded by my family when he came in.

When Ryan arrived, he was met with so many big, stunned, staring eyes. No one seemed welcoming. I was thankful Jasim and Nathan were there to break the ice and welcome him, because no one else had the ability to do so. My almost seven-year-old Nora was looking at him with big brown eyes. He smiled at her sincerely. I even noticed his eyes filled with tears. Was he really genuine, or was he a skillful actor like his brother? I was skeptical about my surroundings. He then brought himself down to be at her same height.

His eyes shone when he said, "Nora, you are so lovely."

She shied away, hiding her face in my blouse with a smile on her face. Nora loved compliments. I glanced at her. She was looking flawlessly beautiful, with her red dress, her long brown hair brushed in straight brown streaks with a white ribbon around it. I was glad that he didn't try to hug her yet; somehow, I was afraid of my own reaction to him being close to her. I needed to get used to the idea of him first.

Jasmine went to make some tea in the kitchen because my mother was mesmerized, sitting across from Ryan, as if she were still grasping the idea that Yusuf's brother was sitting in her living room.

Jasim broke the silence by saying, "How do you like Canada?"

Ryan's facial expression looked tense. He was most likely overwhelmed with all the scrutinizing eyes around him.

He said nervously, "I like it. It's different from California."

"Oh, so you are from California! I was there many times. It's a beautiful place."

"Yes, it is."

"Do you have a family?"

"I don't. I was married once, but it didn't work out and no kids."

I was just listening, my eyes darting between them.

"When was the last time you saw your brother?"

"It was almost twenty-five years ago. I was still a kid."

"You don't have any other brothers or sisters?"

"No, I don't. He was my only brother."

I could tell that he was nervous. Little later, Jasim and Hady took Nora and my twin brothers to a fast-food restaurant, and Nathan also left with Jasmine, simply to give Ryan freedom to speak on the delicate subject. I told Ryan that he could speak in front of Mother and me.

On her deathbed, Yusuf's mother expressed some guilty feelings toward her eldest son as she acknowledged to Ryan the truth about her past.

She met a man at a college party one night. She had had too much to drink. A couple of months later, she found out that she was carrying a child from that one-night stand with a nameless stranger, and the only truth she knew of him was that he was from the Middle East. And since she was an orphan herself, she decided not to give away her child for adoption. She had to quit school and work full-time to support herself and the son she decided to keep. Because of her misfortune in life, she was always angry and harsh with him, always punishing him as he always misbehaved. She even used to lock him up when she went to work, because she couldn't afford a babysitter. Yusuf was always an angry boy.

Through work, she met an immigrant from Palestine. He was kind and loved her sincerely. He married her, giving her a home and a stable life. Ryan was born, and his mother's attention went straight to him. She spoiled him the way she never spoiled Yusuf, catering to his every need. As a teenager, Yusuf had a very angry, explosive temper. He was always getting kicked out of school because of ongoing fights. Soon, he got involved with stealing and drugs and was constantly in and out of jail.

Ryan's father was kind but couldn't fix his damaged stepson, while his mother was always telling him that he came out of nowhere to wreck her life. One day, she asked him to leave and to never come back. And so Yusuf left ... and never came back. A few years passed, and the mother felt guilty, realizing that she could have been the reason behind her son's behavior and was terrified to hear of his death. She could've saved him if she had been a better mother, but then it was too late, because she never heard from him ever again. She lost her husband to a massive heart attack, and a few years later, she found out she had cancer. She fought it for five years, and on her deathbed, she recalled her lost son. She cried over him, and so Ryan promised his mother that he was going to find him. Finding Yusuf became Ryan's mission after his mother died, and he didn't stop until he finally did. But then it was too late, Yusuf was already dead.

I just listened, afraid to speak. It was so easy picturing Yusuf as an angry teenager; he was always angry, up until he passed away. Recalling the accident, I quivered when I heard Ryan's mother's confession to Yusuf. "He came out of nowhere to wreck her life." I felt the same when I met him. He really came out of nowhere to finish destroying mine. I wondered if his controlling behavior toward me was because of how he felt toward his mother. Did he want to hurt me because he hated women in general? Was he angry because he didn't know his father?

The many forms of abuse I received in my past came in different shapes. They wounded me from various angles. With my new scar from Aiden, I would forever be in pain. Yusuf's way of getting off was by hurting and placing people in despair; it was his way of getting revenge, I supposed. Maybe because he enjoyed their agony … Was Aiden the same? Well, from what I had gathered, his ex-fiancée cheated on him and was after his money, so to him, I was another poor, insignificant money-hungry creature.

My way of coping was to try to wrap that horrific effect and hide it somewhere deep. For a while, I thought I was becoming normal, especially since I had met Jasim. After I met Aiden, I ignored all the voices in my head, which reemerged constantly. But then I was faced with my fears. After what happened with Aiden, I could never trust again.

Ryan expressed his hope to see Nora right before he went back to California. I hesitated at first but accepted it. He didn't really look dangerous to me. He was different from Yusuf. Ryan hardly looked me straight in the eyes, as if he knew how uncomfortable that made me. Ryan could meet Nora at our home, but since I didn't have much space to entertain anyone at my small basement apartment and as Jasim always told me that his home was my home, I decided to invite him to Jasim's. He could spend a couple of hours; I was still reluctant to ignore the idea of how much he reminded me of Yusuf.

Before the meeting, I knew I had to go and look for something. I had hidden it a while back in Mother's house.

Mother, Jasim, Nora, and I sat at the same table with Ryan, having dinner. He was more at ease this time. He spoke to Nora, trying to keep a gap in between them. Maybe he was afraid to get attached to her. Nora was being her usual self, delightfully sweet and girly. We didn't speak of his brother during dinner. We spoke of casual subjects and Ryan's company, which specialized in selling security systems, computers, and spy gadgets. I recalled Yusuf's spying gadgets, which he always hid from me. How ironic that his younger brother had similar interests. The only difference was Ryan made it his career and Yusuf made it his way of life in order to control and scheme people out of their life savings and dignity.

Right after dinner, Ryan said something to Jasim, who got up and offered to give Mother a ride. Nora was watching TV in the living room. Ryan stood in front of Jasim's backyard, watching the faint light coming from the dusk in front of him. I wondered what he was thinking about. I waited for him to turn back, because I had something in my hand for him. I gave him a small envelope. He opened it. Right away, he had tears in his eyes. It was so hard watching him cry. Could a picture of his brother holding him as a toddler affect him that much? It was one of the few belongings Yusuf left behind. He pulled himself closer, and then he changed his mind, pulling back. I was glad he didn't pursue hugging me. I didn't think I could bear it, at least not yet.

"Thank you," he mumbled.

"No need to thank me. This picture should be with you." My lips curved into a smile.

"I am sorry to know what Joe did to you ... I mean, it's very depressing and sad that he was capable of harming a lovely sweet young woman like you."

My heart raced.

"It happened; he did." I had to ask him a question that was bothering me. "You found me on your own?"

"Yes, I did. Of course, it helped that I had some connection with my type of work."

I frowned, recalling Jason's unnecessary search.

"Did you happen to call me a while back?"

He stared at me for a few long seconds. I had to break my gaze.

"I had to confirm and match your name to the address I got, since you moved around quite a bit."

I smiled cynically, recalling the gypsy lifestyle Nora and I endured. He smiled sincerely. It was as if he already understood my mystifying smile. Just the way his brother did once, he had the ability to read me, but I didn't feel alarmed by him. He reached for his jacket pocket and took out an envelope. "Nora is my only niece. I already set up a trust fund for her and put you in charge of her account. You should be expecting some forms and calls coming in from my lawyer's office. Once everything is set up, you can expect some investment money to come in your name as well. It's a little complicated, but the lawyer will explain it to you better."

I shook my head. "I don't think …"

He interrupted me. "That money should've belonged to Yusuf. Our mother's will was to find Yusuf and give him half of her estate from her life savings and half of the life insurance I received after her death." He placed a hand on my shoulder. I tried so hard not to pull back. "I know of the life you had because of my brother and the damage he's done. Some of that money should be transferred directly to you, to help you get on your feet again." He walked toward the front entrance. "In this envelope, you will find the summary of the money you should expect." I felt lost in my surroundings. Was this happening to me? We stood in front of the front entrance. "I know it's hard, but please find it in your heart to forgive Joe. Call me anytime, or maybe even visit with Nora."

I smiled at that. I knew I couldn't bring myself to do so, at least not for a while.

I mumbled, "We will see what happens. I will try and forgive Yusuf." I just couldn't call him anything else.

"Don't hesitate to call me if you need anything, anything at all." He then opened his arms, expecting a hug.

I held my breath, walked forward slowly, and felt his arms around me. There were a few long seconds, during which I couldn't breathe. I pulled back smiling lightly, and then I watched him leave.

I walked to Jasim's kitchen table, placed the sealed envelope on it, and sat on a chair. With shaky hands, I opened it. I examined the numbers over and over again. Was this even real? I had never dreamed in my whole entire life of owning even a fraction of this money. Nora was going to be looked after. I didn't know if I should take it.

Yusuf, I closed my eyes. Like a movie trailer, I recalled him—a tall, arrogant, good-looking man walking with confidence, sitting at one of the many empty tables. I was that young, naïve, nervous-looking girl, who was trying her best since it was her first day as a waitress. I didn't know how long I sat there, buried in my memory. I felt Jasim's arm around my shoulders.

"Are you okay, Hannah?"

I glanced at the envelope in front of me and mumbled, "Apparently, I can afford to pay you full rent soon." My lips curved into a smile.

"You do know that this was the least of my worries? You help me around the house; we had a deal, remember?"

"I know. I just feel bad taking this from Ryan."

"Why? It's Nora and your natural right. She is Yusuf's daughter, as you were his wife." He gave me a reassuring smile and squeezed my hand tight. "You will be okay. Think positive, Hannah."

I smiled back to his face. I needed to think positive, if only I could forget about Aiden.

Chapter Twenty-Five

The next day painfully passed by. I glanced at the phone periodically all day. I didn't want my emotions to fail me and to find myself calling Aiden's cell phone. I even felt reluctant checking my email. A few times, my cell phone rang, and I found myself running to it. I loathed the emptiness that I felt then when it wasn't Aiden.

I also reviled the feeling of redundancy that filled my days with worthlessness and dejection. I had to keep reminding myself that Aiden merely saw another woman in me. If only I could pick up and go, start fresh somewhere else, but I knew that was impossible.

As the days slowly passed by, I tried to forget Adrianna's degrading, hurtful words, and Aiden, he was someone I needed to forget, just like Yusuf. The refection of my disastrous destiny with men filled up my chest with a pent-up seething.

What had happened to Mary? Her constant warnings were playing in my head like an impenetrable puzzle. I knew she was hiding a secret, but what secret? I shook her out of my head. I had to also stop thinking of her and only focus on the positive. At least I knew where Yusuf came from. He had a real first and last name and a brother who lived in California. I recalled the number I had read off of the document Ryan gave me before he left. Soon, I was going to be relieved financially. With the trust fund that was set up, half was going to savings and half was going to help me look after Nora better. The extra one-thousand dollars monthly installment could make a difference in our lifestyle, especially after I started working for Nathan. I could spend more time with her and take her on vacations; I wanted her to have all the things I once dreamed of having. Perhaps, in a couple of years, I could even go back to school, and get a degree—then land a good paying job—that would make my dream come true. We were not close to being rich, but we would be settled.

I was recalling how low of a life we had had to endure so far. I remembered the draft of one thousand Debra once gave me, which helped me escape from Vancouver. The lump sum of money I was going to receive soon was going to help me restore my credit and buy a decent car. I was going to put the rest of the money in my savings account, for rainy days just so no one could treat me like trash anymore.

I had learned in my life that money didn't grow on trees, and I was already planning not to indulge myself. I had also decided that I wouldn't be moving from Jasim's place. To me, my small apartment was my home, a place where I felt safe and loved. I had a good family, a mother, a sister, brothers, and a brother-in-law, and I also had Jasim. I didn't know what I would have done without him being by my side. Right then, he was my strength.

One day, I got a call from a lawyer's office asking me for my information, SIN (social insurance number), and banking information so they could transfer funds. At that time, I was by the door, leaving to pick up Nora from school. It was probably from Ryan's lawyer, but I had to make sure; briefly recalling Yusuf's schemes, I quickly went online while I placed the lawyer on hold and researched his name and phone number. I breathed when I found out that the lawyer worked for a legitimate Canadian firm. I tried to feel better; at least I could try to pick myself up from the bottom and move forward. If only I could erase Aiden from my head.

***

ONE FRIDAY AFTERNOON, I PARKED my car by Mandy's after picking up Nora from school. I even brought us each one latte. I noticed a little blue Porsche in her driveway. I hesitated. I wondered who was visiting her.

Somehow, the sight of new expensive cars brought me chills. I recalled Adrianna's and Aiden's BMWs and Jason's Porsche.

It had been a few weeks already since my breakup with Aiden. I was slowly getting used to the idea that he was also a part of history, just like Yusuf. From that moment on, I would live my life to the fullest without any man to interrupt it.

Mandy was now planning her wedding with John; she asked me to be her maid of honor, and I accepted of course. How could I not? She was my best friend. Dealing with Mandy's wedding brought memories of Jasmine's last year's wedding, causing Aiden to swoop through my mind. I dismissed him; just the same way I used to dismiss Yusuf when he soaked my mind. Now it was Aiden's turn. For the last couple of weeks, I had either been at the gym, sweating my brains out, or at Mandy's or Jasmine's, lazing around, and after picking up Nora from school, I always went back to Mandy for more mingle time. At night, I played backgammon with Jasim. I was hoping I wouldn't become way too lazy by the time I started my new job with Nathan.

I couldn't help the disturbing reflection I created in my head of Adrianna and Aiden having sex, especially when I lay in bed. I wondered if they were now wrapped in each other's arms, being intimate. Was he indulging her with more expensive gifts or possibly having dinner at some nice, expensive restaurant? I recalled Adrianna's phone conversations where she would talk about all the gifts from Aiden, how hard he tried to get back with her, and his defensive line. I hated when I felt unworthy and inferior.

I had to shake a memory off. Nora began to whine in the backseat of the car; she was anxious to see Tiffany. As soon as I stepped out, Nora ran toward Mandy's front entrance, and then I felt a little animal zooming in between my legs. I jumped. I placed the two lattes on the top of my car. *What was that?* I wondered.

A tall, good-looking man with a short brown hair emerged from behind a tree, calling, "Charlie! Charlie! Come back!"

I looked around to find a little Chihuahua running around, while the tall man was trying to chase him. It was an amusing sight. "Can you help me catch him please?" he yelled out nervously. I scanned around to see if I could catch sight of the dog, and then I ran to the other side to catch him. I saw a car coming all of a sudden, and I got alarmed. I bet the driver wouldn't see the little dog zooming back and forth on the street. There was no time to scream. I ran as fast as I could toward the car, which stopped suddenly after hitting me lightly on my thigh. I fell on the ground, facedown, scratching my hands and elbows, which saved my face from hitting the hard ground.

I noticed that Charlie the dog was terrified right in front of me, as if he realized what he'd done. I grabbed his light body. I noticed he was shaking hard. I was glad that I was able to get up without difficulty. The owner of the car was still shocked. Her hand held a cell phone a few inches away from her ear. She was obviously too distracted to notice that she was about to kill a dog and possibly a human. She yelled out with a concerned tone asking if I was okay. I just waved my hand. I was glad I was able to save that crazy little Charlie.

The owner of the dog first looked shocked and then smiled happily. "Oh, how can I thank you? Thank you! Thank you!"

"No worries. I am glad your Charlie is safe."

He lifted Charlie, who covered his face with slimy little licks.

"My name is Jeff." His brown eye still looked anxious.

"Hannah."

"Are you friend of Mandy's?"

"I am. You know Mandy?"

"I am her cousin. I just came over to her place with little Charlie. She needed to have her wedding dress altered drastically, but Charlie decided to discover the neighborhood on his own."

"Oh. You do alterations?" I was thinking he could alter a couple of my pants I had just gotten for myself. He stared at me for a moment.

He gasped, rolling his eyes. "I am a designer, my dear. I designed Mandy's wedding dress and so many celebrities'," he said proudly.

I frowned. He was being abrupt and arrogant with someone who risked her life to save his dog. What was the big deal with designing celebrities' clothes?

I said tonelessly, "I see."

"Let's get you cleaned up," he said while rubbing Charlie's short brown-and-white fur. I followed him to the house. As soon as Mandy showed up, Jeff exclaimed, "Your friend is awesome, amazing! I love her already. She saved my little Charlie from being run over by a car!"

I frowned again. His character was strange. He was going from abrupt to happy, changing his tone sarcastically.

I replied, "It was no big deal."

"Not a big deal! You risked yourself by standing in front of that car that hit you instead of Charlie. It's a big deal!"

I laughed at the way Charlie was now licking his arm. Only a few minutes ago, he was running away from him.

Jeff then turned to Mandy and said, "I think you should find something for your friend to wear and get her wounds cleaned up." His tone was bossy. I could see Mandy's frustration on her face. A few minutes later, I wore a different shirt and had a clean bandage on each of my elbows. My upper thigh, where the car had hit me, was a bit blue and sore. We were on our way to Mandy's living room. Mandy and I each held a takeout latte.

I turned to Jeff and said apologetically, "I'm sorry; I didn't know you were here. I could've gotten you some coffee."

Jeff said, "That's okay. I mean, Mandy should've told you that I was coming." He sounded fussy. Mandy rolled her eyes and walked toward the kitchen.

My eyes grew wide when I saw her wedding dress. If Jeff designed it, he was indeed talented. It was a strapless, off-white mermaid-style dress, with satin around the chest-waistline area and a beaded design. I just stood there staring at it.

Jeff asked, "Do you like it?"

"I love it. Wow." I couldn't take my eyes off of it.

"I will design you one for your wedding one day." My heart sank. "My treat for you, for saving my little Charlie."

"You don't owe me anything, really."

Mandy came back with a cup in her hand. I guessed so she could share her latte with her fussy cousin. I insisted that we both share our latte with Jeff. I found out over the conversation that Jeff had just bought a house not too far from Mandy's. He was almost practically her neighbor.

She exclaimed mockingly, "Lucky me!"

He said proudly, "Of course, you are lucky. Now I will make sure you dress better."

Mandy said defensively, "What's wrong with my clothes?"

He sighed and replied, "Nothing. John is feeding you better these days."

I could tell her tone was getting heated when she said, "Jeff, I may not be as skinny as your scrawny models, but I am not fat."

"Whatever."

The unusual conversation was interrupted by Mandy's cell-phone call. I could feel her relief when she excused herself. I continued my conversation with Jeff. I found out that he was the only cousin to Mandy and her sister. He was different from anyone I had met so far. I didn't feel inhibited while I was speaking to him. Over the last few days, I was starting to develop a liberated feeling—possibly since I didn't have to worry about a horrific job working under Adrianna. My past was already exposed; even Aiden knew all about it now. From now on, I wouldn't hide myself anymore. Mandy came back. She looked refreshed. She was probably speaking to John. She said excitedly, "Jeff, do you have a nice dress for Hannah?"

He studied me from head to foot.

He said, "I may. Why?"

I was listening as if I were not part of the conversation.

Mandy replied, "Because we are invited to this cocktail party tomorrow. You can come too. I think you know a couple of people in there." He stared at her for a long moment; she added, "Hannah did save your Charlie's life."

He said, "I will forever owe her for that." He smiled sincerely.

She added, "Well, we need the dress by tomorrow, before noon; just in case you need to alter it."

Jeff said, "I don't owe you anything, Mandy. Don't boss me around, dear cousin." I was glancing between them again. It was as if they had forgotten to include me in their conversation.

"You don't owe me, but you owe Father, right!"

I knew that Mandy's father was a plastic surgeon.

He glanced at me and said while touching his nose, "My nose, he simply fixed my nose because it didn't go well with the rest of my stunning features."

I couldn't help myself. I heard myself giggle.

He frowned, adding, "What? You don't think I am stunning? Dear Hannah …"

I cleared my throat and said, "You are. I was going to mention that to you." I tried not to roll my eyes. He was acting strange again.

Jeff said, "I'm kidding." He giggled. "You girls are crazy." He then turned to me adding, "I am good-looking. All my admirers say that."

This is a very entertaining conversation, I thought. I found myself forgetting about all my troubles.

Mandy said, "Father is a good plastic surgeon …"

The conversation continued, and I found myself listening mostly to the both of them while they delicately and skillfully criticized each other. I was surprised that neither got offended, maybe because they were confident and full of themselves. I should learn to be more like that, I decided. I really wanted to be an individual, strong-minded person. I didn't want anyone's criticism to destroy me anymore.

When John arrived, they stopped with their playful way of talking and were more serious. After dinner, I helped Mandy with her guest list for her upcoming wedding.

***

The next day, at half past noon, I stood in front of Jeff at Mandy's place, wearing his beautiful dress. At first, I was scared when he handed it to me. I was afraid of all the layers and colors. As soon as I put it on, I had to hold my breath. I was shocked to see my reflection in the mirror. It still looked different but classy. The dress was off-the-shoulder and tight around the chest, with pink, orange, and off-white. It tightened around my narrow waist with a little off-cream belt, only to flow in three different folded layers to my midthighs. It was short and weird but superb, and of course, the five-inch heel added some more legs. Well, I still had to keep the bandage on my elbow, but that was okay. It wouldn't be that noticeable. I couldn't help myself. I turned to Jeff and hugged him.

He pulled me away, saying, "Easy, girl! Is this, like, your first dress?"

I laughed and said excitedly, "No, but for sure the most interesting one!"

He smiled. "You like it. I know I am a genius."

"You are," I said. I wondered what Aiden would say if he saw me wearing this. All of a sudden, I felt my heart sink. I had to keep on reminding myself that Aiden was gone from my life. To distract myself from his painful recollection, I focused on the dress I was now wearing. I didn't care that slowly I was becoming an airheaded woman, since thinking merely caused me agony.

Later on that day, I started to relax that Jeff was coming along. I liked him, even though I found him very arrogant and strange, but somewhat interesting; also, Mandy and John could have some time alone. Right before getting ready for the party, I went to take out money from the bank. I knew that I was already almost broke. I wished I hadn't spent so much money on impressing Aiden with my expensive clothes and makeup. What was I thinking? I shook him out of my head. I withdrew a hundred dollars and almost decided not to look at my balance, but then I did. I should have almost four hundred dollars left. According to Ryan's statement I had read, I should get some money transferred in a couple of weeks. I would be okay until then.

I glanced twice at the amount. The machine must have given me the wrong receipt. I inserted my card again and printed the balance—same balance. I shook my head in disbelief. Something was definitely wrong. I printed another receipt with the last twenty transactions. I studied the long receipt. There was a transfer to my account a couple of weeks ago, with thirty thousand dollars. Maybe the lump sum had arrived earlier than anticipated. *Wow.* I smiled at the printed number on the paper in front of me. But the amounts didn't match. I was supposed to get sixty thousand dollars. I only got half. Maybe it was supposed to be in two payment installments. I would have to call the lawyer during the weekday to confirm this transfer and inquire about the rest of the money. I felt a little happier. At least my financial burden was resolved. I could instantly fix my credit. That deliberation gave me some confidence.

I styled my hair and makeup while the girls were looked after by the babysitter Mandy had hired for both of them. This time, I insisted I pay my share.

***

Mandy looked awesome with her blue strapless dress, which matched the color of her eyes, and she wore her blonde hair long and straight. I placed my hair in a loose side bun, letting some strands flow around neatly. I really looked different that day.

Jeff sat next to me in the car. He was speaking of his upcoming fashion show. I glanced around, realizing that life had taken me on a scary roller coaster ride. I was glad I was still walking straight.

John parked the car right across from a large, upscale restaurant. The tinted glass entrance was large, reminding me of the last firm holiday party I'd had to attend, minus the holiday decorations. That was the same night I met Aiden; I scowled. I walked next to Jeff toward a man wearing a tux. John gave him our names.

Mandy whispered to me, "I am glad you decided to come instead of my parents. Mother and I are disagreeing about my wedding guest list."

I turned to her. "Was that why you insisted that I come?" I whispered back.

She smiled mystifyingly and ignored my question.

Waiters wearing tuxes were walking around with trays full of drinks. I took a tall champagne glass, which was really refreshing. I was glad Mandy had insisted that I come. Some of the elegant guests were walking, and others were sitting around neatly set-up tables. I forgot to ask Mandy about the occasion. And I didn't see any banners around.

Jeff was walking next to me while Mandy and John met up with a couple of their friends.

I asked Jeff, "So what is the purpose of this cocktail party?"

He said, "The purpose is welcoming someone taking over a business. I don't know, a reason to party, I suppose."

"Who do you know around here?" He looked around him, while touching his chin lightly with his long, slender fingers.

"I know the host's daughter. She loves fashion shows. She wants to be a designer too, but the poor girl has no talent." He looked around, adding, "I wonder when they are going to bring the hors d'oeuvres?" He then glanced at me and said, "I forgot to mention, you look phenomenal."

I smiled, blushing.

"Thank you." I looked around.

Jeff said suddenly, "Oh, I see something. Come with me." I felt myself being pulled lightly by my arm. I didn't know at first where he was taking me until I noticed that he was apparently walking toward a waiter carrying an hors d'oeuvre tray.

I was later sipping on my second glass of champagne, walking around with Mandy and John. I wanted to leave them alone, so I decided to excuse myself and look for Jeff.

I found him. He seemed to be in the middle of a conversation with an older, short, stuffy man. I hesitated at first but slowly walked toward them. When I got closer, I noticed that Jeff and the older man were speaking of a famous Lebanese designer. Jeff was speaking of his exquisite work, but soon, the older man said that some Lebanese were troublemakers and went on to speak of someone he knew through his work experience.

The man was saying to Jeff, "These people are always angry. I think it's in their nature, as if they want to fight the whole world. You can even see them on TV sometimes shouting."

Jeff said defensively, "That's not true. Maybe that man had a reason or was born that way?"

"I don't know; he was still new to Canada, as if he came from a muddle far away. I heard he lost his relatives during the war, but that's not an excuse. I think most people from that region are just too complicated."

My heart sank as I recalled my torn-up country and the many lives that the war stole away. I bit my lip nervously while Jeff turned around; they noticed me, and soon Jeff introduced us.

"George Melisso is hosting this marvelous party, Hannah, my lovely friend."

We shook hands. I tried not to stare at George, while faking a smile. So that was George Melisso! *The famous flirt—*

After turning to greet me, George said, "Hannah, how lovely to meet you!"

I said politely, "Nice to meet you too, George. I heard you are building a couple of lovely homes."

George said, "Yes." He smiled, adding, "It's for my kids. I already have a home." He then examined me with a mischievous smile.

Jeff said to him, "Congrats. I heard your daughter is getting married."

George said, "Thank you. Finally, in a few months, I will feel liberated."

He then turned to Jeff and said jokingly, "If only I was twenty years younger, I would ask your lovely friend for her number right now." He also gave me a wink.

I blushed lightly, recalling what I had heard of him. After all, he was a flirt.

I said tentatively, "My number is complicated, I am afraid."

George giggled. "I love solving complicated numbers." He turned to Jeff and said, "We were speaking of complicated people, right, Jeff?"

I tried not show displeasure. I was from Lebanon. I bet he didn't know.

George continued with his sentence, "… always using some lame excuse of war for their bad behavior."

I knew that there was no excuse for ill manners, but then again, I didn't lose all my family to the war. I didn't know how it felt. A long time ago, I decided not to judge people.

Then I heard myself hesitantly ask George, "Have you lived during a war?" My tone was low.

Drawing his ears closer to me, he said, "Excuse me?"

Then I repeated myself with more confidence.

George said, "Of course not. Canada is a peaceful, beautiful country with a great government."

I took a deep breath and said to him, "That's because you are lucky; you were born here. Others aren't that lucky; they have to fight just to exist."

George frowned.

I gulped hard. I stuttered lightly when I continued, "I mean, you, um, you didn't choose this peaceful, beautiful country; your parents did, on your behalf when they chose for you to be born here."

George said defensively, "But I chose to educate myself and work hard. I chose to have good manners ... Sometimes, it's a matter of choice."

I stared at him, thinking how clueless some people could be! "Imagine if you were a kid who lost his parents and house and all his belongings, then what? How are you going to educate yourself? Who is going to raise you?" He had no answer. "You can't judge people unless you went through what they went through and were able to pull through alive, educated, and well mannered."

He nodded. George's frown disappeared. "Hannah, where are you from?"

I mumbled, "Lebanon."

He frowned and then said sincerely, "I hope I didn't offend you. I didn't know you were listening!"

I blushed. I didn't mean for him to realize I was eavesdropping. "No, not at all. Some people are bad mannered even if they were raised in a castle." I recalled Adrianna. "And some people become bitter from horrific experiences." I could right then think of so many people.

He smiled and said, "You are too wise for such a young lady."

My lips curled into a smile, and I said evenly, "I'm not wise. I have seen enough to perceive things from a different perspective."

To my surprise, he tipped his drink to mine and added, "Indeed you do. You are so fascinating." Jeff became speechless and seemed stunned.

George said to Jeff, "I'm taking your friend home with me tonight. I don't care what you say."

I smiled. George was being polite and charming. There was no way he liked me after what I had told him. It was as if that night was my revolution night. I was finally striving toward someplace, but I had no clue where. I hoped not as a sack of potatoes out of this cocktail party. After all, George was the host.

To my horror, he held my arm, turned to Jeff, and said with a playful tone, "I'm serious. She is coming with me for the rest of the evening, and she is going to help me host this party."

Help host this party! How did that happen? I started to quiver lightly and glanced, horrified, at Jeff, who was still taken aback.

As I walked next to George, his arm was still wrapped around mine. I found myself answering questions about the war. Was he really fascinated by me? I didn't get why. I was being honest about my upbringing. I decided I didn't want to feel embarrassed or ashamed. Why should I? I had no husband, no father, and no boss to answer to. I was free, liberated. I had always been dreaming of that moment. But that idea all of a sudden wasn't appealing to me. If only I had one particular man to answer to, I thought, recalling Aiden and my skimpy bikini incident. He was a jealous man, at that time, and I was more than happy to please him while living momentarily in a fantasy land I had created in my head. After all, he wasn't mine to keep; he was someone else's. I sipped more of my drink. I had no clue how to get him out of my mind now.

I was soon being introduced to different people throughout our conversation. I learned that George had lost his wife many years back. He had a couple of kids and one grandchild. He owned a few businesses and many properties. In other words, he was loaded.

Jeff had already told me about the purpose of that cocktail party, but I decided I would ask George, if only to open up a conversation. "What is the purpose of this party?"

His tone was gruff. "An excuse to celebrate, it was my son's idea, since he is going to take over one car dealership, and I just sold my other one."

To Aiden, I remembered. Why did Mandy bring me here? At that moment, I wished I had told her what exactly had happened between

Aiden and me. I decided only to mention to whoever wondered about our breakup that there was a misunderstanding between us. I really felt degraded by both Aiden and Adrianna. The real story would gain me tons of pity, and I hated pity. I noticed that George was approaching Mandy and John, Mandy's eyes opened wide in shock, seeing me with my arm wrapped around George's.

He glanced at them and said, "John, I would like you to meet my lovely young girlfriend."

I smiled shyly at John's astounded expression and mumbled, "I know John and Mandy; they are my friends."

George said jokingly, "Really! Fascinating, I guess you know that John is the brain behind my kids' dream houses." He gave me a wink saying, "If he does an awesome job, I want him to build our dream house, darling. What do you think?"

I giggled lightly, so did everyone around me.

I said jokingly to John, "John, make sure you do a good job."

Our conversation continued. I remembered when George was referred to by Aiden. I was there, sitting next to him. His hand was on my thigh from under the table almost the whole brunch. I sipped more champagne. I needed to forget about what had happened a couple of hours after our brunch. *How foolish was I!* I heard from Mandy that John's parents had already arrived.

John asked, while looking around, "Where is Aiden? I haven't …"

I could tell that he wasn't supposed to mention Aiden, because his sentence was deliberately clipped. Was Aiden supposed to be there? Was that the reason Mandy brought me along? She hid her gaze from mine right away.

George said, "Last week, when I spoke to him, he told me that he will try to come tonight. I haven't heard from him ever since. He didn't even answer his calls or emails. Maybe he is stuck and was caught up with last-minute paperwork and legalities back in Victoria."

My heart sank. I wondered what had happened to him. I didn't dare ask. Soon after speaking with Mandy and John, I walked along with George. As we strolled around, I caught sight of Jeff, who totally overlooked me, as he was in the middle of a conversation with another handsome man.

Later, I found myself circling with George. I met up with many faces, and each time, he introduced me as his young girlfriend. I had one question in mind for George. After all, the vacation to Cancun was his idea.

I hoped my question sounded casual and would raise no suspicions. "I'm surprised not to see Jason or Adrianna from Simon Miller's firm here!" I breathed out. I decided that this particular question was a good way to start my list of inquiries.

His eyes narrowed. "Where do you know Jason and Adrianna from?" Aiden did mention once that his father dealt with Simon Miller's firm; I was now sure they handled Aiden and George's business transaction.

I didn't want to lie. "I used to work at their firm."

He smiled. "Really!"

I nodded, looking around.

He added, "How long ago was that?"

"I left weeks ago." I looked at his expression, which was impassive.

He said, "It's a long story. I really didn't want clashes between a couple of my business associates, so I decided not to invite the Miller family." That answer didn't get me anywhere. "But then I heard that something was going on with Jason. He hasn't even been around for a while now. I like him better than his sister."

"Really?" I tried not to frown. I was afraid to ask him what had happened. I didn't want to sound like I was hunting for information, at least not yet. So I asked casually, "You seem to know Aiden well."

"Yes, I do." His eyes narrowed. In a dubious tone, he said, "And how do you know Aiden?"

I looked away. "Through my friends, you know, Mandy and John."

"Right." He drank from his glass. "Aiden's father was my friend, Neil Harris. He died last year." He looked away. "I like that boy; he's just like his old man, very ambitious and shrewd in business."

After taking a deep breath, I said, "I heard that Adrianna and Aiden are dating." I wanted to throw out this statement just to hear his answer. I knew I sounded like a detective who was fishing for information.

"I don't know. I know Aiden wasn't happy to know that I had invited her and Jason to join us at the resort. Their father was a good friend of mine too, Simon Miller." He sipped some of his square glass. "But then again last year, Aiden brought her along to a few of our gatherings and introduced her as his good friend."

It was as if the world had stopped turning. Aiden didn't invite them? It was all George's idea? Aiden was bringing Adrianna to George's gatherings as his good friend and not a girlfriend, but that was last year, possibly before I even met him. My head was spinning.

I said cautiously, "I remember booking the resort for Adrianna for one week, Royal Cancun, right?" My heart squeezed.

"Yes, beautiful resort." George was probably puzzled by my questions, which explained the way he was looking at me. He added voluntarily, "Strangely enough, Jason never showed up. I heard he was feeling ill from some food poisoning the day before, only Adrianna with Jason's girlfriend Katie." He twirled his glass and added, "Aiden never showed up the first week at the resort either. He said he had to fly to Victoria instead." He then looked at me, mystified. "Or maybe he wanted to avoid some clashes and battles with a certain girl and wished to stay away from Adrianna. You know he canceled as soon as he found out she was coming."

I looked away. What was I doing? George was, after all, a very sharp man. I couldn't think anymore. My head was buzzing; Aiden hadn't lied when he had said he went to Victoria instead.

He continued, "Right before the week passed, I found out he paid for my extra week and only showed up after everyone else was gone. It was supposed to be my treat to him, and it became the other way around." George then added jokingly, "It would have been better if we had a female companion, someone fresh like you."

I giggled too loud for my liking, because I felt I was on the verge of crying. What a strange night.

George led me to a round table. I was glad I got to sit, since my knees were trembling hard. His voice now came as an echo. He was telling me about his travels and businesses. He was talking while I listened, and sometimes, I said things that were apparently funny, because George was chuckling constantly. Maybe he found me really amusing. Well, at that point, I really didn't care; I was finally that carefree woman I always wanted to be—untroubled with the way people perceived me and thought of me.

Soon after, I found myself greeting more people. I held on to George's arm, just so I wouldn't fall down. I didn't know how the evening ended. I did, however, remember taking many photos with George and many other people. Videos of that event were being shot as well. I was next to him when he cut the cake. I met his son, Mathew, and daughter, Lea, and during his speech, he even thanked me for coming to the party. I felt everyone's gaze was on me that night. I was indeed the center of attention. I laughed and joked around as if my insides weren't being ripped apart by the agonizing thoughts of Aiden and the enigmatic mystery around him.

Chapter Twenty-Six

A COUPLE OF DAYS HAD passed. I tried to put the cocktail party behind me but decided to keep George's business card. He also insisted on taking my complicated number. I called the lawyers to check on the transfer that I had already received. Lately, I had spoken to couple of lawyers, in regards to the trust funds and money transfer. A couple of times, I had to fax my banking, along with mine and Nora's personal information. I was waiting for their call back; then I called the credit department to know how I could clear my credit immediately. After being on hold for at least half an hour, I found out that my credit was already cleared. Someone had already looked after it. That was odd. Who could that be? Could it be Jasim? Or could it be … *No, that can't be,* I thought.

Some of Jasim's other tenants, who lived in other rented properties he owned, moved out. He asked Mother if she wanted to move in along with the twins. When she mentioned that she couldn't afford it, he told her not to worry about the money; she could pay the same amount she was currently paying, while enjoying a much bigger house. The very next day, Mother and I went with Jasim to look at his house.

Mother was taken aback by the size, which was much bigger than her town house's size. It was obviously bigger than the current house Jasim and I lived in. We walked to the kitchen, which was already filled with new appliances and was large enough to accommodate Mother's dream to cook in a spacey gourmet kitchen. As soon as she stepped into the backyard, she started to cry. She was probably overwhelmed with how she could instantly fill the space with colorful flowers. Jasim and I watched. She turned back to face us with a stunned, wet face, as if she was still in disbelief that she was about to live there. After all, that was her dream house.

The four bedrooms were empty but spacious; the living room could look stunning with the right furniture.

I wondered about Jasim's generous offer. I dismissed the possibility that rang in my head like a beautiful symphony. Maybe not. I bet Jasim really appreciated Mother's delicious food; plus, he also mentioned that the last tenants didn't pay him on time and completely trashed the house. He needed someone reliable who could look after it the right way, since this house was his last purchase for his property investment and he wanted to protect it. I looked around the house. Jasim must have fixed it before asking Mother and me to look at it, since it looked immaculate and there were no signs of damage from previous tenants.

That same night, I saw Mary in my dream. She was looking for me. Nora cuddled right beside me in bed while I gaped at the sparkly ceiling. Now I could think better, without allowing my emotions to wash my face each time with the terrible memory. I recalled Mary's many warnings. What she was doing was odd; it was as if she was … protecting me? But from whom? I could then tell when Adrianna went outside the café to speak on her phone that Mary merely spoke of work, as if she was worried that our conversation was being taped.

Then I recalled Aiden when he said, *"You have to listen; I got a couple of weird warning texts. They are starting to make sense now."* Weird texts! Just like the one I got. Now I wished I had opened those blocked-sender texts while searching Aiden's phone for Adrianna's calls. Who sent them? I realized that Aiden wasn't lying, as I had suspected him to be—ever since my conversation with George. Mary could hold some clues. Maybe I should try to call her once again. I watched the clock move to morning. At 8:00 a.m. sharp, I called Mary. Her number had been disconnected. I was annoyed. How was I supposed to reach her now? I reached for the phone to call the cops. *Should I report Mary's disappearance?* I thought about it for a bit. Maybe not, I decided. I wouldn't know how to interpret my suspicions to the cops anyways.

***

A few days later on a Saturday morning, only two weeks away from Mandy's wedding, Jasim was working in his garden while I prepared breakfast. I opened all the windows around the living room to invite the sun in. I watched him, wondering if he could be the one behind transferring the money and clearing my credit. The lawyer responsible for Nora's trust and money transfer confirmed that no money had been transferred as of yet and that I should expect the money right on schedule—the middle of the following week. I was still waiting to hear back from the very first lawyer who called me and asked for my SIN and banking information. Jasim was considered comfortable financially. He had invested his money well and wasn't depending on a paycheck. A thirty-thousand-dollar bank transfer to my account plus twelve thousand dollars to help with credit recovery was a lot of money. I hated when things didn't make sense to me. Nora was playing with one of the games Aiden had given her. I couldn't take away all the expensive games he had bought her for my own sake. I had to learn to endure the pain while I watched her play with them.

The phone rang in Jasim's kitchen. I answered almost immediately. It was probably one of his old buddies inviting him to play golf again. I was glad that Jasim was going out more often with his friends. I loved seeing him happy. He was even looking better with his new clothes and always smelled of cologne. Sometimes I wondered if there was a woman behind his drastic transformation, I felt my heart squeeze over this consideration. I would love but hate that idea at the same time. Then again, I wanted him to be happy.

I was surprised to hear a familiar female voice.
"May I speak to Hannah?"
She had a thick accent. "Speaking." I frowned.
"Hi, Hannah. It's Elaina, Aiden's mother."
I froze. "Hi, Elaina." I was silent after.
"I haven't heard from you. How you are doing?"
I took a deep breath. "I'm okay. How are you?"

"I'm good, my dear." At that moment, I wondered how she had found my number. There was another awkward silence.

"Are you busy today?" she asked.

"Why?" All of a sudden, I felt uncomfortable.

Her tone was light. "I need a favor from you, if you have a few hours to spare." I held my breath. She continued, "You mentioned last time that you speak French?"

I scowled. "Yes, but not as fluently as before."

"You don't need to be fluent; I just need you to write me a few thank-you notes in French."

That was strange. Didn't her son have many bilingual staff at his disposal?

"If you can't, I would understand."

"What time?"

"Whenever is convenient for you."

I decided to come up with a valid excuse. "I don't have a babysitter for my daughter."

"That's not a problem, my dear. Bring her along; I miss seeing Nora."

Elaine met Nora once over dinner at a Mexican restaurant. I felt in a tight spot. She was too sweet for me to refuse.

"Sure, no problem." I really hoped Aiden wouldn't be there. I wasn't prepared to see him again.

"I will be there in a couple of hours." I stared at the backyard window in front of me for a few minutes. I was lost in my contemplations for a while, before calling Jasim to tell him that breakfast was ready.

I wore a casual light-blue summer dress, and my hair hung wavy-loose on my back, with shorter front layers. I kept my makeup classy and simple. Then I glanced, satisfied, at my reflection. I looked exactly how I wanted to look—confident. I kept Aiden out of my head; he was probably out of town again.

As soon as I drove through the majestic gate, I felt my heart sink. But I didn't see Aiden's BMW in the parking lot. I wondered where he was. I knocked on the door. Nora was looking around her in astonishment. I played with her hair nervously while waiting.

My heart raced as soon as the door opened, and I saw Elaina standing with a big smile on her face. She even gave both of us hugs. She asked me to follow her, so we both did. She led us to a large room, with many cushions, toys, dolls, and books. There was even a large flat-screen TV mounted to the walls. I didn't remember seeing that room before. Aiden must have skipped this room somehow the first time when he took me on a tour. Then I saw a young girl with a wide smile. She said with a strong accent that she was going to look after Nora. After settling Nora with toys, I followed Elaina to a large, bright office. A question was playing in my mind constantly. *Why am I really here?*

I was trying to make polite conversation with Elaina, while we had some tea and delicious sweets, sitting on her comfortable cream-colored sofa. We spoke of Spain, Lebanon, and Nora; we also talked about baking, since she loved baking all types of sweets. We didn't, however, speak of Aiden. I wondered how much she knew of our breakup. And I didn't want to ask her about when we were supposed to get to work. I didn't really wish to seem pushy. Half an hour later, she led me to her computer chair and asked me to translate what she was about to tell me to French. Half an hour later, we were done.

I turned to her and asked, "How did you know where to find me? I mean you called Jasim, my landlord." Did Aiden give her my number?

"Finding you was easy, my dear." Her eyes narrowed, and she said calmly, "I like you, Hannah. You remind me of my younger self. I was once young and poor, back in Spain ..." She started with her tale.

Elaina was only twenty-two years old when she met Neil, Aiden's father, during one of his vacations to Spain. He was then with his girlfriend. Elaina was one of the hotel maids. She worked hard to help support her sick mother. Neil was so taken by her that he had a fight with his girlfriend, who soon went back home to Canada all alone.

Neil married Elaina during his next visit to Spain, and a few months later, he brought her back with him to Canada. At first, she thought that only Neil's love could help her push through the trouble she was facing, due to the big social and cultural gap. She felt timid and worthless.

Neil also had numerous fights with his family, who refused to welcome her as their daughter-in-law. She spent a couple of years wishing she could go back to her humble life in Spain, but then something happened; Neil got into a big accident. He was in a coma for a while, during which she stood by his side in the hospital.

Elaina then prayed and made a promise while he lay helplessly in front of her, that if he fought to survive, she would then fight for her existence with him. A couple of days later, he woke up from his coma. Days later, he was able to talk. He fought to survive, so Elaina had to fight to exist.

With time, she became stronger and more assertive, realizing that all she needed was more confidence and belief in herself.

I didn't understand the reason behind her story. She obviously had a hidden message in there for me. Well, our stories weren't comparable, because her son loved to hide away from me. He didn't fight for me the way his father fought for Elaina. Aiden seemed to be worried about Adrianna's reaction to finding out about me, but why? Then I recalled someone from Aiden's past.

I asked, "Tell me about Aiden's ex-fiancée." I didn't want to beat around the bush anymore; if she didn't want to speak of her, she could simply say so. But I was surprised when she continued her story instead.

"When Aiden was born, he was everything to me. But I feared for him becoming a selfish and proud man because of his father's wealth. I wanted him to be humble and build himself up. And so I encouraged him to get a job and earn his own money as soon as he turned sixteen years old. He worked for a fast-food chain. He cut our neighbors' grass in the summer." She sipped more tea. "I wanted him to learn the value of money and respect the less fortunate. He wasn't even influenced by the many arrogant rich friends he had, but then I got worried when he went away to university and then to Law school with a girl I wasn't fond of. I knew she always had a crush on my Aiden from the time they were kids."

My heart raced rapidly.

"One day during Christmas holiday, Aiden brought Chelsea along with him, a lovely girl, whom I liked right away. She came from a poor family. She was sweet and full of life." Did she remind her of herself too? Because all of a sudden, Elaina's gaze was looking into the void as she continued, "She was perfect for him, and I could sense that she loved him endlessly."

I was afraid to speak up, trying to imagine what Chelsea would look like, from the way Elaina was describing her—fair, petite, with long, brown hair and dark eyes.

She continued, "During that summer, after they both graduated from Law school, Chelsea shared a place with a girl and got a job at Neil's friend's law firm." Did she mean at Adrianna's firm? As Elaina sipped some of her tea, I noticed that her hands were shaking. She continued, "During that summer also, Aiden announced his engagement to her. I was happy because I knew he couldn't find a better girl. I didn't care that they were both still young. Neil at that time was teaching Aiden his business, so they were always traveling together." She was silent. I was quiet too. I could right then picture the whole scene in my head. "Chelsea was left to spend time alone with some of Aiden's friends."

Aiden's friends, I thought while frowning lightly.

Elaina added, "She was young, pretty and smart. Her only problem was she was still vulnerable despite all the terrible life she went through as a child."

My eyes grew wide. That was a twisted story.

She continued, "She was overwhelmed with Aiden's friends and their lifestyle and was somehow sucked into it."

"Where was Aiden to guide her? If Chelsea was poor, she probably felt discomfited and out of place." I recalled how I felt when I first entered his house. She probably felt deserted and timid.

"Like I said, Aiden was very busy that particular summer, traveling with his father. I don't know what happened between them exactly, but from what I read, she was part of an ugly game."

"A game, whose? Aiden's? An old friend's?"

"Not exactly. At first, I had my suspicions about some of Aiden's spoiled friends, but Chelsea lived with Trish. Trish was a very bad influence on her."

I frowned. Trish? I had guessed wrong. I really deduced that her bad influence was Adrianna. That was unusual.

"What did Trish do? How was she a bad influence?"

"I don't know the details, but Trish held parties at her place … These parties were full of alcohol and substance abuse. Chelsea got sucked into it."

"How could someone get sucked into this against their will?" I recalled when I overdrank a few times. That was with my will; no one forced alcohol on me, but then again, if I hadn't gone to clubs and parties and special dinners. I would probably never have touched alcohol.

"I don't know how, but according to Chelsea, she found herself unconscious one day and woke up …" she paused for a few seconds.

I could tell how hesitant she was. I shook my head. This was a distorted story.

She carried on, "Aiden found her in bed with another man." My jaw dropped. I could now imagine Chelsea. Could she have been a cheater? No, she couldn't be a cheater.

"Did Aiden break the engagement after?"

Elaina took a deep breath. "He did worse; he started dating the man's devastated ex-girlfriend."

"Trish?"

She stared at me. "No, not Trish. He started dating Adrianna, who was the man's girlfriend."

My heart started to race. "Adrianna!" I said blankly. Had Aiden always been in and out of a relationship with her since then? I closed my eyes. Nothing was making sense to me anymore. I didn't know why, but I felt myself running out of breath. "Just like that, he started dating someone else." *How could he?* I thought.

She said defensively, "Aiden was heartbroken and devastated. He only dated Adrianna for a week before realizing that he was still in love with Chelsea." She sighed. "I didn't hear from Chelsea for a couple of months after. But one day, during one of our parties, our guests turned to look disgustedly at a very thin, frail woman. At first, I didn't recognize her, but then I did. It was Chelsea." Elaina started to shed tears. "She looked nothing like herself. She seemed lost, on drugs, or so I assumed. Her face was scrawny. Her clothes were dirty and ripped, and her hair was matted and slimy. She looked so pale, so sick—"

I interrupted her, irritated, "Were Aiden and Adrianna there?"

"Only Adrianna, Aiden was out of town." She continued after a brief pause, "The whole room became still all of a sudden. Chelsea ran to the open buffet and started to shove food into her mouth. She looked like a hungry little kid." I watched, stunned, as Elaina wiped her tears. "I was the only one who came toward her, took her by her hand, and led her toward the kitchen." Suddenly her tears were turning into sobs.

What had happened to Chelsea? I felt my heart was about to stop.

She continued, "In the kitchen, I hugged her little skinny fragile body. She was shaking hard. She didn't say a word. Instead, she pulled herself away from my arm, placed a diary book on my kitchen table, and fled the kitchen."

"What happened to Chelsea?" I demanded breathlessly.

Elaina cried some more and then tried to dry some of her falling tears. She said thickly, "She was found dead the same night at the bottom of a deep valley. She was in the same car Aiden had given her months earlier." I didn't know why, but I felt myself sobbing for that story. It was as if I had just lost someone dear to me. I couldn't believe I was starting to feel jealous of someone so frail, so weak, so damaged and dead, someone who reminded me of myself.

"What happened to her diary?"

Without a word, Elaina went to her desk. She opened one of the drawers using a key. I felt shivers seeing the pink diary. My hands shook when I held the book. I glanced at Elaina briefly. She got up from beside me and said, "Take your time. I will be back in a couple of hours. I think I need some time alone." She then left the room.

I started reading the first page.

All my friends at school have a diary and so I decided to have one too. I just don't know how to start using the damn thing.

I skipped a few pages and then something caught my eye. She was probably a teenager then.

Today, I hate my home. I hate living in a filthy trailer. I hate all my neighbors. I hate my friends at school for bullying me. I hate Mitch for hurting Mom. He's a sick bastard. I knew he was in my room at night once again, probably masturbating. I wish I could just disappear from here.

My blood ran cold. Was Mitch her father? I recalled Adrianna's words: *I think he's still hooked on his trailer trash.* That conversation was stuck in my head like glue. She was speaking of Chelsea and Aiden! I skipped a few more pages.

I wish Mitch would just disappear. I don't know why Mom still keeps him. He's useless. All he does is lay around and drink beer all day. I hate him. My God I hate him. I don't understand why Mom didn't believe me when I told her her boyfriend is a psycho. He is so disgusting and awful."

My heart started to race. I skipped a few more pages and continued reading.

I was so close to calling the cops on Rob for bruising Mom again, but then again, it's no use. She will defend him as always. I can't wait till I'm out of here. I hate my life.

I wondered what happened to Mitch. It seemed that Chelsea's mother was hooked on finding abusive boyfriends. At that moment, Debra's sad story zipped through my head. I skipped a few more pages.

Today I met Will. He is so cute …

I took my time reading this one. I felt that we shared the same fears and anxiety I felt when I was a young teenager. Her sentences made me recall Majeed at the beach. I skipped some more after glancing though her first bad experience with an abusive boyfriend and got to when she went to university and then Law school.

> Today, I am on top of the world. I did it. I am here at the best Law school I could ask for with a full scholarship. Today is a happy day for me. I don't want to think of tomorrow or yesterday. Today is great ... I just want to skip and dance!

She must have really worked hard and been a top student to get that scholarship. I recalled when we escaped from Lebanon to come to Canada. I had shared the same feeling. I went back to the diary.

> I can't believe how spoiled some of the people around me are. Maybe I found the wrong crowd to hang out with.

I skipped to find some familiar names, and then I stopped at this:

> Today, I like Jason. He is way nicer than his twin sister, Adrianna. She is always bitching and whining about something.

Adrianna. Seeing her name made me sick to my stomach. But I kept on reading.

> Today, I met Aiden. He's gorgeous and sexy. I caught him looking at me a few times, but then someone like him won't be interested in me ...

I froze and then took my time reading about her feelings toward him. I scrutinized her words to find my true deep feelings from when I met Aiden the first time. *This book could belong to me,* I thought. It was as if I was the one who had written it. Her first date with Aiden, their first special intimate moment, the expensive gifts he had bought her, the romantic trips they took ... It was painful to read, and then I got to this page of her diary.

> I am going to this concert, with my handsome babe. Adrianna is trying to fix me up to look stylish and ready to rock.

I frowned. Chelsea had become Adrianna's friend? But how? Chelsea seemed smarter than that. Then I recalled Adrianna's words the last time we talked. *"You know what they say. Keep your friends close, but your enemy closer." That was also Yusuf's way of living,* I thought, recalling all the friends he had had in the past, friends he had scammed out of their life savings. They were disposable, meaningless to him. Was Adrianna playing a game with Chelsea? I knew she was good at changing her facade skillfully. I remembered Mary's constant warnings. I went back to the diary.

I love Trish's modern and large apartment. It is convenient and close to work, not too far from Aiden's family's house. Trish is all right, I guess. The only thing I hate about her is the wild lifestyle she lives, as if tomorrow doesn't exist in her agenda.

I frowned. Where did Trish come from? What was her purpose? I skipped to where Aiden and she got engaged, her exquisite diamond ring, the happy moments when Aiden spoiled her by giving her a credit card to go shopping on a shopping spree, a brand-new car, all that jewelry … I could tell that Aiden really loved her, and surprisingly, I wasn't jealous, though the way he spoiled me was not even comparable to the way he spoiled Chelsea, even before they got engaged. Then something just hit me. Adrianna always knew about me and Aiden, from the time she asked me to be her personal assistant; it was only to spend more time with me. I recalled her phone conversations with her friends during few of the car rides speaking of her ex and his gifts, and how he wanted her back, at any cost. Was it only a game? She knew I was listening. Was it because she was very jealous of the way Chelsea was spoiled? I wondered if Chelsea flashed Aiden's gifts to her, so she decided to give me a taste of the bitter jealousy she felt then. Was Adrianna that twisted? Was she still jealous of a dead woman? Or maybe she was angry because she still couldn't have Aiden the way she wanted to? I skipped a few pages.

Aiden is gone again for another few days. I am glad because I feel really tired. I can't sleep and feel withdrawn all of a sudden. I can't even eat … I don't understand what is going on with me. Could I have cancer like Mom? I'm even afraid to see the doctor. I know I have to book my appointment soon. Or will it just pass? I should ask Trish to make us tea tonight. It always makes me feel better.

That was weird, I thought. I skipped to when I saw the name *Adrianna*. I found it.

Today is my birthday, I feel old for twenty-five years old. Aiden is taking everyone for dinner. I'm not looking forward to seeing Richard. I wonder if I should tell Adrianna that her boyfriend is constantly hitting on me, or maybe not. That will hurt her feelings for sure, especially after going on and on about how much she loves him …

Seriously, I thought. While reading Chelsea's diary, I could almost feel the oddity that surrounded her. I faced back the page in front of me.

… I can't tell Aiden either because he's now friends with him. Maybe I should just try to cancel the dinner. I have absolutely no energy anyway.

I flipped the page and then the second, third … My heart raced. This was it? Was that her diary? I was angrily flipping some scrabbled, torn-up empty pages. Then at the very end of the diary, I found a page. I realized it was the very last page. My throat was dry when I swallowed. I noticed there were discolored dots. I wondered if that was from Chelsea's tears. Even her writing was wobbly. I started to read.

My scary face, this is me now, a filthy drug addict. Hell is my past, my present, and most likely my future. I was stupid to think that life was finally smiling at me. I was so foolish not to distinguish a sincere from a mocking smile. My last sight of hope vanished when

Aiden walked away from me after trying to explain what happened. How could he not? After seeing me in bed with someone else? How? How could I explain what really happened when I don't even know myself? I know I was drugged. I had to be drugged. But why? Just to wake up naked next to Richard!

Then I recalled when Aiden told me once when I was drinking at the last New Year's party, "Drink as much as you want only when you are around me. This way, I don't have to worry about you … doing the wrong things." Chelsea was always in the back of his mind. To him, she was doing the wrong thing. She didn't see the dangerous, designed plot she had been placed in; and Aiden was too busy, travelling around to realize what was going on. I continued reading.

Who let Richard in Trish's apartment, and why? Why?

She repeated "Why?" at least thirty times. I recalled Aiden getting angry when he found out I went out with Jason on a date. Richard was his friend at that time. Who were Richard and Trish? Where were they now? I continued reading.

> I'm too tired to think why … After today, I wouldn't want to know why because tomorrow, I will be resting in peace.

I closed the book. Tears fell all over it. I got up. I recalled seeing a photocopier in Elaina's office.

I placed the copied paper in an envelope that I had found and put it neatly in my purse. I sat by the window, crying, not really seeing out onto the beautiful landscape, recalling Chelsea's words that I had read. I decided to read every chapter of her life, every sentence, and every word. I wished she didn't remind me of myself, but then she did, and I was more than positive that Adrianna had skillfully planned Chelsea's ugly ending.

Chelsea's despair led her to end her young life abruptly; she had no one around her for support. She was surrounded by darkness, so she started using drugs. I decided that I would wait for Elaina to wake up before I left. I still had a couple of questions for her. A few minutes later, she walked in; her eyes were swollen still. She must really have cared for poor Chelsea. She stared at my messy face, since I had spent the last hour crying. She came closer and sat beside me; she reached to hug me, and then I heard myself weep on her shoulder.

Fifteen minutes passed. We were sitting next to each other, each wrapped up in her own surroundings. I hesitated before I asked her. "Did Aiden know of Chelsea's diary book?"

She sighed. "At that time, I decided not to tell him." She then added defensively, "You should've seen how he shut himself off after learning of Chelsea's death."

His feelings of despair, in my opinion, couldn't be compared to Chelsea's, who chose ultimate darkness over life.

"Aiden is still angry with the knowledge that Chelsea had cheated on him, and he thinks she would do anything for money." I recalled how he hated cheaters and women who did anything for money.

"Aiden now knows of Chelsea's diary, I gave it to him right after your breakup. I already know how late I am." She was silent for a bit. "Aiden was then devastated to learn from his friends that Chelsea had sex for money after selling most of the jewelry he had given her to buy drugs after he broke off his engagement."

I felt my body cringe. I wondered who these friends who told him were. Aiden should've read the diary a long time ago, despite what she had to do for the money. Elaina should've known better and shouldn't have been so selfish and only cared for her son's shattered feelings, especially since Chelsea trusted her with her own diary. Aiden needed to learn of his friends' scheme that led to her death ages ago. *Poor Chelsea, no one cared for her.*

I said breathlessly, "Couldn't she sell the car he gave her instead?"

"Legally, she couldn't; it was a leased car, but you're right." She was silent. "Aiden was still disturbed with the knowledge at that time."

"Aiden told you of our breakup?" I asked evenly.

"He didn't have to. I came back to a madhouse one day, and Aiden was sleeping in his office." I felt my heart squeeze. She added, "You need to know one truth, my dear. I never had imagined that Aiden would love again; especially after seeing how wretched he was after he broke the engagement with Chelsea." She was looking for my gaze, adding, "After you left, he was so shattered—like never before. He also told me that because of him, you had a miscarriage. I think he was finally ready to be a father."

I refused to believe that Aiden loved me. I shook the thought away; maybe it was because he wanted to be a father, like Elaina confessed.

I said, "My miscarriage wasn't Aiden's fault; it just wasn't meant to be." Then I recalled something puzzling. I said confidently, "Adrianna, Aiden's old friend, I think she is behind what happened to Chelsea. I mean I know enough since I worked for her."

Elaina sighed. "I told Aiden last year when she started hanging around him most of the time, there was something baffling about her. I just didn't know what it was and couldn't trust her. She is surrounded by obscurity."

I remembered sensing Adrianna's obscurity too; I knew she was someone I needed to stay away from.

I asked, "Did Aiden date her last year?"

"Not that I know of, I know she tried to be around him most of the time after his father passed away. She strived to be as helpful as she could be." She squeezed my hand. "Aiden had changed. Ever since he settled his business in Victoria, he has seemed very lost. I think it's the effect from Chelsea's diary and losing you."

I nodded. It was probably from Chelsea's diary. I could imagine the effect on him. As if he were bringing her back from her grave, he was definitely rethinking the way he portrayed Chelsea in his mind all these past years—the drug addict, gold digger, cheater was possibly just a victim. He was probably suffering from self-loathing because he was no hero to her; instead of listening to her, he listened to his friends. He had made a decision to ignore her pleads, and with that—he had lost her.

"I don't think Adrianna will leave Aiden alone. I think she will keep on trying with him and will destroy whoever comes near him."

Elaina nodded. "Aiden's isn't a weak man."

"Adrianna is dangerous person with many faces and talents."

She was quiet. After all, she didn't know Adrianna the way I did.

I added, "What's done is done, Elaina." Then I recalled my miscarriage, the baby that I lost during my nervous breakdown. I felt a squeeze in my chest and repeated, "What's done is done …"

Elaina squeezed my hand and added, "Don't give up on my son. I know you still love him, and he really loves you too." She sounded serious. "Trust me."

I was silent while I felt hot tears on my face. I didn't want to get hurt anymore. I was just starting to feel normal again. I didn't want Aiden to ruin the new comfortable surroundings I had quickly managed to form around myself.

Half an hour later, I said good-bye to Elaina and politely refused her invitation for dinner. Her house still reminded me of the day Aiden and I last fought.

Chapter Twenty-Seven

A FEW DAYS HAD PASSED, during which I examined Chelsea's diary just like I had said I would. I even formed an image of her in my head, especially on her last day, right before she ended her young life. I imagined her just the way Elaina described her—scrawny, dirty, ripped clothes, matted and slimy hair. She was shattered by her destiny, which was caused by some ugly, scary faces hiding behind their masks.

Who were those faces? Was it Adrianna for sure? Trish? Richard? I didn't know why Mary's face came back to me. Her attitude toward me had changed but merely to give continuous warnings. Thanks to those warnings, I didn't go to any parties. I didn't date Jason and kept myself formal with Adrianna's friendly approaches at first. What was Adrianna planning for me? I now knew she had planned an ugly scene. I had an ugly part in that scene, but what was the part? By the time I was done putting this peculiar puzzle together in my head, I had an idea of what could have happened then.

Adrianna was very smart; she had always wanted Aiden, who had fallen for Chelsea. Trish and Richard must have been her friends. Maybe they even worked for her. She proficiently designed and applied suspicion-free plans.

Trish was slowly getting Chelsea into drugs. I even looked up the different types of drugs and the different methods Trish could've used. She had probably added it to her tea, since Chelsea found it soothing to her pain. After all, they had lived together; it was a slow, convenient process—this way, no one would notice, until it was too late and Chelsea became addicted. But I just couldn't understand the reason why—maybe she hoped Aiden would leave her, thinking that his fiancée was facing an addiction, but there was a possibility that he would still have supported her by sending her to rehab. But then, it was all connected and applied after skillful calculation.

Chelsea was drugged one night and woke up naked next to Richard. Aiden was there to see. The drug was already in Chelsea's system, having been planted slowly from at least weeks earlier. Chelsea was then facing the worst time of her life. She was going to need those drugs to make her forget what had happened, especially since her body all of the sudden was aching for them. All Adrianna needed to do was make them available in abundance for her, and this way, no one would suspect her. I wondered if Chelsea really had sex for money. Was she that desperate? *Possibly,* I thought. Drug addiction could take over one's brain.

Was Adrianna planning to execute the same deadly plan with me? Mary had always protected me, warning me about Adrianna, and I never felt withdrawn from any drug while working at the firm, but Adrianna did invite me to parties. Maybe she would've then inserted something into my drink. Mary asked me to lie and make excuses for not showing up; that was way too confusing.

I found myself walking tensely around the house, picking my brain a piece at a time. What had happened to Mary? Why did she disappear? Where was she now? At that moment, I wished I had her personal email address. Later on that day I found myself calling the cops, I really should have reported her disappearance a long time ago.

***

Couple of days later, during dinner on Thursday night, I glanced at Jasim periodically and then at Nora, who was sitting next to me enjoying her food. My thoughts drifted to Mary, I still haven't heard back from the police; where could she be?

Earlier that day, I got a call from Ryan's lawyer confirming the money transfer, from both the lump-sum of sixty thousand and the first monthly installment of one-thousand dollars—I was finally relieved financially.

I recalled Chelsea's story; she probably was too despondent and didn't find anyone around her during the worst time of her life. I was thankful I had my family's, including Nora's and Jasim's, and my friends' support.

I just remembered something, so I asked Jasim, right after wiping my lips with a napkin, "Jasim, be honest with me. Did you hire a lawyer to help fix my credit history?"

He stared at me a few long seconds.

"No, why?"

My heart raced. There was no point asking him about the thirty-thousand-dollar transfer. I really wanted to doubt my suspicions at first—I didn't want to think that Aiden was behind fixing my credit and this money transfer, and I still hadn't touched a penny of it, but why help me now?

I sighed, thinking of all my unfortunate events. I said thickly, "Jasim, I think my life is full of wretched events. I can't seem to have any peace. I really don't think that happiness exists."

He narrowed his eyes and said, "Do you think that you would enjoy life if it was always peaceful and sweet?" He drank some juice. "Happiness is to accept the balance of your bittersweet life."

I glanced at him, with a murky smile. Nora had just finished eating. I smiled at her small frame as she skipped to go and wash her hands.

He was probably watching my expression. "You love Nora, right?"

I sighed and smiled. "More than anything."

"Now imagine your life without her; let's say you didn't meet her father."

I felt a tight squeeze. I couldn't imagine myself without her. That was impossible.

I said calmly, "I can't." I knew what Jasim was getting at. "I would do it again, for the sake of having Nora."

He nodded.

I sipped more juice and then added, "Jasim, can you explain to me why men in general like to control the women they are with?"

He gaped at me for few seconds. "Only some men want to control, without any reasoning; they probably become dangerous if their women defy them."

Men like Yusuf, I thought.

He continued, "Some other men, they could become overcontrolling when their women allow them." He sipped more juice. "A woman needs to learn when to draw the line and become more assertive, to believe in herself and know how to stop any man from overpowering her."

At that moment, I recalled Elaina's story about herself, I knew she then had a message for me, and I just didn't recognize it until now; it was the same message Jasim was feeding me. I had to be more confident, to believe in myself, and not to allow anyone to trash me or make me feel inferior.

Jasim reached to place his hand on my shoulder and said kindly, "You are a good kid, Hannah. I know you are wise and will make the right decisions for yourself and Nora."

I dismissed Aiden from my brain.

He continued, "Look at what you have accomplished so far. You are a one strong-minded woman; you just need to rebuild your trust in yourself."

I smiled right before getting up to start clearing the table. As soon as I settled Nora in bed, my phone beeped, announcing that a text message had arrived.

The message was simply a few words from a blocked sender. It said, "Check your email."

That was odd. Right away, I reached for my laptop and opened my email. I had to face it since I hadn't come near it since my breakup with Aiden.

My heart pounded hard as I glanced through my unopened email. There was an email from Aiden, from one week earlier. I opened the message. My heart sank as I read it.

My Dear Hannah,

I didn't mean to, but yes, I did compare you to someone from my past. Declaring it is as painful to me as it is to you. Her name was Chelsea, and I loved her. Chelsea decided to take her own life a couple of months after I broke up our engagement. I couldn't figure out where I went wrong with her. After all these years, I recognize now how foolish I was since I had allowed myself to be influenced by a few people—I believed they were friends at that time, making me believe that Chelsea was a gold digger, a cheater, someone who used me because I was happy to give her everything; her love came with a price. After we broke up, she became someone I despised, but still the mystery behind her death completely destroyed something in me. I just couldn't figure out what had changed her suddenly and what exactly had happened to drive her to destroy herself completely before her suicide?

I thought by treating you differently, I could maybe keep you by my side. Now I accept the fact that I have lost you too.

After reading Chelsea's diary, many years too late, I realized that I was one of the reasons behind her death. I wasn't there during the time she needed me the most. With that ugly truth, I must now learn to live with myself.

Adrianna never meant anything to me. We were never in a relationship. What we had was a one-night stand only a week before I met you the second time. I had so much to drink and don't remember much of that night, merely bits and pieces. I was in a state of a shock when I woke in the morning next to her.

Since I started avoiding Adrianna continually, she became a different person. She even stalked me around; she showed up at my dinner parties, my offices, and she even came to see me in Victoria right after New Years.

That was the reason I wanted to hide you away, because I was afraid you would get hurt. For some reason, I had this strange feeling after I learned that she made you into her assistant, I just couldn't trust her.

Adrianna lied about everything that she told you, including the firm's party that I never went to. My aim was to stay away from her, and I was only worried about you being around her, which was the reason behind trying to persuade you to change your job.

I'm not asking you to be with me again; I know you are better off without me. I just want you to know that I will always love you and will look after you. Your future is secure; you will never have to struggle again.

You will always be my birthday girl.
Love, Aiden.

My tears start falling. What was this odd message? It was as if he had lost all hope. I didn't want Aiden's money. I always looked after Nora and myself, and was determined to make a better future for us. I was, as Jasim said, a one strong-minded woman. I just wanted his love; if only he knew how much I did love and still loved him! Money, cars, jewelry—they were all insignificant and materialistic.

I then noticed another email; it had just arrived fifteen minutes earlier. I opened it. I blinked twice when I saw the sender's name.

"Meet me at 568 John's Road. In two hours."

I didn't hesitate. At first, I looked up the address. I then made a couple of phone calls right before I asked Jasim to look after Nora, who was sound asleep. When he got downstairs, he asked me worriedly where I was going. I gave him a hug and said that I wouldn't be long.

As I drove, I recalled so many events. Now there was no turning back.

I still had a half an hour to spare, so I went to a convenience store that had a photocopier and copied Chelsea's diary. I had brought it with me.

The address was a small coffee shop. I nodded when I was greeted by the fair, petite night waitress. She had an oversized brown-and-black uniform. Her hair was tucked under a hat. She wore thick, black-framed glasses. I noticed her braces when she smiled. Her face was bare of any makeup.

I sat by one of the many tables after I bought a tea. I looked around; there was only one customer. He was minding his own business, reading a newspaper and drinking a coffee. The waitress came to clean a table not too far from where I was sitting. She was removing a couple of dirty cups and the napkin dispenser, because there was a couple who came to sit at the now clean table.

I glanced at my watch. I noticed that the person I was supposed to meet was late. Another hour had passed. I sent a couple of texts around. Maybe I had been fooled, and no one was going to meet me there.

I was on my way out. For the last fifteen minutes, I had been the only customer around. The place was now deserted, but I decided to wait for another fifteen minutes. I ordered another tea and sat back at my table. Ten minutes had passed; I glanced at my watch again while sipping the rest of the tea. Only five more minutes, I told myself. I yawned and felt my head spinning. My head felt as if it weighed a ton, and my body all of a sudden was stiff. *What was going on with me?* I wondered.

I got up to leave, but I felt the room whirling. I sat on the chair and placed my hand on my head. As if I were watching a dream, I saw the night staff locking the coffee shop after turning off the light. I swallowed my fear, because I couldn't move an inch to defend myself. The waitress came toward me; she emptied my purse's contents. She grabbed my cell phone and was feeling my body. She then helped me up. I felt myself with difficulty walking toward my car. I was then pushed toward the backseat. I couldn't even think since my head was blurry. My body was moving as the car was driven away, and then I blacked out.

I was behind a steering wheel with matted, slimy hair and dirty clothes. My head was spinning as I was approaching a ditch or a deep valley. The car was going faster and faster, and then I felt myself flying. I knew I was going to die. This was it. I heard myself scream loudly. I woke up. My head hurt badly, as if I had been run over by a bus. I looked around in a panic; I lay in my small car's back passenger seat.

It was still dark, but I was surrounded by trees. Where was I? In the middle of the forest? The sight in front of me gave me the illusion of being part of a mysterious dream. It felt unreal and terrifying. There was a woman sitting in the front. She was the waitress from the coffee shop. I felt my heart race, and my throat was already dry. She still wore the same uniform.

She glanced at me and said in a familiar tone, not the same friendly voice she used when I purchased my tea, "You are finally up."

Panicking, I looked at her and gasped, saying, "Mary! Is that you?"

She took her hat, her glasses, and her braces off; it was her. Was she here to hurt me in the middle of nowhere? I glanced at her again, without her fine makeup and expensive clothes. She looked nothing like the Mary I knew at the office. What had happened to her all of a sudden? I felt shaky once again. What did she want from me? Did she drug me? Was that why she asked me to meet with her in the middle of the night? Did she have the answers for the questions that were playing in my head like clipped, annoying beats? Or was she only there to harm me or even kill me? I knew I had to say something. She didn't reply to my question. My heart rapidly raced as I asked, "Mary, what do you want from me?" She turned, smiling blankly. She still looked pretty even without all the colors on her face. She also looked fragile and weak.

She spoke in a low, calm tone. "You think you are very smart and thought ahead, bringing spies and probably a few recorders and video cameras to the shop?"

I frowned. How did she know? I thought I had planned it perfectly by calling Mandy, who sent John. He pretended to be a customer, sitting a few tables across from me, with a phone camera, and Nathan and Jasmine were sitting across from me with another phone camera. I didn't have time to buy myself a wire or purchase more spying material from a security store. I knew there was something weird going on, and I needed to be taped. I was thankful I didn't have to explain myself too much to my amateur spies for them to come with me. But after nearly a whole hour of waiting for Mary, who never showed up when she was supposed to, I sent them a text suggesting they leave.

Mary added, "If I wanted to hurt you, I would've; trust me!"

I breathed out. I said evenly, "Why didn't you hurt me?"

She said calmly, "I'm not here to hurt you, Hannah; you know that."

"What are you doing then? I always had this feeling that there was something between you and Adrianna."

She reached for Chelsea's diary from beside her, showing me the pile. "You know more than I thought you knew."

I said, "Were you planning to make that my diary too?"

She said defensively, "No, of course not."

I didn't trust her still. I shook my head, looking around me. I never guessed she could be dangerous. I thought Mary was my friend, and the only person I could talk to at the firm; I really believed she cared about me.

She continued, "I just wanted to talk to you alone."

"That's why you drugged me? I know you put something in my tea."

"I just put you to sleep, Hannah. You were asleep for exactly one hour."

I said tentatively, "Is that your way of having a private conversation with someone?" When I got no reply from her, I added, "I get it; you and Adrianna work together as one organized mafia team, just like Trish and Richard."

"I'm not saying I'm not guilty. I am."

"Why did you want to talk to me alone?"

She said tactfully, "You are smarter than I thought. I'm really impressed." She looked away. "Not everyone was as smart or lucky, I should say."

I started breathing hard. I wondered how many people she had managed to hurt already while following Adrianna's orders.

I said thickly, "Maybe lucky, I would say. I escaped death before by luck; the last time it was a split second away." Recalling my country Lebanon during the war and the painful near-death accident, I added, "Did you have orders to hurt me, all because of some woman's jealousy?"

My mind went blurry. Her tone was calm. "You were just caught in the wrong place, at the wrong time, with the wrong people. That was the reason I advised you to stay away from Jason."

I laughed. I knew already how Adrianna worked. I recalled Chelsea's diary.

Mary added, "Was Adrianna jealous? Maybe. But what makes her really dangerous is that she loves to be the director of her own life; people around her are like feeling-less characters, easily disposable."

I didn't get it. "Were you Adrianna's assistant, the one who did her dirty work?"

"We both did dirty work." She stared into space. "I was dragged into doing dirty work; when I realized what was happening, it was too late."

"What type of dirty work?" She turned to face me, but she remained silent. "Why am I here? Why are you confessing to me?" I looked around frantically. She sighed. She was still quiet. I was getting frustrated. What was she waiting for? I snapped, "Who else did she hurt besides Chelsea?"

She sighed. "His name was Chan. He was my husband. Her name was Carla, and she was Adrianna's stepmother."

I tilted my head back, so there were other people, but why?

I felt breathless when I asked, "Are they dead?"

I waited through a couple of minutes of silence. Before Mary started speaking of Chan, her husband, her sentences were to the point, no sidetracks. I was listening intently. I was hoping she wasn't confessing because she had other plans for me.

Mary was recovering from alcoholism in a rehab center when she met Adrianna; they were both recovering from alcoholism. They bonded. Mary opened up about her husband's abusive behavior. A few months later, ironically, they connected at a bar. Mary was then separated from her abusive husband, who was supposedly hiding his money away from her before he divorced her. Adrianna came up with a plan, which at that time was appealing to Mary, to slowly drive Chan back to his heroin addiction and then to his overdose death. Mary agreed during a drunken moment.

A month passed. The police came searching for her. Chan had been found dead from an overdose just the way it was planned, but Mary didn't kill him. That same day, Adrianna called her. She had something to show her.

It was a tape of Mary planning to kill Chan. She was drunk then, but she had no way to prove that she was innocent, since Adrianna's voice wasn't heard, only hers. Adrianna had planned well after all.

Adrianna threatened to give the tape to the police if Mary didn't follow her orders precisely, which was to kill Carla.

Carla—an alcoholic diva—was always in and out of rehab. She also had a dominant, ruthless personality. Carla could possibly inherit Adrianna's father's firm and all his millions. With Mary's help, Carla's death was supposed to seem like an accident. After almost a year of planning, Carla drove herself to her death, hitting a tree. The investigation showed alcohol and drugs in her system; she was stressed that day after finding her husband in bed with a girl half his age, but the police didn't dig further. Mary had expertly mixed her alcoholic beverage with drugs. Adrianna knew Carla so well, to the point she could predict her next action.

But the story became more perplexing when I found out that Carla wasn't just Adrianna's stepmother.

I hated that I couldn't see Mary's reaction when she spoke, since we sat in the dark still. I exclaimed, puzzled, "Her aunt?" I could then comprehend the similarity in their ruthless, dark dominant personalities and their alcohol addiction. I continued, "What happened to her birth mother?"

She said, "Here is the baffling part. I discovered that she died during a weekend getaway at her sister Carla's house, from alcohol poisoning."

"Carla! Could she have been the reason behind her sister's death?"

Adrianna could have been seeking revenge and not only her father's firm and money. I was silent, recalling the few victims that I had just heard of—Chan, Carla, and Chelsea. Adrianna sounded to me like a serial killer, which was disturbing. I wondered if Mary was being paid heftily for her services.

"Knowing all that and yet you still worked for a killer." Well, I realized that they were both considered killers.

There was a long silence. "It was greed, I suppose." She admitted. At that moment, chills traveled my body. I wondered if there were more victims. Was she still a danger to me? Adrianna could've used Mary many times over, which explained why she kept her close. But why did Mary disappear all of a sudden?

I asked, "Was she trying to hurt you?"

She sighed. "Yes, that's why I had to disappear without contacting anyone." Adrianna couldn't find her; that explained her tantrums after Mary's sudden departure. I said breathlessly, "Then you do know what Adrianna's plan was for me."

"Yes, it's not what you think." She sighed. "But then again, it was hard for me to guess her motives, since she had stopped revealing things to me a while back, which got me worried about her planning for my next accident. I was no longer needed."

"Why did she tell you to invite me to a party at your place?"

"Only to introduce you to heavy drinking and handsome men and take some pictures. At that time, I didn't understand the reason behind her request; then I dug further and found out that you were dating Aiden, Adrianna's ex lover."

She probably would've sent the pictures to Aiden, to show him that all the girls he chooses are cheaters. My heart raced rapidly.

"Why couldn't she just fire me?"

"Adrianna does things her own way. She did want to destroy you first."

And that was exactly what she did. It was hard to figure out what she was planning; she was always a few steps ahead. *Just like Yusuf.* She continued, "During the meeting at the café across the street, right before I disappeared, she already had doubts about my loyalty to her, but then again, she didn't know that I knew her real next intention at that time and that I was already in contact with the police detective."

"What was her real intention?" I asked breathlessly.

"Jason, he was her next victim."

I felt nauseous. Jason? She wanted to get rid of her own brother? "Where is Jason?"

"To Adrianna's misfortune, he's still alive." She sighed. I got it. She wanted her own twin dead now; he was yet another disappointment for her, and she wanted him out of the picture completely. "Since last year, I have been digging into Adrianna's life. I wanted more evidence against her to hand to the cops. A few months ago, I went to the cops and told them everything, and since then, she has been under surveillance."

"How did they know that she was after her own brother, without any physical evidence?"

"Adrianna is very sharp, but I know her approaches when she plans for the next victim. She studies them well. Last year, I found out that she had her brother's financial statement. I then discovered that he owned double her firm's share. When I started digging further, I detected that she was watching his every move."

So Adrianna's motive was Jason's share in the firm. I wondered if her father suspected his daughter's deviant behavior, and in his will, he decided not to put her in control of his firm.

My brains were working rapidly; it was giving me a headache. I was trying so hard to absorb what was going on around me.

"Overnight, Adrianna became a kind and understanding sister who simply wanted her brother to be happy. I even felt skeptical about them going away together to a resort, where she didn't have to explain a murder in Mexico as much as she would have to here in Canada."

I remembered that Jason never went to the resort because of a sudden case of food poisoning.

I asked, "Did you have something to do with Jason staying in Canada?"

There was a silence. "Maybe." She did. I knew it. She continued, "A couple of weeks ago, Katie had a sudden severe allergic drug reaction. She was at Jason's house, panicky. He called the ambulance, but the cops had already placed his house under surveillance. They were in his house almost immediately."

I said, stunned, "Wait a minute, so the cops already knew that Adrianna was after her own brother? Why couldn't they just arrest her?"

"I raised their suspicions with all my evidence. Suspicion isn't enough to make an arrest. I agreed to help them until they caught her."

Was Mary helping the cops hoping to get a sentence reduction? After all, she helped kill Carla, the only crime she confessed to.

She continued, "Adrianna always knew how to cover her tracks well, but this time, she didn't plan for Katie to have a drug reaction, so the cops searched the house and arrested a man with a gun and found out that he had already managed to open Jason's combination safe but never had a chance to empty it; they also found a drink mixed with drugs."

I said, "Was the man's name Richard?"

Her answer was quick. "No."

"Didn't the man confess to the cop?"

"During his long interview, he admitted to the cops that he was supposed to empty the safe, kill Jason, destroy the drink mixed with drug evidence, and flee. He said he was working for a man by the name of Carlos."

"I don't get it, why did she use Katie in all this?"

"Jason was supposed to be dead from a shotgun blast. The man was supposed to flee with the money. There was also a large money transfer that was made from Jason's account to an anonymous account overseas. It was linked to Katie's just a couple of hours earlier; she wanted her to be the main suspect in Jason's death during the investigation." That was a messed-up story. Mary continued, "After recovering from her allergic reaction, Katie knew nothing about the money." I could read Adrianna's plan, which was for her brother to be dead while Katie was still hallucinating only to wake up next to a dead body. The cops at first would think it was a robbery, but after digging into his account, they would then find the transfer. Adrianna was definitely behind the money transfer too.

"Where is Adrianna now?"

"Since that night, the police haven't been able to find her." *What!* A criminal like her on the loose! That was frightening.

I said worriedly, "Why are you telling me this? Could we both be in danger now?"

She sighed. "I am in danger for sure. I think you are too, only because it's really hard to predict her next move." My heart sank further. After a long silence, she added, "Aiden, however, is in real danger."

My throat was dry when I swallowed. "What? But why?"

She turned to face me. I felt that my blood had escaped my body.

"I'm guessing because he was a disappointment to her, since he always fell for someone who wasn't her. Adrianna hates to be the loser."

So Adrianna did whatever it took not to lose. I recalled Aiden's email. I had sensed it right; it was as if he had lost hope. Was that because he knew of Adrianna's attempt to hurt him? I quivered hard, not Aiden, even when we were no longer together. I couldn't stomach the idea of him getting killed or even hurt.

"How do you know all this?" I asked breathlessly.

"When I found out that Adrianna was stalking him, I started sending him warning messages. I even showed up at his work after Adrianna's disappearance, and we talked about everything. He sent me a copy of Chelsea's diary." So Mary was behind those weird blocked messages.

"Wait a minute! You already know of Chelsea's diary?"

"Aiden told me about your fight, and what he heard from you that day was disturbing. Right after he read the diary, he figured that Adrianna had something to do with Chelsea's drug addiction, and that she was part an ugly scheme." She continued after a brief pause, "We were in touch up until yesterday before he disappeared."

I froze. Then I shook my head in disbelief. That couldn't be. Aiden had disappeared! Could she have killed him? I didn't know what had happened to me.

I screamed, "No! No … God, please! Not him!" Suddenly, I felt as if I were suffocating.

She said worriedly, "Calm down, Hannah; no time for emotions now. The police are searching for him. We need to think where Adrianna could have taken him." Mary added, "You needed to know what was going on, just in case she came after you too. It's really hard to figure out her moves while she's in hiding." My brain froze as she continued, "He was last seen yesterday. He left his car dealership at five; he was supposed to meet me soon after. He never showed up." It was so hard to think straight. She continued, "He was your boyfriend. Do you know of any place where he could be staying?"

Aiden was afraid to even mention his ex-fiancée to me.

I wiped my tears and said, annoyed, "You should know of Adrianna's hiding spots; you were her partner in crime." I knew I sounded harsh, but that was the truth.

She spoke calmly. "The police searched her cottage, her house, and her offices, with nothing to show for it. They even searched Jason's properties …" I looked into blankness, drinking the tears that were falling on my face. I couldn't think with my fuzzy brain cells. The thought that Aiden could possibly now be dead were slaying my feelings. I was numb. Where could he be? I closed my eyes. I recalled Adrianna's attitude toward me from the beginning. I was afraid of her, even when I met her at the club. I couldn't bring myself to greet her. I stopped crying. I recalled when I was stuck waiting in the washroom. I presumed she had been referring to me when she said, *"I think he's still hooked on his trailer trash."* But then she asked someone to meet her at an address. She called it a new place and said to meet her in an hour. I closed my eyes. That sentence had been in my head for a while now, along with the address. I was searching my brain. Then yes, it came to me.

I said in a loud tone, "Did the police searched at 1649 Kartar Drive?"

Mary turned to look blankly at me. "I don't remember hearing this address. Where did you get it from?" I told her briefly. She texted something on her phone, and we were soon on our way, following the GPS device I had in the car. I felt my heart race. I hoped Aiden was still alive. *He was alive.* I could still feel him in my bones.

We circled around the area for at least an hour before we reached our destination, but we were still in the middle of nowhere.

Mary turned to me. "Are you sure you heard this address right?"

I looked around and then said, "Yes. I even made note of it in my head." I could tell she was rolling her eyes, even in the dark.

She looked around and then stopped my car in a hidden corner. She said, "Let's park the car. We need to go on a long walk. I think there is something behind these bushes and trees." She pointed in one direction.

"Did you let the police know?"

"I did. They're going to be circling the area soon too. I really hope there is a house to this address. We are following an address you heard months ago. It may not even exist."

I tried to recall that night at the club. *Did I hear it right?* I really hoped so. I walked right next to her. I noticed that she carried a gun.

She gave me a knife, just in case I needed to protect myself, which was absurd. I tried not to think of tonight's outcome. We walked for at least forty-five minutes toward the woods. My heartbeat was pacing with any sound. We tried to move steadily and with minimal sound while walking the deserted semiforest. I could see a shabby little house. My heart raced rapidly. Could this be the address? A couple of old cars were there, but there was no sight of a BMW anywhere. Quietly, we approached the little run-down place. Dirt covered the driveway, making it barely discernible. Mary asked me to keep my head low as she approached the covered window. She whispered that she was going to the other side and for me to wait for her. I wanted to remind her to call the cops, but then I didn't want to shout.

At that time, I wished I had my phone with me, Mary still had it. *Crap!* I stepped one step closer, and then I fell into a leaf-covered hole. Without thinking, I screamed. The hole wasn't deep, and I was able to get out quickly, but I hated the noise I had made falling. I was worried that someone could've heard my scream. I felt my heart racing as I heard the front door swing open while I was trying to look for the knife that had fallen. I froze and saw a man with a beard and moustache standing tall only a few feet away from me, watching me. It was hard to tell his features in the dark. I hesitated as my heart pounded really hard.

His voice was gravelly. "Who the hell are you?"

I froze for a second and then stammered, "I-I was lost. My car stopped. I ran out of gas, and so I was looking to get some help."

"Are you fucking kidding me?"

I heard a familiar female voice. "Marcus, what the hell is going on?" I saw a wicked gaze glaring at me. Was that Adrianna? As if the world had just stopped. It was as if I were looking at someone much older than she was. I tried not to look horrified when I glanced behind her and saw Mary help herself into the house.

She snapped, "What the hell are you doing here?"

My heart jumped and raced in different directions. I swallowed hard.

I said, terrified, "Adrianna!" That was all I could pull out of my dry as a bone throat.

Then I heard her say to the man, "Bring her in. Tie her up. I don't want to hear her. Then I want you to search this whole area." I felt myself being pulled. I pushed and screamed. I bit hard. I still ended up with tied-up hands and legs. I was carried like a sack of potatoes to a dark room.

He said sarcastically, "Mr. Harris, you got a surprise visitor." He then threw me to the floor. My body ached as it landed on the rough ground. I looked around frantically. It was too dark!

I heard a faint voice a few feet away from me. "Hannah! Is that you?"

I hissed, "Aiden! Aiden ... you are alive."

His tone was low but croaky, "God no! Don't tell me the bitch got you too!"

I wet my dry lips. I wanted to laugh and cry. How could I explain how I had found myself there? The blinds covering the windows were thick and dark. The place looked like a dungeon. I heard a noise coming from Aiden, as if he were moving with difficulty toward me. I closed my eyes. That could be it for me. My life events flashed back—the war, my father, Yusuf, the accident, and then Nora. My tears came rolling down when her beautiful face landed in my mind. I would probably never see her again. I would never hug her tight, brush her hair, read her bedtime stories ...

I had conjectured that Yusuf was one of a kind but now realized that many people like him existed—different genders, different races. I wondered if Adrianna was planning to kill us right then and hide our bodies. I hoped she would have some mercy and kill us quickly. At that moment, I wondered how painful dying was. I was running out of breath from the terrifying images of death that occupied my mind.

Aiden, I could feel him closer. I said in a wobbly voice, "Do you think she is going to kill us?" He was silent. How would he know? Adrianna was someone who callously took people's lives. No conscience was going to keep her up at night. "I'm sorry, Aiden. I didn't believe you."

His voice came out as panting. "She planned everything skillfully. She's evil in disguise." I chewed on my lower lip. I really hoped she wouldn't get away with it. I felt Aiden's tied-up hands on my leg, as if he were looking to touch a part of me. I was slowly getting used to the dark. I pulled my body closer. It was hard since both my hands and my feet were tied. I placed my head in between his tied-up arms. I felt a little safer around him.

I whispered, "Aiden. I never stopped loving you. It had nothing to do with your money. I just want you to know that."

He took a deep breath. "I'm sorry for getting you into this. I'm sorry for everything." He sighed. "I love you Hannah, more than anything. I should've been more honest with you about my past, and at the hospital …"

I interrupted him. "Don't mention that day, please. I want to remember happy days." I squeezed myself closer to him; inhaled his cologne mixed with faint sweat smell. I didn't want to think of bad things at that moment. They would probably come up when Adrianna came to the room to torture us. Then I remembered Mary. Where could she be right that moment? Could she also be captured? Did she really call the cops? Maybe they were on their way to rescue us; maybe there was some faint hope left. I realized that being stuck in the bathroom that day when I heard Adrianna talk was part of my strange destiny. Never in a million years did I think my good memory would be the reason behind my death. For now, I was still with Aiden. His arms were around me, and we were both still breathing. I needed any happy thoughts, even thinking about my life without me.

Nora was going to be looked after with Ryan's mother's money; at least she wouldn't starve. Jasmine, Mother, Jasim, Mandy … she had many people to help raise her. Would she miss me? I started to cry at that. Aiden tried to squeeze me as tight as he could with his tied up hands. I wondered how much time had passed since I was captured, maybe fifteen minutes. I heard the door open wide. The faint light from the next room illuminated the filthy, run-down room. I pulled away from Aiden to look at Adrianna's figure standing tall by the door. She was wearing dark blue jeans and a tight black shirt. Her hair was in a messy bun, and her face was bare of makeup. She looked at least fifteen years older. Her eyes seemed cold, and her face was impassive.

"It's nice to see you cuddled in each other's arms before you say your final good-byes." She opened the door wider, adding, "My lucky day, Aiden. Your choice in girls is uncanny. They can't even think for themselves, and they are too eager to die."

I mumbled, "Why are you doing this?"

"A girl like you shouldn't ask a question like that. The reason why is too complex for your narrow brain." I could hear Aiden controlling his breathing. "So, since you are both here, I wonder who I should kill first."

Aiden said in a steady tone, "You may kill me. Do whatever you want to do with me; I was the one who let you down, not her. She has nothing to do with us."

Adrianna's piercing laugh was sickening to the ear. "Too late for that. I didn't find her. She came knocking on her own death's door." My heart felt bruised from all the heavy pounding.

Aiden's voice was fierce. "And how do you plan to get away with it?"

Her tone was cold and sarcastic. "Don't concern yourself about that. You should only worry about which girl to pick in eternity, her or Chelsea."

His voice was loud and clear. "Eternity is a million times better than being with you! You will spend your life in a dark jail cell; you won't be able to hide forever."

She laughed and then said in a low, even tone, "Aiden, after today, I won't even fantasize about you." She came closer to him and hissed menacingly, "I like my men hot, not stone cold." I tried at that moment not to look behind Adrianna, who then turned to me. "Are you going to tell me how you found this place?"

I stuttered, "I-I was there, one day at the club; I was sitting on the toilet when I heard you tell someone to meet you here." I hesitated. "I was positive that this was your love nest with Aiden. I wanted to surprise him because he lied to me about you." Why not play dumb and foolish? That was the way she regarded me anyway.

She rolled her eyes and snapped, "Stupid! Can someone be more dumb?" She turned away. "I don't buy it. Are you going to tell me the truth, or maybe you would like to watch your true love bleed to death!"

My heart was about to jump out of my chest. "This is the truth. I'm not making up any stories."

Aiden said, "Why are you doing this? You have everything you desire. Money, power—"

She interrupted him. "I don't have what I really want." She laughed and then said calmly, "You won't understand."

He said firmly, "Try me." She brought her eyes to his and stared at him.

Her tone was cold when she said, "I am not explaining myself to you yet, maybe while the light in your eyes is fading away."

I swallowed my panic as I recalled her sentence once again. *"It's a delightful feeling, knowing the sight of your hope with Aiden is finally slipping away."* She was a cold-blooded criminal. She would become more dangerous with time. No one was safe around her. I heard noises coming from the front door; so many heavy steps were running around the house. *The police!* My lips curled into a smile. I felt my body being lifted. Everything was happening quickly. I couldn't think while she was trying to balance me, pushing the cold gun metal into my face. Terrifyingly, I was now in front of so many large uniformed men with guns facing Adrianna and me. I couldn't even breathe anymore.

One tall uniformed police officer said loudly, "Put the gun down."

Her voice was shaking. My heart raced faster when she said, "Don't come near me, or I will kill her."

The policeman's tone was calmer when he said, "What do you want, Ms. Miller? We can negotiate after you put the gun down."

Adrianna said tautly, "I don't believe you. I know your games. You are not smarter than me."

I heard a few gunshots from behind me. I screamed, and then Adrianna's body became rigid. Her gaze was lost in space. I was released from her hand to fall to the ground while quivering violently. Adrianna's stiff body fell right next to me. I turned my face to look at Mary, who was still holding the gun. She looked frozen and pale. Mary had saved my life. I couldn't even cry. It was as if the world had stopped. I knew she had sneaked into the room when Adrianna came in leaving the door open; thankfully I was able not to reveal Mary's presence in the same room by looking behind Adrianna. I was hoping Mary would make her move while hiding behind the door before it was too late, but I guessed she was waiting for the cops to arrive. I glanced at Adrianna's motionless body once again, recalling her threats from only minutes earlier. She was now a stone-cold body. I had no remorse for her.

Half an hour later, I was wrapped up in Aiden's arms in the back of the ambulance. I was still shaking while he held me tight. I couldn't believe that we had remained alive during this horrific episode. Aiden didn't look as immaculate as usual. His clothes were rumpled and dirty, and his hair was all over the place. His face and arms had many bruises. Well, I didn't look much better. My faded jeans were ripped in many places. My white, short-sleeve shirt was also ripped open, probably from fighting Marcus while he was trying to tie me up. The cops gave me a light jacket to wear. I knew that my body was covered in bruises too, but that didn't matter. Right that moment, I was doing much better than Adrianna.

Mary was being held by the police for more questioning. By confessing and helping the police with Adrianna's case, she was going to get a sentence reduction. Aiden told me that she killed Adrianna in self-defense. She wouldn't be charged with murder; however, he was going to hire the best lawyer in town to defend her. After all, she had saved both of our lives. He added jokingly that it wouldn't be from Simon Miller's firm.

He asked me, "How exactly did you find this spot?"

I didn't want to lie.

I said, "What I told Adrianna was indeed the truth. I was at the wrong place at the wrong time. Stuck in the women's restroom. She was talking on the phone, asking someone to meet her at this address, and when Mary told me you disappeared, the address came back to me."

His lips curled into a smile. "Twice over, you were in the wrong place at the wrong time—both times in the restroom. The first time, you were lost and you stole my heart; and the second time, you were way too alert and you saved my life."

Did I really steal his heart the first time? I was tongue tied; and all I could do was hold him tight and kiss him on his face and lips …

He mumbled, "Hannah, don't, I probably stink badly—"

I interrupted him saying, "No, to me, you smell just like heaven, you are my heaven Aiden …"

Chapter Twenty-Eight

Only a little over a week later, on a late Sunday afternoon, I glanced over at my family as they sat around the exquisite table. My maid-of-honor dress was long and bright-green with an open back and a long slit up the leg. The shoulder straps were tight, and the top was fitted. I knew Mother didn't approve of it from the way she examined me with a scowl. My hair was expertly styled in a loose side bun, with a little flower design applied to the side of my hair. Mandy's makeup artist had applied my exquisite makeup. That day, I simply wished to impress one man, and he was sitting in front of me. His table wasn't too far away. Aiden sat next to Jasim, who sat next to Mother and then my brothers. Elaina sat on his other side. John insisted he bring Elaina to his and Mandy's wedding. Jasmine and Nathan also sat at the same table. Nora was next to Tiffany and was sitting at Mandy's parents' table. Soft music played after everyone had given his or her speech. I sat at the table right next to the bride and groom. They looked really happy. Mandy looked stunning with her mermaid dress, and John looked handsome and seemed proud being next to her. I felt my heart squeeze. Aiden glanced my way a few times. Mother noticed his staring, and she also looked my way. I moved my eyes away from her stare. I bet she understood just then that there was something going on between us. I was glad she didn't frown.

My mind traveled back in time to the day I was briefly held hostage with Aiden. It was still traumatizing me. I knew it would take time before it became part of my history. And I was glad that once again, I came out from my trauma still breathing. The first thing I did after being dropped off at home by the police was to find Nora, hold her tight, smell her hair, and cover her with kisses. Only a few hours earlier, I thought I would never be able to do that again. Soon after, I turned to face the many faces that were worried sick about me. I smiled, wondering how I was going to explain what had happened to me in just a few sentences, since I had no energy to talk.

That was an experience I hoped never to go through again. Aiden had kept his distance from me the last week, only calling me once to confirm his attendance at Mandy and John's wedding with his mother and to deliver the latest news about Adrianna's case.

After the police investigation, the man who was caught at Jason's house confessed that Carlos and Markus were the same man; Aiden once knew him as Richard, Adrianna's ex-boyfriend and the man he found with Chelsea. All that time, he still worked under Adrianna. Trish, the other partner in crime, had jumped to her death twenty floors down years earlier. I wondered what happened there. Did someone push her? But I was glad to know that justice prevailed.

The place Adrianna fled to was purchased through a different name. If it hadn't been for my good memory and my being stuck in the restroom while listening to Adrianna's conversation, the police might have never found out about it.

Mary was most likely getting a reduced sentence since she helped with Adrianna's capture. With her sharp brain, she would definitely make a good detective.

A couple of days earlier, I had received a special delivery from Aiden—a sporty, shiny, red Lexus. I didn't know what to do with it, so I parked it in Jasim's garage. Only the day before, I got another delivery—a designer watch and a full set of jewelry, with a message that said: "To Hannah, with love."

Perhaps Aiden thought I was jealous after reading about Chelsea and being trashed by Adrianna. Well, maybe I was a bit jealous at first; I was, after all, a woman with feelings. But after what had happened with Adrianna and poor Chelsea, I learned that all the money and gifts in the world could never breathe life into an empty soul.

Aiden and I were going through withdrawal from what had happened. But I was glad he was able to make it to celebrate a good event. I couldn't help but glance toward Aiden, who was speaking to his mother. Watching him from afar, made me realize how much I had missed him. I knew he missed me from the way he was looking at me. I could now read his eyes clearly. I just couldn't wait until I was alone with him. That day, he was a mix of power, class, and sex in his dark suit and crisp white shirt. He was tanned, as if he had spent the last few days under the sun. I could hardly see the bruises on his face. I wished I didn't have to sit so far from him. I looked around myself annoyed.

Soon, the DJ started to play some music. First, the bride and groom and soon other couples started to get up on the dance floor. After dancing briefly with John's best man, Tad, I went back to my seat and glanced toward Aiden, who had an impenetrable look on his face. I waited for him to make his move and take me to the dance floor. Maybe he was worried about Mother's reaction after my talk with him right before her surprise birthday party. Half an hour passed. I looked over to check on Nora and Tiffany; they were both playing with their iPads. *Thank God for technology!* I thought happily. I looked over to where Aiden sat. He wasn't there. I then looked around. I didn't want to see him dancing with someone else. I sighed, annoyed.

A few minutes later, the music stopped, and I heard the DJ calling for someone to come up to the dance floor. The name was familiar. He called again. My eyes grew wide. Why was he calling Mother's name? I tried not to frown as she walked toward the DJ's stand. She looked stunned too. The hall was suddenly quiet. I glanced over at Mandy. She was laughing while whispering something into John's ear. Did they know what was going on?

A skinny man, covered in tattoos, his blond, thinning hair in a ponytail, said in a loud, fun tone, "Mrs. Shaheen, I have a request from Mr. Harris to give you the microphone." He then walked toward her and handed her the microphone. Mother looked really nervous. My heart was racing. What was Aiden up to? Then I saw Aiden; he was approaching the dance floor, which had been cleared immediately.

His voice was clear and confident when he said, "Mrs. Shaheen." I tried to contain my quivering body. "Before I met you, Hannah told me that you are lovely and kind, and I have to agree with her." He glanced at my stunned face.

How embarrassing! I thought. Now everyone around turned to face me with a grin on their faces.

He continued, "I wanted to tell you something that I couldn't keep to myself any longer." He lingered before he continued with poise. "I love your daughter Hannah and will always cherish her." He glanced at his mother, who had a big smile on her face. "My mother here is my witness, and so is everyone around." My tears came rolling down my cheeks. "I want to ask if I may have her as my wife."

Mother wiped a few tears off her face before she turned to me. She asked in a shaky voice, "Hannah, do you love … um …" I bet she had forgotten his name in her nervousness.

He said quickly, "Aiden."

She cleared her throat. "Aiden?" I couldn't say anything; I was about to choke on my tears and my shock. I just nodded, gasping for breath. She then turned to face Aiden saying, "Okay." This was it?

He then strolled toward me, a small classy black square box in his hand. He went on his knees and mumbled, "I now have your mom's permission." He smiled as he opened the box. He added, "May I?"

I nodded. I gasped when I looked at the ring as he lifted it. It was a beautiful platinum-gold ring with a square, twinkling diamond. He slipped it on my finger, and kissed me on my boiling, wet cheek. People cheered around me. I felt as if I were part of a fairy-tale moment. Then I heard a song, "Breathe Again," the same song we danced to when we first met. *Our song*, I thought. He pulled me to my feet. I was shaking hard. I had to hold on to him.

He whispered in my ear, "May I have this dance with my birthday girl?"

All I could do was nod; he then led me to the dance floor, where I held him tight and cried on his shoulder.

Epilogue

I STUDIED THE PICTURES FROM the album as I fiddled with the diamond star pendant, Aiden's first gift, and the half-moon pendant, Jasim's birthday gift. I loved my wedding dress. Jeff designed it as he promised. It was strapless, with French lace, and was tight-fitting around the bust and waist, only to flow evenly around the hips and thighs. We had a backyard wedding, or should I call it a majestic backyard wedding, since it was at Aiden and Elaina's house?—Well, my new house too …

I remembered then how my knees went weak when I first saw him that day. He looked so handsome in his dark, crisp tux and white shirt. I touched the picture of us kissing; a month after our wedding, I could still feel tingly, especially since Aiden was exactly what he promised to be, a caring and loving husband. He treated me with respect and never once made me feel inferior. Well, perhaps my character change could have helped a little, because I had gained some confidence and became more assertive.

There was a picture of Elaina holding Nora. They had already connected. Nora could enjoy the love of another grandmother. My heart squeezed, recalling the day Nora was born. I got my girl, my lovely Nora.

A picture of Jasmine and Nathan—Jasmine was now expecting her first baby. They both looked really happy. I smiled.

A picture of Hady, Wissam, and Hisham—my handsome brothers stood around my mother. She looked proud as they all smiled at the picture.

Another picture of Henry, George Melisso, and Jeff—they were smiling while tipping their glasses. I was glad they had found each other. I figured they would bond since they had so much in common—well, maybe not Jeff. I bet George was going to ask Henry to join him on his next trips.

Mandy and John—Mandy's wedding was merely a few weeks before mine; she was back from her honeymoon, still wrapped in John's arms.

A photo of Jasim with his arm around Aiden—I smiled at that.

I smiled widely at the most beautiful picture in the album, Mother with my bouquet of flowers. I recalled when my sister then laughingly insisted Mother stand with the rest of the single ladies. Mother stood reluctantly since Jasmine nagged her to accept, looking a little discomfited. After I threw the bouquet, I turned around to see that my bouquet of flowers had somehow landed in her arms. We all laughed. I could then even witness a couple of young girls rolling their eyes. Later on that night, my sister grabbed me away from Aiden. She wanted to show me something. I felt goose bumps all over my body. Happy tears dropped on my cheeks when I saw Mother sitting in one corner next to Jasim. Her hand was wrapped in his. How did I miss all the signs of their affection? My heart skipped and skipped happily …

***

That day was another special day. Earlier, over a small gathering at our house, Mother insisted on a simple, quiet evening as she and Jasim tied their special knot. She looked happy and vibrant in her off-white suit. I could never have imagined that Mother could look as stunning as she did that day. Jasim looked a decade younger than he did the first day I met him.

But I had planned a little surprise for them; I had to include the belly dancer and the drummer from both my and Jasmine's weddings. Well, every wedding needed a big entrance to announce the arrival of the couple in love.

My wedding album wasn't complete yet. One day, I needed to add Nora's wedding pictures when she found her loving man. Happy women, at last! As we deserve to be.

I closed the album and then glanced over at the large bed. I remembered how uncomfortable I felt when I saw Aiden's place the first time, but I was surprised at how quickly I adapted to luxury. I heard loud thunder outside, and then another big rumble followed. I closed the blinds, because lightning was illuminating the room. I was glad that the rain and thunder happened after Mother's wedding. I turned off the lamp and then walked toward the bed.

I snuggled next to Aiden, hugging him tight when I heard another loud bang of thunder. I sighed. Mother Nature was angry that night. But that didn't bother me one bit, because next to Aiden, I felt warm, calm, and most important, safe.

About the Author

SARAH SALEM IS A DAUGHTER and a mother of one. She was born in Lebanon and always knew that nothing was impossible or unachievable.

Since her early childhood, which she spent in Lebanon, she has enjoyed books and listening to stories. Writing a story was one of her life's dreams, simply because she wanted to write novels that readers would love and find interesting.

Books by Sarah Salem

Twisted Forms of Love
Bittersweet Tones of Love